MORE BY THE AUTHOR

THE RAVEN'S JOURNEY

Book 1: See Me
Book 2: See Me Revealed
Book 3: See Me Go
Book 4: See Me Believe
Book 5: See Me Overcome
Book 6: Hawk
Book 7: Ronan
Book 8: Stolas

I0585587

LOOKING THROUGH THE SHADOWS

The Underbelly
After the Wreckage
We Always Fight

I S.P.I.

I S.P.I. Mischievous Magic (Volume 1)
I S.P.I. Spicy Sorcery (Volume 2)

SHORT STORIES & MORE

Where Realms Collide
Unnerving Descent
Unnerving Eclipse
Unnerving Wicked
Super: Unexpected Heroes Arise
Rise Reflection
Rise Resurrection
Rise Revolution
Rise Recreation
The Space Between Us
The Pulse (The Haunting of Orchard House)

Michelle Lee on the Web

Michelle on Facebook at
tiny.cc/MichelleLeeWrites

or write to
MichelleLeeWrites@gmail.com

THE RAVEN'S JOURNEY
BOOK SEVEN

Michelle Lee

BLUE FORGE PRESS
Port Orchard, Washington

Ronan
Copyright 2020, 2022
by Michelle Lee

First eBook Edition April 2021
First Print Edition April 2021
Second eBook Edition May 2022
Second Print Edition May 2022

Cover photograph by Michelle Lee
Cover design by Brianne DiMarco
Interior design by Brianne DiMarco

ISBN 978-1-59092-891-2

For information about film, reprint or other subsidiary rights, contact: blueforgegroup@gmail.com

Blue Forge Press is the print division of the volunteer-run, federal 501(c)3 nonprofit company, Blue Forge Group, founded in 1989 and dedicated to bringing light to the shadows and voice to the silence. We strive to empower storytellers across all walks of life with our four divisions: Blue Forge Press, Blue Forge Films, Blue Forge Gaming, and Blue Forge Records. Find out more at www.BlueForgeGroup.org

Blue Forge Press
7419 Ebbert Drive Southeast
Port Orchard, Washington 98367
blueforgepress@gmail.com
360-550-2071 ph.txt

For my family—
for the way we all pull together
to get through the hard times.

RONAN

Michelle Lee

Chapter One

"ey, Dega, how's married life?" Ronnie grinned at the man as he walked into the house.

"It's fantastic." Degataga smiled. "Better than I'd dared hope for, I love it. How's the filming going?"

"There are good days, and then there are days demons besieged us. It's hit and miss, but ratings are way up, so we must be doing something right," Ronnie stated, closing the door behind him.

"Onida said Stolas has a pretty good network in place now in case of a major movement."

"He does? Wait, she's talked to Stolas?" Ronnie frowned at that information.

"Not directly, through Winnie she has. I guess he's still working on it, but something is in place, at least. He hasn't talked to any of you?" Degataga paused in the living room to stare at the picture above the fireplace.

"It gets me too," Ronnie admitted, looking with him. "That day, things shifted. She opened up to me," he said as he remembered the day at the beach with perfect clarity. The picture Jax had gotten of her with her wings silhouetted in the ocean spray, and hair gently blowing was stunning. Everyone that came through the room stopped to stare at otherworldly beauty that Jax had captured.

Degataga shook his head as if to clear it. "When is the last time you saw him?"

"Who? Stolas?" Ronnie tried to get back on track.

"Yes, Stolas."

"After the skinwalkers." Ronnie carefully watched Degataga's face. That was the first time he'd genuinely seen Degataga unravel. Now that he thought about it, Stolas had come unglued too.

"That was over three months ago," Degataga said in concern. "Onida has seen him since then, so have I."

"Well, if Airiella has seen him, she hasn't mentioned it. Why would her not talking to the demon worry you?" Ronnie crossed his arms and leaned against the wall.

"He's deeply attached to her," Degataga answered plainly. "You know that."

"So is everyone who has ever met her," Ronnie laughed. "It took Taklishim meeting her once, and that hard façade of his crumbled."

"And you held out so much longer?" Degataga sounded almost smug.

"Nope. The moment she opened that hotel room door and my eyes fell upon her; I was in love. Wait, that's not true; the moment she walked into that interview room, I fell. When she opened the hotel room door, it sealed the deal." Ronnie revised his declaration.

"Honestly, she had all four of us in her hand that first meeting. Onida was probably the longest holdout, but she still had us all."

"What brings you out here today?" Ronnie righted himself and led him into the backyard that had an unmatched view of the ocean.

"Airiella, of course. Onida and I have both felt something off with her. Has anything come up? Any new abilities surfaced? Or creatures for that matter?" Degataga had the grace to wince with the last question.

"Not that I have seen. Maybe you are picking up on wedding stress? Combined with the shooting schedule we've been on recently, it's a lot."

"It doesn't feel like that. I'm surprised you aren't feeling it too." Degataga rested his elbows on his knees as he stared out at the ocean.

"I'm in a different place right now," Ronnie admitted, embarrassed.

"Meaning what?" Degataga shifted to look at him.

"I'm not ready for this wedding. To let go of Airiella."

"Why do you think you need to?" That was the question Ronnie wasn't sure how to answer and was dreading getting asked. One, they all kept asking him.

"I guess I feel like it's not fair to Jax for me to be in the picture if they are married and committed to each other. But the flip side of that is when I think of not being able to crawl in bed with her because I need to feel her, I almost have a full-blown panic attack."

"From the things I have gathered, nothing leads me to believe you still couldn't do that, even if they are married." Degataga frowned. "Is this a personal choice, or has Jax told you that?"

"Personal choice. I don't know what to do, Dega."

Ronnie let out a dramatic sigh.

"I'm probably the last person you should ask for advice on this. I walked away from the love of my life once, and it took me years to get back in her good graces. The two of you need to talk. I'll say this, the situation with all of you isn't a normal situation by any means, so I don't think that what society considers normal should apply to you."

"There's a part of me that wishes she was marrying me and not Jax. It's a small part, but the love I feel for her is anything but small. I'm an awful friend. Scratch that, awful human, because I'm pretty sure that I'm in love with Chrissie."

"You need to talk with all of them. The only reason Onida gave me a second chance is that Airiella intervened."

Ronnie flopped back on the chaise lounge and tried to get his erratically beating heart under control. "It is even possible for me to love them both as I do?"

Degataga laughed. "Ronnie, I can't believe that question even came out of your mouth. Look at the situation you are in with your friends and Airiella and tell me if it's possible."

A sheepish look came over his face as the ridiculousness of what he said dawned on him. "Shit, okay, yeah. I'm not just talking about that, though, and there's a physical aspect to it. Before you say it, I know Airiella was physical with all of us, and she maintained it fine. I'm losing this argument, so I'm going to shut up now."

"Talk to them, Ronnie." Degataga laughed gently. "That's the best advice I can give."

"I'm running out of time to do that, too. The wedding is less than a month away. Shit, that means I need to talk to Chrissie about it too, and it's so awkward."

"Where is Airiella?" Degataga tried to change the subject.

"Out shopping with Chrissie for a dress. Jillian and Mags are with her too. She hasn't had a whole lot of time to do that part of it all since we've been out filming." Ronnie scrubbed his hands over his face.

"Then, where is everyone else?" Degataga looked around.

"Babysitting. I saw you pull up and left the guys to it. It takes four of us men to care for three babies when Mags does it all by herself. Sad. In our defense, they are crawling and into everything the moment we look away. Guess which one is the worst?" Ronnie grinned.

"Angel?" Degataga guessed with a wry smile.

"Nailed it. Airiella said she would be, that girls are demons themselves. It makes me laugh that Taklishim is having two of them. Speaking of, you know what you are having yet?"

"A girl and a boy." Degataga's face lit up when he talked about them. "How are you with Chrissie's boys?"

"I flat out love those kids. The middle one is with them; the other two are in Aedan's house with the rest of us. I think because of my history with my father; I can identify with them easier. They are great kids. After they talk with their dad, it takes a little work to get them back to themselves. It's hardest with the oldest, Jayson. He likes to be called Jace. He's such a serious kid after those phone calls." Ronnie felt the sadness start to creep in.

"They see more than we give them credit for; I'm sure he has scars inside from things he's observed," Degataga said gently.

"I know he does. I did. I think they all do, except the

youngest one maybe. He was too young to understand what was happening. Out of the three, that one, Bryce, is the least serious. He's kind of a jokester and binds the other two together. The middle kid, Rafe, is the most sensitive. It's odd because they have no relation to me at all, but I still see pieces of me in them." It was something that made Ronnie's heart soar, too.

"It's not as odd as you think. You are around the boys all the time, and you share a common thread. Airiella could find pieces of her in other cancer survivors, or other survivors of different situations," Degataga countered.

"Maybe so. Rafe went with them today because Chrissie had another phone call from him, her ex, and he must have said something to make her upset because Rafe wouldn't leave her side. She didn't say anything to me about it, but then again, she never really does. She doesn't talk about him much to me. Only to Airiella."

"I'm surprised one of you didn't go with her today." Degataga turned back to the ocean. "You guys never leave her alone."

"She pointed that out. Told us no guys were allowed. I argued the loudest and got shut down the fastest. She closed down all our connections when she left too. Maybe that's why I can't feel what you guys are feeling? Or maybe it has to do with your mysterious native ways." Ronnie waggled his fingers at him, half laughing.

"Onida kicked me out today too, said I was hovering too much. She and Tama are shopping for baby stuff. Taklishim almost came with me but got called into a town council meeting with the Chief. I think he wanted to play with the boys."

"They would have loved that. Out of everyone, it

surprises me how much those kids adore him. Well, they are pretty enamored with Tama's cougar too." Ronnie smiled. "I love how kids have no fear sometimes. As an *adult*, the first time I met Taklishim, he intimidated the hell out of me. Seeing Tama's cougar for the first time was just as frightening."

"It sounds to me like you are pretty invested in these kids, maybe even Chrissie too. Why do you think you aren't ready to take the next step with her?" Degataga switched the focus back on to Ronnie.

"I'm starting to regret coming out to let you in," Ronnie mumbled. "That's a fucking question I haven't been able to answer myself."

"What are you afraid of?" Degataga pushed him.

"Plenty of things. I'm human." Ronnie was uncomfortable under the direct gaze of the wise man he considered a good friend.

"Ronnie, you asked me for advice." Degataga sighed and held his hands out innocently.

"Yeah, and you told me you were shit at it, basically," Ronnie countered. "Is this medicine man voodoo you are using on me now?"

"Two different things, voodoo and medicine men, you know better. All I'm doing is reading your energy." Degataga turned his penetrating gaze back on Ronnie.

"I'm afraid of things not working with Chrissie and being left alone, losing the kids, not being able to go back to Airiella," Ronnie spit out in a rush, tired of its weight pressing on him.

"One, do you think that Chrissie would keep you from seeing the kids? Two, relationships are hard and take work; it won't ever be perfect all the time. Three, what makes you think Airiella and Jax wouldn't let you back in as you put it?" Degataga asked point-blank. "Fear is irrational, and if you really thought through those questions and answered them honestly, you'd be able to conquer those fears easily. Want me to give you the tea mix that helps you fix things?"

Ronnie shuddered, remembering Airiella and Jax drinking it, and how hard it had been to see. "No, thanks. I don't want to be another failure of a male figure in those boy's lives," he added.

"I'm just going to point out again that you need to talk with the parties involved. Communication and honesty are important. How often did you call Airiella out for not being open with you about the stuff she had going on inside her? And what makes you think that she isn't already aware of how you feel? She's quick to point out that she already knows when we try to keep stuff from her."

"Her knowledge and me verbalizing it are different things. She won't push me to talk about it, unlike me, who badgers her until she gives in. Shit, even if I go to Jax first, she'll still know. We've had this talk before, her and I. Even Jax and I."

"Matters of the heart are tricky beasts. So is fear for that matter. In my own opinion, you have the best people possible to talk with about both. She's going to always be in love with you, Ronnie. Even married to Jax, she will still be in love with you. Jax, Airiella, and Chrissie are the closest people to your heart. Talk with them." Degataga stood up. "Have Airiella call me."

"Are you leaving?" Ronnie stood up as well.

"Yes. I don't know when Airiella's coming back, and a coastal storm is brewing, I don't want to get stuck somewhere and not be able to get home."

"There are no clouds, no wind," Ronnie pointed out, gesturing to the bright horizon splayed out before them.

"The energy tells me otherwise. A storm will hit today. One that isn't caused by your angel," Degataga added sarcastically.

"She loves them. Sits right on the balcony of her room and absorbs it." Ronnie pointed to the balcony above them.

"I can understand that. The pure energy of it calls to Airiella. It's cleansing for someone like her."

"Is she in danger?" Ronnie asked nervously, voicing the thought that had snuck into his head.

"I don't know. I'd counter that with when is Airiella not in danger?"

"Good point. Let's not jinx it. I'll have Airiella call you," Ronnie promised, leading Degataga out into the front.

"Remember, Ronnie. Talk to her. It's not honoring who she is by not including her when it affects her."

"Yeah, yeah, I heard you," Ronnie groused.

"For the sun loved the moon so much, she died every night to let him breathe," Degataga said softly, reciting the quote that felt like a sucker punch to Ronnie's soul.

"She's the sun and the moon." Ronnie fought back a wave of emotion. "Depending on the situation. I get what you are saying."

"Maybe you don't." Degataga stood behind his car door. "Put the different people in your situation into those roles and think of why they would choose to die every night. You might find some answers there."

Panic started to rise in him, swelling fast, and

RONAN

Ronnie's breath flew out of him in a whoosh as he doubled over unable to catch himself as he fell face-first to the ground, his head filled with screams and white noise he didn't understand. "Airiella..." he choked out.

Chapter Two

Ells, go back to the first one," Chrissie told her thoughtfully, studying her in the mirror and trying not to laugh at the expression on her best friend's face. "I know, you are in pure hell right now. There was something about that dress."

"Which one was that one?" Jillian kicked back, sipping on the glass of wine the bridal shop offered them.

"I know which one she's talking about." Mags crossed her legs. "The romantic looking one, right?"

"That's a good word for it," Chrissie agreed, marching over and flipping through the dresses on the rack until she found the one she was thinking of; "This one. Put this one back on."

"It didn't fit," Airiella whined. "Too tight across my boobs, and too wide across my hips."

"I'm not looking for the fit, that's what alterations are for, I'm thinking about the look." Chrissie pushed her back into the fitting room. "Stop arguing with me."

Mags giggled. "Fat chance of that happening."

"What's wrong with this one?" Airiella turned to look in the mirror.

"It's not you. This dress is way too girly for you," Jillian added helpfully. "It's pretty, but not you."

"And you hate sleeveless," Chrissie reminded her. "You are just saying that because you don't want to try on anymore and will settle for anything to make it stop. I know you, Ells."

Jillian burst out laughing. "Now, I get why she said she liked that hideous one!"

Airiella flipped them all off and went back to the fitting room. "You think this one is the one?" Mags asked Chrissie.

"I do. But I need to see it again. Something about it stuck out in my mind. Of all the ones we've forced Ells to try on, that's the only one that has stuck. I know she doesn't care what she wears, and she'd be happy to wear leggings and a t-shirt of Ronnie's. But I want her to have a perfect day; she deserves it."

"She does. My friend agreed to do the flowers, by the way. I gave Jax the info to talk about for payment." Jillian took another drink. "I'm not sure why I'm drinking, really, but I'm starting to feel drunk."

"Then give it to me, I'll finish it." Mags took the glass from her and gulped the wine down.

"I think they give it to us, so we don't beat the bride senseless for arguing with everything," Chrissie joked.

"I can hear you," Airiella called out.

"I know," Chrissie replied, checking on Rafe, who was sitting quietly on the floor, coloring in pictures Jax had drawn for him. "Doing okay, honey?" she asked him.

"Uh-huh," came the distracted answer. Rafe had asked her this morning why Ronnie couldn't be their daddy because Ronnie never hurt their feelings. Chrissie had cried countless times at the things her ex made those poor boys endure.

Chrissie looked back at the closed fitting room door, noticing how silent it had become back there. "Ells put the dress on."

She heard the huff of frustration and movement begin again. "How'd you know she wasn't?" Mags wondered.

"It was too quiet. You know Ells hates shopping, right?" Chrissie looked back to the women.

"Yeah, I know. I always have to force Airy to come with me." Mags giggled again. "I made her go to a certain store with me for some fun adult toys, and she about blew a gasket even though her interest was piqued."

Chrissie let out a laugh. "Oh man, I would have loved to see her face then."

"I can still hear you," Airiella muttered.

"I still know," Chrissie replied. "The faster you get that on, the faster we will be done and can get some food to put in Jillian's belly, so we don't take her home drunk."

"Smitty won't care," was the muffled response. "He'd probably like it. They are the pervy pair."

Jillian snorted. "She's not wrong."

Chrissie's breath caught as Airiella stepped out of the fitting room. "Yep, that's the one."

Like magic, the sales lady appeared and fussed over the dress on Airiella. "I can let it out here, and take it in here." She pinned the gown at the hips, so it draped over her curves. "How quickly do you need it?"

"In two weeks," Chrissie told her, firming up her voice. "Can you get it done?"

"That's awfully fast," the lady hedged.

"Well, she works on a TV show, and they've been off filming, so her schedule doesn't allow for much time for this," Chrissie used her mother tone. "If you can't get it done, I'll find someone who can."

"I can do it," she answered quickly. "I thought you looked familiar," she said to Airiella with a new interest in her voice.

"Great." Chrissie stepped closer. "Take the measurements, then give us a few minutes of privacy, please. Complete privacy, meaning no hiding and spying on us."

The lady blushed and measured Airiella fast, who at least had the good grace to say nothing to contradict Chrissie. "I'll need to measure with the shoes on."

"She won't be wearing shoes." Chrissie crossed her arms, and Mags and Jillian smothered laughs. "It's a beach wedding."

She finished measuring and scurried away. Chrissie waited a few minutes then looked around the corner. "Rafe, stand here and watch that lady. If she comes back here, tell me, okay?"

"Like a spy?" He smiled at the thought of a game.

"Just like that, good boy." Chrissie turned back to Airiella. "Let your wings out."

Airiella turned, and her gigantic black wings took up the room. Mags squealed and dropped the wine glass. "That's the dress!"

Jillian gasped. "No question about it, that's the one. Good eye, Chrissie."

Chrissie studied her. The gown was simple. Tight across her chest and cinched below the bust line, fitted down her torso and then flared out below her hips, falling straight to the floor. The back was open in a circle, exposing her shoulder blades where her wings came out and closing at the neck. The material was a satiny white with a soft gauzy material over the top of it for the skirt with pearl-like beads sewn in.

She motioned for Airiella to spin around. Chrissie liked how the sleeves were the same gauzy material, but opaquer while still being see-through and draping gracefully down her arms. "Walk for me," Chrissie commanded her and watched the way the dress moved as she walked.

It flowed with her movements, not restricting her and not loose enough to trip her up. Even without her wings, the dress made her look like an angel, especially with the wild mess of curls framing her face. Her tan skin set the look off exquisitely.

She looked over at Mags and Jillian. "Veil or no veil?"

"No veil," they answered in unison.

"Maybe a few ornamental pins randomly in her hair." Jillian circled Airiella.

"Mommy, she's coming," Rafe called out, not quietly.

"Wings back in," Chrissie snapped out. Thankfully it was in enough time the lady hadn't seen. She waited until she was in the room, and Chrissie reached in her pocket, pulling out the credit card Jax had given her. "Ring it up."

Nodding politely, she took the card and walked back out. "Can I put real clothes back on now?" Airiella growled.

Mags laughed and stood to undo the zipper, so Airiella didn't mess up the pins that were in place, and she helped her step out of the dress, then she carefully hung it up and brought it out to the front of the store.

"Thanks for your help, Rafe, you did a great job." Chrissie ruffled the boy's hair as they waited for Airiella.

"Auntie Ells looked pretty," Rafe replied, picking up his pictures and crayons. "Why couldn't the lady see that?"

"We didn't want her to see the wings. Remember how we talked about that? How her wings were a special secret?"

"I 'member," he said, smiling.

Airiella came back out, looking relieved to be in her jeans. "Come on, kid." She scooped up Rafe. "We deserve ice cream after that torture."

"Can I mommy?" Rafe looked over Airiella's shoulder at her.

"After lunch, Auntie Ells knows the rules. Besides, Auntie Jilly needs real food. If we don't take care of her, too, she might get sick."

"Killjoy," Airiella muttered. "You thought I looked pretty, Rafe?"

"Yep. Like an angel." Chrissie melted at the look on Rafe's face. A flash of anger hit her again as she remembered the call from her ex earlier, how hurt Rafe had felt after.

"Easy, Chris," Airiella cautioned, catching the emotion as they met Mags in the front of the store, who handed back the credit card to Chrissie.

"Two weeks," she reminded the saleslady. "I'll be back to get the gown."

"The bride will need to be here too, a final fitting,"

the lady argued.

"I'll take care of that. The bride won't be in town, so just get it right. I picked this store because you had good reviews." Chrissie gave no room for argument.

Mollified, the lady smiled and agreed all would be ready. They headed out, and Airiella was asking Rafe what he wanted for lunch. Chrissie knew the answer would be grilled cheese. She swore Airiella, and Rafe could live off that.

Chrissie pulled out her phone to look up what restaurants were in the area and saw three missed texts from her ex. She growled as she ignored them while Airiella gave her a curious look as she got Rafe buckled into the car.

"Travis," Chrissie answered the look.

Airiella shut the car door so that Rafe couldn't hear her. "Ignore the bastard. He doesn't deserve the wasted emotions."

"He was high when he talked to the boys this morning. Jace told me. He's nine, and he shouldn't have to know what his father sounds like high. He also gave him a huge guilt trip about not wanting to see him." Chrissie spoke quietly, but Jillian and Mags both heard and moved in closer.

"Want me to kick his ass?" Mags asked, her face angry.

Chrissie had to laugh. "You'd have to stand in line. I think Airiella would beat us all to it, given the opportunity."

"Damn straight; I would," she snarled and pushed Chrissie to the door. "Get in."

They got in and got settled while Chrissie continued to look for a suitable place to eat. "Here's an upscale diner, so they have food Rafe will eat and food that more refined tastes would like too."

"Is that another dig at me for liking grilled cheese?" Airiella asked, laughing.

"Maybe. You two can eat that, us grown-ups will eat something better. Before you ask, yes, they have ice cream."

"Good, Rafe deserves a treat for keeping my wings a secret." Airiella smiled in the mirror at the boy. "And for saying I'm pretty."

"Hey, we tell you that all the time," Jillian cried. "Where's our treat?"

"You got wine," Chrissie told her. "After lunch, we need to go to a store that will have light strings." Chrissie was again searching on her phone. "Party store should have them," she mumbled.

"I thought you already got those." Mags leaned forward to speak between the seats.

"I got as many as they had, but I need more."

"What about a photographer?" Jillian added.

"One of my friends that I used to work with, his husband is a photographer. I asked if Jamie could do it, and he said he would," Airiella answered quickly. "I love Jamie's wedding photos."

"We don't need a DJ since Jax and Smitty wired up the backyard for sound, we can just stream music." Mags checked that off her mental list. "Jillian has the flowers covered, and now we have the dress."

"Makeup and hair thingies are still needed," Chrissie said out loud.

"What?! No." Airiella pushed back. "No makeup."

"Oh, shut up. You put Chrissie in charge, and you'll do what she says." Mags put her foot down.

Chrissie smirked at Airiella. "Regretting that

decision yet?"

"Airy, remember a while back when we all dreamed of you with wings?" Mags changed the subject.

"That was a long time ago. Back at the beginning, before we knew what messes we were getting into," Airiella remembered with a sad sigh.

"That dress reminds me of that vision of you," Mags said with a smile.

"I hope that's a good thing," she remarked dryly.

"Stunning. Chrissie called it right. That means you just need to do what she says." Mags had a way of quieting Airiella down that was magical.

"Something is hitting my radar, ladies. Please keep an eye out for anything that looks odd," Airiella said quietly, and the car went silent as they drove.

Chrissie fought the impulse to text Ronnie that information; he probably knew if Airiella was feeling it. He'd wanted to come with and, at the time, she had agreed with Airiella, that they needed a girl's day. Now she wished she'd fought to have him come. She felt safe with him around.

"Stop it, Chris. I'm perfectly capable of keeping you all safe," Airiella told her quietly.

"Yes, I know. But who will keep you safe?" Chrissie brought up the question that Jax and Ronnie used against her when they were trying to get her to see reason.

"Myself. I'll let the others know if something comes up." Airiella's tone had hardened slightly.

"We are not even remotely close to home. We are on the other side of the peninsula, and it's not like they can be there to help you. Maybe we should keep heading back and find somewhere closer to home."

"We aren't that far away from Tak and Tama. They have people in this area if I need help," she reminded Chrissie. "Relax, please. I only warned you because my radar pinged, it's not close."

"Fine. I won't be the one to answer to Jax and Ronnie if you get hurt."

"I will," Mags offered. "They are scared of me. Airy is fine, Chrissie. She'll let us know if it's close."

"After lunch, we'll switch and have Mags drive, and I'll use my soul sight to see if I spot anything else the rest of the day."

"I thought you just said it would be fine. If that's the case why, are you making plans that say otherwise?" Chrissie was getting worried. The trauma of seeing her best friend without a pulse the last time hadn't worn off. Coupled with the nerves of speaking with her ex, she was feeling a bit on edge.

"Have you not met Ronnie? He's drummed it into me to have plans ready. That's all I'm doing."

"Covering her ass is what she's doing because that will be the first thing Ronnie asks when you get home," Jillian said. "Oops, sorry. I forgot about Rafe."

Chrissie shrugged it off. "He's heard worse from his father."

They got to the restaurant where Airiella and Rafe were goofy and having fun, both so relaxed that Chrissie felt her tension easing. They got through lunch and the rest of the stores they needed to go through with no problems.

Airiella did have Mags drive, and once they were finally on their way home, she lay her head back against the seat and closed her eyes. "Ells, everything okay?" Chrissie tapped her on the shoulder.

"Yeah, soul sight for a long time tends to give me a headache. I'm just resting my eyes."

Chrissie felt terrible for dragging the day out for so long. Airiella hadn't even been home a full day before Chrissie pulled her back out. Their filming schedule had been grueling. Through Ronnie, Chrissie knew she'd had to fight off demons more than a few times.

"Mommy, can I get the mail?" Rafe asked as they pulled up to the mailbox.

"Auntie Ells is going to get it," Chrissie answered, seeing Airiella halfway out the door already.

"It's cool, come with me, Rafe. You can unlock it for me. Your mom wore me out; my hands might not work." She smirked at Chrissie.

Mags was already opening the gate and starting to pull in when Chrissie caught rapid movement out of the corner of her eye. She turned in time to see Airiella diving in front of Rafe and wrapping her arms around him. At the same time, her son of a bitch, ex-husband stabbed a needle into the angel.

She heard Rafe crying, "No, Daddy. Stop."

Chrissie's heart froze, and her throat closed up, all she could do was pound on the window as Travis pulled Rafe from Airiella's arms and threw him into a car she hadn't even noticed, and then drag a now limp Airiella to the car and shove her in. To her horror, he pointed a gun at their vehicle and fired twice.

Distantly, she heard Mags and Jillian screaming. Chrissie's head swam with dizziness as she watched her child and best friend get abducted, ten feet from her. There wasn't a thing she could do about it.

Chapter Three

Ronnie! Get up!" Degataga shouted at him. "That was gunshots!"

Ronnie heard Mags screaming and scrambled to his feet. "Airiella!" he yelled. He distantly heard the thumping of footfalls behind him and knew Jax was on his heels. They ran down the driveway, following Degataga and saw Airiella's car pulled halfway through the gate and another peeling off down the street.

"He has Airiella and Rafe!" Mags screamed, her face contorted with fear.

Ronnie stopped in his tracks. "What?"

"Some guy just took them!" Mags was frantic, tears falling from her eyes.

"Was she shot?" Jax pushed him out of the way, flying down the driveway.

"No, he shot the tires out," a voice came as a shaky Jillian crawled out of the back seat. "He injected her with something."

"Who was it?" Jax's eyes were wild. "Shit! I can't feel her at all!"

"My ex." Chrissie climbed out and fell to the driveway in a boneless puddle. "Travis Nielson."

Ronnie flew into motion and grabbed Chrissie. "She's in shock. Dega, help her."

"Mags, what the fuck happened?" Jax demanded, his tone tinged with panic.

"I don't know; I was driving. Before lunch, Airy told us something hit her radar, but she said it wasn't close. We switched to me driving so she could use her soul sight, but nothing happened the rest of the day. We pulled in here, and Airy got out to get the mail, and Rafe wanted to help. That's what they were doing. I didn't see anything else."

"Jillian?" Ronnie jumped in. "What happened?"

"We never even saw the car," she stuttered. "She dove in front of Rafe, grabbing him, and the guy injected something into her neck. He grabbed Rafe and then her, shot the tires out, and then took off."

Jax was shaking violently. "Why can't we feel her?"

In Ronnie's arms, Chrissie started to come to, her eyes just as wild as Jax's. "Rafe, Ells. We have to call the police. Now."

Jillian had her phone out and called 911, reporting the incident as Smitty came tearing down the driveway. She threw herself at him, breaking into heavy sobs.

"I can't help them as Airiella can," Degataga apologized to Ronnie. "Even Tama could help better."

Ronnie's arms tightened reflexively around Chrissie. "Why would he take Airiella?"

No one answered. It didn't make any sense why Chrissie's ex would have taken her. "Mommy?"

Chrissie struggled to get out of Ronnie's arms, and he set her down gently. "Yes, baby?"

"Why are you crying? What's wrong with Uncle Jax?" Jace stared at the group wide-eyed while Jax shook, and Smitty tried to hide Jillian and the hysterical Mags from sight. "What was that loud noise?"

"Baby, when you talked to your dad this morning, what did he say?" Chrissie tried to control her voice, but Ronnie heard the panic underlying the words.

"The same thing he always says," Jace said bitterly. "That we need to be with him, and you took us away. You kidnapped us. I told you he was high."

"I know, Jace. Was there anything else?" Chrissie bit her lip, and Ronnie moved closer to her, sliding his arm over her shoulders.

"What's happening?" Jace demanded to know. His stance, so like his mother's it was almost comical. "Tell me the truth."

Chrissie sobbed, turning into Ronnie's chest, and he again fought back the feeling of panic rising in him. Ronnie held Chrissie, his heart torn between worry about Airiella and Rafe, and Chrissie and Jace. "Buddy, I'm sorry. Your dad showed up here and took Rafe and Airiella. He might have hurt her."

Fury took over the small boy's face. "Why would he hurt her?"

"That's what we are trying to figure out. Do you remember anything important in your conversation with your dad?" Ronnie tried for reasonable, but his voice held the same note of panic that Chrissie's and Jax's did.

Degataga knelt in front of the boy bringing him close to eye level with him since he was so tall. "Think hard,

Jace. Think of all the conversations lately that you have had with him and try to remember if he said anything about being here or taking any of you."

Jace got an uncomfortable look on his face, and he shifted from foot to foot. "I don't want to be a tattletale."

"It's okay, no one will get in trouble," Degataga told him, his tone gentle and reassuring.

"Bryce told Auntie Ell's secret," he spilled.

"What do you mean?" Degataga had a way with kids, that was for sure.

"He told Daddy she was an angel." He looked apologetically to his mom. "I tried to take the phone away, but he got mad at me and ran away with it. He was talking about the magic she can do. When I caught up to him, he was describing her wings."

"Chris." Ronnie moved her away a little bit so he could look at her. "What would he do with that information, and would he even believe it?"

"Why wouldn't he believe it? He's an addict; Travis thinks he's suffered alien abduction when he's high. I have no idea why he would take her unless he thought that he could get something out of it," Chrissie declared, and her face was stone-cold. "Travis is going to try and sell her. That's what he did with the abduction he claimed. He tried to sell his story."

Jace burst into tears at that, and Degataga scooped him up and tried to console him. "I'm taking him back to Aedan's."

Ronnie nodded, a sense of dread filling his chest as his eyes met Jax's. "You think he will out her for money?"

"An addict will do anything for money for their next score. It's why I divorced him so quickly," Chrissie spoke truthfully.

"How? Who would he sell her to?" Ronnie desperately wanted this not to be true.

"Is there a market for angels?" Jillian asked through hiccups.

"No." Smitty's tone had a harsh bite to it. "But there is for wild stories in the news."

"Fucking shit!" Jax exploded. "Stolas!" he screamed maniacally. "Help!"

Ronnie flinched at the pain in his friend's voice. It was the same pain in his heart, and he could only hope the demon would answer. He hadn't been around in a while, and he wasn't sure what exactly Stolas would be able to do.

"You bellowed?" Stolas appeared, leaning on the mailbox casually.

"Airiella was abducted along with Chrissie's son. We can't feel her, and we think he took her to expose her for money." Jax stalked over to him, his body rigid.

Stolas straightened, and his expression changed, giving Ronnie a chill deep inside him. If he had ever wondered about the depth of feeling the demon had for his angel, his facial expression answered the question. "He was able to capture her?"

"They said he injected her with something." Jax's fists clenched tightly, and they heard sirens in the distance.

"I can smell the chemicals." Stolas spoke in a tone so cold that even Jax backed up.

Stolas looked around in the grass and found the syringe. "Tell me fast before they get here."

Jax relayed the information they had in a rush and waited while Stolas examined the syringe, smelling it and dropping it back in the grass. "Can you help?"

"Not directly, this isn't the work of a demon or a creature from Hell, yet he belongs there. He injected her with a mix of a sedative and heroin. It's a lethal combination, and I can't speak as to what it will do to her. She's not exactly human. He didn't inject the boy?" Stolas spoke in a manner that left no doubt about how angry he was with this situation.

Jillian shook her head no. "Only her that I saw."

"She wouldn't have felt danger from him if he was high. If she tackled the boy out of the way, she felt something off and that the danger was to him. I'll ask around and be in touch." He disappeared as the cop's cars came into sight.

Ronnie felt the aggression building in his body. "There has to be something we can do."

Smitty pulled out his phone and called up the footage on the security camera. "We have video proof of what Jillian saw, as well as a view of the car he drove. I'll give it to the cops, but it also gives us something to search on as well," Smitty told Ronnie before the cops got out of the car.

Ronnie nodded in answer, knowing that pursuing this on their own would get them into trouble with the law. They went through the story again with the cops, Smitty showed them the footage and then pointed to the empty syringe that Stolas had dropped in the grass.

Not surprisingly, the demon didn't show on any of the footage, and Chrissie didn't want the police to question Jace. Degataga came back out and gave his statement. They spent over an hour interviewing Chrissie on Travis, his habits, behavior, and anything he had said to her in recent weeks.

She repeated that she hadn't known he'd been in the state. She thought he was still in in St. Louis, where he had disappeared to avoid warrants out for him. All of their phones chimed as an amber alert went out for Rafe with his description, Airiella's description, and the car information. It was only a matter of time before the media caught wind of it.

So far, they had managed to evade being found by those that sought them out; Ronnie didn't want their location to get found out now. "Can we move this inside the property? We'd like not to be found by members of the media."

Smitty ran to get their SUV to tow the car to the house while the cops agreed to move inside. "Media can help sometimes," one of the policement told Ronnie.

"Not when you are on a TV show. They just want to invade your privacy, find out where you live, and try to set up surveillance on you," Jax snarled angrily.

"I understand. I'm sorry, I didn't realize you were on a TV show. That changes things a bit. Are you sure your fiancée didn't get taken because of that? To ransom off? Meaning that maybe the son wasn't the target," the cop tried to reason out.

Mags face changed to a stunned one. "We didn't think of that. We just assumed since it was her ex that he was after her sons."

"That could very well be true. Mr. Nielson could have also seen an opportunity with Ms. Raven and decided last second to take her too."

Ronnie felt sick. "The reason doesn't matter right now. We just need them both back safely." He couldn't go telling the cops she was worth a fortune to media outlets because she was an angel.

"This is a small community, I'm certain he will be spotted quickly," one of the other cops broke in gently. "We will do our best to bring them both back unharmed. I'm also going to have this tested to see what drug got administered to Ms. Raven."

They already knew from Stolas that it was lethal. He didn't know if the reason they couldn't feel her was that it killed her or knocked her clean-out. He didn't want to dwell on it because his reaction wasn't going to be one he could control. Jax was in the same boat.

Ronnie left Chrissie with the others, grabbing Jax and Degataga and pulling them outside, out of earshot of the cops. He repeated what Stolas had told him about the contents of the syringe, and Degataga stiffened.

"He said it was lethal?" Degataga was stunned.

"Yep. What will it do to Airiella?" Ronnie hated the helpless feeling that came over him.

"She's still human; she's just extra. If it's lethal to humans, it will be lethal to her. If Chrissie is correct and Travis took her to expose what she is for money, and she dies and comes back from that and Travis gets it on film, there's no stopping the media storm that will happen. Even if he only took her to ransom her back to Jax, seeing that happen will change things drastically."

Jax deflated. "She's supposed to be safe here. There has to be something we can do." Ronnie saw Jax breaking down before it happened and moved to put a supportive arm around him.

"Taklishim is on his way; he said he was going to mobilize animals throughout the area. A few will meet him here. We'll need something with both their scents on it, he said. They've helped out with countless missing children cases along this area." Degataga sounded numb.

"Won't that only work if wherever they are an animal can go?" Ronnie wondered.

"Not necessarily. Taklishim can answer that better than I can. From what I understand, those that can shift to an animal have a naturally heightened sense of smell, sight, or auditory response, depending on the animal."

"Why can't we feel her, Dega?" Jax mumbled, losing his mental grip.

"Heroin is a dangerous drug and can harm the brain in various ways. Combined with a sedative, depending on what got used, it can shut down Airiella's responses. Don't assume she is dead. Lethal or not, she's extraordinary; this is a very tricky situation, as well as dangerous in a variety of ways."

"Rafe just turned six. He's a little boy and idolizes Airiella. I can't imagine what he's feeling after seeing her like that," Ronnie murmured. "Especially if she dies."

Degataga dropped his head. "Let's not borrow trouble. Kids are resilient, these even more so given the things they've seen and been a part of; times like these, we need to hold on to hope."

Jax broke out in sobs. "I failed her."

"It's not just you, bro. We all failed her in this one." Ronnie sat next to him.

"She wouldn't see it that way." Chrissie spoke from behind them, her face streaked with tears and ravaged. "You both know that. If you could speak to her, she'd tell you the same thing. Jax, I can't imagine what you are feeling right now, I know how I feel, and it's killing me. I'm sorry I put you all in this situation."

She moved to sit next to Jax, reaching her hand out to him, and he shot to his feet. "Don't touch me!" he bit out sharply.

Ronnie wasn't sure what to think. Jax had never reacted like this before. He stood facing him. "Jax," he began and was halted.

"Not you either. I can't take it right now. I'll fucking break." Jax stepped away out of reach.

Degataga watched him in concern, shaking his head at Ronnie, who started to go after him. "No one will touch you, Jax."

Ronnie turned back to Chrissie, who was crying silently into her hands. "I'm so sorry."

Ronnie himself was about to break. Degataga rushed back into the house and came back out with Smitty, who took one look at Jax and moved to Ronnie's side, putting a gentle hand on his arm. "Sit down."

"This is my fault." Chrissie tried to stand, but Ronnie held her in place, unable to deny it though he knew it wasn't her fault. He was just too emotional at the moment to set her straight.

"That's bullshit Chrissie, and you know it," Smitty told her, speaking Ronnie's thoughts for him.

"He wouldn't be here if it weren't for me."

"If you want to play that game, then it's my fucking fault for bringing you here," Jax snapped, clearly at the end of his rope.

Ronnie felt the world unraveling around him. "Stay with me, Ronnie," Smitty said quietly. "I can't have you gone too, hold it together for me, man."

"She's fucking gone, Smitty." Ronnie felt the first crack inside him. "A little boy I love is gone, too."

Chrissie exploded, the force of it causing Jax to stumble, and Ronnie started to lose control. "God damn it! Stop! All of you!"

"Ronnie." Smitty grabbed his head and made him face him. "Look at me. Focus. I feel it too, but if we don't hold it together, we have no hope of helping. Stay with me. Breathe."

Ronnie stared at him, hot and angry tears slipping out of his eyes. "I'm fucking cracking, man," Ronnie warned.

"Later. Break later. Chrissie, look at me," Smitty demanded, his voice rougher than necessary. "There is no way you are to blame for the actions of someone else. Not one person here blames you because your ex-husband is a drug addict and deranged, possibly psychotic." Smitty's voice cracked a bit. "All of us are hurting and scared right now for both of them. If Airiella is conscious, there is no way Rafe is in danger. She will protect him with her life."

"What if she's not and she's the one in danger?" she whispered brokenly. "I put my best friend in the line of fire."

"No, you didn't. Airiella puts herself in the line of fire all the time; this has nothing to do with you directly. That's the fear in you talking," Smitty told her, ever the voice of reason.

"He's right, Chrissie." Degataga squatted down in front of her. "This isn't your fault. You've got to hold it together for your other two boys who are beyond scared right now. Jace needs you. Airiella needs you to be strong. I believe she knew what she was doing getting out of that car. And if she didn't, Smitty is right, Rafe being in her presence is the safest place for him."

RONAN

Ronnie knew that wasn't true if Airiella wasn't conscious. It was the most dangerous place for him to be, alone and scared. The panic rose in him again. Smitty tightened the hold he had on Ronnie's arm as a warning to calm down. "You are one of the very few on the shortlist of people that can bring Jax back from the edge, you've got to calm down," Smitty whispered urgently. "If that darkness shit comes back to him over this, we are beyond screwed."

Aedan came upon them, his face pale and his arms full of clothes, he walked past them and to the side of the house and came back, squatting down next to Smitty. "Chrissie, Bryce is scared, and I can't get him to calm down. The police cars are having quite an effect on him."

"Shit," Ronnie swore and glanced up as Taklishim came around the corner and walked straight to Jax, standing before him and in his way of pacing. Ronnie got ready to move if Jax got aggressive with the warrior.

"Let him be," Aedan said gently. "They need each other right now."

Jax collapsed against the large man they've grown so close to and fell apart, which sent Ronnie flying over his edge, and he stood and bolted, running straight to the gym. This time was different. None of them were with her this time. They had no lines of communication, and no information on whether or not either of them was okay.

He started punching, trying to bleed out the emotions that were taking over, in a way that could be bad for all of them. Alcohol was a crutch he couldn't afford to turn to, to get through this. He needed a way to numb everything, and it was all his brain could focus on, telling him just to take a shot to calm his nerves.

He hit harder and faster, his moves becoming a blur

of aggression that didn't ease. He didn't hear Aedan come in over the sounds of his fists thudding into the bag, the cries coming from his throat. The sight of Jax breaking down, Chrissie was blaming herself, Ronnie's pain and worry, the absence of one of the most treasured people in his life, and an innocent little boy that he had grown to love so much.

It was too much. Ronnie fell to his knees and screamed, letting the rage take over his vocal cords, his voice bouncing off the walls. It wasn't until Aedan put his hand on Ronnie's back that he fell silent. "She can't fight him if she's drugged," he whispered weakly.

"Jax just said the same thing. Ronnie, she's the strongest person we know, she'll find a way to either come out of it or back to us somehow. You've got to believe that. You need to go back out to Chrissie; she thinks you're mad at her."

Help.

Chapter Four

Chrissie jolted as Jax cried out, she looked up from her self-pity to see Smitty, Jax, and Degataga's eyes wide. "What?"

"She just said help," Smitty told her kindly, his voice tight with tension despite the kind tone he was using.

"She's alive then?" Chrissie felt a shimmer of hope.

"I think we'd feel it if she weren't," Smitty hedged. "That's all we got. At least that's all I got."

"It's all I got, too," Degataga said softly. "Chrissie, can you go get something of Rafe's that has his scent on it. Like an unwashed piece of clothing?"

She nodded robotically and went into the house, each step up the stairs feeling like the weight of the world was on her shoulders. She got up to her room, went through the clothes basket, grabbed a shirt he had worn yesterday, and something in her chest tightened, her sweet little boy.

She had to hold it together. She went to Airiella's

room and grabbed the shirt she had left on the bed that morning that she slept in and went back downstairs and out the back door, handing them both to Taklishim. "Please find them," she whispered as her legs buckled.

She found herself in Ronnie's arms again, somewhere she was all too fond of being, yet felt like she didn't belong. Not anymore. Not after this. "I'm sorry, Chris. I lost it." He kissed her temple.

She tried not to get her hopes up. "You don't need to apologize. I accepted a long time ago that she and Jax were first in your life."

His chest rumbled under her ear. "We need to talk, just not right now. I'm not much good right now and will completely fuck it all up." He set her on her feet. "Go get your boys and bring them out here."

"Is that a good idea with everyone's emotions so high?" She wanted to be there for them all. Airiella got taken trying to save her son. That was something she knew for a fact, and she didn't want her other two to be damaged by that.

"I think if they are out here, Jax will rein it in better. I know I will." He leaned his forehead against hers. "Smitty was right; no one blames you. This situation isn't your fault."

"Easy for you to say, much harder for me to believe," Chrissie scoffed at him, her heart breaking wide-open again.

"You two are so much alike; it's scary sometimes." Ronnie gave her a small smile.

Chrissie felt fear swamping through her again, and she clutched at Ronnie's shirt, bunching it up in her fists. "She'll be okay, won't she? Besides my boys, she's all I have left."

"That's not true, Chris." Ronnie dropped his voice. "You have me, and you have all of us here."

"He won't hurt Rafe, at least not physically. He never has before, anyway. I can't say the same about her," Chrissie admitted, terrified for her friend. "He's gotten violent with me before; I have no reason to doubt he would with her either."

Ronnie's face went hard. "Go get the boys." His voice held a dangerous edge to it. "We'll talk about that later."

"God, I'm so stupid," she muttered. "Why would I say that? I'm sorry, Ronnie. I'm hoping she will be fine."

"I'm not angry because you said he'd hurt her, I already figured that. You misunderstood my reaction. Go get the boys," he repeated, trying to tamp down the anger.

She backed away, unsure how to take what he'd said. Her emotions were frayed and raw. She headed towards Aedan's house as he fell in step beside her.

He put his arm around her shoulders. "He's angry because you just told him you suffered abuse. He's upset about what happened to you. He's upset about Airiella too, but what you just saw was because of you." Aedan tried to explain it, but it wasn't sinking into her head.

"She'll be okay. If she can get a message out, I have to believe she will be okay," Chrissie repeated.

"Chrissie! Snap out of it. Look at me," Aedan demanded as they got to his porch.

Startled, she looked up at him. "What?"

"Ronnie isn't mad about what you said. Take a look around. Notice that everyone relaxed a bit after they heard her? They know she's alive. If she's alive, she will find a way to fight. We've all been through enough shit with her to know that."

"It was only one word, and that word was asking for help." She still wasn't getting it.

"It's confirmation she's alive. It's exactly what Ronnie and Jax both needed to come off that edge. That look you saw on Ronnie's face was not because you said Airiella would be hurt. It was because you said *you* were hurt. The big dumbass might be in love with Airiella for the rest of his life, but if you can't see that he is also in love with you, I can't help you."

"What?" She couldn't have heard that right.

Aedan sighed. "You heard me. Go get your boys." He pushed her in the house, and Bryce catapulted into her arms.

"I'm sorry, Mommy! I got Auntie Ells hurt!" He cried into her shoulder.

"Jace, why did you tell him that?" Chrissie tried not to snap, realizing Jace wasn't in any better of a place than Bryce was.

"Sorry," he mumbled in a small voice.

"Come on, outside," she ordered him, carrying the crying child. Ronnie had been right; their presence helped bring her back from hysteria. She looked questioningly at Aedan as she walked past him, recalling what he said.

"Yes, I was serious," he told her, correctly interpreting her expression. "Ronnie's right, you and Airiella are eerily similar in a lot of ways."

"We share some of the same experiences," she told him sadly.

"That right there, is why he got upset. We all might have known that on some level. But you just verbally confirmed it, and that is an extremely sensitive topic among all of us."

"He loves me?" She dared to ask.

"I'd bet my marriage on it," Aedan said seriously. "Give him time. Separating from Airiella is hard for him. She's his first real love, and he's scared."

"Of me?" Chrissie stopped in her tracks, Bryce's head smacking into her chin.

"Partly. If you know what to look for with Ronnie, you'd see it too. He wears his heart on his sleeve, but trust me, he's in love with *you* and your boys." Aedan's words soothed Chrissie in a way she hadn't known she needed.

"Thank you," she said gratefully and started walking again.

Ronnie met her halfway and took the emotional Bryce from her arms. "Hey, little man. It will be okay. Your auntie is one tough lady."

Chrissie had never had any doubt about how Ronnie felt for her children. Aedan was right about him wearing his heart on his sleeve. It was apparent every time he was around them, which was a lot. She had been less sure of his feelings for her because she was always comparing it to how he felt about Airiella.

Chrissie didn't begrudge him that, she understood it more than he gave her credit for; she also had no problem with it. She saw how it was with Smitty and Aedan. None of them had issues with Airiella being close. Every one of them admitted to being in love with her.

It wasn't until Aedan told her Ronnie loved her that she realized there was room for her. Smitty was head over heels in love with Jillian, and she also knew without a shred of doubt that he was in love with Airiella too. It was just in a different way. Now she just needed to figure out in which way Ronnie was in love with her.

She wondered if that was what Ronnie wanted to talk to her about; if so, he was right, this wasn't the time. Not with her child and best friend missing because her douche of an ex-husband was looking for a score.

She looked around, trying to find where Jace went, and her heart caught as she saw him holding Jax's hand. His little face devastated, but he was trying to be brave. Jax understandably didn't want Chrissie around him, so she stayed back while he talked with a cop that had come into the yard.

Smitty walked up to her this time. "Jax isn't mad at you, Chrissie. He didn't want physical touch because the sympathy would have tipped him past the point of no return."

"Are you sure? He seemed pretty angry." Chrissie was more willing to listen now that Jace was with him.

"I'm sure. It's not the first time Jax has been at that point. It hasn't been since she took all that energy from him, but we are all familiar with where he was. Notice he didn't want Ronnie touching him either."

"He let Taklishim touch him," she countered. Jace moved closer to Jax's leg.

"Taklishim has an interesting relationship with Airiella. You know that. They both needed each other at that moment. He would have reacted the way he did with you if *anyone* had tried to touch him. He did it with Ronnie too; you heard him," Smitty repeated.

"Jace feels responsible for this," Chrissie told him, ashamed and feeling like a bad mother.

"I know. Jace told Jax he was sorry he couldn't stop

it. He also told Jax that he would help him be strong. You've got quite a kid in that one." Smitty hugged her.

"The only good things that came out of that marriage were those boys. And he damaged them too." Chrissie got angry again. "I swear I could just kill him right now."

"Seems to be the popular opinion at the moment," Smitty agreed. "You know about Ronnie's past, right?"

"I know some of it." She looked at Smitty through narrowed eyes. "His father was abusive to his mother and him because of alcoholism. He hasn't told me specific events, but having an addict for an ex-husband lets me know more than you think."

"Did he tell you he, himself, had a bit of a substance abuse problem?"

Chrissie felt her heartbeat slow. "No," she answered with a controlled voice. Her face must have given away something because Smitty started moving.

"It was a long time ago, Chrissie. He hasn't touched anything since Winnie died. But if you want to understand why he was losing control like that, you need to understand where he came from; he drank and smoked weed to escape the pain his father caused."

"Okay, I can see that. It's what Ronnie lived with, so he had easy access to it," she hedged, now nervous about her feelings for Ronnie. She couldn't do another relationship with an addict.

"He also started fighting then. After his father got arrested, he stopped smoking weed, but he still drank. We got him involved in boxing and channeled his emotions into that. When Winnie died, he stopped drinking immediately. He straightened all his shit out, talked out issues, and became the first line of defense for Jax. He took care of him through everything. He won't even take a celebratory drink now."

"So then, just a bit ago, when he took off, what was that?" Chrissie wanted to know.

"My guess is he was fighting the urge to take a drink to numb the emotions that were flooding him. Notice he channeled it all to the gym. He's sturdy and stable."

"I'm assuming that he knows Airiella's ex-husband is an alcoholic?" Chrissie asked carefully.

"Yes, he knows that. Airiella also knows about his past, and she trusts him with her life, remember that. I only told you so you'd understand. This blood bond we share with her makes this hard on us. We felt her panic and then felt her disappear. If she gets hurt, we'll know. The separation from her is a physical pain we endure. It also gave us part of her empath skills; we now feel all the emotions of those around us, which was pretty overwhelming. Not just for him, for all of us."

The ball of anxiety that had gathered in her gut slowly dissipated. "I understand."

"None of that was personal or against you. Ronnie loves you, and *none* of us blame you. We all want a piece of your ex-husband now, but none of us blame you."

Her eyes filled with tears. "I don't know how you can't blame me. I blame me."

"I know you do. Airiella would be the same way, and we would tell her the same thing."

"So, what do we do now?" Chrissie took a deep fortifying breath.

"You need to go over there and sit with your man. He's freaking out about Rafe," Smitty said honestly.

"He won't hurt Rafe. Travis took him to hurt me."

"Then go over there and think about where he might have gone. What his next steps will be. You are the only one here who knows him. We have to figure out a way to get a step ahead of him to get them back."

Chrissie smiled. "You truly are the voice of reason."

"At your service, my lady," Smitty bowed.

Chapter Five

Ronnie felt a blast of pain come through the connection, his arms instinctively tightening on Bryce. His gaze flew to Jax, who has doubled over again, Jace crying out in alarm. A second wave hit, more potent than the first, followed by intense nausea.

Degataga appeared and plucked Bryce from his arms, and he leaned over the chair and vomited. "It's the drug, it's either wearing off, or he gave her another dose," Degataga explained as Ronnie wiped his mouth off.

Chrissie walked up with a bottle of water, blanching. "The pain is from the drug?"

Ronnie shook his head. "No, that was something else."

"I didn't want to be right about that," she whispered in horror. "Aberdeen!" She stood up and yelled at the cops. "He loves Nirvana. Aberdeen has a huge heroin problem. He would have gone there."

"Drugs are everywhere, ma'am," one of the cops

said as he looked skeptical at her outburst.

"Yes, but there are also more people there and more places for him to hide," Taklishim backed her up.

Another round of pain slammed into Ronnie. At least he knew she was still alive. That gave him a thought. If she was getting through with her emotions, he should be able to reach her.

Angel? Can you hear me?

Ronnie? Help. It's so dark, and I can't use my powers, came an incredibly weak reply. *He's coming.*

Angel, where are you? All he heard was that white noise again.

He looked up at Degataga, who nodded in reply. She had broadcasted to all of them. "What's the white noise?" Ronnie was afraid of the answer.

"I think he drugged her again," he replied softly. "I don't know how much of that she can take, Ronnie. Don't ask me to guess. It took three hours for it to wear off, she's metabolizing it fast, but it's already in her system. A second dose of that so close together is dangerous."

Jax looked sick, and Ronnie wobbled, trying to stand. "Who would have thought demons are easier to fight?" Ronnie managed to say before dropping back in the chair.

"Demons are predictable." Taklishim came up to him and pulled him up. "Drug addicts are not. Stolas is out on the beach. Jax, I don't think he should go."

Ronnie moved, grabbing Chrissie's hand. "I'll go."

Taklishim staggered backward as a wave of energy slammed through them. Degataga braced his friend, looking at Ronnie. "I think he's unhappy."

"No shit, you think?" Ronnie gasped for breath.

"He's in love with Airiella too. He didn't look like he took the news so well. I'm not surprised."

"Go, get him out of here. That's going to be hard enough to explain to already edgy cops that aren't used to dealing with a drug addict kidnapping two people," Taklishim ground out, trying to maintain his control.

"Get it together, Tak. You can't fight the demon," Ronnie reminded him. "He's not here to harm anyone."

Degataga motioned for him to go, and Ronnie took off, pulling Chrissie behind him. "Oops, sorry. You should probably stay, too."

"I want to go. It will make me feel like I'm doing something at least," Chrissie pleaded.

He looked back at Degataga. "I'll cover; take her."

Chrissie's phone rang. She pulled it out of her pocket, suddenly surrounded by cops. She looked helplessly at Ronnie, who glanced back out to the beach, torn. "Answer it," he told her, still holding her hand. He glanced at Smitty and nodded to the beach.

He saw Smitty take off as Chrissie answered, putting it on speakerphone. "Hello?"

"Give me back my boys," he heard a man tell her.

"Travis, let them go. You've committed multiple felonies already," Chrissie said forcefully. "You are only making this worse on yourself. Don't do this to your children."

"I didn't do anything, you did," he sang. Ronnie heard the tone and knew the guy was high as a kite.

"Let them go," Chrissie repeated.

"Would you be jealous if I fucked her?" he cooed in a revolting voice.

Chrissie looked sick, and Jax and Ronnie both went

rigid at the question. "You'd do that to another human being in front of your child?"

"He's blindfolded. He wouldn't see anything."

Rage tore through Ronnie, and the only thing that held him back from snapping was Bryce and Jace's faces. Jace might have been the only thing tethering Jax. Tears fell down the boy's face. "What do you want, Travis?" Chrissie's voice shook.

"I want what's mine. Rightfully mine." Travis was back to singing his sentences. "My wife and my boys. Little boys need their fathers."

Ronnie saw the moment Taklishim lost control, and his warrior took over. He dropped Chrissie's hand and dove, tackling the man. "Tak, no. How the fuck would you explain yourself. Think about it," Ronnie whispered angrily to the furious warrior.

"How can you listen to this?" Taklishim shoved him off violently.

"Why do I hear other men, Chrissie? You fucking whore! You dirty goddamn fucking whore!" Travis screamed through the phone.

Now it was Taklishim holding Ronnie in place. "Maybe with the demon was the safer place for us to be," Taklishim snarled, maintaining a delicate thread of control.

Aedan grabbed Jace and Bryce and took them into the house, rage on his face. The cops were motioning for her to keep him talking, and Ronnie wanted to scream.

"I'll just fuck her since you are a fucking little whore," came the next singsong statement.

"If you fucking touch her or that child, I will rip your balls from your body and stuff them down your throat," Jax roared.

Shit, with Jace gone, nothing was holding Jax back. Silence came from the other end of the phone, and Chrissie blindly handed it to a cop and wrapped her arms around Jax, her face pale, mouth trembling, and body shaking.

"Who's this?" Travis asked, finally.

"I'm the man that is now after you because you took two people you shouldn't have. You'd better hope I don't find you, and if I do, you better start praying hard if I find either of them harmed," Ronnie broke in.

"Well, you aren't the same one who just yelled." Travis almost sounded sober for a moment. "You'll never catch me, I'm the gingerbread man," he sang, his voice tinged with insanity.

"Got it, Aberdeen, downtown," called one of the cops.

"Oh, Chrissie. You'll regret this." The phone went dead.

Taklishim pulled out his phone and walked away, his body tense and anger rolling off of him. Degataga moved to follow him, glancing back at Chrissie, who hadn't let go of Jax. Ronnie pulled her away from Jax gently, gathering her to him.

"Jax." Taklishim stalked over and pulled him away.

Ronnie held Chrissie, trying to calm his blood down. "Did he rape you and beat you?" Ronnie growled.

There was no response from her. She just held Ronnie tighter and trembled in his arms, her body cold. He didn't honestly know if he wanted an answer or not; if he could handle it. His control was hanging by a thread thinner than the one that was holding Taklishim in place.

Smitty came back up, jogging. "Stolas is a very pissed off demon and flat out scary as hell," Smitty said as he got closer. "He wants one of us to tell him when Airiella's found, and where she is."

"Chrissie was right, Aberdeen, she just got a call that they traced," Ronnie said between gritted teeth. "We should let him take care of the problem. It's no less than he deserves."

"Rafe is there," Chrissie cried softly.

"He wouldn't hurt your son," Smitty confirmed instantly. "Stolas isn't a bad person."

"I know, but I don't want him to see or hear something awful. More awful than what he just heard his dad say, I mean." Chrissie fumbled with her words.

"What did he say?" Smitty looked at Ronnie. Ronnie could only shake his head. Repeating it wouldn't help his sanity.

Ronnie glanced back at the house and saw Mags and Jillian in the doorway, their hands over their mouths and their faces full of the horror they overheard. Smitty would find out soon enough what was said as he saw him head over to Jillian.

"Rafe is my sensitive boy. Hearing Travis say those things will hurt him so badly." Chrissie looked up at Ronnie, her eyes filled with a pain so deep it tore at him.

Taklishim walked up. "I've got a friend on the force in Aberdeen who is also a wolf. I've given him the general area to start looking in. We'll find her. If something has happened to either of them, it won't go well. I've given him a kill order." Taklishim's voice was cold and hard; the anger under the surface at a boiling point.

Chrissie gasped. "He's still the boys' father."

"He just threatened to rape Airiella in front of your son, and you think he's worth saving?" an astonished

Taklishim asked Chrissie.

"You aren't a murderer, Taklishim, and that little boy loves you. Don't sink to that level," Chrissie pleaded, and the warrior caved, pulling his phone out and texting something. "He's damaged."

"He was damaged before the drugs if this is where he has gotten to," Taklishim told her. Ronnie agreed with the man. To hell with his not wanting to hurt people, Ronnie wanted to kill this fucker himself. Not only for what he threatened to do to Airiella, for what he has done to his own children, and what he did to Chrissie.

"Even if that's true, he'll answer for his crimes. Just don't let it be by you or one of your people. Hurt him if it makes you feel better, don't kill him. Airiella would be pissed." Chrissie spilled the truth neither man wanted to accept.

She had a point, Airiella would be angry. As Ronnie had that thought, another pain passed through him, at a soul level that dropped every one of her connections to the ground. Sorrow washed over him, Airiella's life was in mortal danger.

Chapter Six

Chrissie lurched as Ronnie dropped. "Are you okay?"
"Airiella," he gasped, his face pale. So this is what it would feel like to have a part of his soul die.

Degataga was the first to recover and helped Ronnie get up. "Onida said her heart is weakening; the drug is too much for it to handle." The news was devastating.

Taklishim came over with Jax. Smitty, Mags, and Aedan followed. "Tama told me to go find her." Taklishim looked around at the cops. "Onida told her that Airiella needs one of us to burn the drug from her system."

"They won't question why you leave," Smitty pointed out. "Any of the rest of us, they would. We were all here when it happened."

"Jax, call Stolas here," Taklishim said quietly.

"What?" Jax looked at him, stunned disbelief written across his face.

"I need help." Taklishim sounded desperate. Chrissie worried what that might mean for Rafe and

Airiella. "If I can't burn it out of her system, he probably knows something that can."

Degataga slowly nodded. "Onida confirmed that. She's also a little frantic, which means we are running out of time before her heart stops."

Chrissie tried to stifle a sob. "Can she come back from that?"

Taklishim still had a hard edge to him, but his face softened as his eyes raked over Chrissie. "We simply don't know. We believed Airiella had a limited amount of times for that to happen, but no one knows what that limit is or if it is even fact."

Smitty cleared his throat. "One thing to consider, if you call Stolas and he finds her, I'm pretty sure that the consequences will be severe. He was barely able to keep his demon magic under control. And he didn't hear the phone call either."

"You know, you keep saying my name, and it does get back to me," Stolas said quietly, appearing out of nowhere.

Taklishim went rigid, and his jaw clenched tightly. "I need your help," he bit out.

"Smitty is right, there will be extremely severe consequences if I find her first," he warned. "What was said in the phone call?"

"I don't care about the consequences. My concern is Airiella and the child. The drug is weakening her heart; she doesn't have much time left. She needs one of us to burn the drug from her system. If there's too much in her and because it's been in there doing damage already, I'm afraid it's not enough. Is there something you know of that we can use to get it out of her system?"

Chrissie felt ice-cold fear as the demon's eyes flared red; the energy radiating off him was lethal, and she took a step back, which he noticed. "My apologies, I mean no harm to anyone here. I can't guarantee anything I can come up with will work." He looked back at Taklishim. "Tell me about the area, and I will meet you there."

Something was nudging the far reaches of Chrissie's memory. "Lightning!" she shouted, drawing unwanted attention. "Oops, sorry." She lowered her voice. "Didn't you guys tell me that when her life is in danger, there's lightning?"

Ronnie's eyes got wide. "I can't believe we didn't think of that. She's right. Follow the lightning strikes."

Taklishim texted his friend and waited for the response. "He says there hasn't been any."

"There's a chance that wherever Travis is, he isn't around Airiella and Rafe at the moment. He could have left them somewhere and went to find his next high. The position they triangulated could only be where you find *him*, not the two we want to find." Aedan's logic stated a truth Chrissie hadn't considered. And truthfully, one that frightened her badly.

"It's the truth, and one that has been bothering me," Stolas said uncomfortably. "I've been toying with an idea." He pulled one of Airiella's feathers out of his pocket and ran it through his fingers.

"You still have that?" Jax asked softly, his eyes glued to the feather.

"It's always with me." Stolas held the feather as if it were the most precious thing in the world. "I've been thinking about asking your friend Kalisha to do a tracking spell using it. I've just not been able to give it up. This feather is a piece of Airiella, and it should point to her, but it will destroy the feather."

"I understand." Jax reached for Stolas's arm with no hesitation. "I'll make sure you get another."

Chrissie, feeling daring, asked, "What is she to you?"

Stolas stared at the feather in his hand. "A reminder of the humanity I used to have. A hope that I always won't be judged so harshly for one bad choice. She's the light that can penetrate the darkest of places inside me and love that I've so desperately missed. Thoughts of her warm whatever shards of my soul remain on those cold nights where the screams of the evil souls that reside in Hell crack me open. She gave me this freely as a sign of trust; me, a demon, a prince of Hell. She trusted me with a part of her that I could have used to hurt her. I don't know that redemption is possible for me, but I would gladly give my life to save hers."

"Stolas, she would do the same for you," Jax told the demon with a sincerity that struck them all mute with the stark truth of the words.

"I know. I'll find Airiella and the child. I'll bring your love back to you, and your child," Stolas said, looking at Chrissie, his voice rough.

Emboldened by the softer side Airiella had told her Stolas had, but that she'd never seen until now, Chrissie stepped close to the demon and stood on tiptoe to kiss his cheek. "In my eyes, you've redeemed yourself."

A ghost of a smile flitted across his face. He turned back to Taklishim. "Tell me where you will be."

Taklishim showed him an address. "I'll need to go there first to get clothes. I'll have to fly there to get there quickly."

"Warn whoever is there, that I will be showing up. I don't wish to harm your friends, but will do so if they impede my finding the two lost souls."

"I'll let him know. Thank you." Taklishim looked like he'd rather swallow his tongue than thank the demon.

Stolas disappeared, and Taklishim nodded at them and walked around the side of the house. Moments later, his gigantic eagle perched on the roof, looking down at them then took off, his mighty wings sending down a blast of air.

"Holy shit! Did you see that eagle!" one the cops cried.

Chrissie almost laughed. She clutched at Ronnie's hand. "There's nothing we can do now, is there?"

"No. We wait and hope to hear from one of those looking; cops, Taklishim, Stolas, someone is bound to find them."

"There isn't much difference between Stolas and us," Jax said softly, his eyes shining with unshed tears. "One bad choice, he said. He loves her the same way we love her."

"He does," Chrissie agreed. "I don't think that's a bad thing. Even if he's using dark magic, he's using it for good. It takes a strong man to keep helping as he does, knowing her heart belongs with someone else."

"We have to talk," Ronnie said again.

"She does love him; maybe I should have told him that." Jax looked out to the ocean.

"I think it would help more if it came from her," Chrissie said gently. "She'll tell him when the time is right."

"He knows," Ronnie interrupted. "She's told him. In

that blunt way, she has. She's told him that she loves him, but won't ever be in love with him."

Chrissie did laugh then. "That sounds like her." Then she started to cry again. "Is it wrong for me to hope that she isn't with Travis, that he did ditch them somewhere? I desperately don't want Rafe to have heard what Travis said."

"I want to go with them." Ronnie itched to put his hands around Travis's neck.

"Me too." Jax's tone broke Chrissie's heart, while Ronnie's made her want to back away it sounded so brutal.

Smitty and Aedan had been unnaturally quiet, and Chrissie glanced at the two men, both appeared brooding and lost in thought. Degataga was off on his phone, pacing along the tree line. There was an unnatural stillness to the air, the kind that happens before an epic storm hit.

"Mommy?" Jace sounded so small.

"What, baby?" She turned to see his tear-soaked face, and he came up next to Jax and retook his hand.

"Daddy's on TV."

Chrissie painfully felt her heart jump as all the large men surrounding her turned their attention to Jace. Jax lifted the boy slowly, then broke into a dead run back to the house, the rest of them following. The metaphorical storm had broken.

Chrissie got to the room in time to hear the reporter talking about the amber alert that had gone out, and an old mug shot of Travis plastered on the screen with the picture of Rafe she had given them. Then they showed clipped footage of the car he had been driving, taking off out of their driveway.

"I edited the footage to make sure nothing was

identifying our location," Smitty said at Ronnie's questioning look.

"In an even more bizarre twist to this sad story, Travis Nielson has contacted us to try and sell a story about a real-life angel. He claims the woman he kidnapped is an angel. We can only hope that she is safe and unharmed, with the child that Nielson took with her. The station has turned over the recording of the phone call to the police as evidence since he admitted to kidnapping her. We don't have the woman's identity yet, but will keep you updated on the story as it breaks. If you see this man or this car, please contact the police at the number on your screen. In a related story, the drug problem our country faces seems to be growing larger every day."

Bryce crawled out of the chair and came over to Ronnie, who picked him up and held him, his eyes unfocused as he stared at the TV screen. Jace was still attached to Jax, who had dropped to the floor in shock.

"You weren't wrong, Chrissie," Smitty broke the silence. "It's a good thing they assume he's just a crazed-out drug addict."

"For how long, though?" Aedan cut in. "The Vatican knows about Airiella."

"Father Roarke is on his way here," Degataga informed them. "That's who I was talking to out there."

"Because of this?" Ronnie finally snapped to attention.

"Yes. Father Roarke was coming anyway because of the wedding; he just moved the date up. There've already been calls from media wanting to ask about claims of a real-life angel; what're the churches' thoughts about that possibility."

RONAN

Chrissie jumped as a roar of thunder shook the house. She desperately wished it had been Airiella that caused it and knew in her heart that it wasn't. "Degataga predicted a storm earlier, guess he was right," Ronnie said to her casually.

"Chris, I fed the boys," Jillian called out.

"Thanks," Chrissie mumbled, another mark in her awful mother column. She hadn't even thought about that. Chrissie didn't know how long they stood there staring numbly at the TV screen, the amber alert flashing across the screen every few minutes. Each time she saw Rafe's face, it felt like she was getting stabbed.

"There's nothing we can do right now." Ronnie turned to her. "Let's go talk, come on." He took her hand and led her up the stairs and to his room, where he quietly closed the bedroom door. "He's asleep," he told her softly.

Her heart gave a mad flutter as she watched Ronnie tenderly put Bryce down on the bed and cover him up, kissing his forehead. At that moment, she longed for Rafe and Jace to be right there with them. She knew her oldest son wasn't going to leave Jax's side. He wanted to help find his auntie and little brother.

Ronnie moved to the foot of the bed and lay back, staring at the ceiling. He patted the bed next to him, and she went and sat down, her eyes raking over his solid body. It was only her sleeping child next to them that made her keep her hands to herself.

Ronnie pulled her down next to him, wrapping an arm around her and nestling her into his side. "Chris, today has been a shitty day. Like, beyond shitty. I'm so sorry that you are going through this."

"Me? All of us are going through this." Chrissie slid

her hand across his washboard stomach, unable to help herself.

"I know, but it's your child. I can't imagine how you feel. He's not mine, but I want to tear the world apart until I find him and then beat the shit out of the man who did this. I'm not proud of that, but it's the truth."

"Rafe is going to be so heartbroken if he heard that phone call." Chrissie felt her lips tremble. "He's only six. He should never have to know what rape is at that age. Or hear his mother called a whore. Sadly, that isn't the first time he's heard that one."

Ronnie's arm tightened around her, and she felt his body tense up. "You and Airiella have had many similar experiences," he said, his voice tight with anger as he repeated those words.

"We have. You might know more details than I do. When we talk about it between us, we discuss more the fall out than the actual events. I know she sees more than she lets on. I also know that she would never have let Rafe out of that car if she had felt danger."

Ronnie grabbed her hand that was roaming around his chest and brought it to his face, kissing her palm. "I've learned a lot about emotions from her, and right now, I have to admit that I've been shit about making them clear to you. I'm in love with you. Everything we've faced today has shown me that. It's also shown me that you weren't aware of that. That you think I only loved Airiella."

Chrissie couldn't deny it. She also didn't want to rat out Smitty and Aedan. She didn't know what to say, so she didn't say anything. He's cuddled with her before, but it felt different this time. She also had to admit to herself that she was scared of where this was going. Yes, he admitted that he was in love with her, but he could also finish it with it still wasn't the right time for him and shut her out.

"I *am* in love with Airiella, too. We all are, and it's different for all of us. I know that you know that, but I know for myself, I've needed to hear it from her on occasion. It's such a strange situation we all found ourselves in with her. It became clear to me today that the love I feel for the two of you is *very* different. Much like for her with the rest of us. I can't lie; I'm always going to need her and always be in love with her. I think it's part of being what she is. The flip side of that is, I need you too."

"I know, Ronnie. I'd never ask you to give her up," Chrissie said softly. "She's told me many times about how the connections and bonds work for her. I understand, and I'm okay with it."

"That's where you misunderstand me." Ronnie rolled to his side so he could look her in the eyes. "The sexual part of my relationship with Airiella isn't necessary. I haven't stopped it because I'm terrified that if you decide this is all too much for you that I will lose everything. I love these boys. I love them like they are my own. I'm scared to lose them, I'm scared I'll lose you, and that I'll lose her."

"You don't lose her, though. You'll never lose her." Chrissie saw the feral fear in his eyes.

"The rational part of my brain knows that. But the part that is ruled by all these emotions doesn't. Today has shown me that while I can't live without Airiella, I can't live without you either. Hearing Travis speaking those things sent me through the roof. I lost control. Not only because of Airiella but because it told me that you've already lived what he's threatening." He sighed. "I'm not doing this well, I'm sorry. You know how she has this unending well of love for everyone, and it never fades?"

Chrissie nodded. She knew it well. Bryce stirred next to them, crying out, and Ronnie rolled over, running his hand soothingly over the boys back, softly humming until he quieted down and drifted back off to sleep. Ronnie was the closest thing to an actual father figure that Bryce had ever had.

"I find myself with that type of well of love for you and her. She is comfort, love, and passion, and while you and I haven't gone there yet, what I feel for you is different. It's almost deeper than that. I can only equate it to the difference between Jax and I for her. For me, you would be my Jax."

"I know what you are saying, but not where this is going. Are you wanting to take this further between us, or wanting it to end because you feel too divided?" Chrissie asked, holding her breath.

"I didn't know the answer to that myself until today. I want to take it further. I promised myself that when Airiella married Jax, I would physically remove myself from the picture, even though they both have told me it's unnecessary. It's not fair to Jax, and more importantly, it's not fair to you." Ronnie bared his soul.

"To me? But I understand the need for it." Chrissie failed to grasp the significance of what Ronnie was saying.

"That may be true, but you deserve more than a divided me. I so badly want to give these boys a stable life, to give you what you deserve. I admit I'll probably still be affectionate with Airiella, but it won't go farther than that."

"Ronnie, she climbs in Smitty's lap, Mags climbs in hers. She kisses everyone, and she's taken naps with all of them, I don't have any problems with any of it. I've seen first-hand what that connection means to her. I have one with her myself, and while neither of us has been intimate like that, our intimacy is on a different level, and I wouldn't give that up. It would be a double standard for me to expect that of you. I understand everything you are saying to me. Believe me, I'm thrilled you want to take this farther and that you've said you are in love with me. The feeling is mutual."

"You wouldn't care if I crawled into bed with Airiella and Jax because I picked up on something she wasn't verbalizing?"

"No, I wouldn't. Airiella's come and crawled into bed with me numerous times. That's who she is. She gives what is needed. If she ever texted me in the middle of the night telling me she needed me, I'd crawl into bed with her myself; there're so many levels of love it's crazy to think about naming them. My past is just that, my past. Does it still hurt me? You bet it does. It's given me scars, insecurities, nightmares, flashbacks, pain, but it's also given me my children. I'd do it all over again for them. Yes, I need to heal, just as she did, and I am; by being around all of you. It has given my children and me a safe place, all of this love, this closeness, the sense of family. It's not just you that's been shit at talking about this; I have too." Chrissie bit the inside of her cheek to try and keep herself from saying too much.

"I feel the loss of Rafe here tonight deeply in my heart, as much as I feel the loss of Airiella. Did you know that?" Ronnie stroked a hand down her cheek.

"I do. I also believe that no matter what drugs Airiella's given if she felt Rafe was in danger, she would bring herself right out of it and slay whatever needed slain.

I can only assume that means that she is the only one in danger. I know what it's doing to all of you because it's doing the same thing to me. I want to take things further with you. With every breath that I take, I want that. I also don't want you to give up Airiella. I want you to do what you think is necessary and to give each other what you need." Chrissie placed her hand over his heart, his skin warm under his t-shirt. "I'm not jealous, not really. Not now that I know you feel the same about me as I do you."

"You were jealous?" Ronnie was flabbergasted.

"Not in a bad way, more a wishful way. Honestly, the times that the three of you have come down together and I know that you were all together, I wanted to be in that sandwich between you and Jax. I mean, have you seen the both of you?" Chrissie teased him.

Ronnie growled, "Nope, not sharing you. Degataga said something to me earlier about putting myself and another person in the place of a quote. The one about the sun and the moon."

"For the sun loved the moon so much that she died every night so that he could breathe. That one?"

"Yeah, that's the one. It made me first think of Airiella, how she's always choosing whatever path is available to save us, even if it means death. There isn't one person in this house that she wouldn't do that for; you know that. So I started putting others in the roles as he said. Mind you; I'm doing this between the shit that's happening, so I wasn't the best focused. Then I did it for you and I. I finally understood the quote even more, and then Airiella herself. I'd do it in a heartbeat if it meant you'd get to keep breathing. I'd do it for Rafe, Jace, or this little guy right here. I'd do it for any of my brothers' downstairs, or their families. I could never choose between you or Airiella, but I would substitute myself for either of you. I love you both that much."

Chrissie felt heat spreading throughout her body at the look in his eyes. "This so isn't the time for me to be feeling this. My child is in bed with us. My best friend and second child abducted by my ex."

"I won't sleep with you anyway until I've talked to both Airiella and Jax. So, we need to get them back first. It doesn't mean I won't kiss you though." He pulled her on top of him and slid her knees to either side of his hips, settling herself on top of a very impressive growing bulge.

He wound his hands around her neck and pulled her down, his fingers tangling in her hair. Chrissie's body reacted to every touch he made, and as he unleashed the full force of his kiss on her, she wanted to strip all the clothes off of him and lick every inch of his body. His mouth was magic.

"Fuck, I want to taste you," he groaned.

She forced herself to move off of him before she gave in. "If you say things like that, consequences be damned. Child in bed or not, I was tempted to let you."

"Will he be fine to be left here?" Ronnie looked over at Bryce.

"Normally, I'd say yes. Bryce got rattled today, though. He used to have night terrors bad when he was a baby. The doctor told me it was probably due to the fights he saw at home. Rafe had them too. We should either put him in his bed or bring him back down with us. I'm assuming that is where you wanted to go?"

"If we stay here, things will go a lot further than either of us are prepared for at the moment."

Chrissie was ready, but she wasn't going to push him. He'd given his conditions, and she would honor his wishes after she touched him. She leaned forward and slid her hand up under his shirt and up that magnificent chest, then back down and right under the waistband of his jeans. Her fingers met the hard velvety skin and she skimmed them over it, his hips jerking at the contact and breath hissing between his teeth.

She pulled her hand back out and kissed him, pulling back before he could tug her down again. "Sorry, but not very sorry. I couldn't help it."

His eyes were on fire, the lids hooded. "We need to find our angel soon. Very soon."

She moved so he could stand, and she openly stared while he adjusted himself, biting her lip and wanting another touch. She stood up too. "Thanks for the talk. Let's hope we find them."

Ronnie lifted Bryce carefully, trying not to jostle him and wake him up. As soon as he was in Ronnie's arms, the boy shifted and wrapped his arms around Ronnie's neck, settling back down with his sweet face turned into Ronnie's neck.

"I don't think I will ever get tired of feeling that." Ronnie's eyes were soft and dreamy. It didn't help Chrissie's libido at all. It turned her on even more to see the love he had for her children. The door flew open right as Chrissie was grabbing for the knob.

Mags looked harried. "Travis shot one of Taklishim's friends."

Chapter Seven

Breaking news about the amber alert for missing child Rafe Nielson. Travis Nielson was spotted moments ago by law enforcement officers following a lead. Nielson fired shots, and an officer was struck, as well as two bystanders. One of them fatally. No update as of yet on the condition of the officer. Again, the following picture is of Travis Nielson, if you spot this man, please call 911 immediately, he is armed and dangerous. There was no sign of missing child Rafe Nielson. Rafe is six years old and thought to be accompanied by an adult female. We still have not been able to confirm the female's identity that got abducted along with the child."

"Fatally? He killed someone?" Ronnie asked the silent room.

Degataga nodded slowly. "One of the tribal people from Tokeland," he confirmed finally. "He had locked on to Rafe's scent and found the car. That's where he got shot."

"Taklishim couldn't heal him?" Ronnie felt Chrissie grip his arm, her nails digging into his skin as the reality of the situation sank in.

"Headshot." Degataga's simple answer landed like a bomb. The room was silent except for the sound of the TV, the news anchor repeating the story and warnings.

"How the fuck does a strung out, high as a kite asshole get a headshot?!" Jillian cried. "Sorry, Jace. Please forgive my language."

Jax was hugging the shaking boy and had pulled him between his legs as if he could protect him from the horror his father was inflicting. Ronnie's heart broke for him, knowing that this would be one of those scars that haunted him forever. Much like his father's acts haunted Ronnie.

Chrissie crossed the room and sunk next to Jax. "Sweetheart, maybe you shouldn't be watching this. Bryce is sleeping, do you want to go to his room and stay with him?"

Jace shook his head and clung to Jax, who looked just as devastated as the boy did. Travis had murdered someone and had Rafe and Airiella. Ronnie walked over and slowly lowered himself to the floor on the other side of Jax, holding Bryce still so as not to wake him.

"Hey, buddy. Can you come with me? Please? What if I tuck Bryce in the wrong way?" Ronnie tried. "I don't know how to help him if he's scared."

Jace looked at Jax, who kissed him on the head. "Go with Ronnie; I'm going to sit with your mom."

Jace first crawled over to his mom. "Dad is bad. I hate him," he said, tears falling down a face that could no longer be as innocent as it once was.

"Hate is never a good thing, baby. Instead of hate, feel sorry for him. Say a prayer for Auntie Ells and Rafe, and for that man's family. Don't hate your dad. You don't have to like him, but don't hold hate in your heart. Can you do that for me?" She kissed his cheeks and wiped the tears.

Ronnie stood, cradling the sleeping Bryce, and held out his hand for Jace, who took it silently. He led them to the staircase and caught Chrissie telling Degataga to put the kill order back on. His heart hurt; he knew how much it cost her to say that. Travis had gone too far.

He took Jace up the stairs and let Jace show him how to get Bryce changed into his pajamas and tuck him in as Chrissie did. He knew the routine was something that was comforting to the boy in its familiarity.

"Why don't you lay here with him? That way, if he wakes up scared, you'll be here to help him?" Ronnie suggested calmly.

"I know what you're doing, and it won't make me feel better. My dad killed someone. He took Auntie Ells and Rafe. He said mean things to my mom." Jace swiped angrily at his face as the tears fell. "He's going to hurt her, isn't he?"

"Who? Your mom?" Ronnie wasn't sure if he was talking about Airiella, and he didn't know how to answer that one.

"No. My dad already hurt her. I mean Auntie Ells."

Ronnie stood and lifted the boy and sat down on Rafe's bed, putting Jace next to him. "I can't answer that, Jace. We don't know what will happen. All we can do is hope they are safe."

"It's not enough. That man's family hoped he was safe too, and my dad killed him. I don't want him to be my dad anymore. It hurts me inside."

Ronnie paused to get control of his voice before he answered. He took a moment to lay back on the bed and scooted over, so there was room for Jace next to him. He was happy Jace took the opportunity and lay beside him.

"You know how I told you that my dad wasn't nice, either?" Ronnie started, hoping he could reach through the trauma.

"I remember. You said your dad hurt you too, but that you got better."

"I did. It took me a long time. My dad used to hurt my mom all the time. He'd hurt her bad. It started when I was about as old as Rafe, and it used to make me so mad, I'd cry myself to sleep. When I was your age, he started hurting me because I told him to stop hitting my mom. I tried to protect her, but it didn't work." Ronnie figured honesty was the only way to go with this.

"My dad did that too. He used to say bad things; then, he'd hit her. He'd cry and say he was sorry and that he wouldn't do it again, but he always did. He would sneak into our house while we were asleep and do drugs because she wouldn't let him in."

Ronnie felt rage well up in him again at the things this kid had witnessed; what Chrissie had gone through. "Drugs make you stupid, Jace. I know. My dad didn't do drugs, he drank instead, and it made him mean. The concept is the same for drugs. It changes the way you think. Do you know why your mom said not to hate?"

"Because hate is bad?"

"Not only that, but it changes the way you think just like drugs and alcohol do. Drugs changed your dad into someone else. Hating him won't change any of it; it will only hurt you. It took me a long time to figure that out too. Do you know how stupid I was?"

Jace shook his head and rolled to his side to watch

Ronnie. He hoped he could reach the boy because this kid's eyes filled with so much pain that it was hard for Ronnie to keep looking at him.

"I started to steal my dad's beer out of the fridge and drink it. When I did that, it made me not care that he beat me up. I kept doing it until the girl I loved died. I did it even after my dad went to jail. I couldn't stop the nightmares, the hate inside me; I even started fighting other people."

"You turned bad?" Jace gasped.

"No, not bad. I didn't want to hurt anyone. I wanted to hurt my dad, and myself." Ronnie gave him the brutal truth.

"Why did you want to hurt yourself?"

"I blamed myself for what had happened. I believed if I was stronger, I could have stopped it. I thought if I had been faster and better, or smarter, or bigger that things would have been different. None of that was true. I didn't learn that until a lot later, though. I kept telling myself if I had only been different, things would have been better. The truth is, none of it had anything to do with me or my mom. It was all my dad. He chose to do what he did because he wasn't happy with himself. That's what you need to remember." Ronnie let his tears fall.

"But, I didn't stop Bryce from telling my dad about Auntie Ells."

"Bryce is a little kid, still. He doesn't understand what he did was wrong. That's not your fault. Neither is the way your dad acts. What he does isn't who *you* are. What *you* do is who you are." Ronnie gently tapped on Jace's chest. "Inside your heart is what matters. You are scared, for your brother and Airiella, right now. You are even scared for your mom. All that is okay and none of it is your fault. What your dad has done is his own choice. Your mom told you to pray for the others because she's a good person. You wanted to help Jax because you are a good person. Your dad isn't you, and you aren't him."

Jace started to cry. "How did you feel better?"

"I talked with an adult, and he got me signed up for boxing, judo, karate, and other martial arts. So all that anger I had inside me, I used it to train. When I was mad or hurting, I went to the gym and learned how to fight."

"Fighting is wrong, though, isn't it?" Jace asked astutely.

"If you are fighting to hurt someone, yes, that is wrong. I wasn't doing it for that. Want me to tell you what I learned from it?" Ronnie leaned forward a little.

Jace nodded slowly. Ronnie could see the boy thinking about the words he'd said and trying to put it together. Sadness hit him hard at the loss of a carefree childhood the boy had endured. It was one Ronnie knew all too well.

"The fighting and training taught me discipline. You know what that is, right?"

"I know mom says she has to discipline us when we are bad." Jace's face screwed up with a look of concentration.

"Discipline means that I followed the rules to get better at what I was doing. It means that there is a consequence for my actions. If I didn't punch the bag right, it would hurt me. So learning discipline and the rules of the different types of fighting taught me the consequences of a bad decision. Does that make sense?" Ronnie explained gently.

"So, when my mom takes away Rafe's toy when he's bad, she's doing it to teach him not to do that again."

"Correct. Fighting also taught me to channel my anger into something productive. What that means is when I felt angry, instead of hitting a person, or yelling, or breaking something, I took all that anger, and I used it for energy to get better at fighting. By the time I was done, I wasn't angry anymore. I was tired and exhausted and just wanted to eat and sleep."

"Does that mean I should start fighting?" Jace asked seriously.

Ronnie chuckled. "No, it means you should find whatever makes you happiest and use your energy for that. I didn't choose boxing on my own. Since I was already in trouble for fighting at school, my counselor chose boxing to channel that aggressive behavior. When he saw it was working, he had me join the other martial arts. It also gave me confidence where I didn't have any before. Kids used to pick on me because I was super skinny, Jax was always bigger than me, and he protected me."

"No way. You are way huger than Jax is."

"I am now. I wasn't when I was your age. After I started training, I grew a lot. I had confidence that I could defend myself, and suddenly I realized I didn't need to. I could walk away from the fight. Those kids were picking on me because they were just mean. I wasn't a mean person inside my heart. Do you understand what I'm saying?"

"I think so. What else did it teach you?"

"That violence is never the answer. I'm probably the strongest one in this house, but I never would hit anyone. I only use my strength to protect people. I don't hit to hurt; if I have to hit someone, I hit only to make them stop, and even then, only if I have no other choice. Do you see the difference between that and what your dad did? And what my dad did?" Ronnie held his breath, waiting for the answer.

"You are saying that it's a choice," Jace said slowly.

"It is a choice. Do you see the difference between you and your dad?" Ronnie pushed a little more.

"I'm not mean inside." Jace chewed on his lip. "How do I get better then?"

"You do what makes you feel good, and you talk to people when you feel bad. Talk about what is making you feel bad with someone else who knows. Learn from them what helped them and apply the lessons to your own life. That's something everyone does, especially adults. Did talking to me help you feel better?" Ronnie hoped like crazy it had helped him.

"Yeah, a little bit."

"Then, when you feel like you did downstairs, come and find me. Talk to me. Talk to Uncle Jax, he understands too. He saw how mean my dad was. He helped me, and I helped him," Ronnie offered.

"What did you do when the person you loved died?"

"That was when I chose to be better. It hurt Uncle Jax bad when Winnie died. I stopped doing all the bad things I was doing and decided it was my turn to help Uncle Jax. He's like a brother to me, like Rafe and Bryce, are to you."

"If the police shoot my dad and he dies, what will I do?" There were fear and sadness in his small voice, with a waver that caused a stab of pain to shoot through Ronnie.

Ronnie didn't know how to answer that. "It's different for everyone. Death is a part of life. What I did, was I remembered everything good about Winnie, and those times when it hurt bad, I thought about her. I smiled when I remembered something funny, and sometimes I would talk out loud to her as if she were there with me."

"What do I do if I have nothing good about him to remember?"

Ronnie's heart broke again. "Think of your brothers. They are good, right? Think of fun times you've had with them and your mom."

"Do you love my mom?"

"I do," Ronnie answered without hesitation. "I also love you and your brothers a lot. Whatever you need, I will do, Jace. I promise you."

"Will you teach me how to box?"

"If that's what you want, sure. Any of us can teach you. I taught all of the guys. I made them work so hard, sometimes it was hard for them to stand up." Ronnie tickled him lightly.

Jace giggled, the first kid sound the boy had made in a long time. "They couldn't stand up?"

"Nope. Their legs shook so bad they just laid on the floor, whining like babies."

"You won't ever hurt us, right?" Jace turned serious again.

"No, Jace. I might make you mad, but I won't ever do the things your dad did. Or the things my dad did. That is my solemn oath to you. I think you are one of the most amazing kids I have ever met in my life."

His face crumpled up. "How come my dad doesn't think that?" he cried.

Ronnie pulled him in and hugged him, letting him cry. "I wondered the same things about my dad. There is no good answer. All I can say is it's not because of you; it's because of him. If you don't believe me, ask anyone downstairs, and they will tell you the same thing."

Ronnie held him tight, knowing that no words he could say would ease the hurt in him. Sometimes it was the simple act of not being alone that helped. Something Jax had taught him when he found himself in this situation. For every loss he felt as his dad slipped farther and farther down that dark path, Jax filled it with love.

Jace eventually quieted down and slipped off to sleep, he gently moved him into bed with Bryce, covering them both and kissing their heads, silently promising to protect them and crept out of the room to find Chrissie sitting in the hallway.

She slumped over, her face swollen from crying, and appeared to be in a restless sleep. Ronnie bent down to pick her up, he planned to put her in the other bed with near the boys, but she woke with a start at the contact.

She flung her arms around his neck. "Thank you."

"For what?" Her sudden movements had him flummoxed.

"For everything that you said to Jace. I've never gotten him to say so much."

"It's a little easier when you share a common thread. I know how Jace is feeling. I can't lie, Chris. It's going to leave permanent scars. I'm living proof of that," he told her, understanding her reaction better.

"You are also proof that you can overcome it and be an example for others to look up to; don't sell yourself short."

"Jax filled the holes my father left in me. So did Smitty and Aedan. Every time I got to a breaking point, or even before then, they turned me around. For every insult that tore me down, they had something to use to build me back up. It's a group effort, and every one of us will be there for your boys to make sure they get through this. That includes you," Ronnie promised her.

"Jax was about crawling up the walls; he said you were hurting. Right after you left."

"He's right. It hurts him as much as it hurts me." He leaned his head down on hers.

"There's been no other news. It's like Travis faded into the night. God, Rafe is probably so terrified right now."

The anger rose again. Ronnie figured it would keep on happening until they found Airiella and Rafe. "You told Dega to reinstate the kill order? Why?"

"It won't ever change with Travis. He took a life tonight. He took the life of someone only out trying to save two innocents. As much as I hate the thought of the boys losing their father, if I am frank, they already have. Death would be a kindness. Being killed by a policeman is better than having to explain that their father died and found overdosed dead in a street. That he always chooses his next high over them. I don't want him dead, not really. I don't want him to hurt anyone else either, and with as far as he's gone tonight, I'm afraid of what he would do next. He has Rafe and Airiella. I'm not willing to risk their lives to save Travis's."

"There's an important distinction here that I feel I need to make. The drugs have altered Travis; it's not him that did that. It is, but it's not." He sat down on the stairs with her in his lap.

"I know, Ronnie. It's also why I gave my consent for Taklishim to reissue his order. It's not Travis that's being taken out, it's whatever has taken over his mind. Travis died a long time ago; this just needs to end. Death will at least bring closure to my kids."

"I think you are a better mother than you give yourself credit for." Ronnie kissed her, seeing the underlying fears she had about herself. As he pulled back, a wave of fear crippled him, making him feel like the blood was draining from his body. His ears started ringing, and his vision swam. It wasn't intentional, but he ended up grabbing hold of Chrissie hard in an attempt to steady himself.

At her gasp, he realized what he'd done and released her. "Shit, I'm sorry." He heard the others crying out. "It's Airiella."

Chapter Eight

Chrissie rubbed her arms lightly where Ronnie had grabbed hold, and followed him fast. His reaction had been automatic, and she didn't fault him, but whatever he had felt had been powerful. Judging by the disoriented group she found when they entered the room, it hadn't been just him.

"She's coming to," Degataga told Chrissie as she hurriedly glanced at everyone, checking to make sure they were all okay. Only Jillian and herself weren't affected. Jax was the only one still dazed. "It's worse for him because they are so connected."

"She's not answering me," Ronnie said out loud.

"Me neither," Smitty called out, his voice shaky.

They all looked at Jax, who still wasn't focused all the way. "She's shackled." His voice was soft and distant sounding. "She said it's dark. Pitch black. The air is still, and she can't use her abilities." He shook his head. "She's not all there. Whatever they gave her is seriously messing with her head." He looked like he was all present now, but extremely shaken.

"Does she have any idea where she's at?" Aedan leaned forward a little.

"No. Rafe is next to her, she thinks he's chained too, but she can't be sure. He's sleeping, she said. Scared, but she doesn't feel pain from him." Jax looked up. "She won't answer me if she is hurt or not. I don't know if she can tell."

Chrissie felt a split second of relief that Rafe was unharmed, only to have the fear slam back home at not knowing if Airiella was okay or not. "Is she in the same location as Travis?"

"She doesn't think so. She's sick. She says she hears no sound, it's cold and smells old and damp." Jax relayed the information.

Chrissie glanced at Degataga to see if he was texting Taklishim. He met her eyes. "I have that same connection with Onida, who is with Tama. Tama is relaying the information to Taklishim the same way. We are all on the same page here," he took a moment to explain.

"Sounds like she might be underground," Aedan said. "Is she on earth or cement?"

"Cement. She said she's afraid to use earth because she doesn't know if something will crash down on her." Jax's voice became tight. "She's naked. She thinks Rafe is too."

Chrissie felt bile rise in the back of her throat, and she shot to her feet. "No," she whispered, her hands fluttering like deranged butterflies over her mouth.

They all doubled over again, Jax retching violently. Ronnie's mouth was open in a silent scream, his eyes tightly shut. She didn't know what to do. She looked over at

Degataga, who had the weakest link to her, and was straightening up. "She's having reactions from the drug," he said and his voice was hoarse.

Jax started sobbing, "She said she's dying."

Chrissie was having none of it. "Jax, snap out of it! You tell her I said this; she needs to suck it up and get her ass back here. Fry the asshole if she has to. I did not plan this wedding to have her get cold feet and die as a way out. You repeat that to her, word for word."

Ronnie chuckled lightly; his cheeks wet from his tears. "I can hear her now. She said she loves you too."

Chrissie dropped down to her knees next to Jax and leaned her head against his arm. "Tell her to come back to me. I need sex advice. I don't care what you say, Jax, just keep talking to her. Tell her if she doesn't come back, I'm going to sleep with both you and Ronnie."

She felt Ronnie come up behind her. "It's working, Chris. She's engaging. You almost got a smile out of Jax on that one, too."

"She's not strong enough to get out of the chains," Jax relayed for her benefit.

"If she can break the chains of her past, she can get out of this. Travis is nothing compared to what she's been through," Chrissie continued, refusing to let Airiella give up.

Smitty burst out with a half-cry, half-laugh. "She's trying to tell you where to touch Ronnie to make him your bitch."

Chrissie choked. "God, I love this woman. Tell Airiella I'm never using her as a babysitter again if this is the type of shit she's going to pull."

Jax reacted slightly to that and gave her an odd

look. "Well played. I can feel the fight rising in her," Jax said quietly. "The other part of me wants to yell at you for striking low."

"I know her well, Jax. I'll use whatever I can to keep her in the game."

"She smells blood." Ronnie started talking again. "Not sure if it's hers or not. She agrees with Aedan and thinks she is underground somewhere, and she said she isn't in good enough shape for a physical fight."

"Tell her to talk to Rafe," Chrissie suggested. "Wake him up. If he's not chained, he can explore the room. He's a smart boy."

"Danger." Jax went rigid again. "She thinks that danger is nearby."

"Play dead. Travis is stoned out of his mind; he won't know the difference if she doesn't react," Chrissie answered sharply, remembering her attacks from Travis. "Why would Rafe be naked?" she wondered quietly.

Ronnie put a hand on her thigh. "Maybe to just keep him scared and somewhat helpless. Don't jump to conclusions."

"Taklishim hasn't seen Stolas in a while. He lost sight as Stolas followed the spell back out of town, so we know that he isn't keeping her in the same place he was calling from," Degataga informed them. "Maybe Rafe didn't hear the phone call then."

Ronnie swore. "No, he heard. He's awake, and he told her that he would protect her, and that's why his dad took his clothes."

Chrissie broke down in tears. Poor kid was going to be devastated after this. "Is he restrained?"

Jax shifted and tipped Chrissie's head up. "Hey, she

won't let anything happen to him. She just said she'd bring down the building around them to keep him safe."

"Is he restrained?" Chrissie asked again.

"He is," Ronnie answered quietly, moving closer. Both Jax and Ronnie wrapped their arms around her, and she let herself cry for only a minute.

"How?" she asked.

"Rope," Jax replied softly.

"Taklishim can heal burns, right?" She looked at Degataga, who nodded. "Tell her to burn it off him."

"Travis is there, she went silent," Jax spoke suddenly. "Can you hear it, Ronnie?"

"No, can you?" Ronnie jolted at that.

"Yes. Travis is ranting; they are in a cellar of some sort, cement walls, ladder going up. The ladder is across the room from where they are. He has a lantern and a gun. He doesn't know she's awake. He does know Rafe is awake," Jax relayed the information quickly.

Chrissie hung on Jax's every word, his body movement, and the tone he was using. It told her what he wasn't saying out loud. She felt the fear creep over him, his body breaking out in goosebumps and the way his muscles tensed around her.

"She can't get her body to respond," Ronnie said flatly.

"Onida thinks her organs might be shutting down. Her blood might be toxic right now. If he injects her again, she won't survive it. Whatever she does, do not let him know that she's awake," Degataga cautioned urgently.

"What's happening?" Chrissie asked as both Ronnie and Jax reacted to something, her senses, and emotions on overload picking up the vibe the two were radiating.

Smitty was the one who answered, his voice vibrating with anger. "The fucking bastard is touching her."

"You can hear too?" Ronnie kept his voice even.

"No. I know that emotion Airiella's letting off. It's the same one that she let off at Northern State when that guy assaulted her," he growled out.

"Jax, don't you dare keep this to yourself," Chrissie said in his ear, vehemently. "This is my best friend and my child. I know you are her mate and all that stuff. But I have years with her over you and that's my ex-husband that's doing this."

"He's threatening to kill them both. Airiella hasn't reacted, but her emotions are going ape-shit crazy right now. She won't tell me what he's doing other than touching her," Jax ground out.

"He's threatening to kill his son?" Chrissie was aghast.

"She wants us to piss her off. She thinks the anger might give her a boost of energy. She wants to let her wings out to protect Rafe," Jax hissed a slow breath out. "She's hurt. Fucker did something to her."

"Tell her to do it. Tell her Stolas is tracking her. Tell her that Travis killed a friend of Taklishim's. Give her the details you don't want to. If she wants to be pissed off, tell her what you are holding back." Chrissie pushed him, knowing exactly how to push Airiella's buttons. "Do it! Travis is a coward! If she shows any display of power, he will back off."

"Not if he's unstable and strung out," Ronnie told her gently. "Don't push Jax, Chris. He always does what Airiella needs, even if the rest of us don't agree with him."

Chrissie bit back a sob and went straight for the

heart shot she knew would get Airiella riled up in an instant. "Tell her Travis raped me. Tell her he raped me while I was pregnant with Rafe. That's why he was born a preemie, not because I had complications. Travis was the reason. One night, he was strung out on heroin, and I refused to give him money to get more. He was coming down and got angry, pushed me down the stairs, then raped me. I was eight months pregnant, and when he finished, I went into premature labor. Tell her the truth I never could, because I am ashamed that I didn't divorce him after that."

The room fell silent after Chrissie's confession, and the two men holding her were so still compared to the violently shaking mess she had become. Tears of shame and anger flew down her face like a waterfall. Beside her, Ronnie's breathing became harsh, and on the other side, Jax shifted.

He kissed Chrissie's temple. "She knows now. Ron, stay with me, bud." Chrissie felt Jax's arm behind her move, and she looked over at Ronnie. His face was full of anguish and savage anger. Behind her, all the others moved, surrounding them.

Chrissie didn't know what was happening, but the tacit support from this group bolstered her in ways she didn't know how to express. Chrissie found herself picked up and set down between Ronnie's legs as the others moved in, all of them touching.

"Someone, please say something," Chrissie begged, feeling utter despair after her bombshell.

"If Stolas or Taklishim doesn't beat her to it, she's going to kill him. She's furious and even madder that your information just broke Ronnie," Smitty said, his face a violent storm of emotion. "Truthfully, you pretty much just crushed all of us with that little story. So, we are doing the only thing we know how to hold us all together, that's just being close and touching."

Chrissie couldn't look behind her to see Ronnie's face, but she didn't need to. It wasn't information she would have shared usually. Airiella didn't need the details to understand the trauma. It was all she could think of to say that she knew was guaranteed to get a spark lit in the woman.

"I told her to draw from the connection," Jax spoke softly. "She still hasn't given away that she's awake, but from what I can hear, he's ranting about how much Chrissie has ruined his life, and it's just fueling the fire in her. From the stabs of pain, I keep feeling; he's either hitting or kicking her."

Chrissie's breath caught again, and Ronnie leaned into her back. "*You* didn't break me, the horror of what you endured did," he whispered in her ear. "Nothing you say here will ever be used against you or repeated. You are safe."

"Where is Stolas?" Chrissie demanded. "Why hasn't he gotten there yet?"

"We don't know." Degataga regarded her carefully.

"Don't treat me with kid gloves, I won't break," Chrissie told them all.

"Oh honey, we wouldn't dream of it," Mags told her, fire in her voice. "Are you sure you and Airy aren't related?"

Chrissie felt a manic laugh bubble up. "I'm sure. If you are going to tell me something similar happened to her, I already know. I don't need the details."

"That's not what I was referring to at all. I can't tell

you how many times she's snapped at these buffoons not to treat her like she's fragile, that she won't break," Mags clarified.

"She's the reason I survived it all," Chrissie revealed.

"No. She may inspire you, she does to everyone. *You* are the reason you survived it," Ronnie corrected her. Something happened because everyone in the circle flinched except Jillian and herself.

Chapter Nine

Fuck!" Ronnie whispered angrily. "Chrissie's right, where the fucking hell is that demon at?"

"Taklishim saw lightning," Degataga announced. "It wasn't close, but he's headed that direction."

"What happened?" Chrissie sounded frantic.

"He hurt her again," Ronnie said, watching Jax. "I can hear it all now that we are all touching."

"Me too." Aedan looked sick, and Mags was furious.

"He fucking shot her," Smitty growled, his temper fraying quickly.

Chrissie's voice went shrill. "What?"

"She said in the leg," Jax answered quickly. "He's losing it. Degataga, can you hear this?"

"Yes, Taklishim knows he's needed."

"What aren't you saying?" Chrissie demanded.

"He did something to Rafe," Mags answered her. "She's not clear on what, but he cried out, and he's crying."

A bolt of energy went through the room, and Ronnie felt a glimmer of hope. She had engaged the connection and drew from them. "She's going to do it, she's going to let her wings out," he told Chrissie. "Nothing will get to him if he's behind her wings."

"Even a bullet?" she asked.

"I can't say we've ever tested that. As far as we went were arrows," Smitty reminded her.

"This is driving me crazy! I'm going to bite that damn woman's neck like a vampire if it means I'll get to hear her," Chrissie mumbled.

Angel, you be careful. I need you both to come back to me.

No promises, Heracles. My body isn't working right inside, but that asshole is not hurting this little boy again. Is Stolas truly coming?

He said he was going to use your feather to have Kalisha do a tracking spell. I think he would move Hell itself if it meant he would find you, Ronnie answered honestly.

Please take care of Jax and Chrissie.

Don't give me that shit, angel; this is not a goodbye, this is merely another epic shitstorm we found.

His blood went cold at the silence from the other end of the connection. Based on the sounds he was hearing, Airiella's wings came out, and Travis freaked out. Smitty was keeping Chrissie informed while the rest listened in horrified silence.

The gunshots rang loud in his ears; the pain was frying his nerves with every injury inflicted on her. Jax gripped his hand in a death grip. Smitty on the other side of him stable and steadfast in his hold on Ronnie, but no less tense.

Stolas is close; I can feel his energy. I'm out of time.

I'm using what I have left to bring the building down.

Ronnie heard Chrissie cry out as Smitty relayed the message. "What does she mean she's out of time?"

"Her energy is gone. If Stolas is close, she's probably hoping he'll be able to get her out." Jax's tone was utterly flat, resolved, and filled with pain.

They heard the rumble of the earth through the connection. Ronnie could make out the sounds of the stone cracking and crumbling. Each impact of something on her sent another wave of pain throughout them, and through Degataga's touch, Ronnie felt healing energy wash through them all.

"Why are you healing us?" Ronnie asked the man.

"I'm not, I'm replenishing energy stores so she can pull more," Degataga explained.

I love you all.

"No," Jax cried, trying to stand. Ronnie held him firm with Aedan on the other side doing the same.

Ronnie felt an immense wave of pain hit him as the noise in his head increased with what he could only assume was the building falling around her and Rafe.

He's safe, came her feeble voice.

"Rafe is okay," Ronnie told Chrissie, his voice thick.

Keep pulling from us, angel.

Stolas, he heard her say. *Help him.*

Where the fuck is he? Stolas boomed out. The menace in his words bleeding through the connection. *Seir! I need you now!*

Ronnie was afraid to say anything, and with a quick glance around him, he saw the others felt the same. For now, they still had an open line of communication with her and none wanted it to disappear. It was their only link to her.

Find me the shadow warrior and bring him! Stay with me, love; help is coming.

Did you use your feather to find me? Ronnie hated how weak she sounded.

I did. I'd do it all over again.

Can you unchain me? Her voice was fading.

I can't, love. It creates too many questions that you will have to answer. I promise you that help is coming. Your friend will bring the police. Just stay with me now.

Raven!

Ronnie felt the emotions he'd been holding in check flood out of him at the sound of Taklishim's voice. He'd do whatever he had to for them to stay safe. Taklishim was his hope that Airiella would come back to them.

Tak, Rafe's hurt, he needs help.

Warrior, you can't heal them, Ronnie heard Stolas tell Taklishim.

Excuse me, demon?

Think about it. A building out in the middle of nowhere, crumbled to the ground. Airiella's blood is on the chains, the earth, no clothes on either of them, anywhere around. And yet here you are when the last time anyone saw you was back at their house. Do you want to answer all those questions and expose yourself and her?

Fucking hell. Ronnie hadn't thought that much about it, and Stolas made way too much sense for Ronnie's liking. "God damnit!" Aedan yelled in a moment of rare unrestrained emotion.

"What?" Chrissie startled.

"They can't fucking do anything to help her." Aedan was losing control rapidly.

"Chill," Jax told his brother. "Tak won't let her die, or Rafe."

Ronnie could hear Taklishim cussing and tuned back in.

I'm not letting her die; Tak confirmed Ronnie's thoughts.

I'm not suggesting you do that. I'm merely stating facts. Do enough to ensure Airiella lives, and when the police are close, Seir will take you back. You can't burn it all out of her, not after seeing the syringe, and there's evidence of the quantity injected into her. Be sensible. I'm trying to help you all here.

I got it. Let me do what I need to do until the police are close. Do you think it's easy for me to see this?

Do you think it's any easier for me? Stolas's voice held barely contained fury. Ronnie remembered what the demon was like when he was pissed.

What about him?

Do you object to me handling it? Stolas was completely livid if his tone was anything to go by, and that was frightening.

No, just not in front of them.

Tak, help Rafe.

The boy is okay, Raven. After the medics and hospital staff check you and make records and notes of what happened, we will heal you both completely. He's right, though, I need you to put your wings back in.

Stolas, take a feather. Thank you for finding us.

Ronnie bristled, his tears hot at the thready tone of her voice. She was barely hanging on.

How much do I need to leave in her? Taklishim was barely in control as well.

Enough to make it believable. Hello little one, you took good care of your auntie.

My daddy hurt us. Ronnie hoped to God that Smitty didn't repeat that. Thankfully he didn't. Jax's hand tightened on his again.

I know he did. He won't anymore; I promise you that.

Raven, draw some energy from me, sweetheart.

Shit. If Taklishim was using terms of endearment, then things were worse than Ronnie thought. At this point, he was pretty sure that the only thing holding him and Jax in place was each other.

It's too late, Tak.

Bullshit, Raven. Pull it, and for once, don't argue with me.

Stay with us, love. This little one needs you still. Don't you?

Auntie Ells, better listen to them.

Ronnie felt a hysterical laugh form, but it didn't have enough strength to make it out of him. The little guy wasn't even aware of the effect he was having on her.

Can you keep us a secret little one?

Yes. Just like Auntie Ells wings.

Excellent, Rafe. I'll see you soon, okay. Taklishim's tone was gentle.

They will be here in less than two minutes, Stolas informed them. *I have some unfinished business I need to take care of; Warrior, Seir, will take you back.*

Ronnie heard a scream that raised all the hair on his body, then silence. A minute later, a naked Taklishim stormed into the house, and Ronnie stood to get him clothes.

"No need, mine is on the side of the house. I just wanted to let you know I was here. Be ready for the phone call."

He sat back down, Smitty and Jax never having let go of his hands. They all heard police sirens and people calling out. Ronnie swallowed a lump at the sound of Rafe's voice, calling for help. Right as they were all getting ready to breathe a sigh of relief, the connection died. Not because they let go of each other, but because Airiella was no longer on their plane of existence.

Chapter Ten

What the fuck do you mean she died?" Chrissie screamed hysterically.

"Ssshh, you'll wake the boys." Ronnie tried to calm her.

"I don't care! I have to wake them to go with you to the hospital. Don't you dare for one second think that I'm not going, that's my son! My best friend!"

"No matter what Stolas told Taklishim, he wouldn't have left her if he didn't think she would pull through," Jax muttered, his face bereft.

"The medics will do their job." Degataga sounded more confident than he looked, and Chrissie wasn't having any of it.

"I only got half the information of what happened down there, and don't think I don't know it. I can read your faces like a book. I don't know what you all are holding back from me, but I will find out." She was pissed and terrified out of her mind.

"Chrissie," Taklishim walked back in, "Rafe will be fine. He's got some cuts, bruises, and a concussion, but otherwise okay."

"And Airiella?"

"She's damaged," he said bluntly, giving a glance at Degataga. "Tama needs to come."

"Mental?" Degataga asked, and Chrissie looked between the two, seeing Taklishim's slight nod.

"I asked Seir to bring them back." He looked unhappy with that too. "I'm headed back out to the yard."

"Them?" Chrissie moved and stepped in front of him.

"Onida too."

Chrissie's phone rang at the same time there was a knock at the front door. Jax went to answer it, knowing it was the police that had been sitting in their car in the driveway.

"Hello?"

"Chrissie Nielson?" a female voice asked.

"Yes."

"This is Sergeant O'Neill with the Grays Harbor sheriff's department. I wanted to let you know that your son has been found and is safe. We are going to transport him to a medical facility to get checked out. The woman with him, Airiella Raven was found as well."

"Thank you. Where are you taking my son and Airiella?" Chrissie demanded, her blood boiling. "Can you tell me the condition of Airiella, please?"

"Grays Harbor Community Hospital ma'am. I understand that you have officers on sight? They can transport you if you'd like." The sergeant answered, ignoring her question about Airiella.

"No, thank you, there are several of us that will be coming. Can you tell me the condition of Airiella Raven, please?" Chrissie repeated

"Are you family ma'am?"

"Not blood, but her fiancée is standing right next to me," she lied.

"I'm not supposed to give information," Sergeant O'Neill said. "However, as a mother myself with a friend that I consider a sister, I'll tell you that they are working on resuscitating her. Her injuries appear to be extensive."

"Thank you," Chrissie whispered, the never-ending supply of tears coming back. "We are headed down there now. Thank you," she repeated.

Jax walked back in as Taklishim came in through the back, this time dressed. "Let's go," he said and his voice was strained.

Chrissie ran to the closet and grabbed her purse as Ronnie came down the stairs with the boys. "I'll drive," he told her. She wordlessly handed him her keys.

"Mags and Jillian are going to stay here with the babies." Aedan strode up to them. "I'll follow with the rest of the group in the SUV."

Mags came over and hugged her. "Text me as soon as you know anything." Chrissie promised and hugged Jillian and flew out the door as Ronnie finished buckling Bryce in his seat.

"Mommy, is Auntie Ells okay?" Jace asked sleepily. "Is Rafe okay?"

"We are going to go find out right now, baby. You can go back to sleep," she said and she looked back at them.

"What about Dad?"

Chrissie didn't know how to answer that one. She

didn't receive any information about her ex. "I don't know."

"I never want to see him again," Jace growled with anger, fully awake now.

"You don't have to, baby."

"The police are going to give us an escort," Ronnie told her as she turned back around.

Chrissie worried when Ronnie slumped forward, his head resting on the steering wheel. "What's wrong?" she asked quietly.

"I feel life. Barely there, but it's there," he said softly. She let out a whimper and held his hand as he pulled out after the cop car and waited while the gate opened. Aedan close behind them.

"Mommy, you are crying again," Jace said quietly.

"Auntie Ells is okay, honey, these tears are happy tears," Chrissie told him.

"Ronnie?" Jace looked from Chrissie to Ronnie.

"Yeah, buddy?"

"Remember how you told me to talk when I felt bad?"

Chrissie held her breath and squeezed Ronnie's hand. "I sure do. You feeling bad right now?"

"Uh-huh."

"How come?" Ronnie asked carefully.

"When your dad hurt your mom, and it made you feel bad, what did you do?"

"When I was your age, I cried. Then I tried to help my mom feel better. Sometimes I would clean up for her, or make her food. Sometimes I talked to Jax about non-important things until I felt better. Are you feeling bad because of Airiella?" Ronnie correctly guessed what was eating at Jace.

"Yeah. It hurts inside when I think of my dad hurting her."

Chrissie swallowed hard, trying her best not to cry at the words that never should have been coming out of her child's mouth. The innocence lost broke her heart in ways she didn't think would ever heal. Travis had robbed Jace of a childhood.

"You know what, buddy? It's not a bad thing to feel that way when someone you love is hurt. It's called empathy. Remember how I told you that you were a good person?"

"Yeah."

"That what that means. When you hurt because someone else is hurting, that means you have a wonderful heart filled with love. The best thing you can do is share that love. When you see her, love on her lots. Make her smile, make your brother smile, and your mom. Airiella is full of love, and if she thought you were sad, it would make her sad."

"Okay. It sounds like you are only saying that to cheer me up, but Auntie Ells is full of love. Thanks."

Chrissie wished she could to talk to Ronnie through a connection. What he was doing for Jace was pure magic and one of the most beautiful things she had ever seen. Ronnie was helping heal her son's heart even if that link became forged because of the horrors they had to face.

She pulled his hand up and kissed his fingers, hoping he understood the gesture. "I know, Chris."

They got to the hospital relatively quickly with the escort and were met at the door by more officers and taken directly back to where Rafe was. Jax was demanding to know where Airiella was, and Chrissie saw how torn

Ronnie was.

"Wait. Hold up. Airiella Raven should be in a room with Rafe," she told the nurse. "Trust me when I say that she will freak out if she wakes up and doesn't see him. That won't be good for anyone. They've just been through a traumatic experience."

Onida stepped through, her doctor face on. "Excuse me, who is the doctor in charge? Airiella Raven is my patient."

"You are a doctor, ma'am?" a nurse asked, looking over to Onida.

"I am, and more importantly, I am *her* doctor."

Chrissie shut up and let Onida take over. Her tone brokered no argument, and the attending doctor rushed into the room. He looked around at the group gathered here and the police in the hallway. "Dr. Cloud, how nice to see you again. Ms. Raven is a patient of yours?"

"She is. Where is she?" Onida barked.

The physician looked at Tama in confusion but quickly back at Onida. "She's down here. She's in rough shape, follow me, and I'll explain what we have."

Onida shared a look with Tama then followed the doctor out of the room. Degataga chuckled, "Have no fear, Airiella will turn up in this room."

Chrissie turned back to Rafe, who was thankfully out. The nurse came back in. "We sedated him; he was scared and worried about Ms. Raven. Will Dr. Cloud be taking over care for him as well?"

Ronnie stepped in. "She will. Is Rafe okay?"

Tama slid past Chrissie and stepped up to the bedside and put her hand on his little arm. She saw the odd look that the nurse gave Tama. "That's Dr. Cloud's twin."

The nurse swallowed and looked at Taklishim, whom Chrissie had to admit, was a bit intimidating at the moment, his worry for Airiella clear on his face. "That's her husband." Chrissie nodded to Tama. "They are fine to be here."

"Of course," the nurse stammered and lowered her voice. "They are something of a legend. Anyway, your son has a mild concussion and we'd like him to stay overnight for observation. He's got bruises that will be tender, abrasions from the ropes that restrained him, and cuts from debris. Considering what he's been through, he's remarkably okay."

"Because Airiella protected him," Chrissie told her. She couldn't help the tone that came into her voice. The woman was fishing for information, if not verbally, by the curious glances she was giving Tama and Taklishim.

Smitty and Aedan leaned against the wall, their arms crossed, and postures stiff. She saw the moment the nurses recognized them. "You're from Shadow Seekers!" she exclaimed, her gaze finally resting on Jax. "Oh! Ms. Raven is your fiancée! No wonder you all look so familiar."

As if she only then realized why they were all here, her gaze turned back to somber. "I'm sorry. Please let me know if you need anything."

Chrissie looked at Ronnie, who had a definite fuck-off vibe. "She didn't recognize you?"

"Oh, she did." Smitty smiled suddenly. "He's just perfected the don't even think about talking to me, look. Plus, he stood so close to you; it was a clear sign that he's not available."

Degataga shifted the still sleeping Bryce he had taken from Ronnie as they came in, and gently lay him on

Rafe's bed. "What do you think, Tama?"

"He'll be okay. He might have nightmares for a while. I took away the parts that were the most traumatic." She looked at Chrissie. "I hope that was okay."

"It is. What did you take away?" Suddenly Jace was at her side, listening to every word said.

"Jace, come with me." Taklishim held his hand out.

"I want to stay here," he argued.

"I know, so do I. Sometimes, we have to let Mom's have a moment." Chrissie shot him a grateful look. She didn't want Jace to hear any more than he had to.

Once they were out of the room, Tama looked back at Chrissie. "I pulled the visions of his fathers' body, the screams, and the memories of some of the awful things that were said. I can't take it all away since it's on the official record, and they may have to question him again, but they won't ask about those details."

"Thank you for that."

"In a couple of weeks, I'll recheck him and build a little construct in there to help him not think about it if I need to. He's still young enough to be resilient in this area. It's traumatizing, and he definitely will have feelings about it, but in my experience with these things, it's best to let them play out and heal in their way. I'll ease part of it for him; mostly, I'll watch. I did heal the concussion. Dega can look too, in case the pregnancy brain overtook my sensibilities, and I missed something. For that matter, I can guarantee that Tak and Oni will both look as well."

Tama rested her hand on Bryce. "Is something wrong with him?" Chrissie got nervous.

"No. Degataga told Oni how stressed out he was; I'm just checking to see if there's going to be an issue.

There won't. Everything he dealt with was either second or third hand."

"Thanks, Tama," Ronnie told her.

"Clear out," Degataga informed them. "Dr. Cloud is coming with Airiella, she'll need room to get her situated, and she's in no-nonsense mode. One of the other doctors pissed her off."

Chrissie and Ronnie stepped to the head of Rafe's bed while the others filed out and lined the hallway, causing a lot of the nurses to swivel their heads. Chrissie almost laughed. She'd had the same reaction when she met them all for the first time. It was a lot of male hotness to take in at once.

Then she saw Airiella, and the laugh died in her throat. Next to her, Ronnie made a strangled sound in his throat, and Jax was immediately behind the bed following it in. His face set in stone and jaw ticking madly.

Onida stepped aside while the nurses got the bed in place and made sure all the IV bags got positioned correctly. Chrissie watched her stride into the hallway and bark at the cops. "No one in this room except the people you see here."

"Yes, ma'am," one of them answered.

"The rest of you come in and close the door behind you." Onida walked back in and waited for the last nurse to leave before her face relaxed. "Sometimes it's hard being bitchy." She stepped over to Rafe and put her hand on him. "I can see Tama has already taken care of him." Onida stroked his face. "He'll be okay, Chrissie. Airiella took the brunt of it."

"That doesn't make me feel a whole lot better," Chrissie told the imposing woman.

"I know, but it's better that it was her. Rafe wouldn't have survived any of that. We might be powerful, but we can't bring back the dead," she said bluntly. She looked over at Jace. "Why don't you climb up here with your brothers, watch over them for me. If anything changes, you let me know," Onida told him seriously in her doctor tone.

"I can do that," Jace told her seriously. "Can I see Auntie Ells first?"

"Sure, honey." Onida's voice went soft. "She doesn't look too good, though. I don't want you to worry too much because we are going to make sure she's okay."

Jace nodded solemnly and walked over to Jax and took his hand. Chrissie covered her mouth and bit her lip to stop herself from crying at the brave look he put on his face. "It doesn't look like she is breathing," he said quietly, his hand hovering like he wanted to reach out to her.

Onida stepped over to the other side of the bed. "She's breathing. See this machine right here? That line that's jumping up and down?" She waited for Jace to nod. "That's her heartbeat. See this tube?" She pointed to the oxygen. "That's oxygen to help her breathe."

"Is she sleeping?" Jace asked quietly, his hand still hovering.

"You can touch her. She's kind of sleeping. In medical terms, we call it a coma, it's a deep sleep the brain goes into so your body can heal," she told Jace the most positive explanation possible, and Chrissie was grateful for that. "We believe that even though it looks like they can't hear you, they can. Go ahead and talk to her. Your aunt is an exceptional lady; I'm sure she will always listen to you."

"Auntie Ells, I hope you can hear me. Thank you for saving Rafe. I'm sorry my dad hurt you. I love you."

Chrissie turned her head into Ronnie's chest and cried quietly, his arms wrapping around her. "That was perfect, buddy."

Ronnie helped Jace get situated next to Rafe. "Onida? Is this the same machine as that one?" Jace pointed to the heart monitor attached to Rafe.

"It is, good eye," she complimented him.

"Okay, I'll watch it for you so you can fix her."

Chrissie wiped her eyes in time to see Tama lay her hand on Jace, and he immediately fell asleep. "Do you want me to make it so that he doesn't have nightmares?"

Chrissie felt torn, but Ronnie spoke. "No. I'm working with him."

"That's great. Jace'll sleep like this until I wake him. You are free to talk." Tama eased down into a chair Taklishim had grabbed for her.

There was a knock at the door, and Taklishim stiffened, immediately moving away from the door. Smitty gave him a look and pulled it open. Stolas walked in and over to Onida. "They let you in after I told them no one but us?"

"They didn't see me," Stolas explained. "Technically, they didn't break your rules. Here, this will help flush the toxins from her," he said and he handed her a container. "Push it through the IV; it'll work fast." He gave Jax another box. "For the pain."

"Did you take a feather, as she told you to?" Jax asked him.

"No. The warrior got them picked up before the cavalry arrived."

"What about Travis?" Chrissie asked him, glancing down at her boys to make sure they were asleep.

"Not something you will ever need to worry about again," Stolas said, his eyes lighting red for a moment.

"I hope he suffered," Aedan snapped.

"I can assure you of that as well."

"What was the scream?" Smitty asked.

"The sound of his soul forcibly getting ripped from his body." Stolas said it so simply and casually that Chrissie stepped back into Ronnie, fear swamping her mind. His glowing eyes rested on her. "It's less than I would have liked to do."

"Is he in Hell?" Chrissie wondered.

"Hand delivered."

"Thank you." Chrissie fought the urge to hug him. He didn't look like he wanted human touch at the moment.

"May I?" He looked at Jax as he gestured at Airiella.

"You found her, brought Taklishim there, and got him out before getting seen. I don't know that she would have survived if you hadn't done that; I've said it before, you are welcome with us." Jax nodded at him.

Stolas knelt next to the bed and rested his head against her arm then kissed her cheek. He stood and surveyed the room. "There's a special place in Hell for rapists. He will be there for a while."

Chrissie felt a chill hit her bones as she watched Stolas. He was more than a demon; there was a kindness to him. She stepped away from Ronnie and stood before him, holding her arms open. He hesitated a moment and then hugged her. "Thank you," she whispered in his ear. "I'm with Airiella on this one; you aren't bad."

There was a soft look on his face as he pulled back from her and gave her a small smile. "You all know how to reach me." Then just like that, he was gone.

Chapter Eleven

Onida pushed the fluid Stolas had given her into Airiella's IV, and Ronnie watched the monitor's numbers improve in a matter of minutes. Stolas certainly knew his stuff, and he had never been happier to have a demon on their side.

"I healed her wings before I had her put them back in," Taklishim told them. "I only had a moment to strengthen her heart a little bit before I left."

Onida nodded. "That's probably what kept her alive. She's here at least overnight, and I can push paperwork to get her transferred to the hospital we run tomorrow."

"No need to transfer her," Jax told her. "If you can get her stabilized enough to get her released, we will just take her home. If it's a couple of days here, that's fine. The less excitement we cause, the better it will be. With the nurses knowing who we are now, there's bound to be media involved. If they see a helicopter land on the roof, shit will go crazy."

"That's from our perspective anyway," Ronnie added. "Medically speaking, you'll need to fill in the blanks for us. Does she need specialized care?"

Tama scoffed. "What do you call us?"

"You know what I meant," Ronnie shot back.

Onida chuckled. "Medically speaking, they ran her blood work and started on a flush right away as well as antibiotics. There will be red flags as that drug did a lot of damage to her organs, specifically, her liver, kidney, and heart. That will show on the blood work. The gunshot wound missed her artery at least, but it fractured her femur, and there's quite a bit of muscle damage. Since that's an obvious wound, I don't suggest we heal that one here. Let's wait until she's home. Same with the cracked ribs. One of the more serious injuries is in her spine; I don't know if they caught that or not or if we got here in time before they did an x-ray. Below her neck, ceiling debris must have hit her; she has a couple of fractured vertebrae in a spot between her wings. Since I didn't see anything on the chart about that, I think we should fix it. Internally, I believe that we need to fix everything internally, and it's a mess. With me as her doctor, they won't ask too many questions. If we leave the visible stuff alone, for now, it will be easier. There's a small fracture to her left cheekbone that we can probably wait on, but I'm inclined to say fix it, or she might have a hard time smiling, laughing, anything that moves her face."

"Damn." Ronnie sighed. "Please tell me that's all."

"Physically, the most important is internal." Onida gave him a look and then looked at Jax. "Tama will have to speak on the mental part." She took in a deep breath. "Jax, they did a rape kit," she said softly.

Ronnie felt his knees start to buckle, and Chrissie shoved a chair under him. Smitty moved to stand beside

Jax, and Aedan moved next to Chrissie. "Spit it out," he muttered.

"They found no semen, but there's evidence of forceful penetration, meaning they found tears."

Chrissie made a strangled sound, and Aedan caught her as she passed out, bumping into the bed behind him. Ronnie heaved violently, and Onida put her hand on his back until it passed. Taklishim was near Jax doing the same thing.

"She probably doesn't know," Onida told them. "The number of drugs that were in her would have kept her out. It could turn out to be a small blessing. I'm only bringing it up because it's in the official report, and when she wakes up, the police will ask her."

Ronnie looked at the beautiful angel lying there so still. A sight that had become all too familiar to him, and he felt sick. Her face bruised and battered, her body having broke inside and out. She was so strong mentally, but he'd felt her emotions firsthand when she relayed her previous experience with rape. Even being told she'd been touched and not remembering it would hurt her in ways he couldn't even fathom.

"Go take a walk," Aedan told him calmly, Chrissie lying unconscious in his arms.

Ronnie shoved out of the chair and stalked out of the room, stopping at the nurse's station. "Can you have someone bring a cot in there, please?"

He didn't wait for an answer, he found the first exit sign he could and flew out the door, his chest tightening with every step Ronnie took until he couldn't go any farther and sunk to the ground.

A keening sound ripped from him, and he rocked

back and forth, never noticing the red-eyed raven that landed not far from him. He lay back on the ground and rolled to his side in the fetal position and cried. For Rafe, Jace, Bryce, and Chrissie, and the awful things they've endured. He cried for Airiella, Jax, and the rest of the team; and wondered how they would get her through this.

"He's suffering as we speak, Ronnie." He heard Stolas's voice.

"How did you know?" Ronnie hadn't been startled by the sudden voice in his ear, that's how far down a black hole he'd fallen.

"I searched his memories after I tore his soul out. I needed to know. Her eyes looked broken when I saw her. Something in them told me there was more to the story."

"Rafe?"

"He was there. Blindfolded, but he was there." A blast of white-hot anger tore through Ronnie, and the smell of sulfur filled the air as Stolas released emotions.

"Did you kill him?" The tormented whisper ripped from his lungs.

"I did. I'll gladly carry that stain. The way I pulled his soul out stopped his heart."

"That's not a stain, that's justice. I'd have killed Travis too," Ronnie admitted. "Does she know?"

"That he's dead? Yes."

"No, about the rape," Ronnie clarified, hating the way the word sounded on his lips. It was a vile word, but it was not disgusting enough to describe the damage it caused.

"On some level, she does. I don't know if she pushed it out of her mind, or only some part of her is aware, but her eyes told me she knows."

"He did it to Chrissie too," Ronnie told him. "When she was pregnant."

"I saw. She endured a lot at his hands. Those two women have a deep bond. Love them well."

"Airiella loves you too, Stolas. Have you not figured that out yet?"

"Whether it is true or not is beside the point. My foolish heart has once again put me in a futile position. The difference is this time, I'm already a part of Hell, and it's where I belong."

Ronnie didn't know what to say to that, and now wasn't the time to have an in-depth conversation about the path that led him to be what he is. "Take your advice. Love her well," he finally told Stolas.

"Did you not hear the part about Hell being where I belong?" Stolas spat.

"Because you belong in Hell means you can't love her well? From what I can see, your love for her already runs pretty deep; you just hide from her until she calls you. If what she went through today hurt you, then make an effort to show up and show her that you care. That's what will get her through this."

"I stay away so that I don't complicate her life."

Ronnie laughed bitterly. "Is that what you think?" He glared at Stolas. "Do you know anything about her? Let me put this simply, how do you grow a plant? You take care of it. Whether or not you believe she loves you, she does. You hiding away from her because you can't deal with that, or the fact that Jax is who she is supposed to be with, doesn't show her that you care much about the effort she gives you in return. You show up when we call you because she needs help, you fall apart when you see how badly hurt she is, and then take off before showing her that you made an effort to be there. Us telling her you were there doesn't tell her much. She sees the good in you and gives you love freely. Your help is invaluable to her and us. So fucking show her that she's worth the time it takes you. Disappearing only tells her you didn't want to take the time to see her eyes open."

Ronnie felt the swell of energy forming in the demon, but he wouldn't back down. Stolas just flat out had his head up his ass this time. He was shocked when the response that came out his mouth was a laugh. "With as old as I am, you think I'd know more about women than I do. Even demons have fear, Ronnie, you've struck on mine. I will take your words of advice and think about them. I appreciate the honesty. Someone is summoning me; I must go."

He couldn't help the wave of relief that washed over him that Stolas hadn't been angry for his outburst. He took a little comfort in knowing Stolas wouldn't set out to hurt him. Emotions had run high tonight, and it wouldn't have surprised him if the demon lost control after seeing those memories. Maybe he had on his way to hand-deliver Travis.

Ronnie stood back up and brushed his clothes clean. He needed to head back in; he was sure Jax needed a walk just as much as he had. He walked back in and waited for the nurses to buzz him back in and saw Aedan sitting in the hall as he came upon the room.

"Everything okay?" Ronnie asked uneasily.

"Yeah. I called Mags. How are you? Calmed down?" Aedan's eyes were showing strain when he looked up.

"I don't know if I'd call it calm, but I'm not going to snap. Thanks for catching Chrissie. She okay?"

"She was still out when I left the room. Think Airiella knows?" He looked back down at his hands.

Ronnie sat on the chair next to Aedan and rubbed his face. "Stolas appeared while I was having a nervous breakdown outside. He confirmed it and said he believes she knows. He said her eyes looked broken when he saw her."

"How did he know?" Aedan looked up again, this time with tears shimmering in his eyes.

"That dude is scary as shit. He told me when he ripped Travis's soul out, he looked through his memories and saw it. Rafe was there," Ronnie whispered.

"Fuck." Aedan looked sick again. "Mags is losing her shit over it; Jillian was crying in the background. I think Jax is borderline where you were; Smitty has turned to stone, the rest are working on healing Airiella."

"Jax won't be borderline if I tell him that." Ronnie hung his head down. "I don't know what to do, Aed."

"Don't lie to him. I'm not saying march in there and tell him right now, but we both know it will come up again. Sooner rather than later if he's dwelling on it, which I'm sure he is."

"Smitty's with him, right?" Ronnie looked at the closed door.

"Yeah. Glued to Jax's side." Aedan leaned against Ronnie in an uncharacteristic display of vulnerability. "It hardly seems fair that someone should suffer so much and still expected to do all that she does."

"She is an angel," Ronnie countered warily. He didn't like how she suffered either.

"I'm talking about Chrissie. Though the shoe fits for both of them."

Ronnie snapped his mouth closed. "You're thinking about what she said while trying to piss Airiella off?"

"That, and listening to the asshole speak on the phone; hearing the stuff he said while with Airiella and listening to Jace talk. Fuck, I'm going to have nightmares for the rest of my life. It makes me sick to think about people like that existing in the same world as the one I am raising my innocent daughter. Fucking kills me even to contemplate the things Chrissie and Airiella have experienced firsthand and yet still have the compassion they both do." Aedan leaned his head against the wall. "Seeing Airiella broken and battered once again, then hearing the words rape kit and Chrissie passing out. How can one person restore balance when things are like this?"

Ronnie hooked his arm around Aedan's shoulders. "We are switching roles now? You are getting emotional, and I have to be logical? A sure sign of the apocalypse." Ronnie looked around. "Okay. Think of the good she balanced it out with for all the bad that we have seen with our own eyes. Your babies, Tama, and Onida's babies, the love she spreads that changes people's lives. The life she restores. Through each person she touches, they, in turn, spread it further."

"You seriously are going to throw out the ripple effect on me?" Aedan asked, dumbfounded.

"Give me a break. It's all I have right now. Both the women I love are in that room and hurting in ways neither of us can fathom. Fuck, my entire team is hurting, and I just had a heart to heart with a demon while lying in the fetal position on the ground." Ronnie shook his head.

"At least tell me you are going to take this thing with Chrissie farther." Aedan turned to look at him.

"That's my plan. I can't imagine my life without those kids in it. Or her. Today painfully drove that home. It was a wake-up call," Ronnie admitted.

"Is it just me, or are their lives crazily similar?"

"They are. Yet Airiella and Chrissie are also different in ways that give them each strength's the other doesn't have. They have the same kind of bond Jax, and I have."

"I can see that. Jace is going to have a bit to work through," Aedan commented.

"He is. I'm working with him on it. He asked me to teach him to box. I told him that any of us could teach him and that when he felt that bad feeling inside, to talk to any of us. Even if it wasn't about what was hurting him."

"Good advice. Poor kid is way older than his nine years. He reminds me a lot of you." Aedan quieted his voice as nurses walked by, eyeing them both.

"I know. I think Jace will do way better than I did, though. He's smart." Ronnie saw the door opening, and Jax stepped out. He patted the seat next to him, waiting for his best friend to join him.

"Better now?" Jax asked cautiously.

"Better than I was. You?" Ronnie gave him a careful look over, watching for the warning signs Jax was going to lose it.

"Destroyed. If there was ever a time I needed a punching bag, it's now. You called Mags?" Jax looked at Aedan.

"Yeah. Mags and Jillian didn't take it well." Aedan stated the obvious with a tone that was glum and desolate.

"Fuck, who would?" Jax bit out. "I had a hard time leaving the room. Smitty was about to throw me out. Tama put Chrissie out, said she'd alter it when you came back in," he told Ronnie. "Aed, nice catch, by the way."

"None of us would have let her hit the floor," he replied, closing his eyes and putting his head back against the wall again.

"What do we do now? How do we move past this?" Jax hung his head.

"A day at a time. Let's get her better before we worry about that," Ronnie told him, unsure of how to put any of it into action.

"It's a part of her getting better, Ron. Think she'll remember?" Jax asked, hesitant.

Aedan nudged Ronnie, then again harder when he didn't answer right away. "Knock it off, give me a minute," Ronnie snapped.

"What?" Jax looked at him weirdly.

"Not you. Aedan. Shoving me with his elbow like I'm not going to tell you what you need to know. Stolas found me outside, and we had a little chat. Short of it is, when he pulled Travis's soul, he searched his memories and found it did happen, and Rafe was there. He thinks she'll remember because when he saw her, he said her eyes looked broken."

Jax shuddered in anger. "Hell is too good for Travis."

"Pretty sure Stolas shares that opinion. Stolas assured me that the bastard was suffering." Ronnie hoped it would ease a little of what Jax was feeling.

"I don't feel even a little stable right now." Jax's voice trembled with the heavy emotions rolling around in him.

Ronnie patted Jax on the back. "I assumed that's

why Smitty sent you packing."

"Told me if I didn't, he was going to have Tama knock me out."

"He probably would have too." Aedan rejoined the conversation. "We've got to get over it. We can't change what happened. For her sake, Chrissie's, and the boys, we need to figure it out. It doesn't change how we feel about Airiella, or who she is. Nor does it change how we feel about Chrissie. She blames herself, and her boys will pick up on that."

"Back to logical now? Already done with emotional?" Ronnie fired back at him, irritated with himself.

"Well, someone has to be, you sucked at it with your ripple effect shit."

"Sounds to me like he's still stuck on emotional," Jax said, woodenly.

"Oh, fuck off, you two. You don't hold the monopoly on emotions," Aedan growled back at them.

Ronnie laughed. "This almost feels normal."

"I'm going back in there." Aedan stood up. "Jax, get some air, you look like shit."

Ronnie watched him go back in and looked at Jax. "Still about to lose it?"

"No. Not how you mean. Maybe on a cracked on the inside emotional level because I can't comprehend the actions, but I'm not going to snap. Tell me what's changed with you. The marked difference between Chrissie and you today."

"Yeah. Figured you'd notice that. Took the actions of today to make me see how stupid I am and how much they mean to me." Ronnie wasn't proud of himself for it either.

"You aren't stupid. Our circumstances are a little unique," Jax defended him.

"Well, I told her I wanted to take things farther, but I wouldn't sleep with her until I talked to you and our angel. I confessed my fears that I wouldn't be able to go back if things didn't work out with her."

"Alright, I changed my mind; you're stupid." Jax sighed. "How many times have we told you we are fine with things as they are?"

"I'm aware. It took the events of today for me to see it. Sadly. Maybe I just needed to hear the words coming out of my mouth. I don't know. Degataga pointed a few things out to me before everything went down." Ronnie drew in a deep breath to calm the storm that rose inside of him again.

"Nothing changed with Smitty except sex. Why would you think you are any different? Especially knowing how strong the connection she has with you is?" Jax pushed at him.

"Marriage to my best friend. Need I say more?" Ronnie grew frustrated but knew he had to let Jax have his say.

"Yes! All three of us talked about this after I proposed. I don't own her; marriage doesn't change that. For fuck's sake, you are a part of me. You are a part of this whole thing. I don't care how many people you date; there is always a place for you in this." Jax's emotions were stretched too thin.

"I know that now. Chrissie made it clear when we talked. Like I told her, it's my choice to end the sexual part of it, despite all of you making it understood I didn't need to." Ronnie tried to calm his tone to help Jax even out a little.

"Ronnie, I support whatever you decide to do. I've always got your back, even when you're stupid." Jax finally sighed, but looked crushed by the weight of everything.

"Great pep talk, bro." Ronnie went for humor.

"So how serious is this?" Jax ignored the humor and cut through the shit.

"Lifetime serious. I'm in love with her, with the boys. I can't imagine my life without them," Ronnie said softly. "I don't want to imagine it."

"Ells will be happy to hear that." Jax sat up, leaned his head back against the wall like Aedan, and closed his eyes.

"I know. I'm still in love with Airiella, and it took me a while to understand there's room for both. It doesn't have to be one or the other. I don't need sex with Airiella to feel close to her. Don't get me wrong, that part is great as you are well aware, it's just not necessary. Aside from the whole, she's supposed to be with you thing; you deserve your marriage to be between the two of you in that regard. Just as Chrissie deserves to have all my attention in that regard, letting go was hard for me."

"What exactly about her being kidnapped, raped, and beaten made you decide not to sleep with her?" Jax looked stricken as he said it, his eyes once again open and staring directly into Ronnie's.

"It wasn't that, you asshole. It was more my need to be there for Chrissie. My worry about Rafe. It didn't push my need to protect Airiella down, it more made me see that my need was just as great to provide for Chrissie." Ronnie frowned at Jax.

"That makes more sense." Jax relaxed again,

exaggerating his movements.

"Jackass." Ronnie was tempted to punch him in the arm.

Jax smiled. "I'm happy for you. I hope that what you have with her is as strong, if not stronger, than what you have with Airiella. I hope that it's as strong as what I have with Airiella. You both deserve happiness. I didn't ever expect you to break up with me, and coming to terms with that isn't easy."

Ronnie laughed again. "Jax, I'll never break up with you."

A nurse walked by at that moment and gave them a startled look and muttered, "Figures, all the hot ones are gay."

"How much you want to bet that's in the tabloids tomorrow?" Jax chuckled. "Back to the situation at hand. What do we do?"

"No idea. I've got to figure out how to make Chrissie understand this isn't her fault." Ronnie sighed and scrubbed his hands over his face again.

"I don't think you'll have to worry about that. Ells will set that straight." Jax leaned into him.

"If you think about it, we may have answered our question; their relationship is like ours. Airiella is going to help Chris, and Chris will help Airiella. Neither of us can understand what it feels like to get raped. Maybe our best bet is to let Airiella approach it on her terms, and we let them know that we can help. Same thing we've always done. If that means listening to gut-wrenching details again, we do it," Ronnie suggested.

"I never really thought about it like that; they are like us. Airiella steps in when Chrissie falters, and vice versa. Seems obvious now. It also feels a little like taking the easy road out of this."

"Not really. Not if we bring it up together." Ronnie thought about it. "We are jumping ahead on it anyway. We can't spring this on her the minute she wakes up."

"No. Welcome back from the dead baby, did you know Travis raped you?" Jax snipped.

Ronnie shoved him. "Not cool."

The door opened again, and Aedan stuck his head out and motioned them in, his eyes drifting to the cops outside the door. "She awake?" Jax asked as he stood.

"No," Aedan said.

"They must have finished with what they can do then," Ronnie guessed, standing and following Jax.

"Or as much as they can with the energy they have left," Jax countered.

Chapter Twelve

Chrissie woke to the sounds of quiet murmuring and feeling vaguely uncomfortable. As her body became aware, she realized she was lying on a hot and hard body. She cracked open an eye and saw Rafe looking at her, and it all came crashing back to her.

Travis, the abduction, Ells, the rape kit, then nothing; at least that explained why she was lying on Ronnie. She would have hated not to remember sleeping with him. She didn't know what time it was, but the nurses had unhooked the IV that had been in Rafe.

Rafe silently reached for her, and she pulled him to her after he climbed over the still sleeping Jace. She again heard the quiet murmuring that had woken her up, but someone had closed the little curtain between the beds, and she suspected it had been the same person that had taken Rafe's IV out.

If Rafe's added weight bothered the sleeping giant under her, he didn't make any sounds to indicate it. She hugged her little boy tight to her and fought back a wave of tears. He was alive and safe; everything else would get handled in time.

She tried her best to slip quietly out of the cot, but since there wasn't a whole lot of room to maneuver, she ended up waking up Ronnie. He saw Rafe awake and in her arms, and he shifted to help them up while hugging them both.

She saw Ronnie's questioning look at the curtain between the beds, and she just shrugged her shoulders and mouthed shower to him. He nodded and stood with her as she carried Rafe to the tiny bathroom in the room.

"Can you get him the clean clothes we brought?" she asked Ronnie quietly. Looking back at Rafe, she said, "Okay, baby, let's get you cleaned up, so you feel all the way better, okay?"

He only nodded at her, his eyes wide and full of sorrow, and she wondered what he remembered or had seen. There was a haunted, hollow look to go with the sorrowful eyes. Ronnie came back in with the clean clothes.

"Can you help him shower? I need to go find a bathroom for myself," she said sheepishly, her bladder feeling like it was going to burst.

"I got it, go ahead." He kissed her on the head and started unwrapping the soap and grabbing a washcloth.

She quietly snuck out of the room and darted out into the hallway, grabbing the first nurse she saw. "Bathroom?" The nurse pointed down the hall, and Chrissie took off at a jog.

She crept back in the room in time to help Ronnie get Rafe dressed. "How do you feel, baby?" she asked, hugging him gently.

"I'm okay. I need to see Auntie Ells," he whispered in her ear.

"I think she's still sleeping, honey, we should leave

her alone for a little while." Chrissie brushed his wet hair back, towel drying it some more.

"I promised," he said and his eyes started to fill with tears, and Ronnie scooped him up.

"What did you promise, little man?" He planted a kiss in the middle of his forehead.

"To watch her and keep her safe."

Chrissie felt her own eyes well up. "That's brave of you."

"He did bad things to her," he said and started to wail, and Chrissie pushed the bathroom door shut. Ronnie sat down with Rafe on the toilet, so there was room for all of them.

"We know he did." Ronnie stroked his back. "It's not your fault, and she will be okay."

Chrissie felt icy cold fear stab her heart. He'd seen more than they thought he had. She heard movement from the room, peeked out to check on the other two boys, and saw Taklishim and Tama make their way past to Airiella's bed.

Taklishim was pulling the curtain back, and Chrissie saw Jax laying behind Airiella, her eyes open. Chrissie squealed, startling both Ronnie and Rafe, and she bolted out of the bathroom to hear a very weak sounding Airiella.

"You're fired, Tak. You missed a spot," she said and she held out her bruised and abraded wrists.

Chrissie's forward momentum halted when the man burst into tears, and Jax climbed out of bed, and Taklishim lay down in front of her. "I'm so sorry, Raven."

Chrissie hadn't even heard Ronnie come up behind them. "Give him a minute, Chris."

Jax came walking over. "She's weak, but said she would be fine. How's this one?" Jax gestured to the weeping boy in Ronnie's arms.

"He's upset," Ronnie answered as all Chrissie could do was stare at the stoic man she had only seen break down when it came to Airiella.

Tama had sat at the foot of the bed, her hand on Airiella's foot as Taklishim hugged her and was murmuring words to her so quietly that Chrissie couldn't hear them. That same icy fear stabbed at her again, and she wondered if she knew what had happened.

"Does she know?" she finally found her voice and asked Jax.

"I don't know. I hadn't gotten there yet," Jax admitted. "I was so happy to see her eyes open and feel her moving that I couldn't make myself ask."

"Probably not the best conversation opener," Ronnie agreed. "Rafe said he promised to watch her and keep her safe."

"You did?" Jax rubbed the boy's head. "That's great!"

"Is that because of the kit?" Ronnie asked carefully, nodding at Taklishim and Airiella.

"I assume so. Well, part of it. Taklishim was on edge about her before that bombshell. I think that just pushed him over. Tama said he didn't sleep," Jax spoke softly.

Chrissie felt her breathing become erratic at the thought of what her best friend had endured at the hands of her ex-husband. Jax took her arm and pulled her out into the hallway. "Breathe, Chrissie."

"Do you know what she's been through?" she whispered harshly.

"I do. I've seen the things Airiella went through. I was in the visions she had of the things she needed to heal from; it nearly made me lose myself completely. If she remembers, she's going to need you to help her get through this. Be there for each other," Jax pushed, his voice commanding her attention.

"How can you be so calm?" Her ragged breath exploded from her lips.

Jax laughed darkly. "Oh, if you could only see what's going on inside, you wouldn't ask that. If Travis weren't dead, I'd do it myself."

The harsh words cut through the hysteria that was trying to take control of Chrissie's mind. "It sickens me. I brought that into her life."

"Knock that shit off. Airiella won't tolerate that any more than I will. She doesn't blame you, and she's all but said so. How many times do I need to tell you that?" Jax's tone was aggressive.

"It doesn't matter how many times you say it, my heart will still feel it," Chrissie said coldly.

"Do you know that she's told me that she feels bad for bringing you into this life and putting you and your boys in danger because of what she is and the target that has become her?" Jax turned the table on her.

Chrissie jolted. "But that's not her fault."

"My point exactly. We learn to accept that some circumstances aren't things that we brought on ourselves, whether we have a reason for why it happened or not; this is no different. You had no way of knowing that Travis was here, or was a threat to you, her or your kids."

"God, Jax, I'm afraid to face her," Chrissie moaned, covering her face with her hands.

He pulled her hands away from her face and hugged her. "Whether she knows or not, she's the same person."

"That's just it. Ells won't be. You don't come through that without it changing you. It doesn't matter how many times it's happened before or if it never has, it changes you. What if she becomes scared of you? Of Ronnie?"

"I haven't been through it; you might be right. I also know Airiella's heart, and I know that she would never be scared of Ronnie or I. Regardless of what has happened."

"Jax, that's my point. You haven't been through it; you don't know what will trigger the fear or a flashback. The memory comes to life inside your mind, and you don't know whether it's real or not," Chrissie argued.

"I'm not arguing that, Chris. I'm trying to tell you that I, Ronnie, or Smitty will know the moment it happens. For sure, I will, whether I'm with her or not. It's how the connection is between us. The moment her busy brain woke up, I was aware of it, and she of me. The hint of fear that creeps into her about any of this, I will know the second it happens. Her emotions tied to rape have a distinct feel to them. Did she tell you that she specifically asks Ronnie and I to do things that would normally trigger her so that she can overcome it?" Jax held her chin in place, so she looked him in the eye.

"No. Ells doesn't talk about her sex life with anyone. She may joke about it, but she never shares details. Is she listening to us right now?" Chrissie worried about the reaction that may happen if she was.

"No. Airiella doesn't have enough energy to be with Taklishim and listen to us right now. She's aware of my emotions, which is why I'm doing my best to remain calm."

"Speaking of that, why did you get out of bed so he could get in? I thought for sure you'd adhere yourself to her." The rare display of emotions from Taklishim had left her unsettled. Her nerves were so raw right now anything would set her off.

"He needs her more than I do right now. I've long suspected they have a connection that neither of them is aware of; Tama believes that too. I don't believe it's romantic, but I know, for sure, he's in love with her in a spiritual way. Tama is the one that pointed it out to me. They are very close, and she loves the hell out of him." Jax gentled his tone.

Chrissie shook her head. "Okay. I'm under control now."

"No, you aren't, not by a long shot." Jax hugged her tight. "I'm not either, Chrissie. But we just deal with it as it comes. I know what you mean to her. I heard her reaction to the news you shared, felt the pain of it. I can also tell you that since she came to, she has been worried about you. Remember, this isn't the worst thing she's lived through, though it certainly isn't an easy one. For any of us. This situation reminded me that she isn't immune to being hurt in ways *we* didn't think about."

She squeezed Jax back. "I'm so happy she has you. Even if I don't understand all the nuances of the connection, the love is easy to see. Even when she didn't want to admit it and was confused by it, I could still see it."

"Get your hands off my woman," Ronnie growled behind them. "I already share one with you, and I'm not making it two."

Jax laughed. "I wouldn't dream of it, bro. Guess that three-way is off the table, Chrissie."

Ronnie laughed at the expression on Chrissie's face. "I'm just joking with him, Chris. Our angel sent me out here to bring you two back in. And I quote her on this, 'Tell them to get their asses back in here and stop having emotions I am too tired to guess at right now.'"

"Did you get a moment with her?" Jax looked at Ronnie over the top of Chrissie's head.

"Yeah, Taklishim is wrecked. Tama knocked him out because his emotions were out of control. Bryce and Jace are awake, and Rafe is in bed with her."

"Oh, no. Poor kid, I'd better get him out of there." Chrissie untangled herself from Jax and moved towards the door only to have Ronnie step in front of it.

"Hang on there. I've got to tell you what Rafe told her," he said and held a hand out to stop both of them.

"Rafe?" Jax asked.

"Yeah. Rafe told her that God told him to watch her and keep her safe. That after the smoky man left, God came before the policemen did."

"Smoky man?" Chrissie repeated dumbly.

"He must be talking about Stolas; sometimes there's smoke when he appears or disappears depending on his mood. It wasn't the best of circumstances, so that kind of makes sense," Jax responded.

"But, God?" Chrissie looked searchingly at Ronnie.

"He's pretty adamant about it," he confirmed. "He said God told him that she would make it through this okay, but that he had a special assignment for Rafe. He needed to watch over Airiella and keep his warrior safe."

"Leap of faith, right?" Jax gave Ronnie a look.

"Anything's possible with her," Ronnie said, his voice casual.

Chrissie wasn't sure what to think. They accepted Rafe's statement without question, and as bizarre as it sounded, she had to admit that with Airiella involved, Rafe might have talked to someone other than Stolas. Was it God, though?

"Speak of the devil," Jax said with a smile.

"Not quite, he's a bit more daunting than I am." Stolas leaned against the wall, a guarded look on his face as he studied Ronnie. "I took your words to heart, and I'm here to check on her."

"Good. About damn time someone listened to me," he mumbled and pushed back in the room, Chrissie following Jax and Stolas.

"Stolas, was there someone else there besides you that talked to Rafe?" Chrissie asked quietly.

"Not while I was there, something was coming through when I left. Did something happen to your son? I apologize for not sticking around, but I had an urgent matter to deal with," he said and he stopped and gave her a look that was easy for her to interpret as to what that urgent something was.

"He said God talked to him," she answered bluntly.

"It's possible. I can't say for certain."

"That's the smoky man, Auntie Ells." Chrissie heard Rafe confirm what Jax had surmised.

"Hi, smoky man. I'm thrilled to see you." Airiella's voice was thick with emotion. "Chris, Stolas, stay; the rest of you, out. Ronnie, Jax, go feed these boys."

Chrissie was stunned that they didn't even argue. Jax picked up Bryce and took Jace's hand, while Ronnie kissed Airiella on the head and pulled a protesting Rafe away, telling him that Stolas would take his watch for a bit.

Her heart stuttered as Rafe gave Stolas a stern look. "Will you keep her safe while I'm gone?"

"It would be my pleasure, little one." Stolas bowed down to Rafe.

Unexpectedly, Rafe launched from Ronnie's arms at Stolas in a perfect leap. Thankfully Stolas caught him readily enough even though he wasn't expecting to have to. Rafe wrapped his little arms around Stolas's neck, clinging to the demon.

"Thank you for helping Auntie Ells. I love you, smoky man." Chrissie choked on a sob as Ronnie gently pulled the boy away, shooting Stolas a look of apology.

"Wait, Ronnie. Hey, little one." Stolas chucked Rafe under the chin. "I think you helped her more than I did, but thank you for the hug. That was the best hug I've ever gotten."

Pride filled the little boy's face before he wrapped his arms around Ronnie's neck and rested his chin on Ronnie's shoulder to watch them as they walked out of the room. "Jeez, Chris, that kid kills me." Airiella smiled.

"Amazing young man you have there," Stolas agreed, his voice a little deeper than usual.

"Thanks." Chrissie shuffled her feet.

"Sit," Airiella told her, pointing to the chair. "You too," she said and she patted the bed next to her, looking at Stolas. "For the record, Jax knows what I plan on doing here, so both of you stop looking at me like I'm fragile, or about to tear you apart."

"I, uh, um, sorry," Chrissie mumbled.

"Stop, Chris. Stolas," she said and she tugged at his arm until he moved sideways a bit, then she pulled him down to lay beside her; she promptly tucked herself next to him and pulled his arm around her. "You saved my life as much as Taklishim did; as much as Rafe kept me from slipping away because of the drugs. Because of you, I'm here right now and have a chance to keep doing what I do, which is apparently scaring the hell out of people with my reckless need to save them all."

"The warrior deserves the credit, not me," Stolas argued, but Chrissie noticed he didn't pull away, and she was glad he didn't. Airiella was right; the demon had saved both Airiella and Rafe.

"Tak wouldn't have found me if it hadn't been for you, and he knows it. Chrissie's son is alive and safe because you did what they couldn't do," Airiella insisted firmly.

"Love, I'm not a good person." Stolas sounded uncomfortable with the praise. "I'm on the wrong side of heaven."

"Really? Are you quoting song lyrics to me now? From one of my favorite bands no less."

"In my defense, I didn't know either of those things." Stolas looked embarrassed at the affection, but powerless against it.

Chrissie smothered a laugh and bit her lip as Airiella stared at him. "The song is called Wrong Side of Heaven. It's oddly suited to you. Anyway, there's nothing you can say that would convince me you are bad, Stolas. I know otherwise. That little boy just declared he loved you. He sees the same thing I do, and if I'm reading Chrissie's face right, she thinks the same."

"I'm a demon," he scoffed, sounding a little unsure of himself, something Chrissie wasn't used to seeing with him.

"I know. One whose soul is so much lighter now than it ever was before." She pushed against his chest and sat up, her wings popping out. "Chris, pull a feather for me."

Chrissie stood up and ruffled her fingers through the silky feathers until she felt one that called to her and gently pulled until it came free and handed it to Airiella, who made the wings go back in and lay back down, her head on Stolas's shoulder and nestled into his side.

"To replace the one you gave up. Ronnie, let me know that you didn't believe I could love you. I had to force it out of him, but guilt works wonders on him sometimes. He's easy like that. I told you in the beginning that trust and love were something you had to earn. You've earned mine. I *do* love you Stolas, you've stolen a piece of my heart." Airiella tucked the feather in his jacket pocket and tipped her face up and kissed him.

Chrissie knew it didn't mean what she was sure Stolas hoped it meant. Airiella was pretty free with her kisses and people she loved; she hoped the man wouldn't get his heartbroken as he wound his fingers in her hair and kissed her back.

"That was more than I could have ever dared to hope for, love. Thank you," Stolas told her quietly. His face was awash with love, his voice tender.

"Now that's out of the way." Airiella put her head back down on his shoulder. "Maybe you can both tell me whatever it is you are holding back."

"I think Jax should be here for this." Chrissie sat up.

"Jax knows I'm asking, so stop hedging around it, Chris," Airiella warned. "He touched me, didn't he?"

Like they were synchronized, both Stolas and

Chrissie went utterly still at Airiella's tone. A tone she hoped to never hear from Airiella's lips again. Violation and pain were simmering below the surface of a memory that may or may not hover in her mind.

"He did, love. He's suffering for it too, I've made certain of that," Stolas admitted carefully, his tone steeped in anger. The energy in the room became palpable.

"Was Rafe there?" Chrissie saw Airiella shivering as she asked the question, and she couldn't take it. She climbed straight over the both of them and lay behind Airiella, her arm creeping around her middle, resting right below Stolas's.

"He was there, love. I'm not sure how much he understood, but he knew you were hurt, and bad things happened to you."

"They did a rape kit, Ells, they found tears," Chrissie confirmed.

"Will I remember?" Her voice quivered.

"I think that part is up to you, love."

"How did you know, Stolas?" Dark shadows filled Airiella's face as the reality set in.

"When I ripped his soul out, I read the memories. We need proof to take souls to certain parts of Hell. I found Travis's and I saw it. If I could change it, I would. There's not much I wouldn't have done to save you from that." His voice was thick, and Chrissie saw his eyes had a sheen of tears he was fighting against shedding.

"Ells, I'm so sorry," Chrissie whispered, feeling the choking energy of anger filling the room level up.

"Stolas, stop, she can feel that," Airiella told him gently.

"My apologies. The anger this causes me is

uncontrollable," Stolas apologized.

"I can't say it's making me all that happy." Airiella's tone held the shadows that her face had shown. "Do you know my past, Stolas?"

"I've never pried, love. From what the others have said, you've experienced this before. I didn't feel it was my place to ask."

"Is there some herbal juju you can whip up, so I forget it all?" Her question surprised both Stolas and Chrissie.

Chrissie caught her breath, waiting for the reply. Airiella didn't usually back down like this, and it made her wonder just how bad it was before. She knew it had been violent, but like she'd told the guys, they never discussed details, only the emotional fallout.

"There is, love, you know that it's not a fix. You should deal with it now and not shove it down for it to all resurface later down the road. I'll do whatever you ask, that's just my opinion," Stolas said reluctantly.

An opinion Chrissie shared with him, though it made her a hypocrite. "Ells," Chrissie rubbed her hand down Airiella's arm, "he's right."

"I know he is, but you don't get to say that, you are in the same boat I am," she said and she started to shake, and both Stolas and Chrissie held her tighter. "I don't know anything about demon magic," she told Stolas, "but open your mind to me, I'm going to share with you, and then I want to know if your opinion changes."

Chrissie wasn't sure what Airiella was going to do, but she suddenly plunged directly into a memory of Airiella's that she never wanted to see. The violence and abhorrence of what she went through left an impression in

Chrissie's head; by the time it came to an end, all three were left shaking and sobbing on the small hospital bed.

"I still have moments where I wish you were mine. Maybe more so, now. I don't want to be the reason you go dark. I'd rather just be a part of the dark that's in you. It's a dark that I know and can help you fight, even if it eradicates myself. I also know that I wouldn't be able to contain my anger over it, as Jax does, focusing on what you need instead of the pure vengeance that would take over whatever soul I have left in my body. While what you suffered yesterday doesn't compare in abject horror to that, it, in no, way diminishes what happened. My opinion is the same, love. Between your friend here and the love they all have for you, it will be far healthier for you to confront this than hide it away." He stroked her face softly. "Heaven chose well in making you one of their warriors. Your light keeps us all going."

"Then I will take your advice," she answered so softly Chrissie could barely hear her. "I can feel it building in you. If you can't get that under control, you might want to leave before it leaks out," she said and she kissed the back of his hand. "I don't fault you for it."

"You've breathed new life into me, love. Going is a wise move. You have only to call my name, and I will come," he said and he sat up and slid out from under her arm. Leaning over, he brushed his lips over hers once more, then kissed the back of Chrissie's hand. "Take care of each other."

He disappeared, and Chrissie felt Airiella move over to make more room for Chrissie. "Chris, stop blaming yourself. There was nothing about any of this that could have foretold us. I'm sorry you got pulled into that memory too, and I can already hear you comparing them in your mind and minimizing the damage done to you. Don't. You can't compare it because you aren't me. Trauma is trauma; there is no better or worse. We both came out the other end of it."

"Ells," Chrissie started, only to be cut off.

"Stop. For once, I'm going to listen to what someone tells me and do as Stolas said. We need to take care of each other through this. Details don't matter."

"They do, though," she argued.

"No, they don't. What matters is we move past it." Airiella's voice trembled again.

"I should go get Jax or Ronnie." Chrissie tried to sit up, but Airiella held her in place.

"They are already on their way up. Cops are here to question me, too. Stay with me, please."

Chrissie couldn't have turned away from her if she tried. It was hard to see someone who was so strong, overcome with weakness and fear. It didn't gel in her mind that Airiella was scared. She was always so fearless.

"You're wrong, Chris. I'm always scared, I just don't run from it." Airiella corrected her as if she could read her mind.

"How do you not hate him?" She felt the wetness on her cheeks and swiped the tears away.

"It's not easy. For now, I'll just let everyone love me through it," she said as the guys walked in.

Ronnie came straight over, his face schooled in a careful mask she saw through. He leaned over and kissed Airiella's forehead, then lifted Chrissie and lay down in her spot, settling her on top of him as Jax crowded in on the other side.

Chapter Thirteen

Ronnie didn't want to bring it up after the anguish that had washed through them while they were giving Airiella space. Nor did he want to mention the deadly emotions that Stolas had put out at one point that caught everyone in the vicinity off guard.

He desperately wanted to see her smile, even a small one. It kept popping up in his head, the moment they had at the beach when Airiella started to come to terms with things in her past, and how hard it was for her. This trauma was still fresh, and he had no idea what she remembered about it, if anything.

Jax had told him she was going to confront Chrissie and Stolas about what they were hiding from her. She'd even asked Jax, who had said they would talk about it later. Ronnie hated this. He was the one she went to for dealing with her emotions, and for him, this was one of those things that could tip him over the edge after the first time she'd talked about rape.

He'd listen to whatever she had to say, he always would. There just wasn't any way that he could hold back the anger and pain it caused him, which he knew was nothing compared to what she was feeling. It wasn't just her; it was Chrissie too.

"Heracles," she called out, the name a gentle reminder to him that he was strong enough for this.

"Angel, want to talk?" He grabbed her hand and held it, jostling Chrissie around in the process.

"No, not really. I know I need to, I'm not ready yet. Your thoughts are pretty loud, though."

He cleared his throat. "Shit. Sorry." He pulled her hand up and kissed the back of it. "So, what was it like kissing a demon?" He tried to get her to smile.

It worked. A small smile appeared on Airiella's beautiful face. "I can call him back here so you can try if you'd like."

"He's got that dark and sexy, broody thing going for him. I'll give him that, but he's not my type. Remember, I'm a Thor man," he joked.

Chrissie sat up and looked back at him, her face a question. "I have more competition? Did you just call Stolas sexy?" She looked over at Airiella. "Am I hearing things? And that kiss was pretty hot, Jax, you are one secure man. He even quoted song lyrics to her."

Jax grinned at Ronnie before replying. "Oh, just ask Ronnie. I was gritting my teeth the entire time. He deserved it; without his help, I don't know that we'd be here right now with her."

"He's been in love with her since the start; we always knew that," Ronnie told Chrissie. "Quoting song lyrics is new. Which song? Angel, open your eyes, please," Ronnie cajoled her, a strange feeling washing through him that he was afraid to identify.

"Let her be, Ronnie," Chrissie pushed back. "It was Five Finger Death Punch."

"Wow. How did Stolas know to quote that? Which song was it?" Ronnie directed his question to Airiella.

"It's fine, Chris." Airiella opened her eyes, her lashes clumped up from moisture. "He's just pulling me back from sinking in this. It was Wrong Side of Heaven."

"Oddly appropriate," Jax said.

"He didn't know it was a song." Airiella defended Stolas.

Ronnie shot Jax a look and felt Chrissie tense. "Ells, did I just hear you in my head?"

"Maybe, I don't know what you heard," she said and she closed her eyes again.

"Baby, what's going?" Jax murmured, and Ronnie felt the panic pull at him.

"I can't decipher what's reality or just horrific scenarios that my brain is concocting because I don't remember." Airiella shifted and rolled to face Jax, burying her face in his chest. "I can't look at anyone right now."

Shame. That's what Ronnie was feeling. She was ashamed. It smacked into him hard. Ronnie heard the whisper of the door and looked over to see Tama standing there. He nodded for her to come in, and she came closer to the bed and took a chair, her pregnant belly huge.

"Hi, beautiful girl. Do you want me to make it go away?" Tama asked her, putting a hand on her leg.

"She asked Stolas to do that, but he thought it would be best for her to deal with it," Chrissie answered.

"He's not wrong, but I will leave that choice to her. She's been through enough."

"He gave her a choice too. In the end, she listened to

him." Ronnie rested his head against the back of Chrissie's neck as he felt the connection shut down. She was retreating into her head, and he wasn't sure that was the best place for her to be right now.

"She said she was having a hard time telling the difference between what was real or not," Jax supplied Tama. "Baby, I'm going to fall off the bed, can you lay on top of me?"

Ronnie shifted closer to the edge on his side and tugged Airiella with him until Jax was farther on the bed, and then she did as he asked and lay on his chest, her face turned away from him. There was only one thing he could think to do to offer her comfort, and he put his hand on Jax's arm, the other on her, and let the connection they shared flow through them.

At the spark that flew between them the moment their skin touched, a small sob broke free from her. "Tell me what you see in your mind." Tama spoke in a mesmerizing tone.

"I can't see anything, but I hear screaming," came the hushed response.

Onida walked in then, police behind her. "How's my girl?" She shot a questioning look at Tama, then Ronnie.

"She said she's having a hard time telling fact from fiction in her head," Ronnie offered up.

"That's to be expected. The drugs in Airiella's system were potent and very toxic. Not to mention that you were in a traumatic situation." Onida was using her doctor tone, which told Ronnie that the police were wanting information.

"Ms. Raven, would you mind answering some questions?" A female officer stepped forward.

"I don't know that I can be of any help," Airiella answered numbly.

Ronnie felt the connection open back up between them, and the fear colliding with the anger inside her was a storm of epic proportions. He kept his hand on her and Jax and looked at the lady cop. "Go ahead and ask, but she's having memory problems."

"Understandable. Ms. Raven, can you identify that man that took you?"

"Travis Nielson."

"Thank you. Can you tell me what you remember?"

"I got out of the car to get the mail and heard movement at the last second. I dove to protect Rafe and felt a burning stab. I think I came to once before I was drugged again. I was somewhere dark, cold, damp, and moldy smelling and chained to the wall. The second time I woke up, I pretended like I wasn't and tried to look around to get more information, but it was still dark. I felt that I was on cement, naked, and that Rafe was next to me. Travis came back in and was ranting. I don't remember about what, just that he seemed crazy, maybe coming down off a high. Travis started kicking me, and then I think Travis did something to Rafe because Rafe cried out; I got angry. When he turned away, Rafe crawled over my leg and sat in front of me. His little body was cold, and he was shivering. Travis attacked us again, and then the building came down around us."

Ronnie wondered why she was holding back and realized it was because Chrissie was listening intently to the words she was saying, and Airiella didn't want to make Chrissie feel worse. Because of the connection, he knew there was a lot more she wasn't saying, and also things she couldn't verbalize unless she were going to out herself.

"Do you remember anything else? Do you remember getting shot?"

"No. Things are pretty fuzzy in my head. Did you catch him? Travis?" Her quiet question hung heavy in the air, even though she knew the answer to that already.

"He won't bother you again, Ms. Raven," the older cop spoke, his voice a little rough.

"Meaning he died?"

The lady coughed a little. "Yes, Ms. Raven. The building collapsed on him."

"Is that enough?" Onida asked harshly.

"Yes, Onida. In my opinion, the matter is closed. Thank you for agreeing to let us see her," the lady answered. "If there's anything else, we will reach out. Mr. Walker provided us his contact information."

Ronnie glanced at Jax, whose face remained tightly shut, his eyes dark and menacing. "Do you still need to talk to Rafe?" Chrissie asked.

"Yes, though, as his mother, you will need to be with him." Ronnie prepared to go with her, but Chrissie stopped him.

"Stay here. Airiella needs you more than I do," she told him, her mouth brushing his ear.

Go with her, Ronnie. Rafe needs to see a stable man with his mom. Jax has me. Don't let her fool you; she's not okay despite what she says.

Angel, as much as I want to go with her and protect that little boy, I'm worried about you. Ronnie squeezed her hand.

Go. I'll need you later. Right now, I need just to let Jax hold me.

Ronnie dropped her hand and stood; Chrissie's face etched with concern. He shook his head a little at her. "I'm coming with you."

I love you, Heracles. Take care of my girl.

I love you too, angel.

"She needs you!" Chrissie whispered to him urgently.

"She told me to go with you." Ronnie put his hand on her back and led her behind the cops. "Trust her. She told me she would need me later."

Chrissie glanced back, then at Ronnie's face. "I don't like this."

"You don't have to, but for now, Jax has her, and that's who she needs. I trust that she will tell me when she needs me." Ronnie hoped she would.

"She won't. Not about this."

Chrissie may be right, but he had the connection to tell him as a backup. "Rafe needs me too, Chris. So do you. She's got Jax, Tama, and Onina, aside from the fact she told me to go with you. Aedan can take the boys to the hotel room he and Smitty got and let them play in the pool afterward."

"Think they will let her go home today?" Chrissie asked in a low tone, so the police didn't overhear them.

"Doubtful. Airiella's not looking great, and her presence is still weak. Not to mention when whatever she's on wears off, that leg is going to hurt like hell. I don't think Onida can swing it yet. My guess is tomorrow, but she will get Rafe released, and we can go home. Give the boys a bit of normalcy." That was his intention anyway.

They came to a small office that Aedan and the boys sat outside of with another cop. "Is she awake?"

"Yeah, go see her," Ronnie told him. "Where's Smitty?"

"Bathroom. Want us to take these two?" Aedan gestured at Jace and Bryce.

"Yes, please," Chrissie answered, lifting Rafe into her arms.

"Ronan Byrne?" The female cop stopped outside the office and looked at Ronnie.

"Ronnie. I don't go by Ronan unless I need to be formal," he corrected the cop.

"Ronnie, then. I'm from a neighboring tribe of Onida's, and I'm doing my best to get this closed up as quickly as possible. I also specialize in sexual assault."

"I don't think Rafe got sexually assaulted." Ronnie felt a prickle of fear tingle in his spine.

"No, I don't believe he was either. But Ms. Raven was. I have several contacts that I can provide for counseling. I just wanted you to know that. Onida and Tama have helped me several times with victims, and unless I am reading the signals wrong, Mrs. Nielson also falls in that category."

Ronnie wasn't sure what to say, so he accepted the card she gave him and slid it into his wallet. "Is questioning Rafe necessary?"

"Unfortunately, yes. I need to make sure the bases are covered here, so there is no doubt about what happened, just in case Mr. Nielson's family tries to make any claims on his behalf."

"Like what? He kidnapped his son and a woman not related to him, violated her, and killed an officer of the law. What could they possibly claim?" Ronnie felt a fit of violent anger take root inside him again.

"Mental illness, wrongful death, false accusation. Sadly, in today's world, they can claim anything, and it will be a drain on resources for the departments involved and cause a media stir that will suck all of them into it. I'm hoping to avoid all that. Evidence backs the story that Ms. Raven told, what we hear from Rafe will only do the same. The conversation will be recorded and witnessed by another doctor and these other two officers."

Ronnie sighed, believing what she said. He hadn't ever talked with Chrissie about her life before moving here. He knew the marriage wasn't healthy, that drug addiction was involved and that she didn't have a good relationship with her ex-in-laws.

"To be honest with you," she continued, "if there are any missteps, Tama's husband will find out, and he terrifies me. I'm playing this one by the book as closely as possible while still protecting both of them."

That got a chuckle out of Ronnie. "He does that to a lot of people. He loves these boys and Ms. Raven."

"I know. The officer killed was also a friend of mine. I know what needs to be protected here, and that's why I'm here. I will do everything in my power to make this as painless as possible."

Ronnie halted at that bit of information. Did she know about Airiella? "What exactly do you mean?"

"Taklishim trusts me, so should you."

"I had no reason not to trust you; that was never my issue." Ronnie studied her carefully.

She nodded at him and entered the office, Ronnie, following and sitting down next to Chrissie. Rafe pulled away from Chrissie and crawled over to Ronnie's lap and leaned on his chest, looking up at him with big, sad eyes.

"Is Auntie Ells safe?"

"She is, kiddo; Uncle Jax is with her, I promise." Ronnie gave him the best smile he could in hopes of easing his young mind.

"Hi Rafe, my name is Officer Rivers. See this here?" She pointed to a recorder, and Rafe nodded. "This is a recorder and will record everything we say here. Do you think it will be okay with you and your mom if I use this to ask you some questions?"

Rafe eyed her with caution and looked over at Chrissie, who cupped his cheek and smiled at him. "What do you think, baby?"

"Okay."

"Great, thank you so much for your help, Rafe. You are a brave boy. Can you tell me what happened yesterday?"

"I went shopping with my mommy and auntie for the wedding stuff that Mom says Auntie Ells needs to have."

Ronnie stifled a laugh at the honest answer and hugged him. "Did she get everything she needed?" Officer Rivers smiled.

"Yeah. Auntie Ells looked pretty too."

"I bet she did. Lucky you that you got to see her before everyone else. What happened after that?"

"I got to eat ice cream with Auntie Ells." A weak smile flitted across his little face, then disappeared in the next second.

"Yum. Ice cream is my favorite; what kind did you get?" Office Rivers was natural with him, and Rafe relaxed a little.

"Chocolate. The best kind."

Rafe gave a tentative smile.

"I think so too. What did you do after that?"

"We went home, and I wanted to help Auntie Ells get the mail. She was going to let me unlock it. That's when my daddy hurt her. She tried to stop him from taking me."

"How did she do that?"

Rafe shifted a little, and Ronnie felt the agitation in his movements. "She jumped in front of me. He stuck her with something, and she fell down."

"Oh, no. Was your Auntie Ells hurt?" Office Rivers watched him, speaking only to him, looking only at him.

"I think so. Daddy put me in the car and then pulled her in. He shot at Mommy too."

"What do you mean by that?"

"He pointed a gun at her and shot. It hurt my ears and made me cry. He got mad at me for crying."

"That's not nice; how did he get mad?"

"He hit me. Right here." He pointed at his cheek, where Ronnie could see a faint bruise.

Rafe got a distant look on his face as he was thinking about what happened, and Ronnie's heart ached for the boy. Office Rivers didn't say anything, just let him think. They had the security tapes from the gate camera at the house, everything Rafe had said matched what the camera showed.

"He drove fast, and Auntie Ells fell off the back seat. He was mad at that too. He stopped and hit her then put a bag over her head." Rafe's arms were jerky as he mimicked the motions. "I was scared because she wasn't moving."

"I bet that was scary," Officer Rivers agreed, not leading the questions now. Rafe was letting the trauma out in his way.

"He yelled a lot. Bad words Mommy always told him not to say." Rafe grabbed hold of Ronnie's arm that was around his middle and held on like he was going to fall off. "He hurt her more. He used to do it to Mommy too."

Chrissie made a strangled sound, and Officer Rivers handed her a tissue from the box on the desk. Chrissie held it to her face and tried not to make any sounds. Ronnie moved his chair closer to hers, and she leaned against him.

"He made me take off all my clothes and throw them out the window."

"Did he say why?" The other officer broke in, startling the boy with his harsher voice. Rafe only shook his head in response. Officer Rivers glared at him, then softened her face and looked back at Rafe.

"He made me get out, and then he pulled Auntie Ells from the car. Her head made a sound when he did. He took all her clothes off her and made a fire with them. He told me not to look, but when Auntie Ells screamed, I did."

"She screamed?" Officer Rivers asked him quietly.

Rafe had tears falling down his cheeks now; they landed on Ronnie's arm like hot little fires stabbing at his heart. "He was on top of her, and she was screaming. I threw a rock at him to make him stop hurting her, but he didn't."

Ronnie didn't want to hear anymore. A sick feeling was rising in his stomach so fast. His ears started to buzz, and he broke out in a sweat. He began to move Rafe away when the boy turned and wrapped his arms around Ronnie's neck.

"I tried to protect her," he cried. "I wanted to protect her like you do."

Stay strong, Heracles.

Fuck, angel. I don't want to hear this. I want to tear this place apart until I find the bastard's body and beat the shit out of his corpse.

I love you. Chrissie is breaking apart right now; I can feel her.

I'm breaking, angel. Ronnie hugged Rafe tight and accepted the bottle of water that Officer Rivers handed him.

I know. I am too.

I'm not stone, Ronnie warned her.

I know exactly what you are; strength, courage, love, loyalty, the list goes on and on. I love you.

Ronnie gulped the water down, hoping it would ease the burning sensation of the tears that he was swallowing. *I love you too. So fucking much.*

"Hey, Rafe. You did protect her. She's still here with us." Ronnie coaxed him to sit back down.

"Do you want to stop talking now, Rafe?" Officer Rivers knelt in front of the boy.

"I want to help Auntie Ells get better. If I talk to you, does that help her?"

"It does, in a way. The more we know about what happened, the better we can all help her."

"Okay."

Officer Rivers got up and sat back down. "What else do you remember?"

"He put his shirt in her mouth. He was mad Auntie Ells was fighting him, but I didn't see her move." Rafe looked at the wall, his hands once again clutching at Ronnie's arm. "He did the thing he did to Mommy."

Chrissie's sobs excruciatingly tore at Ronnie, and she stilled against Ronnie at Rafe's statement. "Can you explain what that means, Rafe? I don't understand."

Rafe shook his head no. He didn't understand, and it almost snapped Ronnie. Ronnie had a sneaking suspicion of what it had been, and the words that Rafe wasn't saying and Chrissie wasn't filling in painted the picture plainly enough. Rafe turned his head into Ronnie's arm as if he was trying not to see it again. Office Rivers looked sick, same with the other two officers, while the doctor attempted to remain impassive but wasn't able to.

"He pulled her hair and dragged her to the building and pushed her down the stairs. I yelled at him to stop, and he told me to shut up. He was so mean. He put chains on her and tied me up. He stabbed her with something again and left us there."

"Were there any lights on?" Officer Rivers guided him a little.

"No, it was dark and cold. I sat as close to Auntie Ells as I could. He yelled when he came back and hurt her more with the gun and kicked me when I tried to stop him. I moved closer, and the building shook and broke, but I was safe with her."

"I think that's enough, Rafe. We have what we need to help your auntie." Officer Rivers stopped Rafe from going farther. She did know, Ronnie realized. Rafe knew to keep her wings a secret, and he didn't think the boy would have told, but she stopped the conversation before he could.

"You won't need to question him again?" Chrissie asked, her voice weak and shaking.

"I don't think it will be necessary," Office Rivers answered her gently. "Rafe, you are a strong and brave young man. You took good care of your auntie, and I'm sure she's proud of you."

Rafe nodded and turned again, wrapping himself around Ronnie, his little body shaking.

Angel, send Aedan or Smitty to come to get Rafe. I need a minute.

Smitty is coming. Just love her as you do me.

That wasn't possible, but he did love her. His love for Airiella was distinctly separate from his love for Chrissie, and right now, he needed to hold Chrissie. What they heard had left them both shaken. As they walked out of the office, Smitty came around the corner and gently took a protesting Rafe away from Ronnie.

"Come on, little man. I'm going to take you back to Auntie Ells. I think she misses you." Rafe immediately calmed and let Smitty carry him off.

Ronnie turned to the doctor. "Is there a private room we can use?" he asked quietly.

"Feel free to use my office. The door locks," the doctor answered, his face pale.

Ronnie led Chrissie back into the office, where she collapsed against him. "The screams she was hearing in her head; they were real. Ells knew. She knew what he was doing. One day Rafe is going to understand what he saw."

Ronnie slowly sunk them both down to the floor and held her while she shook and cried. "What was the shit that he did to you?"

"Oral sex. Travis forced it. He didn't call it rape. He said since we were married, it was something I owed to him. He had marital rights."

"Chris," he said and he started to talk, and she interrupted him.

"Don't. I divorced Travis after that. I had no idea

that Rafe saw it, that sickens me. Whatever torture Stolas has lined up for him isn't enough. He'd never even met Airiella before."

"You mentioned earlier that you heard her in your head?" Ronnie had waves of revulsion flowing through him, and he was fighting against it hard.

"I heard the screams."

"I hate the sound of those. I'm sorry, Chris. I'm sorry this happened. That you had to live that hell, that Rafe had to see any of it, to you or her. I'm sorry for all the men that think this shit is okay. I'm sorry for everything. I'm sorry you had to hear all that." Ronnie felt like if every man in the world apologized, it wasn't even close to enough.

She sat in the circle of his legs, and he felt himself trying to make himself smaller, so she didn't feel intimidated by him. "Ronnie, stop that. You don't scare me, nor do I believe you could ever be part of something like that. If anything, you've shown me how great a man can be."

"I will never do anything like that. It's heinous."

"She showed Stolas and me the memory of her attack," Chrissie told him, her voice wary.

"She did?" Shocked, Ronnie pulled back and looked at her. "Jax saw it. I almost wasn't able to pull him back."

"Now, I know why."

"Ah, now I get the wave of Stolas anger that slammed into us," Ronnie murmured.

"He cried. We all did. Stolas has a deep love for her. What Travis did, though, has the potential to set her on a downward slope, it can trigger those memories. It's already doing it to me."

"She's in a lot better of a place now than she was then. Out of all of us, I think you have the most power to help her through this. You both have this common wound. We *all* will play a part in getting her through it. I plan on helping *you* get through it as well."

"You are an extraordinary man, Ronan Byrne."

Chapter Fourteen

Jax and Ronnie had tried to postpone the filming schedule to allow Airiella time to heal mentally, but she shot them down, citing the distractions she needed. She'd allowed a week only to be home, and every night was nightmare riddled, from Rafe and Airiella both.

Chrissie was exhausted. She didn't want them to go, but she had hoped that the distance would keep those nightmares from spilling out into Chrissie's head. She was either awakened by Rafe crying out in his sleep or the screams in her head that she couldn't tell if they were real or not.

Ronnie was running back and forth between them all trying to help, and he was even more exhausted than Chrissie was. She knew that Smitty, Jax, and Ronnie all heard the same things she was hearing, and she suspected those three heard and saw more than they let on.

They just stoically bore the burden, their emotions barely simmering beneath the surfaces of their faces, and they worked out whenever they weren't needed, venting their anger and pain on the bags in the gym. Airiella had been faithful to her word with Ronnie; when she needed him, she told him.

Now it was just Chrissie and the boys in the house. She still had a few finishing things to do before the wedding, which Airiella had also be adamant about not postponing. Physically she was all healed, Taklishim and Degataga had taken care of that when she got released.

The mental wounds were still quite fresh. Travis's parents were now adding their form of abuse by demanding custody of the boys, threatening to sue her because they had rights, and she was refusing to abide by them. Office Rivers had been correct in her assumption that Travis's family would cause a backlash.

They also tried to blame Chrissie for his death. Office Rivers had shut that down quickly, her intervention a lifesaver to Chrissie. She couldn't fight for Chrissie on the custody part. Ronnie had left her numbers for the lawyers the show retained, and she called them and had set up an appointment. She also used the name for a child counselor that Officer Rivers had given her for Rafe.

After Airiella had left, he had become desolate because she wasn't where he could protect her. It was spiraling out of control, and she worried that Rafe was going to run away to find her. The last thing she needed was for Rafe to disappear and give her ex-in-laws ammunition to use against her.

Now she just didn't know if she should call to talk to a counselor herself or not. She didn't think that talking to Airiella about it was the best course of action, not with what she was dealing with herself. Ronnie argued that it would help pull Airiella back into the moment if she did, her natural inclination to help everyone would take over, and in assisting Chrissie to deal with it, she would be dealing with it herself.

He had a point, but it felt grossly selfish to Chrissie. She spent hours on the beach with Bryce letting him play in the sand and tide pools while she tried to sort her emotions and thoughts. She wished, not for the first time, that she had taken the initiative when Ronnie was there and pushed the physical aspect of their relationship.

Her feelings for him helped her ground herself in the present, and she craved that intimacy in a way that probably wasn't healthy but was necessary to her well-being. She'd known that he'd talked to Airiella about moving things forward with Chrissie, and Airiella had been thrilled by that. On that same train of thought, she'd also known there had been nothing physical between Airiella and Ronnie since he'd told her that.

He had spent nights in the room with Jax and Airiella, between nightmares her and Rafe had had. Even Smitty had crammed into the bed with them. All of them crowded around her as if their large bodies could keep the nightmares at bay.

She'd seen it when she went looking for Rafe and hadn't found him in his room. He'd curled up in front of Airiella, her arm protectively around him and the three men around her. Airiella's face, even in sleep, had been ravaged by memories threatening to surface.

Which, in turn, brought it all to the forefront of Chrissie's mind. Each time Travis had lashed out against her in some way, all the disturbing things he'd said and done. Every time he'd chosen drugs over her and the boys.

She looked down as her phone rang. "Hi Ells," she answered.

"Why do you think distance keeps me from knowing how you are feeling?" her silky low voice asked.

"I was hoping it would give you a reprieve, at least."

"Chris, we've always been connected. I can feel the resentment in you building. Are you upset that Ronnie has been spending so much time with me?"

"What? Please tell me you are kidding me with that question, Ells." Chrissie was horrified that thought even came out of her mouth.

"No, I'm serious."

"The resentment you are picking up on is because Travis always chose his next high over me and the boys. It's because his parents are now trying to find a way to take my beautiful boys from me. It's because we both have been dealt shitty hands in the things we've had to deal with; it has nothing to do with Ronnie and you. I promise you that."

"I miss being around you," she said and her tone was heartbreaking, and Chrissie understood every nuance that was in there. While she needed the space, Airiella leaving left her feeling lost.

"Me too, Ells. Maybe these stubborn men had it right, and we can help each other get through this," Chrissie capitulated.

"Don't tell them that. Those men will never let us live it down if we tell them they are right."

Chrissie laughed. "I think they already know. Jax and Ronnie know every thought that goes through that chaotic brain of yours."

"Sadly, that is true. I haven't been able to block Jax or Ronnie out like normal." She went quiet. Chrissie knew she was picking through her thoughts, trying to choose the right words to say. "I hate this feeling of knowing he touched me and not knowing what happened."

"Maybe not knowing is the best thing. I know everything Travis did to me, and I can't forget." Chrissie wished she could. "Since it's happened, every single thing he did is on replay in my head. Knowing he did some of that to you, drives me to the point of madness."

"Same here. I remember the pain, screaming, and my imagination fills in the rest. Then I hear your voice in my head telling me you know exactly how I feel because you've been there, and I get so angry that lightning builds in my body. They keep waking me up before I light the room on fire."

"I shouldn't have told that story," Chrissie said quietly.

"It was just what I needed to hear to get me through that hellscape. You should have told me when it happened. I would have come out there to help you."

"That's why I couldn't tell you, Ells. I didn't want you to get hurt, trying to help me. He wasn't stable, and I had my hands full trying to keep the rest of us safe. I knew I could call you. I was scared to call; I was ashamed."

Chrissie heard Airiella choke on a cry. "Worst feeling ever. Feeling shamed over something we had no control over. Something that ultimately scarred us permanently that we would have to live with for the rest of our lives. Always making us wonder what we could have done differently to have kept that from happening. Feeling stained, dirty, and believing the ugly things that were said."

"Nothing, Ells. The answer to that is nothing. We couldn't have done anything differently. It wasn't us. You taught me that." Chrissie wobbled in place, fighting to keep the memories at bay.

"I know, Chris. God, I know. My fucking brain won't stop. You can't even lie to me and tell me that you aren't dealing with the same thing. I can feel it. We both know it wasn't our fault, but it doesn't stop that stupid voice inside."

"I hate that voice." Chrissie threw a rock at the waves.

"I haven't let Jax touch me since it happened. Sexually that is. I'm so afraid that he will be disgusted by me."

"You know goddamn well that isn't true," Chrissie blew up.

"I know. The fear is overwhelming me. If Jax were to turn away from me, I don't think I could stand it. It would destroy me."

"Ells, not one of them would turn away from you. Ever. The love that man has for you is what fairytales are created from; have you talked to him?" Chrissie forced the question she already knew the answer to, trying to push.

"I can't."

Her simple words broke Chrissie's heart. Travis's actions had destroyed Airiella's confidence in the worst way possible. She had never backed down from fear, and Chrissie hated that she was going to have to give her a dose of tough love, but she didn't know what else was going to snap Airiella back. "Not talking to him is letting Travis win. I've never known you to back down from fear. Nor have I ever known you to doubt what you have with Jax. If you don't talk to him, I will. You are discrediting him by believing he would turn away from you."

"I know all the arguments. Reality is far different

from the ruling emotions, though."

"That's the truth," Chrissie agreed softly. "Doesn't change that you need to talk to Jax."

"He stripped me, Chris," she said and she could hear Airiella crying. "How could a strung-out drug addict that has never met me know that to render me useless all he had to do was take away my clothes? I failed to keep your child safe because my fear kept me oblivious to the shit that was going on!"

"Ells, you did keep Rafe safe." Panic flooded Chrissie's veins at the tone she picked up in Airiella's voice. She was teetering on edge, and Chrissie didn't know what edge it was.

"No, that was Stolas who did that. And Taklishim. I didn't do anything other than bringing a building down around us. Recklessly and irresponsibly. I could have killed us both." Airiella was sobbing and bordering on hysterical, and Chrissie wondered where Jax and the others were. "One whore is as good as another. He said that. I remember that."

Chrissie's eyes were stinging with tears; she refused to let them fall. "You are, or never have been a whore. Neither have I." Chrissie pushed the mute button on her phone and put it on speakerphone while she texted Ronnie to find Airiella. She took it off speakerphone and put the microphone back on.

Her phone chimed with a return text that told her they couldn't find her. She'd shut them out, and they'd been looking for her. That wasn't good. "Ells, where are you right now?"

"Hiding," she answered. "I couldn't let them see this."

"They are trying to find you and are worried, either you let them back in and tell them where you are, or they will end up doing something drastic. You can't deal with this alone," Chrissie ordered her.

"I can. I always have. So did you."

"No, neither of us did. That's why you had to drink that magic stuff Degataga sent you, to force you to deal with it. You did it then because you had them there to back you up. It's no different than now other than the timeline. I didn't deal with it either. I did the same thing you did, shove it down and figure out how to keep functioning. We both are a mess right now. They are right; we will help each other. Stop shutting them out." Chrissie's tone was a little harsher than usual, but worry tightened her gut because she knew from personal experience that where Airiella was mentally was a dangerous place to be. Especially if she was hiding.

"I'm so scared," Airiella whispered.

"I know, honey. I am too. You've got me, though. Do you want me to come out wherever you are?"

"Yes," she answered and the anguish in her voice was so heavy that Chrissie wondered briefly if her best friend had dipped into suicidal territory. Chrissie had at one point, and the tone in Airiella's voice was leading her that way.

"I'm coming. You let Ronnie find you. Promise me that, Ells." Chrissie stood up and ran to grab Bryce.

The phone was silent. Airiella had hung up. "Shit!" She swept Bryce up and ran back to the house, Mags coming out the door of her home.

"Leave him with me. Aedan is texting your flight information right now. I'll take care of the boys."

"How did you know?" Chrissie momentarily halted.

"I knew she went missing. Aedan texted me to see if I had heard from her. Then he told me that you had texted Ronnie. Right as I was coming out, he said Jax had a lock on her because she opened the connection back up. I put the rest together. Go on. I've got them. Jillian is on her way back, and we can handle this."

Chrissie hugged her tight, kissed Bryce on the head, and took off to get packed up, her phone chiming with flight information from Aedan as promised. Ronnie would get her from the airport. She broke down on the front porch waiting for the Lyft car to come to get her.

"Hey, chin up," Stolas said from next to her, making her jump. "She needs you. Bad enough that she called me to keep her from hurting herself. She's with Jax right now, and I knocked her out." He handed her a container. "If you need to forget for a little while, use this."

Chrissie wiped her face on the sleeve of her jacket. "What is it?"

"Just an herbal mix that will allow you to block out that which you don't want to think about; I've had to use it myself more than once. It's temporary. A few hours reprieve."

"Is she okay?" Chrissie was afraid of the answer.

"I don't know. I don't have the insight into Airiella's head that they do. She wasn't doing too well when she called me. I'd have to say that the fact that she did reach out tells me that not all hope is lost, and she is trying to fight it. She needs them, but she needs you more right now. You represent safety to her more than they do."

"Not possible," Chrissie argued against that. "I've seen how she is with them."

"It's true. For this, Airiella needs you." Stolas stood up and dropped a kiss on her head. "Take care of each other. You need her just as much as she needs you. I'll keep an eye on your boys as well."

Chrissie stuffed the container into her carryon. "Thank you, Stolas."

Jillian pulled up with the Lyft driver right behind her. Jillian flew out of the car and practically tackled Chrissie. "We've got this, go help. They are terrified right now."

Chrissie hugged her back, noticing Stolas had disappeared. "I'll call when I land. Jace's bus drops him off at 3:45, Rafe will be with him."

Chrissie moved robotically, and when the plane was finally in the air, she finally relaxed back into the seat, leaning against the window and closing her eyes. Stolas had a point, she had told Chrissie she needed her, and she called Stolas. She was trying to fight it, in her way.

She woke when the plane was landing, and she got off as quickly as possible. Getting outside, she searched for Ronnie, her heart leaping in her chest as her eyes found his green ones. She flung her arms around his neck as he lifted her right off the ground.

"She's still out," he told her, putting her gently back down and taking her bag. "She was on the phone with you, wasn't she? Is that why you texted me?"

"Yeah. I was starting to get scared, Ells tone was off, and the words weren't her. Stolas said she called him," Chrissie told him.

"She did. Stolas waited until Jax showed up and then gave her something to knock her out. Fuck, Chris. It was bad."

"What do you mean?" She let him help her into the SUV and waited until he was in the driver's seat.

"Airiella was in the pool maintenance room, in the corner, surrounded by chemicals that she had opened up. I'm not sure what she was planning on doing with them, but it didn't look good. Not only that, but she also had a box knife in front of her."

Chrissie shivered. "She won't kill herself. Trust me when I say that. Hurting herself is another matter. She's so deeply in grief right now that she isn't thinking clearly. I know that the smell of chlorine is calming to her; she loves being in the pool, and she associates it with happy and safe memories. To me, that explains why she was in the pool maintenance room instead of the pool. There are people in the pool, and she wanted to hide, hence the maintenance room. If the chemicals are open, maybe she was just trying to bring out the smell of chlorine a little more. It invokes happy memories for her."

Ronnie slumped over the steering wheel. "I don't know how to help her. Jax came unhinged when she opened the connection back up, and he felt her. Smitty and I literally fell to our knees."

"Can you stay in Jax's room? I'll take yours, with her, or vice versa, wherever she currently is."

"Are you sure? She might not want to be away from Jax."

"I'm sure. I can guarantee you Ells doesn't feel safe. I don't feel safe. Even more so after it happened, and while she knows that she isn't in danger with you guys, there's a part of her brain that is only sensing a male. Since she doesn't remember what is happening, my best guess is she is stuck in this bad mental place because she can't get herself to feel safe."

"I don't think many people realize just how much something like this affects." Ronnie looked at her. "I hate that you know this. She told me before that she always felt safe with me, never threatened."

"I don't think she feels threatened by you. For me, it was the vulnerability. Sleep makes you vulnerable. Travis drugged her, so she wasn't aware, kind of like sleep. There's a lot of parallels that you can draw here. I truly don't believe that she feels you or any of the others are a danger to her, it's that vulnerability of being asleep, or in the dark, and that irrational fear part of her brain sensing a male that she can't see. Right after it happened the first time for me, I didn't sleep more than two hours a night for over three months."

"She knows it's us, though." Ronnie was trying hard to piece it together.

"Fear isn't rational. Those drugs messed with her body and mind. Tama told us there was damage, and it would play out in nightmares. If she's having a hard time separating reality from memory, then it doesn't matter. The irrational fear will win out with a muddled brain. Shit, it even wins out with a rational one if it's a strong enough fear, and trust me, this is a big one."

"This is so fucked up. Okay, you explained away the location and chemicals. What about the box knife?"

"I don't know. I don't believe Ells would kill herself. She may have thought about it, but I don't think she would follow through with it. If I had to make a guess, I would say a self-defense measure and chalk it up to the irrational fear thing. She is a weapon herself, but with feeling violated as she has been, she probably isn't realizing that. She wasn't able to use her abilities with the drugs in her system."

"I wish this didn't make sense. I feel sick. Why do you think Airiella's thought about killing herself?"

"Do you honestly want the answer to that?" She looked at Ronnie and waited for his answer. When he hesitatingly nodded, she took a deep breath. "First, because she's told me. Thoughts are only that, thoughts. It happens to the best of us. Death is an escape, and when things are as bad as they are, it's an easy answer when you are desperate. I've too been in that spot." Chrissie looked out the window as he drove them back to the hotel.

"Sorry, Chris. I didn't even think to ask how this is all affecting you. How are you doing with all this?"

"Feels weird to be the one Ells is leaning on; it's usually the other way around. On the flip side, all those feelings I've pushed away just to do what I need to do to survive are coming back with a vengeance. I think right now, I'm just trying to cope." In a twisted way, helping Airiella was helping her.

"Did you feel suicidal?"

"Yes. More than I'd like to admit." Chrissie felt that the only way to answer that was honesty. It was cliché but true that you didn't truly understand unless you'd been through it.

"Do you still feel that way?" He glanced over at her.

"No. My future looks a lot more promising right now than it did before."

He pulled into the parking lot and parked. Ronnie was out of the SUV before Chrissie had her seatbelt off and to her door, opening it and pulling her into his arms. "I love you. I love both of you, and this is fucking killing me to see you both with these looks on your face. I want to smash things, and I don't like that I don't understand all the things underneath what I am seeing. Despite that, I am so happy you are here."

Chrissie's breath caught as he kissed her, intensely, pouring his emotions into the kiss that swept her into a tidal wave of longing, and she found herself trying to get closer to him. She reluctantly pulled away. "I don't think a parking lot is the best place for our first time, even though I don't give a damn right now."

His breathing was ragged, and his eyes were hooded. "Right. Give me a minute to calm my body down. That means you have to stop touching me, Chris."

She smiled and moved her hands. "Sorry."

He groaned. "Me too."

"Did she talk to Jax at all?" Chrissie tried to change the subject to get the heat to cool between them.

"I don't think so. Why?"

"She's afraid he will leave her over this." Chrissie cupped his cheek.

"That's ridiculous," Ronnie exploded.

Chrissie stroked her thumb over his stubble. "Irrational fear, remember? She feels marked again. I know she's told you that she's felt that way before. It was something I forced her to admit when I first met you."

"Fucking hell! That didn't even occur to me! That's why she has a hard time looking at anyone, isn't it?"

Chrissie nodded slowly, watching his face. "Be gentle with her. Or maybe, don't. I don't know. I guess I won't know until I see her, and she opens up. I incline to go both ways. Gentle in some regards, and hard in the other. I'm not afraid of telling her what she doesn't want to hear, and it may come to that. Do you have and Jax have adjoining rooms?"

"Almost always. Habit."

"Then, if it goes sideways, at least you both will be close. What about Smitty?" Chrissie asked to get an idea of the layout if she needed backup.

"He's across the hall. Aedan is next to him. Every instinct I have is telling me just to pick her up, hold her close, and run away from everything. I know that's exactly what she doesn't want, too."

Chrissie hopped out of the SUV, and Ronnie grabbed her bag. "Has she eaten?"

"Barely. Not enough to make any of us happy, but just enough to shut us up."

Chrissie laughed at that. "Okay. Have some macaroni and cheese sent up, a grilled cheese sandwich and a Diet Coke."

Ronnie matched his stride to hers. "That's an odd choice."

"Her favorite comfort foods. Whatever she doesn't eat, I will."

Jax met them at the elevator doors and wrapped Chrissie in a giant hug. "She asked you to come?"

"She did. Don't stress, Jax. It's not that she doesn't want you, she's scared. She's afraid this will make you want to leave her. She feels stained again."

His eyes clouded with tears. "I wondered if that was it. Am I doing something wrong to make Ells think that?"

"Not at all. It's just fear. You haven't made a move to touch her except comfort, and Ells is reading too much into that. Mind you; this is all assumptions off of what I know of her, what little she has said, and her tone."

"You're bunking with me tonight, bro." Ronnie put

his arm around Jax.

"That's fine. Thank you, Chrissie. Any idea why she called Stolas?"

"No. Best guess is she was afraid of your reaction and of hurting herself. A fine distinction to note there, Jax, hurting herself, not suicide. In my experience with her, it's not intentional; she's just too far lost to be aware that what she is doing might be harmful. She called him probably to ask him to make her forget long enough for her to get some sleep."

"He did say that," Jax admitted.

"She's trying to fight it, Jax. If she weren't, she wouldn't have opened the connection back up, wouldn't have called me, or Stolas, and wouldn't try to sleep. She knows she's in a dangerous place. She's trying to claw her way out of it. I told her to talk to you."

"She only said she loved me, and she was sorry."

"It's a start." Chrissie saw the raw grief etched into every line on his face and the shadows under his eyes. "Give me the key," she said and she held out her hand to Jax. She looked at Ronnie. "Go order the food."

"She was still sleeping a few minutes ago." Jax handed the key over while Ronnie went into his room to order food.

"I'll let her sleep until the food gets here. Sadly, I have experience in this myself, and she and I are similar in temperament on some things. Stay close by; if she opens the connection and feels you far away, she'll probably flip out. Is Smitty in his room?" Chrissie rattled off instructions.

"Smitty is behind you," came Smitty's friendly tone. "Hi, Chrissie. Thanks for coming."

"Voice of reason, right?" She turned to look at him, smiling.

"So she's said."

"I might need you," she said and she looked guiltily at Jax. "Not saying I don't need you, but there's a shit ton more emotion involved with you and Ronnie, Smitty appeals to the side that pulls her back from slipping into the crazy."

"Don't apologize, I understand."

Chrissie stood on her toes and kissed them each on the cheek. "Okay, big girl panties on and into the lion's den I go. Hopefully, we both will come out on the other side."

"Before you go in there," Smitty stopped her, "tell me where you are on this?"

"What do you mean?" Chrissie asked, confused.

"Mentally, are you okay?" Smitty searched her face, his eyes probing her own.

"Not really, but I'm okay enough to have sense. Pretty sure I'll have to dive into the shit in my head to bring her out," Chrissie admitted reluctantly.

Jax swore. "I'm such an asshole. I'm sorry, Chrissie. I didn't even think about what this is doing to you."

"Not an asshole Jax. You are worried about the love of your life. I get it. Remember, none of you should be alarmed at any big emotions that come from the room," Chrissie thought to add.

"How will we know if you need us?" Ronnie reappeared.

"Well, you'll either hear one of us screaming at the other, she'll tell you through the connection, or I'll throw something at the wall to get your attention. How's that?"

"Let's not go with the screaming," Smitty suggested.

Chrissie smiled. "I'll probably just text you."

"Don't go deep enough that you are both lost," Jax pleaded.

Chrissie smiled a sad smile and turned from them before they could see her eyes swim. She took a deep breath and opened the door and slid in. Jax had left the bathroom light on, so it wasn't dark in the room. Chrissie surmised that she was freaking out about the dark and poked her head back out.

"Jax? Is Ells reacting to the dark?" Chrissie asked.

"She has a couple of times. Since we aren't at home, I didn't want to take the chance that she woke up and got scared."

"Good call."

Chrissie closed the door and looked at Airiella. She didn't look well. Her face was pale, and there were deep shadows under her eyes that almost looked like bruises. She'd lost at least ten pounds in the past week, and her hair was stringy in a way Chrissie hadn't ever seen before. Lack of nutrition was most likely the culprit there.

She put her bag down and sat in the chair, listening to her breathe. Even in the sleep that Stolas had put her in, it didn't sound natural and regular. There were periodic spurts of rapid breathing and the harsh struggle for air type of breathing.

Chrissie dove into her mind and searched back through the years of schooling in psychology and her years of counseling to get through her issues, which she never really did. She went to counseling because her job demanded it after she broke down at work a couple of times.

Half an hour later, there was a soft knock on the

door, and Chrissie got up to let room service in and signed for it, locking the door behind him and turning on the lights. Chrissie sat next to Airiella, pushing off the hair that had tumbled across her face when she tossed and turned.

"Ells, wake up." Chrissie kept one hand on her arm and stroked her face gently. "Ells, it's me, Chrissie. I'm here, hon. Wake up."

The way Airiella bolted awake let Chrissie know the sleep hadn't been as deep as Stolas had intended. "Chrissie?"

"It's me. I've got food here, and you are going to eat and not argue with me. Right? Because if you want your wedding dress to fit, you need to eat."

"What if there is no wedding?" Airiella's eyes were wide with fear.

"Why wouldn't there be?" Chrissie asked pointedly.

"Jax could have anyone, why would he want this?"

"I have no idea; you are pretty scary looking right now. But yet, Jax is in the next room, worried sick about you and head over heels in love with your sad self. Eat."

Chrissie pulled the covers off the food and poured Airiella a glass of water and pushed the tray closer to the bed. Airiella pushed it back and stood up. "I don't want crumbs in bed."

"Then come sit over here and eat. I'm not budging on this. You look like hell." Chrissie crossed her arms and glared at her best friend.

"Thanks. Love you too."

"I know you do. Want to explain how Jax found you?" Chrissie wanted Airiella to tell her firsthand the reasons she was the way she was when Jax found her.

"Are they mad at me?" Airiella asked fearfully.

"God, no. Terrified because you aren't in your right mind, but not mad." Chrissie pushed the tray closer to her and waited until she picked up half of the grilled cheese. She stayed silent until the sandwich was gone. "Explain."

"There were people in the pool. I had intended to put my feet in the water to try and center myself, but I couldn't. There was a couple in there, and they were all over each other, and my brain freaked out. I just went through the first door I found, and the corner felt safest to me."

"Because no one could come up behind you there," Chrissie supplied.

Airiella nodded. "I always felt safe in a pool, but I wasn't feeling safe. Not with the people there. I guess I wanted to see if I could make the room smell like the pool instead of a dusty maintenance room. I told myself if I closed my eyes, I could pretend I was in the water. It didn't work."

"Was the box knife because you felt like you needed a weapon?" Chrissie pushed. She needed to know if that wasn't the answer.

"At first, yes. Then before I called Stolas, while I was talking to you, I started to think about stabbing myself with it to just focus on something other than the shit in my head."

"So you called Stolas to stop you from doing that? Jax would have stopped you." Chrissie was trying to find the trail through her thought process.

"No, I called him because I needed to forget for just a little bit. I was at that desperate point where I would have done anything to not think about it."

Chrissie bit her lip. "I hate that feeling."

Airiella drank the water down. "This is way too much food."

"I wanted you to have a choice." Chrissie peeled the orange that Ronnie had added and split it with Airiella.

"Did you do it? Hurt yourself?"

"I did." Chrissie stood and pulled her pants down, exposing her thigh. "I put a hot hair straightener against my leg. It didn't work. Then I was just in pain with dark thoughts in my head and a screaming child because my yell scared him. Now I have this ugly scar as a reminder."

"I'm full of ugly scars. Shit, I am an ugly scar."

"Ells, stop. No, you aren't, and there is a room full of men on the other side of this wall, which are only too happy to remind you that it isn't true. You are not what has happened to you. How many times have you told someone else that?" Chrissie switched back to tough love.

Airiella didn't respond, and Chrissie could see that she was arguing with herself. "Do you think I'm ugly because I burned myself with a hair straightener?"

"You are one of the most beautiful women I've ever met, Chrissie. Inside and out."

"Look in the mirror, angel. Well, maybe not right now," Chrissie joked.

She got a small, crooked smile out of Airiella. "I keep telling myself that if I just knew the details, I could get over this easier. I don't think that's true, though."

"I know for myself; sometimes, I didn't want to remember the details. I wished I had been unconscious and didn't remember. Other times, I was unconscious and couldn't remember and needed to. It was different each time. You remember everything about the other times, and that didn't help you."

"How many times did he do this to you, Chris?"

"Too many to count. Even after I divorced Travis. It was when he was clean and promising to stay that way and would come to spend the best afternoons with the boys that my heart would slip, and I'd give in and let him stay. Only to wake up in the morning and find him high as a kite after the boys went to school and daycare, and he'd get violent and force it." Chrissie blinked back the tears.

"Why didn't you tell me?"

"There wasn't anything you could do, and we were half a country away from each other. I was too ashamed to tell you what a failure I was and how stupid I'd been to believe Travis again." Chrissie gave the brutal truth, one that she knew Airiella was feeling as well.

"I had bruises and bite marks on my breasts. Did he do that to you too?"

Chrissie only pulled off her shirt and unsnapped her bra to show the side of her left breast, scars in the shape of teeth marks. "He used to get excited when he broke the skin."

Airiella's horrified look made Chrissie wonder if she went too far. "I remember the biting. That was when I screamed the first time." She sucked in air as if she hadn't been breathing. "They healed all my marks. I won't have the scars like that."

"Ells, the memory is scar enough. Do you know how many times I have wished that I never came here? If I hadn't, he wouldn't have ever come into contact with you. You wouldn't have ever had to feel that." Chrissie whispered the admission harshly, her guilt slamming into her with enough force to make her shake.

"It's not your fault Chrissie. If you hadn't come

here, I wouldn't have gotten to know your kids."

"Where do we go from here, Ells? Pretty sure we are both screwed up." Chrissie pulled her clothes back on.

"I can't sleep. When I do fall asleep, I immediately go into a nightmare, or a memory, I'm not sure anymore. If it's not about that, it's about before because those wounds are triggered, even though I thought I dealt with them. When I eat, I feel sick, because I start thinking about things and then can't eat anymore. I can't focus because I'm so worried about someone coming up behind me that my wings came out on location yesterday. When I'm around the guys, I'm so worried they are only going to see what happened to me and not that I'm here under this shit trying to find my way back out of it and to them."

"Ells, they know that, and that's not what they see when they look at you," Chrissie reminded her.

"Logically, I know you are right, but I can't get those sides of me to meet. I convinced myself earlier that Jax was going to call off the wedding. That I would drive Ronnie away, and we'd both lose him. That Aedan and Mags would be so disgusted with me, they'd never let me see the babies. That Smitty would give up on me."

Airiella broke down in tears. By the sounds of something sliding against the door, Chrissie figured that Airiella's walls had come down, and the men were sitting outside the door. Chrissie stood and knelt in front of Airiella and put her head on Airiella's knees.

"I love you. You are so crazy, and yet everything you said makes sense to me because I understand it. I want you to listen to me though, can you do that? I mean, really listen."

Airiella bent her head down until it rested on the

back of Chrissie's. "I'm listening. Me, not the fear."

"I am willing to bet that right at this minute, every single one of those guys is sitting outside that door because all they can do to help is to make sure you are protected and to feel somewhat closer to you," Chrissie told her, hoping she truly was listening.

"Why would they do that?"

"Because I'm guessing your walls came down when you started to cry, and it hurt them that they can't help make this go away for you." Chrissie stood up and walked to the door and opened it. Four sets of startled eyes looked back at her. "See? What does that tell you? Smitty, come in here, please."

Smitty rolled to his feet and slowly came into the room. Chrissie dropped kisses on the heads of the other three before shutting the door again. He didn't say anything, he let Chrissie take the lead, and he stood against the wall.

Chrissie motioned for him to go to her, and he was across the room in two steps and had her lifted and sitting in his lap in one smooth motion. "Baby girl, talk to me, please?"

"Why were you out there?" she whispered. "Was someone out there?"

"No, baby girl. We are out there because your heart calls to us, and that was as close as we were willing to get without your invitation. Ronnie said it might make you feel safe if we were protecting your door, so that's what we did."

"How did you know?" Airiella looked at Chrissie.

"I didn't really. It was a guess based on how these men feel about you. Do you still think that they couldn't love you because a strung-out addict asshole raped you?"

Smitty winced at her words, but they sunk in for Airiella. "Smitty, does this change anything for you?" Airiella asked him.

"Not a goddamn thing, baby girl. It pisses me off that it happened, I'm proud as hell that you survived it, hurt that it's damaged you, but it doesn't change the way I feel for you. Or about you. Does this mean you feel like you ruined again?" he correctly guessed.

Chrissie was surprised by his question, not that he asked it, but that she had told him she had felt that way before. She wasn't going to answer for Airiella; she needed to do it for herself.

"I do."

"Are you afraid of us?" He stood up and sat back on the bed, laying down so she could curl into him.

"I don't think so. I'm more afraid that I will lose all of you because of this."

"Won't ever happen. Do you think that little of us?" Smitty was going to play hardball on this with her. Chrissie was impressed.

"No. I know it's not logical, I know it's fear, but I can't combat it," Airiella cried.

"It's been a week, baby girl. Give it time. You are way too hard on yourself. It makes the rest of us not know how to approach anything with you. We all want to help you get through this; we just don't know how. Why don't you tell me what you are afraid of; we can address each one specifically."

Chrissie saw the moment that fear took hold of her, and she bolted to the bed and put a hand on her back. "It's okay, Ells. If you don't want to say them out loud, you don't have to. You are safe here."

Smitty gave her a wide-eyed look. "Is that it? You don't feel safe? Is it only with us, or is it all the time?"

"It's all the time," she said quietly. "I couldn't protect Rafe or myself. I never even saw it coming."

Chrissie saw the realization light in Smitty's eyes. "You think you should have felt him before you did, and now you don't trust your judgment." Airiella nodded. "So your brain is jumping to conclusions on its own that you aren't safe because you couldn't tell last time which is keeping you on edge and making you overreact."

Chrissie was impressed at the way he put it together so quickly. She understood more of their connection now and how he engaged her with reasoning, slowly pulling her back from the brink. She relaxed slightly under Chrissie's hand. "You are safe here," Chrissie repeated. "There's a wall of muscle outside that door."

"And one under you soaking up your tears," Smitty pointed out with a smile. "Can I ask you something, baby girl?" She nodded again. "Were you trying to hurt yourself?"

Chrissie held her breath, and when Airiella didn't answer, she stepped in. "It's not as easy as that, Smitty. There're layers here, and I'm not going to answer for her. I'll tell you about me instead, and maybe that will help you understand a bit better."

"I'm listening," he said and his voice was kind, his eyes hurting for the both of them.

"When I was married to Travis, he used to rape me. I didn't call it that because we were married, and I grew up believing that sex is a mandatory part of marriage. I know now that's not true, but in the situation, it's harder to understand. Abuse breaks a person down, the longer you live with it, the harder it is to deny the accusations lobbed against you. They start to become a reality. I will cop to being suicidal at one point. In my eyes, that's different from what Airiella was trying to do. It's also different from other points in my marriage, and even after, when the pain was a distraction."

She stood up and pulled her pants down again to show the scar she had shown Airiella. "There was a day that he had raped me, calling it his due because I hadn't been in the mood while he was high and trying to beat me. He waited until I was asleep to force himself on me. Jace was asleep in the next room. When Travis finished, my brain filled with nothing but dark thoughts. They weren't suicidal, but they were dark. I used my hair straightener to do this to myself, hoping the pain would force those thoughts away and focus on the injury instead. I wanted to burn them away. Those moments are hard because you are so desperate for relief from your thoughts that rational thought disappears. It doesn't work; it never does because the thoughts always come back. Instead, I got to deal with the pain of this, and a screaming child and thoughts that were dark enough to drown me."

Smitty swallowed hard. "Pull your pants back up, Chris. Please, come and lay on this side of me. I just need to hold you both right now."

Chrissie did as he asked because she needed the touch and comfort just as much as Airiella did. Exposing those thoughts and actions weren't easy. "Did that help explain any of it?"

"More than I thought it would. Baby girl, were you trying to get away from the thoughts?"

Chrissie had her head resting on Smitty's chest, his

arm tight around her, and she saw the nod of Airiella's head. She wished she had the connection with her that they did, that she could just talk to her inside her head.

"You don't have to face those thoughts alone. I'm here, use me. I'll help you find a path through them." Smitty's voice had thickened. "Chrissie, that goes for you too. Fuck. We want to help you both so much, and we don't understand where you are at because you shut us out. I know why you are doing it, and you don't need to. There isn't anything ugly about you, the pain you bear, the scars you have, or the wounds that bleed that we can't see. Both of you."

"Thank you, Smitty. I love you," Airiella whispered brokenly.

"I only accept that if you stop shutting us out," he warned her.

"I'm working on it."

"I know you are. These arms are always open to you and will get filled with nothing but the love we share. Will you let Jax come in and take a bath with you?" Smitty tried.

Chrissie intervened. "Send in Aedan first."

Airiella glanced at Chrissie, her eyes filled with fear. "Stop, Ells. Why on earth would you be scared of Aedan?"

Smitty looked alarmed at that thought. "You're scared of Aedan?"

"No. Aedan just sees more than I want him to," Airiella admitted weakly.

"Good." Smitty kissed her, then turned and kissed Chrissie's cheek. "As you wish, my lady." He stood up and opened the door slowly, Ronnie and Jax falling backward slightly before they caught themselves. "Aedan, you're up."

Chapter Fifteen

Ronnie looked back in to see Airiella's ravaged face and Aedan climbing on the bed and wrapping himself around her. He looked back at Smitty. "What did you do to her to put that look on her face?"

Chrissie squatted down near him. "He didn't put that look there, she did it on her own. She's afraid to talk to Aedan. Smitty got her to agree to take a bath with Jax."

Ronnie felt a sharp tug on his heart, and he tried to keep the hurt look from his face. "I guess that's good." He'd always done that for her as a way to bring her back to him.

"It is," she whispered into his ear, "it gives me time to take one with you. Do you have one of those stars with you?"

Ronnie's brain tore between the heat of her words and the fear her asking for one of his throwing stars invoked. "You think you need one?"

"Not for what you think," she said and she held out her hand, and he pulled one out of his pocket and handed it to her.

"How did you know I had them?"

"Because you are out here holding a watch." She kissed his cheek and stood up, closing the door behind her.

"What the hell just happened here?" Ronnie muttered.

"Just go with it," Smitty poked him.

"Did she talk to you?" Ronnie pulled his thoughts back in as Jax looped his arm through Ronnie's.

"Hardly. Airiella didn't talk a whole lot. She listened, cried, and answered some direct questions. I talked; Chrissie talked. By the way, she has just as many scars as Airiella does, be aware of that."

"Are you talking literal or emotional?" Ronnie was confused by that.

"Both. Chrissie showed me a scar she has and told me the story that went behind it as a way to explain Airiella's lack of answering a question I asked."

"What the fuck did you ask?" Jax hissed out.

"If she was trying to hurt herself."

"You called her out on the box knife?" Jax was astounded, his eyes wide.

"Not really, I just asked. Airiella didn't answer that one. Instead, Chrissie told me about one of her experiences and showed me a scar she had and why she put it there. After I understood the implications better, I revised the question to ask if she was trying to make the thoughts go away, which she answered yes to by nodding her head."

Ronnie let out the breath he'd been holding. "So, the knife just wasn't because she felt like she needed a weapon?"

"It might have been the reason she grabbed it, but somewhere along the line, she was going to do something, cut herself or whatever, to try and redirect her thoughts away from where they were," Smitty clarified. "I'm guessing that's when she called Stolas, so she didn't do it."

Jax sagged against Ronnie, and Ronnie leaned into him, drawing comfort from each other. "We are in way over our heads with this," Jax mumbled.

"Sexual assault is a different beast from regular assault," Smitty reminded them. "None of us has gone through that. The closest we can get is Ronnie's situation as a kid."

"So why is Aedan in there and not Ronnie then?" Jax wondered aloud.

"He's logical and can help her find roots in the path I used to pull her back from the edge, roots outside of emotion. As soon as she took down that wall between us, I could feel the void her emotions were pushing her to. Ronnie, Chrissie is on that same path, but she's a little more rooted in the now than Airiella is."

"Did you learn how to get through to her or how we can help her?" Ronnie hoped something came out of Smitty's time in there.

"It's assumptions, but I saw what Chrissie was doing with her, how she spoke, and how my reactions made Airiella feel. I think that we need to reassure her that our feelings for her haven't changed. Before I would have said we all needed to sleep with her, that was before Chrissie or Jillian, though." Smitty ran his hands through his hair.

"I haven't slept with Chrissie yet; I can do that." Ronnie offered.

"I'm not sure it's the best way," Smitty continued. "She doesn't feel safe. If we all came at her being all touchy-feely, it might have the opposite effect we want. I think we need to let her come to us with physical touch. She doesn't need sex from us; she needs comfort and safety. With Jax, it's different. She needs a touch from him to remind her he still desires her. With us, she needs safety. The reminders that she's still the same person to us."

"What do you propose then?" Ronnie was more than willing to try anything to bring his angel back from where she was stuck.

"Hugs, kisses, reminders that she is safe when she gets that look on her face. Maybe more practice time with her abilities until she realizes that they didn't fail her and Rafe. We have to love her through it. Those eyes of hers will always show us how she's feeling, even if she blocks us."

"And Chrissie? How do we get her through it?" Ronnie hadn't forgotten about her needs; he was trying to figure out how to juggle both.

"I'm less sure about that, but it's my own belief that the more she talks about what she went through, the better off she will be. From what I can tell, it's the first time she's airing details like she has been. After the scar thing, I asked her to lay on the other side of me so I could hold them both, and she didn't hesitate. She's probably feeling the same emotions that Airiella is, except the safety thing."

"She has insecurities," Jax added. "It's clear to me anyway. I'd apply the same logic to Chrissie that you are to Airiella. It's on all of us to make them both feel safe and loved. Chrissie's a part of our family, so are her boys. We love them *all* through it. Maybe we start asking the hard questions they don't want to answer and let them answer how they want. If they both understand that we want to know and it doesn't change anything, it might make it easier for them both to let go of what is holding them down."

"Shit, you sound like Aedan." Ronnie was immensely proud of Jax and how far he had come.

"He and Smitty were bound to rub off on me at some point. Logic and reasoning might be able to keep them off the edge, but we are going to have to work on the emotional parts of it as well, so the cycle stops. I've learned from Airiella that the triggers are always there; they don't have to be potent like that, though."

"If she takes a bath with you, that's a big step with her being scared," Ronnie said quietly.

"I know she usually takes them with you, is that bothering you?" Jax astutely asked.

"A little. It does give me alone time with Chrissie. Physical comfort and feeling safe are big things with our angel. It's always been something I've been able to provide. That separation right there is what's bothering me most about this whole thing. Moving into that part of the relationship with Chrissie is great, it's saying goodbye to the other that I'm having difficulty with." Ronnie found it a little easier to admit it now.

"I did at first too," Smitty broke in. "I can honestly say that nothing changed in how we interact. She's crawled into bed with me and snuggled right up into me when I've been naked, and it's never gone farther. I'm aware Jillian doesn't care if it does, but I haven't felt the need. Certainly, she can still turn me on in a heartbeat, and she has purely to torture me, but I don't feel like I'm missing out. It gives my relationship with Jillian a deeper meaning to know I'm only sharing that with her."

"You miss it?" Ronnie looked at Smitty.

"Sometimes. Not as much as I thought I would. It's times like this that I do, because I know I can offer her what she needs. On that same thought, is Jax can offer it too. And he needs to."

Ronnie felt Jax stiffen up and moved to intervene. "He's not telling you what to do, Jax, or that you aren't giving her what she needs, he's simply saying it needs to be you, not us."

"Whatever Aedan is doing is making her cry," Jax said in the way of an explanation for his body language.

"I felt it too," Smitty said. "I think it's a good cry."

"I don't know." Ronnie felt like a dick for not catching on to the change in the emotions rolling in him. "There's a deep ache in there."

"There is," Jax agreed. "There's also a little less chaos now too."

"Chrissie is strategically using us and our strengths with her to knock down her walls systemically, so the truth is clearer to her," Smitty explained.

Jax looked at Ronnie. "Well, you certainly have a thing for strong women."

Ronnie chuckled lightly. "It seems I do. Chrissie doesn't see herself as strong. She sees Airiella as the strong one of them. You've got to admit, Chrissie knows our angel better than any of us, and she's getting through in a way we couldn't."

They sat there in silence for a while until a group of girls came down the hall towards them. Ronnie thought they looked in their early twenties. They purposely asked for rooms at the end of the corridor so that no others had a reason to come down there.

Ronnie heard them whispering about who they were and knowing it was them. Jax must have heard it too; because his body language went from casual and relaxed to rigid and cold. "Chill, Jax. Smile and turn them away. Maybe they only want an autograph," Ronnie said quietly.

"You are the Shadow Seekers, aren't you?" the loudest of the whisperers called out as they got closer.

"We are," Smitty replied with calm ease.

"Want to have dinner with us? There's four of us, four of you, the numbers work out well," the bold one coyly pointed out.

"Sorry, ladies. We are all spoken for." Smitty tried to keep them at a distance, but they kept getting closer.

"I don't see any women here with you, where's Aedan? Besides, what they don't know won't hurt them."

Ronnie flinched as the door opened behind them. He didn't have to turn to know Airiella was close by; he could feel her anger. She didn't step out of the room, however. He looked back and saw her curled up on Aedan's chest.

Chrissie was the one who stepped out in front of Ronnie and Jax. "Aedan is in there with the other member of their crew. Each of these men belong to her and me. If you don't leave, I will call security. None of them want to have anything to do with you."

"You don't speak for them; they look interested to me," one of the others replied. Ronnie could smell alcohol.

"I speak for myself and my girlfriend," he said and he stood, his arm sliding around Chrissie. "I also speak for my best friend who is engaged, and for my other friend, who is also engaged. We aren't interested."

The bold one raked her eyes over Ronnie. "Oh, the things I could do for you." She was practically purring the words.

"I totally get how you feel now when slime balls hit

on you after you've made your disinterest clear," Ronnie said, looking down at Chrissie's angry face. He kissed her to make sure they got the picture. They didn't.

"He ain't got no ring on his finger," she said and she pointed at Jax, whose gaze had gone hard.

Ronnie was pushed from behind and saw Aedan standing there cradling Airiella to him, his face a mess of swollen eyes and cold anger. Ronnie moved to the side so Aedan could step out, and he moved next to Jax, handing Airiella over, who instead set her feet down on the floor and faced the four women.

"His ring will be there in a couple of weeks, how's this one instead?" Airiella held up her hand with the engagement ring Jax had put there. Then she took Aedan's hand and held up the one with his wedding ring displayed. "Or how about this one?"

"You look like a train wreck," one of them snickered.

Ronnie was about to lose his shit. Smitty stepped closer to him and put a hand on his shoulder, and all of them closed in around Airiella. "You should go on your way now," Smitty told them firmly.

"Seriously? You choose these two over us?"

Ronnie felt the blast of uncontrolled anger that rushed out of Airiella. "What would you look like if you got kidnapped with your best friends' child, drugged, raped, beaten, and chained to a wall?" she snarled.

Not good. She was in protective mode, which was good but not controlled by irrational and chaotic emotions, that was bad. He slid his other arm around Airiella. "Angel, breathe for me, slowly," Ronnie whispered in her ear.

Jax had his arm around her, Aedan and Smitty

touching her as well. The connection flowed between them, and her emotions were seeping into them all. The fire in her he loved so much burned fiercely but for the wrong reasons this time. She was going to end up hurting these idiots who didn't have enough sense to back off.

"Go, none of us want you," Ronnie repeated.

"You got raped?" one of the women asked Airiella softly.

"It's none of your business," Chrissie stated stonily.

The woman ignored Chrissie and stepped closer to Airiella, and Ronnie felt the air around them stirring, a defensive precaution he wasn't sure she was aware she was doing. He kissed her temple. "Easy, angel."

"I was raped too. These guys made me go out with them as a way to distract myself. It's not working. I can't stop thinking about it. I don't know how to deal with this," she said and she started to shake, and her voice trembled.

"Drinking isn't the answer." Airiella moved out of their hold and embraced her. "Whatever happened isn't your fault. Focus on that. Find what makes you feel safe and hold on to it until you can think clearly. One day at a time. Don't give up on yourself."

Ronnie saw the confusion in the faces of the two outspoken women. The other one that had remained quiet stepped forward and put her hand on the woman Airiella was hugging. "I'll take you home," she told her. "Thank you," she said to Airiella, who had released her.

The two instigators still stood there gaping at Airiella. "Maybe you were trying to help her, and maybe you are just two selfish people looking for fun. If she is truly your friend and you care about her, work harder at showing it."

A blast of air had them stumbling back down the hallway the way they had come. Aedan turned Airiella around to face him and held her tight, then kissed her gently. "Remember that I love you. So does Mags."

I need you to help me with something.

Anything you need, angel; Ronnie was happy to be useful.

Cut our fingers, please? Mine and Chrissie's. She wants to be able to talk to me this way.

"Chris, where's the star I gave you?" He looked down into her eyes.

"In my pocket, why?"

Ronnie reached into her pocket and found it. "Trust me?"

"Yes."

He pricked her finger and squeezed it gently. *Is this enough?*

Slice it a little bit. Not just a prick.

He gripped the star a little harder. "Sorry, I need to do a little more." He slid it down her finger a little, opening a wound. To her credit, she said nothing. He turned to Airiella and did the same.

"I heard you, Chris. I know you want the same connection. Press our fingers together; let our blood mix."

Thank you, Heracles. Now I need one more thing. I know you want to help me, and I do need you. But what I need more is for you to take care of her. She's hurting inside. She's doing better than I am, but all this is hard for her. She's being forced to face it all the same way I am, just with the memories. Show her. Show her the way you showed me that it's possible to forget. That not every act by a man is vile. Show her who you are and how you love.

What about you?

I need to let Jax show me. I want it to be you, but I want it for her more. She's yours. I need to learn that I can feel safe with others; it doesn't always have to be you.

Can I have a moment with you first?

Of course.

Airiella finally pulled her finger away from Chrissie, and Aedan handed them both a tissue. "It's not the same as what she all has with you, is it?" Chrissie asked them all.

"No, it's a different connection, but you'll be able to talk to her in your head now." Smitty applied pressure to Airiella's finger.

"I need a moment with Ronnie." Airiella turned and walked back into the room. "Chris, go sit in Ronnie's room."

Ronnie kissed her on the head. "I'll be right there."

He followed Airiella in and closed the door behind him. "Angel, I need you to look me in the eye and tell me you are better than you were."

She looked him directly in the eye. "I'm more stable. I'll stop shutting you out. Aedan and Smitty got me back down." She sank on to the bed. "Can you hug me, please?"

Ronnie swept her up into his lap and cradled her the way he had needed to. "God, you have no idea how much I needed to hold you like this."

"Why didn't you?"

"I didn't want to push you." Ronnie buried his face in her neck. "It's been killing me. Every scream you cry out in your sleep, I want to smash the door down and just hold you until you knew you were safe."

"I wanted you to. I just don't want to pull you in this shit anymore than you already are. It's ugly in there,

Heracles. I hate that she's bleeding with me. Every story she tells, scar she shows me, pushes me closer to the edge while at the same time grounding me because I want to help her. I hurt. I'm so damn scared, too."

"Scared of me?" Ronnie needed to hear her say no.

"Never of you. I'm scared all the time now that my senses will fail me again, and what if it means one of you gets hurt this time? I'm scared that you think you are losing me, and I admit, I'm scared not to have you as I have. I want you and Chrissie to be together so badly, but I feel selfish because I don't want to let go. Then this happened, and I'm both pushing you away and trying to pull you back. There is no reason for me to be afraid to rely on Jax, and I'm not really. I mean, I am, but I'm not."

"I'm your security blanket," he replied quietly.

"That sounds awful. You are so much more than that. I could have easily married you and been happy and secure for the rest of my life. I love you that much."

"I love you that much too. I also know that Jax loves you more than that." She slid her hand up inside his shirt, the same comforting touch she'd given all of them so many times before. "Smitty and Jax were both right, that this between us doesn't have to change. We will always have this." He settled his hand over hers.

"She's so beautiful and fragile, Ronnie. She thinks I'm the strong one between us. She doesn't see her strength. I need you to show her. Just like I need to let Jax show me." She turned her face into his chest and cried silently, her shoulders shaking ever so slightly.

"He won't go dark again, angel. Trust him." Her wings came out and wrapped around them both, the first time she'd had them out since Travis, voluntarily. They were in their little world under her wings. Just the two of them, and it was perfect.

"I need her tonight," she whispered against his chest. "I don't think I'll make it through the investigation tomorrow night if I don't do this. She's helping."

"Did Aedan help?" Ronnie brushed his lips over her forehead.

"He did. You all are. It might not seem like it because I've kept you all locked out, but you are. Rafe could have died because of me; I need to come to terms with that."

Ronnie could have gotten knocked over with a feather after that statement. "Angel, you kept him alive. As shitty as this is to say, with the focus being on you, he was safe. He may have seen things no six-year-old should ever have to see, but his needing to protect you kept him grounded and present. He's hurt inside, just like you are, and it's not either of your faults."

"I do hurt, and it's bad. I thought I had healed all that shit, but it's still there." Airiella's voice wavered.

"I know, angel. I feel it too. We all do. No matter how much you try to block everything, we still feel it. What hurts you hurts us. The only way through this is together. Let us help," Ronnie beseeched her.

"Does Jax still want to marry me?"

"More than he wants oxygen," Ronnie replied with confidence.

Chapter Sixteen

Thank you for that moment, Chris. I needed him.

She wasn't sure she was going to get used to that.

Can you hear my thoughts?

Yes. I could before, too.

Does this mean I'll be able to hear yours?

Probably, unless one of us shuts down the connection, Ronnie can show you how to do that.

So I'll know if you are fading out again?

Most likely. You'll probably be able to feel me more now too.

I noticed that right away. What's next?

I'm going to take a bath with Jax. Ronnie is coming to you. I asked him if I could have you tonight, do you mind?

Nope. That was my plan, anyway.

Okay. I'm shutting down the connection now. I need to be with just Jax. Love you.

Chrissie could feel the absence. Ronnie walked in

then, went straight to the bed and pulled his shirt off. "I know this is going to sound weird, but can you pull your shirt off and just lay on me?" His voice was frayed.

She didn't question it, just did as he asked, and at the contact of their skin, he sighed as if it had brought relief to him. "Is this like a substitution for Airiella?"

"No. I'm completely aware that it's you and not her. It is something I learned from being with her. The skin on skin contact with someone you love is better than a drug. Her trauma is palpable; the pain she's feeling inside leaks into me and feeling you like this calms it in me."

Chrissie wasn't about to complain. She was shirtless on Ronnie's chest. His skin smelled faintly of the forest and was warm. His muscles hard under the soft skin, his tattoos beautiful in their precise artistic lines. He was broad and long, her own body feeling small in comparison. Much like Airiella had said, Ronnie invoked a feeling of safety in her. One she hadn't ever felt with anyone else before.

She pushed herself up off him and pulled off her pants and undid his, pulling them off him. "Get on the bed then," she told him and waited until he pulled himself up, then climbed back on him.

He wrapped his giant arms around her. "You are amazing."

"Maybe I'm just taking advantage of your vulnerability."

Ronnie chuckled. "I'd be okay with that too."

She pressed a kiss into the middle of his chest. At least this way, he didn't see all the scars on her body, self-inflicted or otherwise. She wasn't ordinarily self-conscious about that; it was different with Ronnie. She wanted him to think she was beautiful, whether she thought so or not.

"There are three people who are allowed to take advantage of me." Ronnie shifted under her and pushed her farther up his body, so their faces met. "Jax, Airiella, and now you."

He gave her a kiss that devastated her defenses against him, and she melted under his skillful tongue, no longer as in charge as she thought she was. She pulled back slightly, her eyes unfocused. "Is she okay?"

"She's worried about you. Truthfully, we all are worried about you as much as we are about her."

That was a dose of cold water to her libido. "What? Why?"

"Because you are just as hurt as she is."

She sat back, her legs straddling his waist as she looked down at him, her brain racing, trying to find a way out of admitting anything. It was a move that she hadn't even thought about, one that put her scars on display. It wasn't until he reached out and traced one that she realized it.

"Breathe, Chris. Do you think your scars bother me?"

"No?" She meant it as a statement, but it came out as a question.

"No is the correct answer." He put his knees up behind her and tugged on her legs until she was leaning back on his. "I don't like how they came to be there, but they are a part of you." He ran his palms up her thighs to her hips and held them there.

"They aren't all from Travis," she admitted honestly.

"I know."

"Did Smitty tell you?"

"He told me you had scars like Airiella did, not

where they came from or any story that you told him."

"I probably don't have as many as she has."

"That doesn't mean anything. I don't know all of the stories behind hers either. Just the ones that Airiella shared because she needed to let go of it. All I need you to understand is that if you need to let go of them, I'm willing to listen. If you want to tell me, that's fine." He sat up suddenly, dropping his knees and winding his arms around her to keep her falling. "You also need to believe that I don't think they are ugly. I happen to think you are incredibly beautiful."

Her breath caught as he shifted her again, and she felt how hard he was under her. "You don't see me and see a damaged woman, pretty in the face or not?"

"Nope. I see another warrior, beautiful and fierce in the ways she needs to be. I wouldn't care if scars covered you from head to toe. They are nothing more than a testament of survival against something that tried to take you down. That goes for the ones inside that I can't see as well."

Emboldened, Chrissie unsnapped her bra and let it slide from her shoulders, the scars on her breasts visible for the first time other than to Airiella earlier. "No one has ever seen my breasts since this has happened."

There was a flash of something that crossed Ronnie's face, but it was too fast for Chrissie to identify it. Heat flared in her as he brushed soft kisses against the scars she'd fought so hard to keep hidden. "How is it possible no one has seen these?"

"I never took my bra or shirt off with the few people I slept with after divorcing Travis," she said, watching his face.

"Shame for them, great for me. These breasts are perfect." He flicked his tongue over her nipple. "They taste good too."

She groaned and ground herself against him. "Ronnie," she murmured as he licked the other one.

"Yes, baby?"

"Don't stop," she said and she tipped her head back as he dragged his teeth against the underside of her breasts and licked back up to her nipples.

"I'm going to taste every bit of you that I can, stopping only happens if you tell me to," he whispered, his voice strained as she pushed down on to him. Their underwear the only thing separating them, and she had soaked through them both.

She shifted her legs, planted her feet on the bed, stood up, pulled off her underwear, then leaned over and pulled off his. Her eyes widened at the sight of him. "Good lord, you're big," she whispered. "She never told me you might not fit. Are you all that big?"

Ronnie laughed, pulling her back down. "I have no idea. We don't compare. I've only ever seen Jax, and he isn't what I want to be thinking about right now. Are you worried it's going to hurt?"

"I wasn't until I saw you, but the thought crossed my mind." Her initial reaction was to back out, but she didn't want to. She felt real with him.

"I promise you it won't hurt. I'm going to do everything in my power to make sure it doesn't. And if it does, all you have to do is tell me, and I'll stop. I'd rather have blue balls the rest of my life than hurt you."

She felt a wave of fear wash over her that wasn't her own and seeing Ronnie's startled reaction; it had hit him too. "Is that Airiella?"

"It is. Airiella's okay, Chris. Let her work through it. Jax will never hurt her, never force anything on her." Ronnie sat up and kissed her again.

"We should go." Chrissie tried to pull away.

"She doesn't want us to. She wants me here with you."

Chrissie froze. "Is that why you are here with me? Because she told you to be?"

Ronnie swore. "No, that came out wrong. I'm here because I want to be here. I meant she wanted to be with Jax, not me. If she wanted me in there, she would have told me so. Same goes for you."

Chrissie felt unsure and very vulnerable. "I don't want you to be here because you feel like you have to be here. I'm not a charity case."

"Chrissie, where do you think I'd rather be?" Ronnie took her hands and placed them both palm down on his chest.

"I don't know. With Airiella?"

"If I wanted to be there, don't you think I would be?"

"But you just said that she didn't want you there. I know I said I was okay with being a second choice, and because it's her, I am. I guess I didn't expect it to hurt this way, though."

"You aren't my second choice. Chris, look at me." Ronnie lifted her chin. "I'm in love with you, and I want to be here with you."

"I'm sorry." She felt like an idiot. The insecurities she kept hidden had just come bursting to the surface.

"Don't be sorry. That was a very raw and honest

response. It also showed me what I needed to see. I'm going to spend a lot of time proving to you that I am not like anyone else that has ever been in your life."

Desire swamped through her, such a drastic change from the fear that she didn't know if it was her own or it was Airiella's. "How do I know what feeling is mine, and what is hers? God, is this what being an empath is like?"

"Yes. Right now, it will probably be hard to tell, but I can tell you Airiella is fighting fear at the moment, so if you felt something else, it's probably yours. Give it some time, and you'll be able to feel her energy with the emotions. What did you feel?"

Suddenly shy, she pushed back until she was sitting on his knees. "Desire."

"Fuck, thank God." Ronnie grinned.

Chrissie pushed him back. "That tasting thing goes two ways, and I need to do that now." It gave her a feeling of control again, and she needed to grasp it to fight back the crap that was trying to surface in her head.

She wrapped her lips around him and lapped up the moisture that had leaked out. "Chris, you need to be very clear with me on what works for you or not," he groaned.

She lifted her head. "Don't grab my head and jam it down on you, other than that, right now, any guidance on what you like helps."

"Guidance you don't need," he said and he gasped as she sucked him down. He stroked her face softly as she licked and sucked, stroking with her hands on occasion. His hips bucked, legs twitched, and muscles went taut the longer she worked at him. The moment she cupped his balls and stroked her fingers behind them, his back arched off the bed, and he came hard.

She relaxed her throat and swallowed him up, gently stroking until he eased back on to the bed, his chest heaving, his hands still gentle on her face. "I hope that was okay." Chrissie rested her chin on his belly, looking up at his hooded eyes. "I needed to feel a bit of control to keep the monsters in my head at bay."

"Well, it's not the way I envisioned our first time being, but it was fantastic. Will you let me return the favor?" His fingers traced her cheekbones. "I've wanted to taste you for a while now." She nodded. "Is there anything I shouldn't do?"

"I don't think so." He lifted her against his chest and kissed her again, and she wondered if he could taste himself on her tongue and if it bothered him. "Does it bother you to kiss me after I did that?"

"Not at all," he said and he nipped at her lips. "Does it bother you?"

"No. It's kinda hot." He rolled her over, so he was on top of her, her legs winding around his hips. "I can't believe you are hard that fast again."

"That's my reaction around you lately," he said and he kissed down the side of her neck. "I plan on taking my time. I like hearing you moan. Drives me crazy."

He kissed every scar he found, and as he circled back to her breasts, she moaned his name. "Ronan."

"Fuck," he whispered. "I like the sound of you saying my name like that too." By the time he made it down her body, she was a quivering mess of nerves and completely soaked. She couldn't even think well enough to be worried he'd think she stunk. She hadn't let anyone go down on her since Travis. He used to tell her she smelled gross and tasted worse.

A ragged cry tore through her at the first lick, and by the third she came, a thundering and blinding orgasm ripping through her body. She frantically pulled at Ronnie's head, trying to get him to stop.

"Chris, baby, what's wrong?" He was there, looking at her.

"I'm sorry!" she cried, her voice a rough whisper.

"Why? Are you crying?" Ronnie gathered her to him while she shook. She didn't know she'd been crying.

"That was probably awful for you," she said when she finally came down.

"I have no idea why you would think that," he answered her softly.

"Travis told me I smelled and tasted bad," she admitted, ashamed.

Ronnie swore again. "He was an idiot. You fucking taste like heaven."

Chrissie stilled. "I'm not gross?"

"Is that why you were crying?" She nodded, shame washing through her again. "Chris, I could happily spend hours between your legs, smelling you, and tasting you."

"After the way that felt, I'd probably let you," she said and an absurd laugh escaped her. "It's been years since I've let that happen."

Ronnie took her hand and stroked it up the length of him. "Does that feel like someone who was disgusted by you?" He circled her thumb over the tip, smearing the moisture in.

"No," she sighed. She loved the feel of Ronnie in her hand. Hot and heavy, smooth, and so hard. The anxiety that had reared up in Chrissie, dissipated slowly, her attention refocused on him and the heat between them.

"I want to go back down there. That little taste wasn't nearly enough. Is that okay with you?" Ronnie kissed her deeply.

"Yes, okay," she agreed breathlessly.

"Focus on the sensations, Chris," he said and he licked her ear and kissed his way back down her body. Every time she tensed, he slowed down until she relaxed. Sex with the few guys she had gone out with after her divorce had never given her the issues that were popping up now.

But they weren't Ronnie, and she didn't love them. Nor had she just seen her ex-husband kidnap her best friend and child and then found out he raped her in front of her child. Anxiety rose again.

"Chris, baby, stay with me. Focus on me, only me. There is only us here in this room. Just you and me."

She listened to his voice, and the tension eased out her body again. "I'm here; I'm back."

"Stay with me. No one else gets to be a part of this. I don't care how chauvinistic it sounds; you are mine. I love you. If you want me to stop, I will."

"No, don't stop. It's just us. You can claim me." Chrissie breathed out as his fingers stroked down her thighs. "Touch me, Ronan."

The sound that came out of the back of his throat was downright sexy. He licked again, slowly this time, and the sensation of his hot tongue on the most sensitive part of her body had her mewling out her pleasure. "God, baby, please keep making those sounds."

She couldn't stop if she wanted to. Ronnie took his time, bringing her up and down, his tongue masterful. "Please, Ronnie," she begged, needing to come.

"As you wish," he said and she could hear the smile in his voice. He flicked his tongue fast, and she exploded with a cry. Her legs shaking with the force of the orgasm as he lapped it up and kissed his way back up until he was looking down into her eyes. "Still with me?"

She pulled him down into a kiss, finding the taste of herself on his tongue somewhat erotic. "Thank you."

"Oh, believe me, that was my pleasure," he purred, settling himself down on her. She wound her legs around his hips, his shaft rubbing that sensitive nub sending shivers through her body. "You want to keep going?"

"Oh my God, yes. I'm desperate to feel you inside me." Chrissie wiggled under him.

He adjusted his hips and slowly pushed his way inside. She felt herself stretching and couldn't wait anymore. Digging her heels into his butt, she lifted her hips into him quickly. He groaned, long and low. "So fucking tight, Chris. I was trying to be gentle."

"I don't want gentle right now; I want you moving in me," she said and she gasped as he moved.

"Slow down, baby, or this is going to be over way too soon." Chrissie watched how his arm muscles flexed as he pumped in and out of her, his body a beautiful machine. "The way you are looking at me makes me even harder."

He bent and nibbled and sucked on her nipples, a jolt of electricity zinging through her body. She felt another orgasm building inside, and she bit her lip. "Ronnie," she gasped as he slid his hand between them, his finger pressing then rubbing against her in a motion that intensified each thrust.

"Come for me. I want to see you lose control," Ronnie murmured, picking up the pace. Like her body listened to his command, she shattered again, crying out and tightening around him. He stopped moving, and she rode out the waves of pleasure that took over.

As she was coming back down, he rolled them, putting her on top. Her eyes widened as he went deeper and let out a groan. "You're going to be the death of me," he said and he thrust upwards as he held her hips while she adjusted. "You're in control now, Chris."

Smiling, she rotated her hips a few times, toying with him. "Does that mean I get to claim you too?"

"Oh, sweetheart, I was yours the minute I walked in that door." His words gave her a sense of security she hadn't felt in years. She started to ride him, flattening her palms on his chest. He met each of her thrusts and she felt him trembling under her. "I'm so close, baby."

"Your turn to come for me," she panted.

"Only if you come with me again," he returned, his fingers back to working that sensitive nub bringing her to a raging crescendo in no time. She tightened around him and straightened her back, taking him even deeper.

"Ronnie!" she cried out, falling headfirst into the most powerful orgasm yet, and he was right there with her, pumping inside her, twitching and pulsing in time with her body. "I think I just died."

"You and me both. That was incredible." Ronnie's ragged response was breathless. A subtle sheen of sweat covered them both.

"That was worth the wait. Thank you for not giving up on me." She cupped his cheeks and kissed him.

"It's you who didn't give up on me. Don't forget that. This, what we shared, is only between us. What Airiella and I have is different, and while I may kiss her, it will only ever be us in sex. You are not, nor ever will be a second choice; this is my promise to you. Me walking in that door was a choice I made to take this further with you, and I don't regret one bit of it."

"I understand. I don't think I need to say it, but it will only ever be you for me."

Ronnie suddenly let out a laugh, and at her surprised look, he explained, "Jax has to sleep in the wet spot."

Embarrassed, Chrissie jumped out of bed. "Oh, my God! We have to call for fresh sheets!"

"Calm down. You'll probably have to sleep in the wet spot there."

She threw a pillow at him. "How is that helping?"

He stood up and picked her up, carrying her to the bathroom. "It's not, but it was funny." He turned on the shower and waited for it to heat up. "Fuck! Chrissie, I'm so sorry! We didn't use any protection! I'm so used to Airiella and not needing to worry about it; I didn't even think."

Embarrassed again, she blushed. "It's not like I thought about it either. I'm not worried."

"What if you get pregnant?" Ronnie stammered.

"Then I guess I have your baby," Chrissie answered calmly, stepping in the shower before he could put her there.

The stupefied look on his face gave her pause. She wasn't sure if that meant he didn't want kids or was horrified about having one with her. She turned her back to him, so he didn't see the tears that filled her eyes again.

"Oh, no. You don't get to drop that bombshell on me, then turn around and cry. Look at me." He waited until she turned around. "I have no idea what look was on my face, but I can assure you that it didn't mean whatever you think it meant."

"Then explain it to me," she demanded quietly, letting the water from the showerhead rain down on her face.

"I've never had someone be that calm about the idea of a pregnancy before."

"You've had scares with other females?" She wasn't sure she wanted to hear that answer.

"No. I've never had unprotected sex before Airiella. I never even dreamed of having children. And when I thought about a long-term relationship with her, it wasn't even a possibility. Whatever look was on my face was me entertaining the idea of a baby that was ours. I liked it."

Now it was Chrissie's turn to be shocked. "You want a baby with me?"

"I'm not opposed to it. Why does that surprise you?"

"Because we just had sex for the first time, and we haven't been in a relationship overnight yet."

"That's where you are wrong. We've been in one since we met. It's just been a slow build. I was serious about being yours." He spun her and started washing her back. "For a while, I thought it would only ever be Airiella. I was in love with her from the moment she opened her hotel room door and saw Smitty and me for the first time. Then I met you, and we had that little vision moment she forced on us. It sat in the back of my mind for a long time. I dismissed it because you were in Kansas. Then you moved here, and we'd all been through some pretty serious shit. Each day I saw you, that idea came closer and closer to the front of my mind. I fell in love with your kids more and more each day. The more time I spent with you, the more I wanted to."

"But you said you didn't realize you loved me until Rafe got kidnapped." Chrissie was confused.

"That doesn't mean I didn't love you before that. It just means I didn't realize it. I'm a forever kind of guy, Chris. Being with Airiella taught me that." He spun her again to rinse her off and started washing the front of her. "There isn't another person on earth that could have taken my focus off her, except you. What does that tell you?"

"I don't know," she admitted. "She's a whole different ballgame than everyone else plays."

"She is. Aside from the guys, she's the only one I ever told I loved, until you. She's also marrying my best friend, and I just had amazing sex with hers."

Chrissie tipped her head back into the spray and laughed. "Yep. That cements it; this is the craziest situation ever. I'm in, though." She looked back at him. "Ronan, I'm yours. Heart and soul. I'm in."

A bolt of terror shot through them both, Ronnie staggered, and Chrissie caught his slippery body before he fell. "Shit, a nightmare."

They quickly showered and cleaned up and got out, drying quickly. "My clothes are in Airiella's room," Chrissie realized.

"She loves wearing my shirts, so why shouldn't you?" Ronnie handed her a clean shirt.

Ells?

Chrissie.

I'm coming. Hold on.

Let me work through it. Jax is here. Let me try. Please.

RONAN

Chrissie sunk on to the bed. "She wants to try and work through it."

"Then let's allow Jax to help. Trust that she will tell you when she needs you."

Chapter Seventeen

Half of Ronnie felt like he betrayed Airiella, the other half of him felt like he was betraying Chrissie thinking that way. He felt like his heart and soul divided, and it wasn't a good feeling. Ronnie loved both of them so much and had been totally honest with Chrissie that she was it for him. He was just struggling with the idea of letting Airiella go still.

It was probably what Airiella was going through and how much a part of her healing process Ronnie had been involved in when she let him in about the other time. It wasn't clear to him why this was such a problem for him. He took the step and walked away from a physical relationship with Airiella.

There was a soft knock on the door, and Ronnie got up to open it. A red-eyed Jax walked in and dropped into one of the chairs, his hands covering his face. "Pretty sure Chrissie is going to avoid me forever now."

Not what Ronnie was expecting to hear. "What do

you mean?"

"Well, when she came in, I broke down crying and tried to explain that I was sorry for what happened to her and Airiella and that we were all here to help everyone through it; that I hated that she knew so much about it. I'm not sure it came out that way." He folded forward on himself and started shaking. "I'm so fucking tired, Ronnie; this is killing me. I don't want to leave her side, and I can't sleep. I'm terrified she is going to disappear again. If I fall asleep, I'm awakened by the terror she's feeling in the nightmares, or by her screams that she doesn't even know she's doing. She wakes up crying, not knowing where she is or who I am."

Ronnie's heart broke all over again. "I said something similar to Chrissie when I went to pick her up. I had no idea all of the fallout that goes along with this. Surviving this, coming out on the other side, not afraid of everything, shows just how strong someone is. So many people would never know." Ronnie sat down in front of Jax. "Did you get her through the nightmare?"

"She flew off the bed so fast that she tripped over her feet and fell. Her eyes had that angel glow and were completely unfocused and wild. Unfortunately, after the bath, she didn't want to put clothes on, so she was naked; so many triggers hit. Anyway, she didn't know who I was and was terrified of me. That was probably the biggest knife to my heart. Fuck. I'm a selfish asshole; it's not even about me." He slid to the floor, facing Ronnie. "I couldn't tell you if it was seconds or minutes, but she finally realized who I was but still wouldn't let me get close to her."

"We can get through this, Jax." Ronnie had no idea how. Jax was falling apart. "How did the bath go?"

"Rough start, but otherwise okay. Airiella wanted me to touch her, to remind her I was safe. For a bit, she was herself, and I had hope. After the bath, though, she asked me to help her forget. Airiella didn't feel fear until afterward. Maybe not remembering is both good and bad. I don't know. I know she's in there, and I know she's fighting to free herself from it. I can see it in her eyes. It's those fucking moments when the fear blindsides her, and she blinks out that take me down."

"I hear you. I saw it earlier. Chrissie had a few of those while we were together too. She came unglued after I went down on her. The memories and insecurities embedded in her mind are strong. I'm glad the asshole is dead. I'm not sure you'd have enough money to bail me out of jail if he wasn't."

"Bail you out? I'd be in there with you." Jax slumped over onto the floor. "How can we have a wedding if she's like this? The flip side of that is, if I postpone it, she's going to think I don't want her."

"There is no good solution there. Give it a few more days. Airiella *is* working on it." Ronnie pulled out his phone and texted Smitty to grab Aedan and come in the room with them. "Let's tackle one thing at a time. She needs to get through the night first. Maybe with some good sleep, things will be easier for her to deal with."

Ronnie stood up and opened the door a crack for the guys to come in before dropping down next to Jax again, this time putting his arm around him. "Airiella's not beaten, nor is she broken."

"I don't know if we can say that, Ronnie."

"I do. Airiella's not broken, dented, yes. Not broken. She didn't hurt herself, she's trying, and she's fighting." He silently begged her not to make a liar out of him.

Ronnie looked up as Smitty and Aedan walked in and sat on the floor from across them. "Okay, we're here. Let's plan this war out." Aedan smiled darkly. "I don't plan to lose. Airiella's too valuable to us all on a deeply personal level, and it has nothing to do with being an angel; this is us fighting this war because she's our family. Chrissie too."

"We've all seen the nightmares," Jax started, his eyes still bloodshot. "Airiella called Stolas to knock her out because she needs relief from her mind. So I think we should start there. It was a good call, Ronnie."

"Well, my thought was if Airiella could get some sleep, she'd be better prepared to deal with shit while she was awake. Her mind would be more clear." Ronnie shrugged. "To me, it seems logical, but I don't know."

"No, you're right," Smitty said, leaning back on his elbows. "We have to take one step at a time, and in this case, I think they need to be small steps. If Airiella can get some sleep on her own, without the help of Stolas, it shows she can overcome it. It will add confidence as well as a less clouded mind."

"Right." Aedan agreed. "So if we can figure out some of the triggers, we can try to work around them."

"Maybe not as easy with nightmares," Jax thought out loud. "It's Airiella's memories that are triggering. We can't combat those."

"No, but we can make the room, wherever we are, feel more comfortable," Smitty mused.

"More comfort or familiarity will put her at ease." Aedan moved and lay on his belly, one of the hotel pads of paper in front of him. "Like, something familiar, so when Airiella opens her eyes, she knows she's in a safe place."

"Yes!" Ronnie crowed. "Jax, print a copy of the pictures on your nightstand at home, those are something we can easily pack around with us."

"Will it work? Airiella had the nightmares at home too," Jax pointed out.

"She did, but the after-effects were a lot less severe," Aedan said mildly.

Smitty was playing with his phone. "I found a place a few blocks from here open twenty-four hours that prints photos. Jax, text me the photos."

Ronnie snapped his fingers. "No sleeping naked; that was part of tonight's issue. Airiella loves our t-shirts. So each of us donates a shirt that we've recently worn but not stunk up that she can wear. Our scent should calm her, even if she's not aware of it."

Aedan added it to his list. "She only wears yours and Jax's."

"That's because she hasn't gotten a hand on one of ours yet." Smitty smiled.

"Easy enough. What about something familiar to put on a door or something that Airiella can identify upon waking up that tells her she's safe. Give me a minute to work this through, I know that didn't make sense." Aedan tapped the pen against his mouth. "Like something she can put across the door, and if she wakes up and sees it there, she'll know no one is in the room with her."

"That could work. What if whoever is with Airiella needs to go out of the room for a minute?" Smitty wondered.

"We just don't. Not until Airiella's over this part," Jax said. "The hotel rooms have a bathroom; we just make sure that when we go to bed, we anticipate whatever we might need. If someone is in the room with her at all times, someone else could get whatever we would have to leave for, and we'd be able to take it down and put it back up."

"I like it," Ronnie said. "Visual cues. Same with turning a light on, the darkness seems to be a trigger too. Jax has been leaving the bathroom light on, and the door partially open, so the room is illuminated enough to see in the dark.

"Smell!" Jax burst out. "On location, the musty smell triggered something, and that's when Airiella's wings popped out. So in the room, let's spray the sheets with some sort of scent she likes."

"Jasmine," Smitty threw in. "We can find body spray at drug stores, and that is a soothing scent and one Airiella likes. It will be easier to find than an ocean scent anyway."

"I was reading an article on anxiety, and there was a number thing that doctors tell their patients to use to get past an attack. Maybe we can alter this method to work for Airiella. Possibly Chrissie too. Pick five things you can see, four things you can touch, three things you can hear, two things you can smell, and one thing you can taste. It's supposed to help ground the mind into a here and now, bring you to the present."

"Okay, so we'd find five things visually that she can spot to help her realize she safe," Ronnie amended. "The photos, something across the door, the light that's three. So we need two more."

"Well, if you count one of us in the room with Airiella, that's four," Smitty added. "Though we could also be used as a feel or hear."

"Airiella's engagement ring and the necklace we had

made might work. They remind her of us," Jax threw the suggestion out.

"That might work, but those are smaller to spot." Aedan tapped the pen again. "Those might be better at things she can touch."

"Airiella's raven," Ronnie thought on the fly. "That would let her know she is safe."

"I wonder if cross-over things work?" Aedan thought out loud. "The raven is a fantastic idea because Airiella can see it, hear it, and touch it."

"Taste will be the hardest." Smitty stood up and stretched. "What about a Diet Coke or a bottle of water?"

"Either would work," Jax agreed. "The Diet Coke would have more of a bite to it because of the taste."

"Okay, let's go back to visual in a bit. What four things could Airiella touch?" Aedan was looking down at his pad of paper and missed the grins the rest had on their faces. He looked up. "What?"

"The obvious answer would be each of us," Smitty laughed.

Aedan laughed. "Okay, true, but that isn't what I was going for; a person we'll count as one. What about the shirt Airiella will be wearing?"

"That's good." Ronnie was starting to see some logic to this method. "The raven would be a third if we are going to use it as a cross over."

"Airiella's ring," Jax supplied. "It will already be on her finger; she just needs to touch it."

"Perfect!" Aedan wrote it down. "Three things she can hear."

"Raven, breathing of whoever is with her, and the air-conditioner," Smitty rattled off. "She always sleeps with the damn thing on in hotel rooms."

"True," Jax hummed. "Those could work."

"Two things she can smell," Aedan went on.

"The jasmine scent on the sheets," Ronnie answered, "and cologne she associates with whoever is with her."

Smitty sat back down. "This might work to pass the panic attack, but will it get Airiella a good night's sleep?"

"Well if we can get her calmed down quickly, her mind will follow, and hopefully she'll be able to relax back into sleep." Aedan sat up, swinging his legs around. "The triggers are mental. If we can get Airiella calm, they should be harder to push in theory."

"I'm willing to try anything." Jax leaned against Ronnie.

Smitty clapped his hands sharply. "I got it. We have the photo place print out a banner on a hard surface that says love wins. We can prop it against the door by the doorknob or find another way to anchor it."

"Do it," Ronnie commanded as Smitty got busy on his phone again. "So, we just need one more visual cue to round out the list."

"The raven that Degataga carved for Airiella," Jax remembered suddenly. "She always has that with her in the little pouch. For that matter, the pouch too."

"Great idea." Ronnie thought about it. "Now, we'll just have to get Airiella to memorize that list of things to do."

"Actually, she needs to recite it out loud. Hearing her own voice will help." Aedan recalled the article. "It's part of the mental exercise; Airiella remembers the cues, reciting them, and counting down."

"This is an executable action plan, guys." Smitty thumped the floor. "All these things we came up with will remind Airiella she is loved and valued, they bring comfort to her, and we can easily provide it."

Ronnie wondered how to make that method work for Chrissie. It wasn't something he could figure out with the guys; he wanted this to be between them, so she didn't feel singled out. He was aware that she didn't like telling the details she had.

"Aedan, want to come with me to get the photos and banner? We can look for the body spray too, and pick up a Diet Coke pack," Smitty asked.

"Might as well. These two look wrecked, and I doubt either want to leave."

Ronnie needed sleep just as much as Jax did. He suddenly remembered his comment about the wet spot and broke out in crazy laughter. The others stared at him like he'd lost his mind.

"Want to share whatever brought that on?" Smitty crossed his arms and raised an eyebrow.

"With Jax staying in here tonight, I told Chrissie that Jax would have to sleep in the wet spot," he spluttered out.

Smitty grinned. "You finally made the step? Congrats, bro! Jax, well, sorry, man."

"To be fair, I told Chrissie that meant she'd have to sleep in their wet spot." For some reason Ronnie couldn't stop laughing.

"You are just twisted." Aedan laughed. "But, yeah, Jax, sorry. I'll wear a clean shirt to sleep in tonight after I shower and set it aside for Airiella."

"Yep, me too." Smitty clapped them on the back.

"I'll text when we are back. If you are asleep, no big deal."

Jax chuckled as the Smitty and Aedan left. "You are an ass. Only you would think about a wet spot in a time like this. It looks like I'm sleeping on top of the covers."

"No, Chrissie had fresh sheets brought up while Airiella tried to work through the nightmare. The expression on her face when I said it was priceless." Ronnie laughed. "Helped me get through it."

"Maybe we can take this one step further." Jax paced the length of the room. "We both know I am going to be there with Airiella every night, what if one other is in there with me, but as she falls asleep, we have her listen to her music. With that playing as she goes to sleep, the songs she loves should put her mind in a better place."

"If those songs don't invoke a sad memory, sure. We'd probably have to create a playlist for Airiella." Ronnie paced with him.

"Don't you already have one?" Jax asked as they passed each other.

"I do." Ronne smiled. "Just wasn't sure you'd want to use that one."

"Why not? Because they are songs that you picked? I don't care about that. You love Airiella, I love her, she loves the songs. Win-win."

"Sounds good to me. With two of us in there, there's a better chance of getting her off the edge. Wouldn't the extra testosterone set her off? Chrissie seemed to think it was the male presence."

"Could be, but maybe with the visual cues and that method, we can bring Airiella down. Chrissie can be on the rotation."

Ronnie thought about it. "Maybe. We'll run it by the

others when they are back. We need to get her to eat too. Lack of nutrition isn't going to help her brain function."

"I know. That's harder to do. Chrissie is good with that part of it. It's just hard to do on the road."

"Aedan may be on to something with this method. It has been worse since we've been on the road. At home, the nightmares were more manageable." Ronnie slumped down into a chair. "Or am I imagining things?"

"The nightmares were the same; the fallout from them was less," Jax clarified. "Tell me about you and Chrissie."

"Like what? You already know everything." Ronnie fought to keep his eyes open.

"True, but there's something you are holding back. I've known you almost my entire life."

Ronnie sighed. "I took the step to a physical relationship, which means I won't have that with Airiella anymore. Now I feel like I've betrayed them both. I can't explain it."

"You don't have to explain it. I think I get it. This bond we all have with Airiella adds a different level to relationships. It takes someone like Jillian or Chrissie to truly understand and be okay with it."

"Chrissie keeps telling me she's fine with it, but earlier when we were alone, there was a moment where something else came into her head, and she blurted out that she didn't want to be a second choice. Fuck, Jax. It just about tore me in two."

"That would be hard to hear. Is Chrissie your second choice? It doesn't feel that way to me."

"It doesn't feel that way to me either, but with Airiella in the picture, it certainly looks that way. If she's insecure about it at all, that's all she is going to see. It took you a while to come to grips with all of us being with her. How did you get past it?" Ronnie remembered the stricken look on Chrissie's face and felt the guilt again.

"I don't know. I'll talk to Chrissie about it. Airiella kept on me; she was always telling me that it was different for everyone, and she had enough love to share with us all. There were times I was insanely jealous she was with you or Smitty. Surface appearances lead some to believe that we all love her in the same way, and maybe that's true for us, but it isn't true for Airiella. She loves each of us differently."

"That's what I tried to explain to Chrissie, but I don't think it came out how I intended it. The last thing I want is her to think I am comparing her to Airiella. I love them both differently."

"Maybe Airiella needs to talk to her," Jax suggested.

"I don't want to lose either of them. Our angel was right all along; I can see a future with Chrissie. A very long one. I used to tell myself I could see one with Airiella too, and while I do, it's a different future than I originally thought it would be."

Jax was rubbing his arms. "Did you turn the AC on high? It's damn cold in here."

"No." Ronnie got up and looked at the control panel. "It's not even on."

Jax gave him an odd look. "You don't feel it?"

"I do, I just figured it was because I haven't eaten and I'm tired." Ronnie glanced at the time. "Should we peek in at them?"

"No. If Airiella is awake, she'll think we don't trust that she's okay. If she's asleep, we could wake her. If something were wrong, Chrissie would text, wouldn't she?"

Ronnie nodded, a vague feeling of unease rolling through him. "We are on the road for another week and a half, and then it's back home for the wedding. Have you talked to Taklishim lately?"

"Yeah. Tak called earlier today to check on her. He's picking up on something too. He told me Tama still offered to "rewire" some things in Airiella's head to get us through, but she declined again."

A piercing scream cut through his head, making his eyes water, and Jax was on his feet, bolting for the door, grabbing his keycard out of his pocket. He fumbled with the lock and finally got the door open, and they ran in.

The room was ice cold and pitch dark. Unnaturally dark. Ronnie ran his hand along the wall looking for the light switch and found it already in the on position. "Jax, we aren't alone," Ronnie whispered.

Ronnie! Jax! Airiella's voice screamed out in their head. Loud and terrified. *Help!*

"She's like an ice cube." Jax sounded panicked. "Chrissie too!"

We are here, angel, in the room with you. Wake up. TRAPPED!

"Stolas!" Ronnie shouted. Cursing the fact that he left his phone behind in the other room.

Jax's phone lit up as he engaged the flashlight app, and he shone it around the room in time to see Stolas striding towards them, his face raw with anger. "Demons," he hissed. "Soul trappers."

"What the fuck does that mean?" Ronnie yelled unintentionally.

A wave of dark energy tore through them, and the lights came back on, the stranglehold on the room released.

241

"It means someone summoned a trapper and tried to sell the souls that didn't belong to them. Jax, she can get them out of this; her soul is stronger than all the trappers combined. She has to fight it. Tell her to fight."

"She said she couldn't. She's stuck in a memory that isn't hers." Jax looked at Ronnie. "Chrissie pulled her in and she's frozen in fear."

Angel, you listen to me, I refuse to lose either of you. You get through to her the same way she got through to you. Fight the fear. You are the bravest damn person I know, and your love can pull her out of anything. You can pull yourself out. Do you hear me?

He heard the sound of her crying in his head, and he switched his gaze to her still form on the bed, Jax hovering over her, trying to warm her skin. Tears were falling from her closed eyes, her skin slightly blue.

Stolas is here. He said you could get both of you out, but you have to fight it, angel. I fucking believe in you. If I could fight this for you, I would do it in a heartbeat.

It hurts so bad. Can't breathe. Rape. I remember. I remember it all. He's doing it to Chrissie now. I can't get out. God, it hurts. Help me.

"Jax," Ronnie choked. "She remembers."

"I know," he said quietly, his face filled with anguish. "It triggered Chrissie's memory."

Another wave of dark energy slammed into them hard as Stolas lost control of his temper. "I will find the summoner. They will pay." The fury in the demon prince's voice raised all the hair on Ronnie's body, his fight or flight instinct kicking in as he backed away. Stolas stroked his fingers down each of the women's faces. "Fight back," he told them.

He disappeared as the door to the room crashed open, and Smitty and Aedan flew in, looking disheveled and frantic. "What the fuck is happening?"

Chapter Eighteen

Why do you make me do this to you?" Travis struck her face as he tried to tear her clothes off her again. "Just fucking love me as I am."

"Travis, stop; this isn't love, this is abuse." Chrissie pleaded with him, her eye starting to swell.

"Now, my love is abuse? You are turning my children against me; they are my boys! They should love their daddy! Instead, they cry and call for you!" He wrapped his hands around her neck, smashing her head into the wall behind her.

"Travis, this isn't you. Stop, please." She could barely speak.

"You wish I were someone else, don't you, you fucking miserable whore. My dick isn't good enough for your stinky pussy. Who?! Who do you think I should be?" He spits in her face.

She couldn't speak; she was losing consciousness. Her eyes locked on the track marks up Travis's arms. The scars, bruises, and freshly bleeding wounds that told her he shot up recently. He let her drop to the ground; oxygen *flooding her lungs as she gulped in air.*

The stink of his unwashed body filling her nostrils as he bent over her, kicking her in the stomach, the precious air she had sucked in exiting in a painful cry. "I fucking hate what you have turned me into!" he yelled at her. "You made me do this!"

He yanked her pants off her and shoved her shirt up. "You are my fucking wife! I own you! Why can't you see that?" He forcefully moved her bra, the wire snapping as he pushed her breast up out of it and bit down hard.

"Every man you fuck will see this and know you belong to me! Then you can tell them how you ruined my life, turned me into an addict, and then refused to let me into my house!" He bit down again and forced her legs open with his knees.

All she could do was hope he was too high to get hard. She clung to her faith and prayed for release from the hell in which she was stuck. Each bite, slap, pinch brought another prayer as she tried to find a safe place in her mind.

He forced himself into her. It hurt, burned, and tore her up, guilt and shame flooding her mind as she choked on the hate taking root in her heart.

"No! Chrissie!" she heard Airiella's voice. Her best friend. She couldn't see this; she couldn't let Airiella see her like this. "Chrissie! I'm here. It's not real. I'm here; you're safe. You're safe. He's dead. Chrissie!"

Dead. That's what Chrissie wished for sometimes. That he was dead, or that she was. This abuse wasn't living; what he was doing wasn't life. This life wasn't what she wished for when she married him. Sickness swept through her as he came, grunting away like a disgusting pig covered in his own shit.

"You might be a whore, but you are a good fuck."
Travis smiled down at her, his pupils blown out. He rolled
off her. "Clean up, your pussy stinks."

The movement hurt; all she could do was curl up
and cry. Why wasn't God listening to her? Why wouldn't
the police help her? What would happen to her boys if she
died?

"God! Chrissie! Listen to me. I love you. It's me,
Airiella. I'm here. Chris, I'm here with you; this isn't real.
It's a nightmare. Or a memory, they are the same. I'm
here. Please, Chris, look at me."

"Why are you in my head, Airiella? Why am I
thinking about you now?"

"Chris! I'm with you. I'm touching you, can you feel
me? I'm real; we are here together. You're stuck in this.
Look at me, please. I'll pull us out. God, Chrissie, I'm so
sorry. You are so brave, and I love you so much. I promise
you, I'll get us out of here, but you have to look at me."

"There is no getting out. Dying is the only way out.
I can't look at you. I can't let you see this shame of what
I've become." Chrissie needed to call the police again. It
hurt too much to move, though.

"Chris, it's my fault you are stuck in this. Please,
look at me. We are in this together."

"Ells, how could this be your fault? I'm imagining
you; if you were here, he would have done the same thing
to you. Not something I would ever wish on anyone, much
less you."

Chrissie could hear her sobbing. "He did, Chris. He
did it to me too. That's how we got here. It triggered your
memory when I remembered. I inadvertently pulled you

into mine, and now we are both trapped in yours. A demon is holding our souls here stuck in this memory."

"How hard did he hit my head that I am thinking about him doing this to you? That's seriously fucked up. I'm losing it. Ells, I'm in Kansas, and he was just here, he couldn't have done this to you too. I don't even want to consider that."

"Chrissie, please," Airiella cried. "We are in a hotel room in Pennsylvania with the guys, shooting a TV show for cable. Remember Ronnie? You love him; he loves you. I'm going to get married in a couple of weeks, to Jax. Please remember."

No. It couldn't be. Something was clawing at the inside of Chrissie's head, painfully ripping apart her mind. "No. I need to call the police. I can't remember where my phone is."

"He raped me, Chris. I brought the building down on him and Rafe. Remember, Rafe?"

"Of course, I remember Rafe. He's my son." Chrissie's voice trembled. Why was there truth to Airiella's words? Why was Airiella in her head?

"I don't know how to do this, Chris. Help me. We live in Washington. Jax moved you out there with the boys. You work at a local school, and we live in a large house, you slept with Ronnie for the first time tonight. I called you because I was freaking out, and you flew out to Pennsylvania to help me because Travis kidnapped Rafe and me."

Airiella was crying. Chrissie rarely heard her cry. She was strong. Chrissie wanted to be like Airiella and get through this hellscape she was living in; she needed to be strong like Airiella. "I can count on one hand the number of times I've heard you cry. The fact that you are crying right now makes me believe I have brain damage. You don't cry."

"I am crying, Chris. I'm terrified. We are both traumatized by recent events, and now there are demons at play again. How can you not remember Ronnie? You are the one planning my wedding!"

Travis's words started replaying in her head, all the disgusting things he spewed out about how badly she stunk, how she ruined his life. Yet there was truth to what Airiella was saying. "Ronnie?"

"Yes, Ronnie. Big, giant, sexy as sin, Ronnie. Ronan. His name is Ronan. He's solid muscle. Super protective, loves your kids."

"Ronan," Chrissie whispered, and reality crashed down on her hard. Everything Airiella was telling her was the truth. Her eyes flew open, and she saw the ravaged face of her best friend. "Ells, oh my God."

Airiella flung her arms around Chrissie and sobbed. "I'm so sorry, Chris. I'm so fucking sorry!"

"You remembered." Chrissie held her tight, looking around. "Where are we?"

"I don't know. The guys called Stolas, and he said I could fight it, but I don't know how. All I can see is your awful memory. How many times did that happen, Chrissie?"

"Too many to count. Now you've lived it as well. In more than one way." Chrissie shuddered.

"We've got a lot of healing to do, but we can't do it here. What happened is neither of our faults. I don't blame you, Chris."

"No, I know that. But you blame yourself, and that's

not right either," Chrissie said softly into her hair, wrapped around each other. "I swear, I can smell you on the air. That jasmine scent you always smell like."

"I haven't worn it since before the kidnapping," Airiella said. "I smell it, too, though."

"Ells, there's a glow coming off you," Chrissie told her. "Like you are sparking."

"Is it on my back?"

"Yes, it's weird. Like a line going up and down your back," Chrissie described. "Makes me think of a sparkler."

"It's Jax; he's touching me. They are trying to bring us back."

"We aren't alone, Ells." Chrissie lowered her voice and spoke directly into Airiella's ear. "Whatever you do to kill demons, I think you should start doing it."

"I don't know if I can use any of my powers. They've not worked since the kidnapping."

"They aren't gone. You used air to get those floozies away from your guys," Chrissie reminded her. "Angry. Get angry, Ells."

"That's just it, Chris. I've been nothing but angry. It's not working."

"Yes, you've been angry, but numb. Get un-numb. I don't even think that's a word." Chrissie looked at the dark shapes around them and tried to push back the fear that was taking over her mind.

"I don't want to feel. Remembering is bad enough. I don't want to remember how it feels."

Chrissie's heart broke. "I don't either, but I just did. And it's awful. When you said Ronan, it broke through to me. He showed me that it's not all awful. Think of Jax, who's touching you right now. These beautiful sparks are the love he has for you. Love is stronger than this shit we've endured. *We* are stronger than this shit."

"Is that when you got pregnant with Bryce?" Airiella's quiet question poked a hole in Chrissie's heart.

"It is. I was suicidal after that. I didn't want to have Bryce. I wanted to abort, couldn't stand the thought of a reminder about how I conceived him. I cried most of that pregnancy. I couldn't get out of the depression I was in; every time I saw my belly was a reminder that my child was going to be born in a living hell." Chrissie let it all out, hoping that it would help whatever Airiella was trying to do.

Chrissie felt it. The stirring of the hot rage that boiled inside Airiella that came out when she needed to protect those she loved. Chrissie hated to do it, but if Airiella needed to feel, Chrissie would stoke those fires in her, even if it meant she had to expose her darkest secrets.

"For a month, I thought Travis was going to stay clean. He started acting somewhat loving again, spent time with Jace and Rafe. Cleaned house. Then close to my due date, he disappeared. Jace found him under an empty house he had been playing with a friend in, passed out with dead rats around him. He had lit a fire under there, and Jace smelled the smoke and went to investigate it. He saw the siding removed from part of the house and shone a light in there. My son had to call an ambulance because he thought his father was dead."

She felt the anger in her own heart grow at the memory. The cops and ambulances that showed up, the devastated look on Jace's face as he realized this was a choice his dad had made on his own. The cycle never stopped repeating. Each blow was hitting harder than the last.

"Can Jax and Ronnie hear me, Ells?" Chrissie asked, worried, and ashamed.

"I don't know. Remember Aedan telling me he would fight this war for me?"

Chrissie nodded. Aedan's words had caught Chrissie off guard because he was far less emotional than the rest of them, and while he had been logical when talking to her, his voice betrayed the sensible words. The event had shaken him and left a mark.

"He can't. He can't fight this war for me. I have to fight it. You have to fight it. They are fighting with us, Chris, but we are the ones that need to strike back. Every single one of them is with us. Every memory that hurts you hurts them. Right now, I know with all of my heart that each of them is with us doing everything they can think of to get our souls back from whatever prison we are in; we have to help them."

"What if that prison is our own minds?" Chrissie's eyes roved over the demon things that surrounded them. They were literally in a cage with these things stalking around them, making weird noises.

"It's not. We aren't in our heads, not at the moment. But they will make us relive every shitty thing we've been through in our lives if we give in to it. That's how they will keep us trapped. I can feel you fighting back the anger in you, don't. Let it consume you. It roots you in the present, albeit an emotional one, but you are aware of where you are."

"Is it consuming you?" Chrissie stopped fighting the anger inside and let it roll around.

"It's starting to. The more you remember, the more

pissed off I'm getting."

"Why aren't you mad at what happened to you?" Chrissie pushed her, stoking the flames.

"I am, but maybe it's still too fresh. It's more pain than anger."

"Travis didn't even go to the hospital with me when Bryce was born. He was off on another strung-out adventure. Travis didn't even know Bryce was born until he showed up two weeks later, begging for forgiveness, telling me he needed help. Travis's parents bailed him out of jail and sent him off to me while he was coming down from a high. With a two week old baby." Chrissie did the only thing she could think to do and told more secrets.

Airiella's wings flew out of her back and wrapped around them both. The silky softness of her feathers was a contrast to the hard and cold memories plaguing her. They also stopped her from seeing a cage around them that probably wasn't even there. Yet wrapped in her wings, she understood how safe Rafe felt. Nothing could hurt Chrissie in here. Not even her memories were more potent than the soft and fierce love Airiella provided.

"This is what Rafe felt like when you protected him. I understand his need to protect you, better than I did before," Chrissie confessed.

"Don't let go of me, Chris." Airiella's voice wavered. "I can't do this without you."

"You are wrong there, Ells. There isn't anything you can't do. I won't let go. Not ever. You are stuck with my kids and me for life. I can't say this has been a fun little side trip, but I know that my life is safe with you."

"Shut up, Chris. I'm what got you here," Airiella argued, crying.

"The same way I brought Travis into your life," Chrissie fought back. The air around them turned blue and static electricity sparked through them, Chrissie smelled ozone.

"Love wins," Airiella whispered raggedly.

Safely ensconced inside Airiella's downy wings, Chrissie didn't know what was happening, and she didn't care. She was safe here, no matter where they were. Her only fear was that while she was safe, Airiella wasn't.

"I love you, Ells. I love that you lived to protect Rafe. I love that you protect the guys and everyone else around. I love that you shared your love with a starved demon and believe he's worth it. I love that you trust me to plan your wedding. I love that Ronnie still loves you and includes me in that because of you. I love how strong you are, and I strive to be like you."

"No, Chris, be you," she replied weakly. "I need you to be you."

Chrissie heard an awful buzzing noise and the smell of burning flesh, heat soaking through the immense cold that had a hold of them and had been settling into Chrissie's bones. She didn't move; she stayed just as she was, clutching Airiella to her.

Gradually she started to hear a voice, "Fight, baby. Fight. It's what you do, who you are. Fight, and come back to me."

"Jax?" Chrissie whispered. "Where are we? Do I hear music?"

"Chris?" Ronnie shouted. "Chris, are you here?"

"Ronnie! Oh my God, Ells, you did it! Ells!" Chrissie pushed back a little to look at Aireilla's ravaged and pale face. "Ells?"

"Angel, you're safe; you can put your wings away," she heard Ronnie say softly.

"I don't think she's okay," Chrissie hesitated to say but gave voice to the fear growing in her.

"She's okay, Chrissie. I think it just exhausted her," Jax said through the feathers surrounding her. "Can you get out?"

Aireilla's arms remained wrapped around her, but she could easily pull free. "I can. Give me a minute," she called out to them.

"Ells, I know you can hear me. It's okay to open your eyes. You got us out of there." Chrissie spoke in barely a whisper. "You kept us safe. I don't know how, but you did it. Now I need you to open your eyes for me; because I have to face these guys just as much as you do. Based on the sound of their voices, they are scared shitless." Chrissie was ready to beg or fan the flames of her temper, whatever it took.

"I remember, Chris. I can't hide that from them."

"You don't have to. Not with these men. They are so much a part of you, just like I am. I saw your hell; you saw mine. Give them a chance to do for you what you do for everyone else. Remember, love wins?"

Chrissie held her breath and waited. The pain of what they both had been through was right below the surface; for both of them. Chrissie knew there were cracks all over that surface they stood on, ready to plunge them to the icy depths of who knows where. She felt every single one of them; they both did. It was a scary thought letting anyone else see the carnage.

"I'm scared too, Ells. If I could, I'd stay wrapped up with you in these wings for days. Eventually, they are going to find a way to crawl up in here with us. We can't hide from it. They don't deserve to suffer because we don't want to deal with it," she said, trying a gentle truth first.

Chrissie felt the wetness of the tears, though she didn't hear the cries. "I love you, Chrissie."

"I know. Let's face this together. There's a room full of hot guys that are dying to see your beautiful face." Chrissie rested her head against Airiella's.

"One of those wants to see yours. Are you going to tell Ronnie?"

"If he wants me to, I will. The same goes for you. You don't have to tell them anything you don't want to. They aren't going to force you to share details they probably don't want to hear. They just want to see you are okay."

She felt the wings pulling away, but Airiella hadn't let her go yet. She didn't need to, Ronnie hugged her from behind once he could, his massive arms wrapping around them both, and she saw Jax over Airiella's shoulder settling behind her, holding them both.

Never doubt your worth, Chrissie.

Chapter Nineteen

Clls, let me get up so Aedan and Smitty can get in here," Chrissie said gently.

Ronnie saw Airiella's arms drop, and Ronnie gathered Chrissie up to him and stood up while Aedan and Smitty swept in. Ronnie sat down in the chair, settling Chrissie in his lap. "Do you want to talk about it?"

"Do you want me to?" she asked in return.

"All we could hear is Airiella trying to get you back." His throat tightened up, remembering the moment he realized it was Chrissie who couldn't tell reality from memory. She'd gotten stuck, and what he had heard had nearly sent him over the edge.

"If you don't want to know, I won't tell you. If you do, I will. It's your choice."

He buried his face in her neck. "I can figure it out based on what we heard. I almost had a heart attack when her wings came out and covered you. I'm surprised you couldn't hear us."

"I couldn't hear anything other than the stuff playing out in my head. I don't know if Airiella could hear you or not. Wherever we were, it was weird, like all feelings around us had been cut off." She burrowed her head into his arm. "A deprivation tank inside an actual cage, that's what it was like, except when her wings were around me. Then it was the only place I wanted to be; I felt completely safe."

"You didn't feel the electricity in her?" The surprise in Ronnie's voice got her attention.

"No. I saw the blue glow, but I never felt anything but safe, protected, and loved."

"She threw off some dangerous electrical currents. Both Jax and I were worried that she would burn you and the bed." Ronnie and Jax had both jerked away when the sparks started flying.

Ronnie looked up as Jax walked upon them. "Switch with me." Ronnie wasn't sure why Jax wanted to be with Chrissie, but he *did* want to make sure Airiella was okay, so he didn't argue. He stood up and placed Chrissie in Jax's arms and kissed her on the head.

He slid on the bed next to Airiella, while keeping an eye on Chrissie, who was deep in a conversation with Jax. "Hey, angel. Did they tell you about our plans to help you?"

"Aedan was telling me a little about it. The jasmine scent broke through to me."

Ronnie filled her in on their plan, Smitty and Aedan providing the details he'd missed and then fell silent while waiting for her response. She was quiet for so long that Ronnie was starting to think she fell asleep again. It wasn't until Smitty pulled her up on his chest and started whispering in her ear that he understood she was crying.

"Did I say something wrong?" he asked Aedan quietly.

"No, unless I'm reading the signals wrong, she's grateful. I think she needs Smitty's voice of reason right now. Do you mind if I have a moment with Chrissie?"

"Nope." Ronnie scooted closer to Smitty and started rubbing Airiella's feet while he watched Jax and Aedan switch spots, Jax coming up on the other side of Smitty and sitting down. There was a broad mix of emotions rolling through him, and Ronnie felt a little lost trying to sort them out.

He went over the conversation that they had picked up on through the connection, and he didn't lie when he said he could piece together what she was reliving. It made him sick, knowing that Chrissie went through that. The cruelty dealt out by someone that vowed to love, cherish, and honor her.

Airiella's yelp of pain brought him back out of his head, and he found Smitty shooting him a dark glare. "What?"

"You might want to let go of her foot before you head down whatever path in your head that made you squeeze it like that," Smitty said evenly.

"Shit! Angel, I'm so sorry." Ronnie looked down at her foot and saw bruises forming. "Fuck." She pulled away from Smitty and curled into Ronnie, her eyes damp and red. Ronnie cradled her, kissing her hair. "I'm not making this any easier for you, am I?"

"This plan you have for me, to help me, will you do it for Chrissie too?"

"I was planning to, should I not?" Ronnie winced at the look Smitty was giving him.

"I think she needs it just as much as I do."

Smitty headed over to Chrissie and swapped out

places with Aedan. "I'm going to go call Mags," Aedan said gruffly and walked out into the hallway. Ronnie heard him slump against the door and knew he'd taken up a position as they had earlier.

"We only heard your end of it, but it was enough for us to put it together," Ronnie said softly, Jax scooting over and sandwiching her between them. "I was trying to figure out how to put something together for her in the same way."

"It was bad. So ugly. Stay with Chrissie the rest of the night, Ronnie."

"What about you, angel?" Ronnie had never felt so torn before.

"I think I need to be with Jax. If things get bad, we can call in Smitty or Aedan. Chrissie has some pretty deep scars and not a lot of experience with someone other than me to help her heal them. Especially a male."

Ronnie glanced at Jax, who only shrugged. "She's in the driver's seat here. I'm going along with whatever she feels comfortable with; if it's you, that's fine. If it's one of the others, I'm okay with that too."

"Can I hold you a few more minutes?" Ronnie asked.

"I'd like that."

Stolas chose that moment to reappear, his face as angry as Ronnie had ever seen it. Waves of dark energy rolling off him aggressively. "Love, you are back."

She only nodded and held out a hand to him. He took it, and Ronnie felt the love she was pushing at the demon until the energy subsided in him, and a more relaxed look came over his face. A single tear rolled down from his eye.

"I failed you, and I'm correcting that situation now," he said and he started and looked over at Chrissie. "The attack was for you, my dear. I'm sorry. I have added that all notifications about intents for anyone from this group get brought to my immediate attention."

"What?" Ronnie sat up, almost dumping Airiella off him. "It was for Chrissie?"

"Airiella got taken along because I am guessing she created another blood bond?" He looked back at Airiella with a question in his eyes.

"I did."

"That's what pulled you with her then." He looked back at Chrissie. "It seems that your ex-husband's parents have connections with people who are familiar with the darker arts. They summoned a demon without requesting a specific one and got a lazy lower level demon who used the soul trappers to steal your soul. If you die, your kids will go to them as they are blood relatives."

"They fucking tried to have Chrissie killed for custody of the boys?" Ronnie shouted, bolting to his feet, Airiella tumbling off to the side on to Jax.

Stolas nodded in confirmation and helped Airiella sit up, him sliding in next to her in the spot Ronnie just vacated. Smitty stood with a stunned Chrissie in his arms and handed her to Ronnie while he pulled out his phone and started to make a call.

Ronnie fumed. "Not the best role models for kids. Who the fuck does shit like that?"

"It was because of me that Airiella almost died with me wherever that place was?" Chrissie whispered.

"They couldn't have killed her, they weren't strong enough." Stolas answered instantly, trying to alleviate her guilt. "They could have killed you, though."

"There were so many of them." Chrissie started to shake.

Ronnie tightened his hold on her. "So Chrissie is being watched out for now?"

"You all are. I added *all* of you to my list, the children, and the warrior also. I'm not without power, though my use of it could be questionable. I'll deal with that if it comes up. Even Hades himself understands that a balance must be maintained. I apologize for the oversight on my part."

"Chrissie, the show's lawyers are now taking on your case and considering it urgent. Obviously, I can't tell them about demons coming after you. I used the kidnapping of Rafe and Airiella as proof that you aren't safe and mentioned threats against you from your in-laws. They will be contacting you," Smitty informed her coolly.

Another blast of energy rolled through the room. This time not because of Stolas, but because of the glowing blue angel next to him. The room shook a little, and Aedan flew back in the room, stopping when he saw Stolas sitting there.

"Angel," Ronnie called out softly. "I don't think that energy is good for Stolas."

The demon looked as if he were in tremendous physical pain, though he made no move away from Airiella. "This is why I say they couldn't have killed her," Stolas commented through gritted teeth. "She isn't even attacking, and the power she wields immobilizes me in a very uncomfortable way."

She immediately relaxed at seeing how it affected Stolas. "I'm so sorry, Stolas. I didn't mean to do that."

He slumped forward a bit. "Your strength has increased, love."

Chrissie pushed herself away from Ronnie, and he set her down slowly. She crawled up on to the bed and sat in front of Airiella. "If I had known that blood bond would do that, I never would have wanted it."

"Stop, Chris. Now that we know what we are dealing with, we'll fix it. We are all behind you on this. Smitty and Aedan can be pretty ruthless on their behind the scenes work."

"Your in-laws will have to get through all of us to get to you." Jax had steel in his voice.

"For what it's worth, I am on your side as well," Stolas told her. Ronnie was oddly pleased by that.

"Stolas, thank you for getting to the bottom of this." Ronnie held out his hand, and Stolas shook it. "You have proven yourself invaluable to us over and over again."

He looked over at Airiella. "Love is indeed a strange thing. It feels good to be on the right side of it after all these years."

"Chrissie, write down their names for me." Aedan handed her the little notepad from the nightstand and waited while she wrote the information down. Then he and Smitty took off.

Ronnie knew an investigation into their backgrounds was about to be put into motion in a way they would never expect. Smitty would leave no stone unturned, and if Aedan were talking with the lawyers, then there would be no slacking off and waiting to see what happened.

His team was hands down the best when it came to protecting those they loved. They'd protected Jax for twelve years from the dark energy that had been inside him, never leaving him alone and keeping things that could hurt him at bay. Chrissie had an army behind her.

With Airiella as a part of them now, they had numerous avenues at their disposal. "If you don't mind, I'd like to have some of my legions do their own investigating?" Stolas asked Chrissie.

"Don't hurt them," she pleaded. "My kids have lost enough."

"As you wish. I will have my legions seek and gather the information that is only available from my end of things."

Ronnie's heart filled with love and pride for this woman. Chrissie just learned that these people sent demons after her, asking them not to be hurt. "They are grieving too," she said and she leaned into Airiella. "They can't have my boys."

"Won't happen, Chris," Ronnie promised vehemently. "Come with me, please, let's leave them alone." Ronnie glanced at Airiella to see her approving look.

"Not demons, not ex's, not rape, not abuse or threats will ever beat us. Your past shapes you not defines you; we fight this together, never alone," Airiella whispered fiercely. They fist-bumped and touched their foreheads together.

Chrissie backed off the bed and reached for Ronnie's hand, and he pulled her to his side. "Angel, you good?"

Airiella shrugged. "Maybe not yet, but I will be."

Ronnie searched her face looking for hints that he should stay here with her but finding only the resolute strength that was so much a part of who she was. *I love you, angel. You know that, right?*

Of course, I know it. I love you too, Heracles. This relationship doesn't change anything between us other than Chrissie now gets to know that Eros side of you.

He felt himself starting to laugh and tried to smother it. *Are you going to let Jax try and help you?*

I am. While this fight inside me might be my own, it's Chrissie's too, in a way. I realized that we need help. You guys can't fight it for us, but neither do we have to sideline you. I'm smart enough to know I can't do this on my own. I need him.

Satisfied, Ronnie bid goodbye to Stolas and Jax, then led Chrissie out of the room back into his. He undressed her slowly, and they got into bed and spent hours talking. Ronnie listened to whatever she had to say, and he told her about their plan to help Airiella. Ronnie asked Chrissie to help him come up with things that would work for her, and together they did.

He taught her how to close the connection with Airiella down, and they discussed a training program for her and the boys to learn self-defense moves and how they could make it fun and beneficial. He promised her a future, and he had every intent on delivering it.

When she finally drifted off to sleep, Ronnie watched over her for a while before succumbing himself. They got some decent sleep in, and he woke to her running her hands over him. His body's reaction was instantaneous.

"Waking up with you is a perfect morning," she said throatily.

"I have no complaints." Ronnie rolled her on top of him.

"I need to go back home today. I can't expect Jillian

and Mags to take care of my kids. Is that okay?"

"You don't need my permission, Chris. I support whatever you decide. You are their mother first and foremost."

"You are almost too good to be true," she whispered. Ronnie damn near bit his tongue off as she slid down his body and wrapped her lips around him.

"Shit, Chris," he growled and hauled her back up and buried himself inside her. "It'll be over before we even started if you do that."

"I don't mind," she groaned, moving on him. "I love those sounds you make when I do that."

He let her take control and focused on her pleasure, doing his best to make sure she came as many times as possible before he did.

Chapter Twenty

I t had been a week and a half of meetings with lawyers, investigators, counselors, wedding details, and more conversations than she'd ever had. She was thankful for the connection to Airiella, and they frequently talked throughout the days and nights.

Every time either one of them fought a memory, they reached out and got through it. Chrissie talked and texted with Ronnie every day, their closeness growing with each conversation. She had never felt this close with Travis, nor had she ever felt this cherished or respected. It was taking a bit of getting used to it.

Now they were due back today, and in three days, Airiella was getting married. She had picked up the dress, confirmed the caterer, the cake, and the tent rentals. Mags and Jillian had helped her get the lights strung how she envisioned, and the landscapers would be here tomorrow.

Father Roarke had arrived last night, and Taklishim had been in touch about the gift that they had gone in on together. She felt like everything was ready, and at the same time like she forgot everything. She wanted Airiella to have the perfect day.

Jax had done so much for Chrissie and had made it so utterly transparent that she was a welcome part of this house and their lives, this seemed like nothing in comparison. The love Jax had for the sister of her soul was beautiful, and they deserved a day to celebrate what they had.

Chrissie dared to hope that what she and Ronnie had would be as powerful as what Jax and Airiella had found in each other. Ronnie had admitted he was nervous about the wedding and that he had mixed feelings. He felt torn because he said it seemed like a door was closing that Ronnie didn't want shut, and he also felt thrilled that it was happening.

Chrissie didn't know how to take that. She wondered if Ronnie still felt hung up on Airiella in a way he didn't want to admit. Chrissie had even asked Airiella about it and gotten total honesty in return that Airiella felt he was just nervous. She knew that Airiella had a view into Ronnie's emotions, and while she would never betray that, she would warn Chrissie if she thought that there was something to be concerned about and help her fix it.

She waited patiently for the bus to arrive and checked over her shoulder to make sure Bryce was still behind her inside the gate. He was happily zooming a dump truck that Jillian had brought him around the driveway. She spotted the bus and breathed a sigh of relief as it stopped, and Jace and Rafe came down the steps.

"Is Auntie Ells back yet?" Jace asked while Chrissie waited for the gate to close behind her. She didn't take chances anymore, even though Travis was gone.

"Not yet, honey. A couple of hours to go."

"Rafe couldn't stop asking about her on the way home," Jace told her softly.

"He misses her. They went through a lot. It's normal, honey."

"Ronnie is going to teach me how to box still?"

"He's going to teach all of us, but he does have a special time set aside for just you two," Chrissie told him as Rafe played with Bryce going up the driveway.

"Mom, are you dating him?" Jace stopped and looked at her, his face serious.

"I am. Does that bother you?" Chrissie held her breath.

"No. Rafe wants him to be our dad. I don't know how I feel about that." He started walking again. "Part of me wants it, and the other part of me is sad about it."

"Ronnie loves you." Chrissie ruffled his hair; the poor kid was way older than his nine years.

"I know. I love Ronnie too. He's cool, and he always has time for me. I want all of them to be my dad's. Can I have more than one?"

"You know what, Jace? I think that all of them would love to hear that." Chrissie's heart broke at Jace's words. "They all love you, boys."

"When will they be back?"

"Should be soon. I believe the plane already landed. So let's get your homework done before the guys get here, then you'll have the rest of the night to play with them."

"Mom?" Jace paused to look at Chrissie.

"What, baby?"

"Do they hate me because Dad hurt Auntie Ells?"

Chrissie squatted down until she was eye level with Jace. "Not at all. What your dad did has nothing to do with you. Why would you think that?"

"Some kids at school called me a son of a murderer."

"Some kids are just mean and petty. You are not the same as your father." Chrissie wanted to demand to know the kid's name so she could call the school and give them a piece of her mind.

"Can I call Ronnie?" Jace kicked at some of the gravel.

"Sure." Chrissie pulled out her phone and sent Ronne a quick text telling him Jace was going to call. She handed the phone to Jace, who took off running towards the house. She caught up to Rafe and Bryce, who were giggling about something.

"What's so funny?" She smiled down at them.

"Bryce thinks Ronnie is his daddy." Rafe grinned, then she saw it falter. "Is Auntie Ells okay?"

"She's fine. She's on her way home right now, so you'll get to see for yourself that she is. You didn't tell Uncle Jax about her dress, did you?" Chrissie tried to get him out of the sudden somber mood.

"No! I kept it a secret like I 'posed to."

"Good job. I think Uncle Jax will like it. Don't you?" Chrissie took his hand as they kept walking to the house.

"Yeah. Auntie Ells looks like an angel when she has it on. Will she have her wings on for the wedding?"

Chrissie didn't know, but it was one of the things she wanted to talk to her about; Chrissie thought that Ariella should have them out. Jax was marrying all of her, and everyone at the wedding already knew about what she was. "Do you think she should?"

"Yes!" Rafe jumped up and down. "Can I tell

270

her that?"

"Of course you can. You can tell Auntie Ells anything you want to."

When they got into the house, Jace was already sitting at the table doing his homework, his eyes showing a little red and her phone sitting next to him. She picked it up and looked at the texts, Ronnie responding they'd be there in under an hour.

"How did your talk go?" she asked Jace carefully, not wanting to push him.

"Good. Ronnie is going to spend some time with me tonight when he gets home. He said Uncle Jax wanted to come too."

"Is that okay with you?" Chrissie wasn't sure if the red in his eyes was because Jax wanted to intrude on their time or because of whatever reason he called Ronnie.

"Yeah. Ronnie promised me alone time, too, if I wanted it. They both did."

Chrissie's heart swelled with happiness at these men. They were exactly what her boys needed to see, and all of them were excellent role models of what a man should be. She dropped a kiss on Jace's head. "Tell me if you need help," she said and went into the kitchen to get them a snack.

She found Jillian already there feeding Bryce and Rafe, both chattering excitedly about all the things they could do with the dump truck she had given them. Chrissie grinned at Jillian and grabbed one of the sliced up apples to bring out to Jace.

Jillian caught her before she went back into the kitchen to rescue her. "When they get here, I need Art for a minute; he and I need to have a little talk," Jillian pleaded.

"It's fine with me." Chrissie gave her a confused look. "Were the boys trying to hijack him?"

"No, I just need backup in case he tries to go off with the boys."

"Got it. Is everything okay? You look nervous." Chrissie thought she looked a little sick, but she didn't want to say that.

"Everything is fine. At least I think it will be. Shit." Jillian pulled Chrissie down the hallway. "Don't tell; he doesn't know yet. I'm pregnant."

The sick part made sense then. "Smitty has no idea? Smitty is pretty in tune with things."

"He thinks my feeling off has to do with Airiella and Rafe. The day you left to fly out there, and I was heading home, I was coming back from the doctor, and it had just gotten confirmed, I'm eight weeks."

"You think he won't be happy? Is that why you are nervous?" Chrissie was trying to understand the emotions showing on the woman's face.

"We haven't ever really talked about kids seriously. More of a yeah, maybe down the road, it would be fun to have one."

"I think you are way off the mark." Chrissie smiled. "He's fantastic with them, both the babies and my boys. I think he'll be ecstatic. I'll run interference for you if anyone heads that way. I'm willing to bet money on his reaction. Over the moon happy, followed by horny."

Jillian burst out laughing. "No bet. That's my gut feeling, too; I'm still just nervous. I wrapped up the sonogram picture in a little box."

"Don't let Airiella see you first, she'll know right off the bat and will probably blurt it out in excitement,"

Chrissie warned her.

"Crap. I didn't even think of that. I was planning on meeting everyone on the front porch."

Chrissie thought about it. "I can tell her not to say anything, that you want to surprise him. If she knows before she gets here, she won't ruin the surprise."

"Okay, do it."

Ells, Jillian has a surprise for Smitty, so when you see her, don't say what you see.

Well, that just brought up a whole lot of questions. What am I going to see? Wait, is this a happy surprise?

Yes, an eight-week surprise.

I've got locked lips. Smitty really has no idea?

Chrissie smiled. "She asked if he really has no idea."

"None, whatsoever."

Jillian says none whatsoever.

I thought for sure out of all of them that he would be the one to notice first when it happened.

That's what I said too. I told Jillian I'd run interference in case anyone headed back out to their house.

"All set, no worries. Airiella said the same thing I did, that she thought he'd know."

"Well, you can all give him hell over it after I tell him. That should be entertaining. Mags doesn't know yet either, though she's been giving me a side-eye a lot lately."

Chrissie laughed. "Mags probably does know. There isn't much that gets by her. Ells said that she's been leaning on Smitty a lot this past week."

"Art said that too. He's able to get her off the ledge easier than the others can. He said Ronnie was helicoptering, and Jax was trying to get him to ease up, while Aedan and himself were using reason and logic to counteract the emotions. When you talk to her, does she seem better?"

"If Airiella's reaching out to me, it means she's having a moment that she can't get through. Overall, I'd say she is better than she was," Chrissie answered after thinking about it.

"The bad moments are still pretty bad, aren't they?"

"They are. The plan that the guys put together is working." Chrissie reached out and put a hand on Jillian's arm.

"What about you? How have you been doing?"

"I think Airiella and I are pretty even on that front. Ronnie and I put a plan in place for me too. When my moments are bad, I call him, and we go through it. Half the time, I don't want to call Ronnie because it doesn't seem fair that he's dealing with it on both ends; I do it because he asked me to," Chrissie explained. It had been a concession for her on that, but in the end, she agreed to it.

"He's got pretty big shoulders, Chris. He can handle it. You can always reach out to me too."

"Thanks, Jillian. I appreciate that." Chrissie smiled at how lucky she was to call all of these people her family now.

"Did you know I've been through it too?"

"No, but it doesn't surprise me. Wait, that sounded wrong. Let me clarify that it doesn't surprise me that you have been through it, in the way that it's become way too common. Not that you put off signals that made me think you've been through it." Chrissie scrambled to correct her statement.

"I have. Probably not in the same way that both of

you have, certainly not in the way Airiella has. But I can identify, and I understand the triggers and how they make you feel. You don't talk about it with Airiella?"

"Oh, I do. It seems like most of my bad moments happen at the same time hers do, or close to each other. If Airiella's coming out of one of hers, I talk with Ronnie first. Jax is taking 90% of the responsibility for Airiella. Smitty and Aedan are backing him up with the logic and reasoning."

"Just don't forget to take care of you in all this too." Jillian's gentle reminder was the same thing Ronnie had told her. For that matter, all of them said that to her.

"I'm good. Do you have everything ready for your big announcement?" Chrissie switched the conversation back to Jillian.

"I think so. I even put a bun in the oven in case Art didn't get what the sonogram was."

Chrissie laughed. "I can guarantee you he knows. I'd start with the oven, that isn't quite as obvious. Have you guys set a wedding date yet?"

"Not yet. Though Art will probably want to do it before the baby is born, neither of us wants a big wedding ceremony. We have talked about that."

Chrissie leaned on the wall. "How about we do what we did for Onida and Dega?"

"That's more in line with what we were thinking. But just us, we don't have any family we want to invite."

"It's easy enough to make that happen relatively quickly, especially since Father Roarke is in town. Think about it. We'll still have the stuff up from Airiella's wedding. Just go get the license."

"You make it sound so simple." Jillian smiled.

"It is. Talk to Smitty about it after your announcement, and I'll make sure not to take everything down right away. Let me know, and I can help you get everything squared away." Chrissie grinned in anticipation.

Jillian's eyes shone, and she wrapped Chrissie up in a hug. "You are amazing."

"Tomorrow night, women's night, we'll have no alcohol since you can't drink, neither will Tama or Onida. She just wants a girl's night instead of a bachelorette party. Weather will be perfect, so we can do a bonfire on the beach and just chill, or we can do movies and spa stuff."

"Why can't we do both?"

"We could. Jax doesn't want to do anything. He said he'd rather stay close by, and he and the guys could just do guy time in the gym," Chrissie explained, knowing Jillian would understand.

"I should have thought about that. No way would he leave her right now. Not even knowing she was with all of us. Smitty hasn't told me any of what she remembered; he's been pretty closed lips about it. I'm gathering it's bad."

"What he did was rape her. That's all anyone needs to know. It's the fallout that's bad, the memories that get triggered, and how it correlates to where she is. She's also associating it with what happened to me. Since we bonded, hers seems to trigger mine, and if I have one, it triggers hers." Chrissie shrugged, not wanting to get into it.

"Shitty situation. We'll get both of your heads away from all that. Anything you need help with food-wise?"

"Nope! Ordered a variety of Mexican food, enough to cover everyone here. We can eat and put on some cheesy rom-com movie and do each other's nails and toes, then go out and chill by the waves with a bonfire if you think we should do both," Chrissie thought out loud.

"Let's do the food and movies first, maybe a couple of movies, giving us a lot of time to let the nails dry. Then let's ask the guys if they want to do the bonfire with us. We can do guys against girl's games."

"Oh, I like that! Great idea! How about how well do you know your partner type of game? We can come up with questions that each side will have to answer." Chrissie got excited about that.

"Perfect!" Jillian cried. "We don't even have to go to the beach to do it; we can do that in the backyard so that we can just wait until the kids go to sleep."

Chrissie heard the beep of the gate opening. "They're here."

Mags came up behind them. "Good timing. Babies went down for a nap."

They headed out to the front to meet the gang, Jace, Rafe, and Bryce, flying out the door ahead of them. The moment Bryce saw Ronnie, he was in motion at full speed, Rafe right behind him veering towards Airiella. Jace was a bit slower but headed towards Ronnie as well.

Bryce launched his little body as hard as he could, and Ronnie swept him up, tossing him up in the air, his delighted squeals making Chrissie's heart light and happy. He fist-bumped Jace then swept him up in a hug too. Surprisingly, Jace let him. Then Rafe jumped right out of Airiella's arms into Ronnie's free one and clung to him.

Ronnie headed for Chrissie and set the boys down, who ran for Jax next. "Hey, beautiful," he breathed and kissed her stupid. "I've missed waking up with you."

"Really?" she said breathlessly.

"Really. Stay with me tonight?"

"What about the boys?" she worried.

"Bryce called me Daddy; I don't think they will care." Ronnie chuckled.

Chrissie saw Airiella herding the boys away from Smitty, who grabbed the luggage out of the back of the SUV. "We need to help get the boys away from Smitty, Jillian needs to talk to him. Alone."

"Everything okay?" Ronnie looked concerned. "Is she upset with how much time he's spending with Airiella?"

"No, not at all, they just need to talk. Don't you worry about it; Jace asked me if I was dating you, I told him I was."

"Is that all you said?" Ronnie's attention was diverted from Smitty to her now.

"What was I supposed to say?" Chrissie was surprised by his response.

"He asked me if I loved you. I told him that I did, that I loved all of you, the boys included. He was satisfied with that. He also asked me for some alone time to talk about things said at school. Jax asked if he could be a part of the training session I scheduled with him and Jace was cool with that."

Chrissie gathered the boys and led them back into the house where Rafe trailed after Airiella and Bryce and Jace followed Ronnie. "Chris, I want to cook tonight," Airiella called back over her shoulder. "Rafe can help me, right buddy?"

"Can I Mommy?" he asked excitedly.

"Just as long as you do exactly what Auntie Ells tells you to do," Chrissie warned him. Her family was home; all felt right in the world at the moment. Love filled the house.

"How about we do a special macaroni and cheese,

but not out of a box, made from scratch?" she heard Airiella telling Rafe.

"Macaroni and cheese is my favorite!"

"Mine too. We have to have vegetables too, or Ronnie will never let me hear the end of it. What vegetable should we do?"

"Trees!" Chrissie laughed at Rafe's response. Moving here had been the best decision she'd ever made, despite the nightmare Travis had created.

She headed over to Jax, who was watching Rafe and Airiella unpack the bags. "Jax, I don't think I could ever thank you enough for what you've done for the boys and me." Chrissie leaned up against him, his arm going over her shoulders.

"I'm happy I did it. I meant it, Chris. You are part of the family. How've you been?"

"Rough spots here and there, but I'm surviving." She was comfortable with Jax, and she finally drew the parallel between Ronnie, her, and Jax that Airiella had mentioned was similar to her situation.

Jax kissed her on the head. "We'll get through it, Chris. Thanks for all the work on the wedding you've done. Anything you need me to do to help?"

"No, it's all taken care of; you can tell me your secret honeymoon plans," she tried.

Jax threw his head back and laughed. "You and Airiella are way too much alike for me to tell you that. She'd know in a heartbeat. Nice try, though."

Chrissie filled Jax in on the plans Jillian, and she had come up with for the next night, and Jax was all for it. "Want me to get Rafe away, so you have a moment with her?"

"No, they both need this. I'm going to have Ells for the rest of my life. I don't mind sharing."

"She lucked out with you, Jax," she said and she squeezed him.

"I'm the lucky one, Chris. She is the reason I am alive. Loving Airiella is the reason for my creation."

Chrissie breathed out. "I can only hope that my relationship with Ronnie will be strong like what you have with Ells."

Jax looked down at her. "You can take that to the bank and deposit it. It's a guarantee I feel more than comfortable making. Ronnie has never lit up for anyone other than Airiella the way he lights up for you. You bring it out in him even more than she did."

"I hope I'm enough for him," Chrissie admitted.

"Why the hell would you think you aren't?" Jax asked angrily. "Because of what that fucking bastard of an ex-husband put you through? Please tell me you don't believe any of the horseshit that was said to you by him."

"Most of the time, I don't. I have weak moments the same as Ells." Chrissie fought back against the shame.

Jax softened. "Ronnie would be lucky to have you and these boys. You are nothing short of amazing, Chris. Beautiful, intelligent, excellent mother, a loving, and intuitive friend, selfless, and funny. I can't think of a more perfect match for Ronnie. You complement each other."

"Airiella is a perfect match for him too," Chrissie said quietly.

"In many ways, but not the ways that you are. Airiella's said it so many times that she could have easily chosen Ronnie and given up on me. She said being with him would be so easy. It's true, it would have been, and I wouldn't have stood in her way. Ronnie deserves love and happiness. Airiella gave him that, but she also brought you into his life. She loves him, and she loves him wholly, and she still needs Ronnie every bit as much as he needs her. Chrissie, what you aren't seeing, is that he needs *you* just as much, if not more."

"I feel like I'm taking him from her," Chrissie admitted shyly.

"You aren't. While it would have been easy to be with Ronnie, she didn't want that. She knows you are the one for him. Sadly, what he needs, she can't give him."

"There isn't anything that woman can't do." Chrissie stood straight and looked at him. She could feel the fire in her eyes.

"Chris, he needs a family." Jax's quiet response threw her off.

"You are his family! Airiella is his family."

"Chrissie." Jax pushed her gently into the hallway. "You don't understand me; you, your boys, a family. He craves that; Ronnie's always wanted children. Yes, things with Airiella would have been fine if she wanted to go that route. There would always be that lacking between them, though."

"Ronnie freaked out when we didn't use protection," she said blandly, her mind racing now.

"If Ronnie freaked out, it was because he was concerned for you. I know Ronnie better than anyone else. He is madly and deeply in love with you. You check all the boxes he has and ones he hasn't even admitted to himself. Airiella doesn't need protection, and he craves giving it."

"You don't want kids?" Chrissie asked, mulling over Jax's words.

"I could go either way with that. My lifestyle doesn't give me a lot of leeway for them. But I'd probably also lean towards adopting one if we decided on that route. When we were kids, Ronnie used to talk about the things he would do with a kid when he had one. He never said if he always said when."

I can't believe you are still worried about this. Never forget your worth, Chris. Ronnie is the one for you. He always has been. Jax is the one for me. I couldn't be more certain about this.

Chrissie cringed. "Damn it, she can hear us; now I'm in trouble."

Jax hugged her again. "Rafe will distract her. I've got a date with Ronnie and Jace now."

Airiella appeared in the doorway, a hard look on her face. "Go get Bryce; he can help me too. You need to get your head on straight. I saw how he was when he talked to you."

"He looks at you the same way, Ells," Chrissie argued weakly.

"No one denies the love we have for each other. Yes, it's there, it always will be. You just deny that the love he has for you is greater than the love he has for me. And that's how it should be."

Chrissie had nothing to say to that and turned to get Bryce. She found Ronnie lying across his bed with his knees up and Bryce sitting on him, leaning on Ronnie's knees and talking about the dump truck. He was so patient and loving with her boys, and Bryce was head over heels in love with Ronnie.

She hated to interrupt, but Jace was waiting for him. "Bryce, come with me. Auntie Ells needs our help in making dinner."

He flopped forward on Ronnie's chest. "But I'm talking with my Daddy."

Chrissie bit her lip, not sure how to respond to that. "It's okay little man. Auntie Ells needs your special help, and I have to see Jace for a little bit before dinner. Then after dinner, all of us are going to go out to the gym and have some fun. I have special gloves for you."

"Really?" he cried.

"Really. Come on, let's go." He sat up, and Bryce giggled, wrapping his arms around Ronnie's neck. He carried him over to her, kissing her softly. Ronnie made her knees weak. She took Bryce from him and set him down, and he promptly took off for the kitchen.

"You don't have to let him call you daddy," Chrissie murmured.

"I kinda love it that he does." Ronnie kissed her again, backing her up against the door frame, his hard body molding to her soft one. "If I don't stop, I'm not going to be able to," he rasped. "I need a cold shower now. God, I've missed you."

Chrissie grinned. "I kinda like hearing that. Go on, take care of Jace. It sounds like you have a busy night."

"This session with Jax and I will only be about forty minutes. After dinner settles, we'll do another forty with all of us, then he and I will spend an hour together. After that, it's you and me."

"Looking forward to it," she whispered, brushing her lips across his.

Chapter Twenty-One

R onnie somehow managed to make it through the night without giving away what he was feeling. He'd had a long talk with Jace, and now nerves were all he had. He had a lot at stake and needed to work everything through. And that's how he found himself on their bachelor time.

They were all joking around, sparring, telling stories, and having fun. Only Jax picked up on the tension that was peeking through in him. "What's going on?"

"Nothing. I'm good." Ronnie smiled easily.

"Liar. How long have I known you?"

"Too long. It's nothing for you to worry about; just shit in my head," Ronnie threw back at him.

"I might be able to help."

"Quite possibly, but then I'd never know if I could take care of it on my own." Ronnie desperately wanted to talk it out with Jax. "If I haven't figured it out by the time the wedding is over, we'll talk. How's that?"

"I don't like it, but I'll accept it."

"And that right there is why our angel is marrying you." Ronnie grinned.

"I hope it's for more than blind support."

"Are you having doubts?" Ronnie stopped moving and gave Jax a close look.

"Hardly. I keep comparing myself to you because of a talk I had with Chrissie. We all know how in love with Airiella you are, and it makes me wonder if it was supposed to be you. If you'd be the better choice and if I took that away from you. I don't doubt my love for her, for you, or what we all have together."

"Jax, please tell me you don't think that." Ronnie was stunned.

"I don't. But I keep wondering."

"If she wanted me, she would have told you no." Ronnie knew that, for sure.

"What if she said yes to me because she believes Chrissie is the one for you?"

Ronnie wasn't sure what Jax was doing here, but it felt wrong to hear him say that. "Airiella has this all-encompassing love for you that nothing else even comes close to; anyone around both of you can feel it. What she feels for the rest of us is a mere shadow. Not to put her love down, it's just different from you. What we all have with her is damn amazing, and I can't imagine life without that. Yes, I'm in love with her. So are Aedan and Smitty. But when we look at the both of you together, it's perfect. You are what we all aspire to be with our chosen one."

"You don't wonder?"

"I did at first. I don't anymore. I can't be what you are to Airiella. None of us can. Not even combined. She was always right in saying that she and I would be easy, it would, and we have enough love to make it last. It wouldn't be right, though. We would always feel like something was missing, and it would be. I'm not quiet because I'm upset about this. I'm working through some other things in my head," Ronnie tried to reassure him.

"Maybe I just needed to hear it from you. I'd call it all off if I thought that this was leaving you hurt."

"You two are made for each other. That could never hurt me. Besides, I am positive that Airiella was right, Chrissie is custom made for me." Ronnie let the grin split his face at that statement.

"Is that what you are working through; are you going to take this farther?"

Ronnie gave him a slow nod. "I have some conversations with some little ones before I do."

"Then, I *can* help you. Come with me." Jax tugged on his arm and gave him an odd look. "Guys, I need a manly moment with Ronnie, we will be right back."

"Manly moment? You two going to go make out?" Smitty cackled in laughter.

"Jealous?" Ronnie called back. "I'll save some for you." He waggled his eyebrows and rotated his hips.

Aedan howled and motioned for them to go. Ronnie followed Jax out behind the gym and listened to what he had to say. A picture started to form in his head, and he began to see it all come together. "Shit, you are a fucking genius. I can't believe you kept this from us."

"I was going to announce it at the reception." Jax grinned. "There's not a lot that you can hide from me anymore, Ronan Byrne. I knew what you were thinking." Jax pulled out a paper and handed it to him. "Go see this guy tomorrow, while things are crazy here with Ells family arriving."

Ronnie crushed Jax in a huge hug. "You are the

best." He heard footsteps and looked behind him to see Aedan and Smitty peering around the corner. "Go with me on this," Ronnie whispered.

"I'm with you."

Ronnie squished Jax's cheeks between his palms and planted a big wet kiss on his lips. At the sound of Aedan's howling laughter, they turned around and saw Smitty standing there with a confused look on his face.

"You seriously were making out?"

Ronnie stepped behind Jax, who was laughing himself and grabbed the hose, quietly turning it on. In a quick move, he stepped from behind Jax and sprayed the two of them then bolted off running around the side of the gym.

While it hadn't been a traditional bachelor party, their group was anything but conventional, and they'd had a blast anyway. Father Roarke, Taklishim, and Degataga had come upon them having a water fight, and it took off from there.

Later, they all sat around the fire pit telling stories about their childhoods and the crazy things they had gotten into; Ronnie was a little surprised by some of the stories that Airiella and Chrissie shared. The two had been fearless and a bit reckless, and their stories had them crying; they laughed so hard.

"Okay, boys, we've got a game for you now. After some important news." Jillian grinned.

"Please tell me it's spin the bottle." Mags laughed. "I've been dying to lock lips with that giant beast there," she said and she pointed at Ronnie.

"Excuse me?" Aedan threw a marshmallow at her.

"I'm joking. Maybe." Mags grinned at him.

Ronnie stood up casually and walked around the fire and hoisted Mags up into his arms. "The least I could do is plant one on you after you named a kid after me. I am pretty legendary," he said and he gave her a creepy smile that had her giggling like crazy.

"Put me down, you big ape. It'd be like kissing Jax." Mags laughed.

"Um, Mags, Jax is pretty good at that, so you'd better find a different argument," Airiella said quickly.

"Ronnie is too," Chrissie added, making a kissy face.

"I'm not sharing, kiss your husband," Jillian stated. "Can I finish talking now?"

"Yes!" Airiella shouted happily.

"Art and I are having a baby!" she crowed, and Mags screamed, jumping at her.

"Given that, we've decided to have an impromptu wedding here about a week after yours," Smitty told Jax. "Chrissie has offered to help get everything set up for us. I just want it to be us here," he said and he gestured to the group. "Onida, if you aren't popping your babies out, we'd love it if you were our doctor."

"It would be an honor," Onida said with a smile.

"Holy shit. Wow..." Ronnie breathed, "...congratulations!"

"Do your thing, baby," Jax told her.

Airiella went over to Jillian and put her hand on her belly and grabbed Smitty's hand so they could hear the heartbeat together. Smitty was practically glowing with happiness. "Come on, the rest of you that want to hear, come here," Airiella told them.

Ronnie was the first there and put his big hand half over Airiella's and half on Jillian. The little fluttering heartbeat loud in his ears brought tears to his eyes. "Amazing. You are going to be awesome parents, and I can't wait to teach this kid all sorts of ways to piss you off."

He went and sat back down and started wishing on stars for his happy ending. "Now, about that game," Chrissie broke in. "Guys against girls. Who knows their partner better. No cheating Airiella, you have to close down your connections."

Chrissie handed them all little pads of paper and pens. "We are going to ask questions, and you have to answer by writing your answers down, and then we will give the responses to Father Roarke since he's probably the only trustworthy one to reveal honest answers." Jillian's eyes were sparkling.

Ronnie felt distinctly at a disadvantage, Chrissie, and he had only recently gotten involved. He must have frowned because Airiella popped into his head.

The questions are fair. Chrissie made sure of that.

Ronnie winked at her. "Who thought up the questions?"

"I did, son," Father Roarke answered happily. "Chrissie had final approval."

"Let's do this." Aedan laughed. "We can share a piece of paper, so we aren't wasteful. Since Smitty is on the end, he can write his answer with his name on it, and so on. Just pass it down."

"Fair enough." Chrissie smiled.

"What is your partner's favorite movie?" Father Roarke read the first question.

Ronnie cringed. They'd only discussed movies once. He thought about it until the paper was passed to him, grinning when he saw Jax's answer. "Wrong one, dude," he told him and scribbled down his answer for Chrissie and then another adding Airiella's name to it.

Father Roarke read the answers, leaving them all in hysterics at Mags and Aedan, who got them both right. Taklishim answered one for Airiella too. Jax had answered Thor, Ronnie had written down Avengers, and Taklishim had written down Justice League.

"There's a theme here." Jillian grinned at Airiella. "I'm sensing a hot guy theme. Which one is it?"

"Well, they are all right; for hotness, I'd say Taklishim was right because well, Jason Momoa. Jax is also right, because, well, Thor. But for entertainment purposes, I'd have to say it is Avengers. Can we just call that one a tie? I'd be hard pressed to pick just one of those."

"No ties," Ronnie called out. "Jax loses that one." He stuck his tongue out at Airiella. "I'd get two points because I got both of them right."

At the end of the night, they were all tied except Mags and Aedan, and Tama and Taklishim. They won hands down. "Relationship goals," Aedan quipped, pointing to himself and Mags. "You should aim to be us."

Jax threw his pen at his brother while Airiella climbed on his lap, looking happier than Ronnie had seen her in the past couple of weeks. Ronnie tossed Chrissie over his shoulder caveman-style and beat his chest, then laughed. "Sorry, I can't pull it off. I'm not a caveman, but I am going to carry her to bed this way. Goodnight, all."

Chrissie tried to quiet her laughter as he carried her up the stairs and to his room. "Tonight, you are mine."

"I'm yours every night," she corrected him.

Chapter Twenty-Two

Chrissie scurried around, making sure Airiella's family got situated as she rearranged the boys sleeping arrangements to fit Nicks girls in, giving her room to Nick. Thank goodness Jax had bought a giant house. It was full up.

Chrissie had initially planned a rehearsal dinner at a restaurant that had a fantastic view, but Airiella's mom had suggested that she and Airiella's nanie make dinner instead. Chrissie gladly handed over the reins on that one, knowing that whatever they made would be fantastic.

All the aunts, uncles, and cousins were situated in their hotels and would come for dinner. Jax's mother had flown in and wanted to stay at a hotel, but would be here for dinner. Chrissie took the cooks to the grocery store, bought the food, and carted them back.

The boys, Nick's daughters, and the babies were all at the beach with Aedan and Nick, and a few of the cousin's kids were in the pool with Ronnie watching over them. Jax had claimed Emma as soon as Stephanie got there, and Airiella was nowhere to in sight.

Ells?

Just needed a moment alone, Chris. I'm fine. She responded immediately.

Where are you?

Hiding in my closet. Chrissie smothered a laugh and sought Jax out.

"Hey, before I go barge in, any idea why Ells is hiding in her closet?"

"She's overwhelmed. The sudden noise and commotion triggered a bit of panic, and the closet was the only place she calmed down."

"Okay, I'm on it." Chrissie turned, and Jax stopped her.

"Airiella's okay, Chris. I wouldn't have left her if she wasn't."

"I know. You should take Emma to play with the babies on the beach," Chrissie suggested.

"I don't want to share her yet. She's so freaking cute I can't stand it." Jax grinned.

His words sunk into Chrissie's mind, and his conversation about Ronnie wanting a family popped up. Jax was a natural and would be a fantastic father. It made her heart hurt that Airiella wouldn't get to experience motherhood in the same way, even if she did adopt.

"Hey, Chris. You don't have a poker face; you know that?" Jax was suddenly by her side. "This is enough for me. Don't be sad for us. We've talked about this a lot, and if she wants to have a child, we decided we would adopt an older one who needed us more than a baby would."

Chrissie but her lips as tears pooled in her eyes. "That's exactly something she would do. She would always go for the unwanted first."

"So would I, Chris." Jax tapped her cheek. "Clear

that up and go check on her."

Chrissie headed back into the house, staying away from the kitchen and not wanting to get in the way. She knew how Airiella's mom was in the kitchen. Once she felt in control of her emotions. she climbed the stairs and went to Airiella's room, closing and locking the door behind her.

Chrissie crossed the room and entered the large closet. She didn't need to turn the light on to know that she would be in the corner; she just felt her way along the wall and dropped next to Airiella. "Your family is still as chaotic as ever."

Airiella laughed. "Why do you think I am in here?"

"Jax said you had a moment earlier." Chrissie called her out on it.

"I did. I'm better now."

"Did you try on the dress?" Chrissie reached over and felt around for Airiella's hand and holding it.

"I did. It fits perfectly. Thanks for all your work on this, Chrissie."

"No doubts?" She pushed, something still felt off to her.

"About Jax? Not a single one. About being the center of attention? Shit tons."

Ah, now she understood. "Did you write your vows?"

"No, but I know what I want to say. Do you think Stolas will come?"

"I don't know, Ells. It might be hard for him to watch you get married when he's so in love with you." Chrissie felt a pang of sadness.

"Yeah, that was my thought too."

"He might come to the dinner tonight, you never

know." Chrissie vowed to call him as soon as she got out of the closet. "You need to see him?"

"Something in me feels like I need to. I don't know why. I don't want Taklishim to go all warrior mode in front of my family, though. The demon battle they saw was enough to scar them for a lifetime."

"That reminds me, the boys, and I think your wings should be out for the ceremony," Chrissie remembered.

"They do?" She sounded unsure about it. "What if there's press hiding?"

"Cameras would give them away. Jax isn't worried about the press, neither is Ronnie, or both would have said something to me. Your nanie and mom are in the kitchen cooking, so don't go in there. Stephanie is here, and Jax hijacked Emma and won't share her."

Airiella laughed at that. "Well, she is pretty cute. And so noted, not going near the kitchen. What should I wear?"

"This is about you and what you are comfortable with; wear whatever you want." Chrissie squeezed her hand.

The light in the closet came on, causing both of them to gasp in fright, and then Chrissie saw Stolas standing there. His face was handsome as ever. "You lovely ladies keep saying my name, and here I am."

"Stolas." Airiella stood and threw herself at him. "I'm so happy to see you!"

Chrissie stood up and kissed his cheek. "I'm going to give you a moment. Airiella, your bedroom door is locked, so we are alone. I'll go wait in the bathroom."

Chrissie left them in the closet and went to the bathroom and checked her little bit of makeup she put on.

She checked her nails and toes and fussed with her hair, just to occupy herself. She kept getting flashes of emotions from Airiella, and she was concerned.

She waited about fifteen minutes before she heard the closet door open, and she peeked out of the bathroom to see Stolas sitting in one of the chairs in the bedroom. She went and sat in the one opposite of him and gave him a look.

"You were right, you know? About me not wanting to see her get married."

"Yet, here you are." Chrissie studied his face for a tell on what he was thinking.

"I'm so in tuned to both you and Airiella that when you say my name, I'm ready to go on a moment's notice, no matter what I find myself doing."

"Me? Why? Airiella, I understand." Chrissie wrung her hands, unsure of what to think about that.

"Why not you? You accepted me and believed the best about me from the start, even though I am a prince of Hell."

"Your heart defines you, not your title." Chrissie caught a flash of something before he controlled his face again. "I can't read you, Stolas."

"In my position, it's a necessity. Regardless, you are correct. I am here. I agreed to be at the wedding; however, my compromise was that I would be attending in my raven form. I'm not comfortable being seen at a holy ceremony, but she has informed me how much it would mean to her. It would be quite selfish of me to deny her request, and both of you make me want to be better."

"Don't change because of someone else; change to stay true to your heart and who you are. The right people will love you." She saw how much this man, demon, fallen angel, whatever he was, how much he loved.

"Why do you, Chrissie?"

"Love you?" She was puzzled by his question.

"Yes."

"Because you have done nothing but protect us, me, my family, Airiella. You've gone out of your way to show kindness to my son, to save them both at risk to yourself; why would I not love someone who puts people that mean the most to me above themselves? You add value to my life, and I have great admiration for you," Chrissie told him honestly.

His face softened. "Both of you have given me a reason to believe in love again. I harbor no resentment for Jax, or Ronnie, as I know that is who you both belong with, yet still, I find love in my heart for both of you."

Chrissie didn't know the story of who Stolas was before he became a prince of Hell, but in her heart, she knew he had been kind. Compelled by his softened face that revealed that side of him, and his solemn tone, Chrissie stood and wrapped her arms around his shoulders in a hug.

"You'll always have a place in my heart, Stolas."

Airiella opened the closet door and stepped out in the skirt she was wearing in a couple of the pictures Jax and Ronnie had taken of her in their early days. She looked like a beautiful, wild, and free soul. Except her eyes were red and puffy.

"Stolas made me cry." Airiella rubbed at her eyes.

Chrissie shot a glance at the seated demon, who smiled genially. "I would do no such thing. This outfit suits you well, love. It's the one I first saw you in."

"Jax bought it for me not long after we met. He said

he saw it and thought of me."

"He was right, he picked well." Chrissie pulled Airiella in the bathroom and handed her some eye drops. "Put these in, then put a cool washcloth over your eyes for a few minutes." Chrissie looked back at Stolas. "Unless you have some magical elixir hidden in those deep pockets of yours that will fix this?"

A smile lit his face, and Stolas pulled out a small container that looked like it had lotion in it. "Rub this under your eyes, and the swelling will go down. The eye drops will take the red away."

"How do you do that?" Chrissie asked, stunned. "You just pull things right out of those pockets that we need."

"I anticipate situations when it comes to this one. Given the events of the past few weeks, I gathered emotions would be high. I also usually have pain gel in there, as well as a mix that takes bruises away, as she usually finds herself needing one or the other."

Airiella laughed. "He knows his audience." She rubbed the lotion under her eyes and on her eyelids, a soft fragrance drifting to Chrissie's nose. "Did you scent this?" Airiella turned to look at Stolas.

"I did, with jasmine. I can't smell that blasted flower without thinking of you now."

Now Chrissie laughed. "Same here!"

"Chris, is there a hairdresser coming tomorrow?"

"Yes, why?" A note of something in Airiella's voice silenced both her and Stolas as they waited for Airiella's reply.

"I think I want to cut this off before the wedding," she said and she held out her hair.

"Why would you do that?" Stolas crossed the room and stood beside her, his fingers lightly holding a ringlet curl.

"I cut it all the time. About every other year, and I donate it to a charity that makes wigs for children who suffer hair loss. Either from medical treatment, like cancer, or a medical condition, like alopecia. I think it would be a good way to feel like I'm starting new."

"We can make it happen, Ells," Chrissie said quietly.

"Never have I seen another quite like you before in all my years. You take my breath away each time we are together in a new way. May I have a lock when you cut it? It will be with the feather, and if I need to find you, I can use it. Also, it's a selfish request for another piece of you."

"Sure. Cut a piece off now if you'd like." Airiella handed Stolas a pair of scissors from the drawer.

Chrissie silently watched as Stolas studied the mane of curls in front of him. "To what length?" he asked her. Airiella showed him, and Stolas clipped a small lock of hair, a perfect curl that showed all the colors of her hair. Airiella handed Stolas a rubber band, and he carefully put it around the lock, and slid it into his pocket. "Thank you, love."

"Are you sure about cutting it all off, Ells?" Chrissie asked.

"I am. It seems fitting to shed the past couple of years the day I start a new journey. It's just hair, mine grows fast, Chris."

"I know, I'm always jealous of that. Jax loves your hair, though." Chrissie stroked the silky curls.

"He'll still love it. Don't tell him, or Ronnie, or anyone," she firmly told them both.

"Got it," Chrissie grumbled. "Your eyes are good

now. If you are putting makeup on, do it now before someone comes up here looking for you."

"No makeup tonight." She ran her fingers through her hair and shook it out a little, the shorter strands disappearing in the mix of the rest. "I'm going as is."

"May I have a last kiss?" Stolas asked.

Airiella grinned and paused a moment. Chrissie knew she was asking Jax, and as she leaned forward and kissed him again, she marveled at how Jax trusted her with other men. Not that Chrissie thought Airiella would ever cheat, just that she didn't believe Ronnie would willingly give her permission to kiss someone else.

Yes, he would, Chris. If you asked him, he would.

Startled by Airiella in her head, she looked up and watched the tender kiss that she knew Stolas was using as a goodbye kiss. "Beautiful," he breathed into her neck before turning away. Chrissie caught the flash of tears in his eyes.

"It's not goodbye," Chrissie told him quietly and stood on her tiptoes and brushed her lips across his. She kissed a demon. Her brain stumbled on that a little bit. "Once she loves you, she will always love you."

In a surprising move, Stolas crushed her in a binding hug, and she realized he was trying to gain control of his emotions. She held him tight until she felt him start to release her, and she looked up at his face. Handsome and back under control. "Thank you for that."

Airiella smirked from behind them. "If you didn't have Ronnie, I'd totally be setting you up with him."

Stolas laughed at Chrissie's blush. "Let's get you to that party down there. Please only introduce me as a work friend if anyone asks."

Stolas held out both his arms, and Chrissie and

Airiella took them and let him lead them down to the party. It went well, and Chrissie found herself trailing Stolas to make sure that he was fine. Ronnie came up to her, catching on to what she was doing.

"You know he can take care of himself, right? He's not someone that gives the impression it's okay to mess with him," Ronnie said with a grin.

"I know, he's just feeling vulnerable, and I want to make sure if it becomes too much, he has a friendly face to lean on," Chrissie explained softly.

Ronnie smiled. "I love you so damn much. Pretty sure Stolas is halfway in love with you too."

He appeared in front of them. "You are correct, Ronan. Though again, I am aware she is yours."

Chrissie blushed again. "I have no idea how Airiella handled all the attention of you men."

"We drove her crazy most of the time," Ronnie admitted. "Always breathing down her neck, and then in her head with the bonds. Man overload. Good thing that you, Jillian, and Mags are close by."

Stolas chuckled. "I think the women rule this group."

"Right you are!" Ronnie threw his head back and laughed. "We all know it too."

"I must go now. I've ignored a few calls already and don't want anyone to come looking for me. The warrior wouldn't be happy."

"You'll keep your promise for tomorrow?" Chrissie watched his face for signs of backing out.

"I will. You have my word."

Ronnie glanced between them and shrugged. "Come through to the front, no people out there, and you can disappear without someone noticing."

Ronnie took off with Stolas, and Chrissie found an empty chair to sit down on for a minute. One of Airiella's cousins, Gabby, if she remembered correctly, came up and asked, "Are you with Ronnie?"

"Yes." She kept her answer simple. She remembered Airiella talking about how Gabby was in love with them all and followed them like a puppy when she was around them.

"He's so hot. I'd be nervous every time he left that someone would hit on him," Gabby babbled.

"I trust him. He's not like that." Chrissie smiled politely.

Ells, if your cousin is going to keep talking about how hot Ronnie is, I'm going to throw her in the pool.

Let me guess, Gabby?

That's the one.

Throw her in. I'm okay with it.

Chrissie smothered a laugh and saw Ronnie approaching. She stood up and motioned him to sit down, and she sat on his lap. Petty, but she didn't care. Gabby just gaped at her and mumbled. "The boys are getting tired," Ronnie said. "Want me to go put them down?"

"I'll help. Stolas get off okay?" She was just ignoring Gabby now.

"He did. You got him to promise to be here tomorrow?"

"I didn't, Ells did." Chrissie saw Gabby moving away. "You know how she is."

"I do. It won't be easy for Stolas. He admitted it before he left."

"I know. Stolas told me too. He's going to be in

raven form. Pretty sure that Airiella will have hers go sit with him." Chrissie leaned against his chest, her neck on his shoulder, so she stared up at the sky.

"You look amazing, by the way. So does our angel. How'd you get her to wear that?"

"It was all her, that wasn't me. Is it bad?" Chrissie had heard a tone in his voice, almost melancholic.

"No, not at all. That's what Airiella wore that day on the beach. The day she faced down her past. I think it might be the only other time that Airiella wore that skirt. That was also the day that things between her and Jax changed. They grew so much closer. So it is a perfect outfit for her to wear, and Jax was so happy to see her in it."

"Airiella's talked about that day before. Not in a whole lot of detail, but she told me how healing it was for her. How you all were there, helping her through it all." It was something Chrissie had to read between the lines on, the things that Airiella hadn't said that told Chrissie just how hard that day had been.

"Airiella took me apart that day. I broke under all those emotions. She released the walls holding them back and took every single one of us down, literally. Then she had to pull them from us again. Looking back on it, I never thought I would love anyone other than her. Now I have you here, and I can't imagine loving anyone more than I love you."

Chrissie held her breath and looked at him. His words were ringing in her head. "You love me more than you love her?"

"I do," he said wistfully. "It's kinda scary to say that out loud. There isn't a person left here right now that doesn't know how much I love Airiella. Knowing that I love you more than that, with all the shit we've been through, terrifies me right down to my soul. I may become that overprotective guy again," he warned her sheepishly.

"It's okay with me. It feels nice. I've never had anyone other than Airiella be like that with me," Chrissie admitted. She loved that protective side of him.

"That right there solidifies my thoughts that Airiella wasn't ever my future, no matter how much I wanted it to be true. That part of me drove her a little crazy at times."

Chrissie felt like taking a play out of Jillian's handbook and proposing to him right now. She was overcome with emotions and felt a weird sensation crawling under her skin. She looked around for Airiella and found her across the yard, watching her closely, a small smile on her face.

What is this feeling?

It's your soul realizing its soul mate. Intense, isn't it?

Did you feel this with each of them? Chrissie couldn't imagine that.

To a degree, the intensity was different with Jax; off the charts crazy. A little intense with Ronnie too, but I always knew that he wasn't just mine. I'm happy you finally see it.

It's making me lose rational thought, Chrissie admitted.

I know. Trust your instincts.

Chrissie took Ronnie's hand. "Let's go put those monsters to bed, and then you can take me to yours."

Ronnie stood in a flash. "No arguments here."

They made quick work of getting the boys to bed, and Chrissie was innately happy that Jax had insisted on hiring a cleanup crew. Chrissie and Ronnie put the night to good use, tasting as much of his body as he sampled hers.

He let her do whatever she wanted, even when it made him feel like he had no control over his body. It was magical, passionate, and fiery. He put every one of her fears to rest. She had never known love like this before, and she would do whatever it took to keep him.

When she woke in the morning, he was still asleep. She kissed him softly and grabbed the things she needed to get ready for the day, sneaking out and heading downstairs to get everything set in motion. As soon as Airiella was up, she shooed Jax away and locked them in her room.

"You sure about the hair?" Chrissie asked again.

"Positive. When is the stylist going to be here?"

"Any minute now. I changed the time to account for the cut. So go shower so your hair will be wet. I need to go grab my clothes from my room and make a few calls to make sure everything is on time," Chrissie ordered her around.

"Love you, Chris."

"Love you, Ells."

Chapter Twenty-Three

R onnie paced, his nerves getting the better of him. "Okay, are you all ready?" he asked for the third time.

Jax laughed. "Calm down. She doesn't know, and she will love it. Do I have this on, right?"

Ronnie checked him over, the tuxedo fitting him perfectly. "You do."

Jillian whistled as she came into the room. "Damn, you men look smoking hot. Jax, a tux suits you."

"They doing okay?" Ronnie asked Jillian.

"I assume so; they wouldn't let me in. Chrissie said no one got to see her until she walks down the aisle."

"No one?" Ronnie was shocked.

"Nope. Not even her mom or dad are allowed in." Jillian giggled. "You should have seen her mom's face when they told her that."

Jax laughed again. "I can only imagine."

Smitty walked in and wrapped an arm around Jillian. "Music's all set, I've got the remote in my pocket, and it's programmed down to the minute, so no one better be late."

It was Ronnie's turn to laugh. "Chrissie would come unglued if Airiella weren't on time, I don't think you have to worry there."

The photographer was the only one Chrissie had let into the room to get some shots of getting ready, and now he was down there with them, posing some and getting candid shots as well. Ronnie tried to bribe him to show him some of the photos, but it was pointless. Jamie had been a fantastic choice for a photographer.

It wasn't long before Chrissie herself came down, looking flushed and more beautiful than he'd ever seen her before, all three boys in tow in their little suits. Bryce leaped into Ronnie's arms, and Rafe clung to his leg.

"What's wrong, buddy?" Ronnie asked him quietly.

"I'm scared."

"What are you scared of?" Ronnie squatted down to look in his eyes.

"There are lots of people here, will Auntie Ells be safe?"

"I promise you she will be. Remember that smoky man?" Rafe nodded. "He's here, and he will be protecting all of us."

"I didn't see him," Rafe told him.

"I'll tell you a big secret, as big as the one's about Auntie Ells that you keep. Okay?" Rafe nodded again, his eyes huge. "His name is Stolas, and look out the window, over there." Ronnie pointed to a tree. "See that big black bird?"

"Yes."

"That's him. He can change what he is," Ronnie revealed.

Chrissie gave him a curious glance at the telling of

Stolas's secret. "It's true, baby."

Taklishim walked up. "I'm here too, Rafe. Everyone here will be safe."

"Are you going to yell at Auntie Ells?" Rafe asked innocently.

Ronnie burst out laughing again. "Probably. He's always yelling at her about something. He hasn't learned yet that there's no point to it."

Chrissie had the photographer take some group shots before she ushered some of the group out to their seats and returned with Airiella's parents. "You guys ready for this?"

Jax grinned. "I've never been more ready."

Smitty cued up the music, and Chrissie sent the boys out of the house first. "Follow the path, Jace, lead your brothers, and then sit where I told you to."

Ronnie felt his excitement ratchet up a notch along with his nerves. None of them had been outside yet to see what Chrissie had pulled off. She wanted them all to be surprised. Chrissie sent Smitty and Jillian out first, followed by Aedan and Mags.

She took his arm. "Ready?"

Ronnie nodded and let her lead him. As he stepped out of the house, he gasped. White lights wound around the tops of the trees, along the path through the backyard, and to the beach. Ronnie saw at least a hundred chairs full of people and a wooden altar that Degataga had made specially for the ceremony.

Chrissie had strung solar lights across the top beams, which gave Ronnie the impression of little fairy's. There was a slight breeze blowing, and the fabric on the corners was swaying lightly, the white satin a contrast to the fiery sunset behind them. It looked like a fairytale come to life.

"Holy shit, Chris, this is incredible," Ronnie whispered as they walked down the aisle and found their seats. He grinned at Father Roarke.

Ronnie turned back in time to see Jax's face as he walked out on to the beach with his mom on his arm. His heart swelled at the look on his best friend's face. Jax was practically glowing, his eyes sparkling with a sheen of emotion. Ronnie's tear ducts filled. On cue, the music changed.

Ronnie didn't realize he was holding his breath until Chrissie whispered for him to breathe. He saw the two ravens fly up first and settle on the sand off to the side, and then she appeared. The angel, she was a vision come to life.

Ronnie looked back at Jax and saw the emotions written clearly across his face, plain as day, tears streaming down his face and a smile that would stop the hearts of any female in the area. Ronnie looked back at Airiella.

The gown flowed with her movements, giving her a floating appearance, and it accentuated the curves he loved so much in a perfect way. She stood there not moving, still enough at a distance that he hadn't noticed her hair yet.

Her parents started to move, and she moved with them, as soon as she reached the chairs at the back, her wings flew out in a rush and Ronnie stopped breathing. *Everyone* stopped breathing at the beauty that walked down the aisle. They were in the presence of love itself.

Not one person he could see had a dry eye. Then he noticed her hair. She'd cut it all off! It flowed freely around her face in a bob, the waves and curls enhanced with shiny white beads that looked like starlight, her face lightly made up in a way they weren't used to but made her look like a princess. She was exquisite in every way.

Ronnie sucked in a breath of air as Airiella passed him, his heart galloping in his chest as she walked up to Jax, her face showing the love she had for all of them; the scent of jasmine floating on air behind her. Chrissie squeezed his hand as they sat. Ronnie caught movement out of the corner of his eye and glanced over and saw Kalisha, Winnie, and Airiella's grandfathers' standing there next to the ravens. It had to have been the work of Stolas.

Father Roarke led them through a small mass in honor of her Catholic family, then started in with the ceremony. Ronnie knew that Jax had been struggling to find the right words to say, and he'd written countless versions down and burned them all up. Looking at Jax now, he didn't seem nervous at all. Just filled with the fantastic love they all knew. His voice was pure, clear, and unwavering, and Ronnie had never been more proud of him.

"I didn't know about the vision of us together when you came into the picture. All I knew was I could feel you the moment you stepped into the room. The two halves of myself were at instant odds with each other. The darkness that brought you into my life was determined to make me hate you and hurt you. The man I wanted to become knew without hesitation that you were his. I've never believed in love at first sight and granted, it wasn't exactly that because of the division in me, but it was the most powerful thing I'd ever felt before, on all spectrums. The more I tried to pull away and avoid you, the more I had to be near you. The more I pushed you away, the more I needed to learn about what was in your heart, what made you tick. I wanted to know what put the shadows in your angel eyes that came out when you thought no one was looking, and I wanted to learn how to make them go away. Without that darkness, I would never have learned the beauty of your light. Without the pain I felt, I would never have known that your soft, gentle touch could drive away those bad parts of me I wanted to hide. Airiella, you are my everything, the reason my life makes sense. I promise always to strive to be the better man that you deserve. I give you my heart and soul for safekeeping, and I promise always to hold yours just as safe. I promise I will never intentionally hurt you and always allow you to be who you are. I promise never to hold you back and to always stand by your side in every decision you make and walk through every fire with you. I promise to always fight for you and not against you. Most of all, I can promise you, without a doubt, that I will always be in love with you. Everything that I am is yours. Love wins." Jax slid the ring on her finger and used his thumbs to wipe away the tears from under her eyes, her feathers fluttering in the breeze.

"Jax," Airiella began, her voice that husky tone that Ronnie knew drove Jax crazy. "I knew about the vision of us together before you did, but I didn't believe it, because I am a firm believer in us choosing our own destiny. I never believed I was worthy of the love that everyone was showing to me, not just the love from you that popped up when I least expected it, but all of the team. I wanted to dislike you,; I wanted to believe that you were as bad as the darkness inside you. I wanted to push you away as much as you tried to push me away. I couldn't. Not when every fiber of my being called out for you, no matter how much I fought it. I was terrified of what us being together could mean for me and my heart, I didn't know if I could survive it. I wanted a savior, and for as many times as I told myself it couldn't be you, I was wrong. What I've learned since is that my heart beats for you. Your heart saved mine. Without you, there is no me, just an empty shell of a person. You challenge me, support me, and give me unconditional love no matter how much I push your boundaries. And I'm sure everyone here knows I do exactly that. I know now our love is limitless. I can't promise you that I will make life easy, but I promise always to put us first. I promise you that my love for you will never fade. I promise that every decision I make you will be a part of; I promise always to let you see me, especially the parts that I am scared to show you, even now. I promise that whatever our futures hold, we will face it together, united and unbeatable. Mostly, I can promise you that no love that I feel will compare to the greatness of the love we share. Everything that I am is yours. Love wins."

Ronnie choked back a sob as Airiella slid the ring on Jax's finger, a blue glow enveloping them both, causing the crowd to gasp in awe. The power of love was at work here, and Ronnie felt it welling inside him.

"We aren't done yet, Siren. The group would like to present their vows. While legally, we can't all be married to each other; we all felt that they deserved their say because they are just as tied to you as I am."

Ronnie looked over at Smitty and whispered, "This is good practice for you." He patted Smitty on the shoulder, giving him a gentle push.

"Yeah, thanks," Smitty fired back, though his smile was as bright as his eyes. He walked up to Airiella and took one of her hands, Jax holding the other. "Airiella, baby girl,

I was your first connection, and it was an experience I'm not likely ever to forget. My vow to you is always to be your voice of reason when things get confusing. I'll pull you back from the edge and wrap my love around you until you can see the path again. Because of you, I'm marrying the love of my life. Jillian and I will always help give your wings a lift." He leaned in and kissed her cheek and then the back of her hand and returned to his chair.

"Well said," Ronnie granted him, giving him a nudge with his elbow. "You're glowing now too."

Aedan and Mags stood up, distributing babies all around and made their way to Airiella. Aedan spoke first. "Airiella, we were your next connections, and Smitty put it perfectly, it's not an experience that is forgettable. The gifts you've brought to our lives are indescribable, and I can find no adequate words to say about how you've changed our lives. You said I brought you a feeling of solace and acceptance. My vow is always to accept you as you are despite any contradictory beliefs I have in my head and to deliver solace in times of chaos. My arms will always be available to calm the storms we face." Aedan too dropped a kiss on her cheek and the back of her hand before releasing it to Mags.

"Airy," Mags clutched at Airiella's hand, "you fill the world with light and love everywhere you go. Every life you touch is changed for the better, whether you know it or not. You told me I brought you a feeling of curiosity, and a sense of wonderment. My vow is always to bring that wonder to your life, that curiosity to try new things, that spark that keeps your light so bright. Life is too short not to feel that way." Mags pulled Airiella in for a hug, then kissed her cheek. "My arms are always ready to grab you and show you something new." The now glowing couple went back to their seats.

Ronnie sucked in a big breath, and on the other side of him, Chrissie squeezed his hand. "You can do this," she told him.

Ronnie stood and walked up to Airiella, his heart loud in his ears. "Angel, there isn't anything that makes me happier than seeing you up here with Jax. I always knew it would end this way; what you two have is beautiful and amazing. I know that my connection with you differs from the others, and what I bring to you is different. You put it to me in one word, vulnerable. My vow to you now and always is to be a place where you can be vulnerable and safe. You brought me to life the moment you entered the room. The very moment you opened that hotel room door, you had me. Until you, I didn't know what life was, what real love felt like, what being vulnerable with another meant." Ronnie felt his eyes fill, and he let the tears fall. "I love you more than life itself. You brought color to me. My vow is vulnerability, something I feel around you a little too often," he repeated, choking up again. "These arms of mine will always be somewhere you can let go and be safe doing it."

Airiella let out a strangled cry and crushed Ronnie to her. "I wouldn't survive without you either; you know that right?" she whispered in his ear.

"I do, angel. I know you need both of us," Ronnie confirmed, pulling back and kissing her forehead and then walked back to Chrissie, sitting down slowly.

"Are you okay?" she asked him softly. "You are glowing, too."

"I am. I'm not losing Airiella, I'm gaining you."

Ronnie reached for her hand and wove his fingers through hers.

Taklishim and Tama rose, and Ronnie was startled; he hadn't expected them to join in. "Raven," Taklishim said as he walked up and they both kneeled at the altar, "we aren't part of your connections, but there is something unique we share with you. We offer our vow of loyalty to you, for all the times you've saved us, fought for us, and given freely to both of us."

"I vow to let you zap Tak whenever you need to," Tama added before struggling back to her feet and winking. Ronnie saw a glow envelop them as well.

Onida and Degataga stood and took their place, and even Chrissie was caught off guard by their additions. "Airiella, Dega, and I offer our vow of health for you and your team. As long as we are able, we will keep you all healthy. You've done more for the world than anyone can ever know, not to mention for us, personally."

Degataga smiled. "I vow to keep you in supply with magic juice."

"Everyone who gave a vow to her is glowing," Chrissie whispered.

Airiella laughed as they walked back to their seats, Jax and her facing Father Roarke again. "Lass, son, I vow to you both to aid you in your future in whatever ways an old Irish priest can."

They fell silent as a glowing Father Roarke finished the ceremony and pronounced them husband and wife. The words held an odd bittersweet pain for Ronnie because it was the final closure on that part of his relationship with Airiella that he needed to start new with Chrissie, memories of their time together flitting through his head.

Tears freely streamed down both Chrissie's face and his own as he felt an overwhelming blast of love come through the connection.

"They did it." Ronnie kissed Chrissie. "They are married."

Chapter Twenty-Four

Chrissie was seated next to Airiella while dinner got served, Ronnie on her other side talking to the boys, who were at the kid's table behind them. "It was perfect," Chrissie said to Airiella.

"It was. The extra vows were just; I don't know, extra." Airiella made a gesture with her hands that Chrissie understood to mean that Airiella was still overwhelmed by it all and processing.

Both Chrissie and Airiella fell silent as Stolas walked up to the table, Jax smiling widely. "Love, I didn't want to go upfront like the rest, but I'd like to offer a vow to you and Jax as well. I vow to do my best to protect you and all those you love with whatever means necessary from my side of things."

"You already do that, Stolas," Airiella whispered roughly, emotions spilling over.

"Maybe, but I felt the need to state it. The wedding was beautiful." He reached out and touched her hair. "It suits you perfectly."

"Stolas, you are glowing too." Chrissie gaped at him.

"Yes, I imagine I am. It's part of what Airiella is.

Our vows are a sign of loyalty to a divine purpose. I believe everyone who gave one will be much harder to defeat now. It comes with some risk to me, but, love, you are worth it." He gave Chrissie a look. "I think for your safety, that you should give her one as well."

Chrissie looked at Airiella. "I vow always to be your best friend, drive you crazy the same ways you drive me crazy, and to love you for eternity. Sisters for life."

Airiella hugged her. "Unnecessary to do that, but he might have been right because you are glowing now too. I would have protected you no matter what."

"We will talk later, love. You need to be aware of the risks now. For today, bask in the glory. Jax, I trust you to take care of her."

"Stolas, I trust you to have our backs." Jax held out his hand, and Chrissie watched them shake.

"Did you think about what I told you?" Airiella asked him quietly before he left.

"I've thought about little else. I don't know that I believe it, but I will keep an open mind."

"I've not been wrong yet. Thank you for being here and a part of this day. And for bringing my grandfathers, I saw them. But unless you want the attentions of my horny cousin who now has her eyes on you, you should probably find a way to exit," Airiella said with a laugh.

"He did bring them," Ronnie whispered to Chrissie. "I saw them and Winnie and Kalisha."

She leaned into him. "I wonder what she told him that he's thinking about; also, I guess he didn't want Gabby's attention because he's gone."

"We'll know when we are supposed to know. I don't think anyone wants Gabby's attention." They ate dinner as quickly as possible, and Ronnie looked at her. "Speech time."

Ronnie stood up and clinked his glass to get everyone's attention. "Unofficially, I'm the best man, so I'm going to give a little speech here. Everyone loves a good love story. But I've got to ask this burning question," he said and he grinned and faced Airiella and Jax. "Where did all your hair go?"

Chrissie laughed with the rest of them, Airiella blushing and burrowing into Jax. "Hey! Leave my wife alone!"

"Wife," Ronnie smiled softly and looked back out at everyone. "Those are words I think myself and the rest of the crew didn't think we would ever hear Jax say. He's been my best friend since we were five years old, more of a brother than anything else. As Jax's lovely mother can attest, we didn't make life easy on her. Sorry, Mrs. Walker. I hate to tell you this, Airiella is worse than all of us combined."

Jax laughed. "Sorry, Mom."

"For Airiella's family, my hats off to you. You raised one fantastic, bull-headed yet beautiful woman."

Chrissie saw Airiella's mom clap her hands. "Bull-headed might be an understatement."

"Luckily, they still have me to keep them sane and on their toes. I'll be there to remind Jax of his many shortcomings and to happily throw Airiella in the pool when she's arguing with me whether she's right or not. Lift your glasses and join me in a toast to celebrate two of the people in my top five list." Ronnie held up a hand and mocked counting. "They might have lost the top spots; I haven't decided yet. Jax and Airiella here's to you and what comes next!"

The crowd laughed and toasted. Chrissie stood up. "I don't think I can top that speech, and I'm not going to try. Airiella has been my friend since junior high school. The number of stupid things we've done is far too high to count, but she's always there for me. When Jax came into the picture, she was still herself, but more. He brought out something in her that only adds to the great person she already was. As for Jax, well, Jax is the reason I'm here. His desire to give everything he can to Airiella to make her life better brought my kids and me to this house. What they have together is what my relationship goals are with the goofball that spoke before I did. Airiella and Jax, your love is the stuff dreams are made of!" Chrissie raised her glass and toasted them.

She sat back down next to Ronnie grinning at her. "Goofball?" he asked.

"Yep. Not sorry."

Jax stood up then. "I know that all of you have been asking me, and also wondering amongst yourselves, what the honeymoon will be. I've kept it a secret all this time, even from my beautiful wife. Man, I seriously like the sound of that. Wife. Stand up with me, wife." Jax pulled Airiella up next to him. "I've never seen a more exquisite person in my life. Anyway, as I was saying, in two weeks we hit the road again for Shadow Seekers filming. The crew doesn't know this yet; the location will be somewhat of a working honeymoon for us. I've been in contact with several places that are in locations that my wife has on her bucket list to see. So, everyone, Shadow Seekers and your spouses and kids, we are all going on a month-long filming trip to Europe. We start in Ireland, then Scotland, over to

Romania, down into Italy, where Airiella and I will remain for a couple of weeks."

Chrissie and Airiella gasped at the same time. Chrissie looked over at Ronnie. "I'm so jealous."

"What? You are coming with me, you and the boys. It's all arranged already." Ronnie kissed her.

"How? I have work, and the boys have school."

"Jax took care of everything. He told me a couple of days ago. We are going to Europe!"

"Not only that." Jax went on after everyone calmed down. "it will also be a honeymoon for Smitty and Jillian who will be married here next week. Everyone, please congratulate the soon to be happily married couple!"

Chrissie was floored and ignoring Jax as she stared in confusion at Ronnie. "We don't have passports."

"Not entirely true, the boys have theirs, yours only needs a picture. Part of the papers the lawyers had you sign was passport applications that Jax had them slip in there in secret. Took some arguing on his part, but they finally relented. Once we get your picture to them, they will get it taken care of; relax, Chris. You get to see the most fabulous haunted parts of Europe," Ronnie joked.

"Seriously? This trip is real?"

"Very real. Do you not want to go?" Ronnie's face turned serious.

"Oh, for heaven's sake, of course, I want to go! I just can't believe it. This trip is a dream. An entire month?" Chrissie felt excitement bubbling up in her.

"We'll have a ton of free time to be tourists, Jax went above and beyond on this. Smitty and I will get started on research tomorrow on the locations and get what we need to have done beforehand done. The rest is interview stuff that Jax will have already researched and talked with the producers on and lined up what needs lining up."

"Money is tight for me," Chrissie cautioned.

"It's paid for, Chris."

"How?" she whispered. "I'm not part of the crew."

"When Jax's dad died, he left Aedan and Jax a considerable amount of money. They both invested and more than tripled the inheritance left to them; he doesn't need to work. This estate is paid off. Yes, we are all on the title as owning it; but with the sale of our house, sale of Aedan's, and Smitty's, and what they both paid out of pocket, this is ours, free and clear. Please don't worry."

"So much. It is so much to take in," Chrissie mumbled.

"Please say you'll come with," Ronnie pleaded, his eyes filled with worry.

"Of course I am going to come! I'm overwhelmed, not stupid." Chrissie smiled.

Taklishim approached her. "Do you mind if we give her our gift now? Tama thinks she's going into labor pretty soon, and I'd rather get her back into our room instead of doing it in front of all these people."

"Shit!" Ronnie stood. "What do you need? Towels? Boiling water?"

"Calm down; it's not happening right this minute, and it isn't the nineteenth century, she thinks within an hour. We don't need anything; Oni's got it covered." Taklishim laughed at Ronnie's panicked face.

"Sure, we can do it now." Chrissie laughed with Taklishim at the expression on Ronnie's face. "They are medicine people. Oni is a doctor; home birth is normal.

Chill, Ronan."

"Jax, Raven, can we have a moment of your time?" Taklishim sounded so formal that it caught Chrissie off guard until she realized he was nervous.

Tama walked up to them, holding a box and gave Chrissie a warm smile, her belly quite huge, and she sat gratefully in the chair that Ronnie shoved under her. "Thanks. Airiella, Jax, we want you to open this now for a specific reason. Chrissie, Tak, and I got to talking a while back after Jax proposed, and we decided to do a gift from all three of us. Believe it or not, it was Tak's idea."

Chrissie saw Airiella's gaze shift to Taklishim. "Does this mean whatever is in there is going to yell at me when I do something it doesn't like? Is it a spy camera?" Airiella joked.

Tama burst out laughing. "That would have been funny. Don't give him any ideas. These poor babies will end up getting spied on."

"Just open it, Raven." Taklishim's voice was gruff.

Tama handed the box over, and Airiella unwrapped it slowly. Chrissie bit back a laugh at the nervous expression on the warrior's face, and Ronnie crowded in behind to see what it was. Chrissie slid a hand over to Ronnie's thigh and put the other one on Airiella's.

She opened the outer box and found three smaller ones inside. She pulled each of them out and looked at them. "Is there an order these need to be opened in?"

"No." Chrissie smiled.

"Well, if you and Tama were a part of this, then at least I know it's safe," Airiella joked again, poking at Taklishim. She handed Jax a box. "You open it."

Chrissie didn't know which one was in which box,

but she grabbed a clean napkin from the table already knowing what Airiella's reaction was going to be. Jax pulled out a beautifully crafted handblown glass rendition of himself and Airiella from a photo Chrissie had found on Ronnie's phone.

"Oh my God!" she cried, her hands fluttering in her lap. Chrissie pressed the napkin into her hands.

The piece Jax had opened was one Chrissie had told the baker they could use as a cake topper. Jax stared in amazement. "This is from that day on the beach," Jax said in a whisper.

"I found the photo on Ronnie's phone. You two were sitting on a rock looking at the sunset," Chrissie said. "The way you were sitting together says so much about how you two are." Jax had one leg under her and the other in front of her as she leaned into his chest. His arms around her protectively, his body language speaking of a love like no other.

"I love that picture. I had planned on having it printed and framed, but never got around to it," Ronnie said quietly.

"This is made by one of our tribal members, who is quite skilled in glass blowing. Tama and I noticed all the glass art that you have. I also noticed that none of it was mass-produced, and each piece was handcrafted. Chrissie told us about your love of glass art since you went to Italy with your family. She helped us figure out which ones to have made," Taklishim said gently.

"I thought this one would be a good cake topper as well," Chrissie told her.

Airiella nodded, tears in her eyes as she stared at the piece. She handed it to Chrissie and slowly took one of the other boxes and opened it. She pulled out the piece Tama had wanted to have made. A glass rendition of the photo Jax had taken that hung over their fireplace.

The detail work was far beyond what Chrissie had imagined what it would be. The artist had captured the color and strands of her hair blowing in the wind perfectly. Her wings, instead of being transparent and outlined like in the photo, were colored as they appeared in real life.

Her legs bent in front of her, arms resting on her knees as she stared out over the water. The piece was just Airiella, but Chrissie had seen the photo so many times, she knew what had captivated that gaze she had.

"Every time I see that photo of you, I'm reminded of how blessed we are to have been able to meet someone like you. There hasn't been another photo I've seen that quite captures the beauty of this moment, and in my opinion, just how unique and special you are." Tama put her hand over Airiella's. "It was the best way for me to explain how much you mean to me."

Jax was unusually still as he held the piece in his hands. "Tama, this is amazing. It's exquisite. Open the last one, baby."

Airiella dabbed at her eyes and pulled the last box close to her, shooting glances at Taklishim. Chrissie knew it meant she was nervous. The first one had been from her, the second, Tama. That left Taklishim, and while Chrissie knew what it was, she didn't know what he had chosen to have made. The bond between the two of them was so unique that she held no doubt it would be something that would make Airiella extremely emotional.

She finally started to open it and pulled out a piece that stunned Chrissie. This piece hadn't come from a photo, at least not one she had ever seen. For some reason, Jax wasn't surprised by it, but Ronnie was.

Airiella was in battle mode, and this made sense to Chrissie because she identified it with Taklishim. Airiella herself was in motion, winding pieces of blue coming off her skin simulating the lightning she called to her. Her hair was floating around her face, which was fierce. Airiella had her wings fully extended, and behind her, a wall of blue flames that protected Taklishim, Tama, Onida, and Degataga. Behind her back foot, sat a black raven.

"Raven, I had Jax draw me this. I didn't tell him why; this is who you are. Fierce, strong, beautiful, and always protecting others while you sacrifice yourself without a second thought. There's a reason I wanted this one made; to remind you, when you feel like you've failed. To remind you that no matter what you face, your destiny is to beat it." He reached for the piece in Jax's hand. "This too is you; the that you the world sees, soft, kind, full of love, and beauty. But so is this. A warrior, unlike any that the world has seen before. Something may hurt this soft one in ways we can't see, but lurking under that, is this girl here."

Chrissie bit her lip to try and keep from crying, the emotions that were rolling off Airiella unchecked were wild and forceful, feelings that Taklishim brought out in her as no one else could. Ronnie moved slowly, anticipating her reaction before anyone else, and cleared the table off quickly, Jax stepping in and moved it out of the way, the glass pieces carefully set aside.

Airiella stood and launched herself at Taklishim, throwing up a wall of blue flames around them, impenetrable. Chrissie was slightly alarmed, but Tama just patted her hand. "Give her a minute. Tak purposely called that out in Airiella; to help ease the storm inside from what's happened to you both. The piece was already made, but it carries more weight now."

"Why the flames?" Chrissie saw the way everyone's attention riveted on them.

"Airiella doesn't want others to see her vulnerable like that," both Jax and Ronnie answered.

"How did you know?" Chrissie looked at Ronnie.

"You didn't feel those emotions?" Ronnie seemed surprised.

"Oh, I felt them. How did you know what the emotions meant?" Chrissie clarified.

"That's how the emotions felt when Airiella was healing," Jax answered for Ronnie. "At the beach."

"Taklishim reminded her of what she's capable of overcoming," Ronnie added. "Which she needed now, maybe more than we knew."

Chrissie looked to Jax. "You drew this?"

"I did. I wasn't sure what Tak had planned for it, but I knew whatever it was, it would get a strong reaction from Airiella."

Chrissie looked at the piece carefully. "It gets a strong reaction from me. Is this how Ells looks when she's fighting?"

"Almost exactly, right down to putting the rest of us in blue flames to keep us safe," Ronnie claimed softly. "The only difference is she isn't covered in blood this time."

"Where are you in this?" Chrissie looked at Jax and Ronnie.

"In blue flames. This scene was before you moved here. Right before Jax proposed."

Chrissie looked at Jax. "This was when Ells thought

you were going to die?"

"Jax would have died," Tama said gently. "Airiella refused to let us help her until we helped him. That was the first time we'd heard her say that we wouldn't have her without him."

"Ells died, didn't she?" Chrissie looked at Ronnie for confirmation.

He sat down and pulled her over to sit on his lap, resting his chin on her shoulder. "She never told you?"

"Not in a whole lot of detail. She wasn't talking a whole lot then." Chrissie remembered how hollowed out Airiella had been when she had arrived.

"Bael gutted her," Jax said quietly. "Stolas to the rescue. Ells refused help until I was stable. Mags went into labor."

"You know why he chose this, right?" Tama looked at Jax.

"I do, I get it, I even agree with it." Jax looked over at Chrissie. "It's a reminder for us all, Chris. A reminder of what matters to Ells, what motivates her, what she can overcome, and what we stand to lose. We've lost her so many times, but she comes back because of the love inside her. It's stronger than anything."

Chrissie ran her fingers over the glass piece. *Drop the flames, Ells. Vulnerability isn't a bad thing.*

Just like that, the flames dropped, and Airiella and Taklishim were exposed. Her wings wrapped around them both as they sat on the ground. Chrissie stood up and went to put the piece of her and Jax on the cake, the colors of her skirt that she'd worn yesterday brilliant against the white frosting.

She stood there, looking back at Jax and Ronnie,

the mix of emotions on their faces as they remembered. Ronnie's face was warier, and she walked back to him. "Airiella's okay."

"I know. I almost lost everything that day, both of them. Right now, these feelings that keep hitting us, those are healing. I know Airiella's okay. What I don't know is how to keep you safe, keep you from seeing what we've seen."

"You don't." Chrissie picked up the piece and held it out to him. "I have one of these inside me too. Maybe not an angel, but I can be every bit as fierce as this. No, I wouldn't like seeing Ells hurt any more than anyone here does. But I have seen it. I've also seen the wounds inside. I like that you want to protect me, and I won't stop you. I will ask you not to keep things from me, though."

Airiella finally stood up and wrapped her arms around Tama. "I can't thank you enough."

"Well, consider it even since I'm about to give birth in your house," she said and she grinned. "Come on, Tak, it's time."

Chrissie laughed as Taklishim shot to his feet, bellowing for Onida and hustling Tama inside. "Tama will be fine, Ronnie. Women have been giving birth for years."

Jax picked up the glass pieces gently. "I'm going to go put these in our room."

Chrissie led Airiella over to the cake. "We'll cut this when he comes back and let the party wind down."

Airiella laughed, wiping her face off. "Do I look like a raccoon?"

"Nope, I used waterproof stuff. You are perfect."

"The party won't wind down after that, you know. I'll have to sit in place so every last person here can come to talk to me."

Chrissie grinned. "That may be, but I don't have to. I can go do dirty things to that hot man in a suit."

"I didn't even know he had gotten this picture." Airiella smiled at the glass. "That was the first time that night that Jax let me touch him, let me claim him."

Chrissie hugged her. "Are you upset that we are all crashing your honeymoon?"

"Hell no! I'm so excited. Besides, being away from them all causes pain. The bond makes it hard, and the farther away we are from each other, the more painful it is. This trip is perfect. Just don't knock on my hotel room door, we'll be busy."

Chapter Twenty-Five

Ronnie followed Chrissie around as she prepped for Smitty's wedding, going over the plans in his mind for the thousandth time. He also couldn't help watching her ass as she bent over to straighten the lights out.

"Ronan," she purred as she turned to him. "Please stop, or we'll be putting on a show for whoever decides to come outside."

"I'm okay with that." Ronnie grinned.

"I've heard. I, on the other hand, prefer a little more discretion. Weren't you going to go pick up the boys?"

"Are you trying to get rid of me?" He brought his body flush up against hers.

"You are a huge distraction," Chrissie said coyly, running her hand between them, his body achingly hard. "And I do mean huge. A distraction, nonetheless."

"I see something I can do right in front of me." His voice took on a husky tone.

"Wow. Are you trying to entice me with a quickie?"

Ronnie roared in laughter. "Okay, okay. I'll go get the boys."

"I'm going to run to town with Airiella and Jillian, so I won't be here when you get back."

"I know." It worked out perfectly for him. The lawyers were meeting up with him and the boys while they would be gone. His plan set in motion, one he hoped didn't drive her away from him. This part of the program had been Jace's.

He pulled her in for a quick kiss but got lost in the feel of her lips. "Damn it, Ronnie," she breathed, "now I want to make Airiella go get them."

Ronnie pulled away and laughed. "The feeling is mutual, babe." He took off at a light jog, detouring through the house and ran into Airiella.

"What are you up to; don't lie to me."

Caught off guard, he could only stare at her. "What do you mean?"

"Something is going on," she said and she narrowed her eyes at him. "You rarely shut me out, and you've done it quite a few times lately, then when you open it back up, I get these weird feelings from you about secrecy."

"Let it go, angel." Ronnie smiled. "I gotta run, I need to pick up the boys."

"I'll come with you." Airiella moved towards him.

"I thought you were going with Chrissie and Jillian?" He thought fast. He could tell her, but he wanted it to be a surprise for her as well.

"Crap. Saved by my forgetfulness. You are only momentarily off the hook."

Ronnie froze. If she asked Chrissie why he was acting strange, it would make Chrissie suspicious. That woman saw everything. He grabbed his keys and the envelope that thankfully, was sealed off the counter. "Walk with me."

Airiella followed him out the front door. *I'm planning a surprise for Chrissie while we are in Ireland,* he told her through the connection.

What kind of surprise? Airiella halted and gave him a funny look.

Damn it, angel, can't you let me ever have a secret?

No, not when it comes to my best friend and you. Are you going to propose?

Yes, and that's all I'm telling you. Live with it. If you spill my secret to Chrissie, I will purposely do everything I can to drive you insane the entire time we are over there.

Airiella squealed and jumped on him. "Lips are sealed. Promise."

Ronnie kissed her on the forehead. "Get off me, you damn pain in my ass. I have children to go pick up."

He heard Chrissie laughing and swung around to see if she heard him. Thankfully she was too far away to have overheard the exchange with Airiella, but close enough that she had heard him tell her to get off him. Airiella grinned. "Sorry, Chrissie."

"Nothing to be sorry for, just not used to hearing him tell you to get off him. It was pretty funny. The pain in his ass part, I've heard from all of them."

"Love you, angel," Ronnie whispered as he got in the SUV.

"Love you, Heracles."

The past week had been more relaxed than he had thought it would be after Airiella married Jax. His body partially reacted to her, still, but not as it did with Chrissie. Smitty had been right; the transition was smooth because nothing changed other than sex.

He made it down the driveway in time for the bus to pull up, and he herded the boys into the car, except Bryce, he was napping with the babies. "Are you ready for this?"

"Yes," they both replied happily.

"Can we get ice cream?" Rafe asked.

Ronnie laughed. "Sure. I'll get in trouble for it, but ice cream sounds good."

They pulled up to the jewelry store Jax had used for Airiella's stuff and filed inside. Jax's friend met them at the counter and pulled the ring out. "Well, what do you think?"

Ronnie thought it was perfect, but he looked to Rafe and Jace. "Think she'll like it?"

"It's pretty," Rafe confirmed.

Jace pulled it out of the box and examined it, the intricate scrollwork on the band masterful in Ronnie's eyes. He had the guy make matching bands to go with; in hopes that Chrissie said yes. Jace finally put it back in the box and closed it. "She will love it."

"Thanks, buddy."

Ronnie pulled out his wallet, and the guy pushed it away. "Jax took care of it. He said to tell you that you had to pay for your honeymoon, and you'd better make it count since they all had to come with you."

Ronnie chuckled; this was the downside to the connection. That was fine. He'd do it. He put the ring in Jace's backpack. "Don't lose this. Remember what to do when we get back?"

"Yes. I have to hide it in my suitcase after it's all packed," Jace recited.

"Okay, let's go." He looked back at the jeweler. "Thanks. Fantastic work."

"Not a problem. You all are keeping me busy. Art should be here soon to pick up his bands."

"You never saw me," Ronnie reminded him.

"Nope."

Ronnie got them back in the car. "Okay. Jace, here is the paperwork for the adoption. We are going to talk with the lawyers and make sure it's all there. Are you sure that this is what you guys want?"

"It's all Rafe keeps asking for," Jace answered.

"I know he wants it, but what about you, Jace? I don't want you to do this if it's not what you want. Don't agree to something because your brother wants it."

Jace looked sad. "It makes me sad that my dad didn't want us. But he's gone now, and you told me this feeling is love. I want it too."

Ronnie's eyes watered. "I loved you all from the first moment I met you, and we played in your backyard."

"You'll be a good dad," Jace said wisely.

"Auntie Ells knows now about part of it. Not the adoption, just the marrying part. So I think we should make her pick out a dress for your mom to wear since she is so nosy."

Jace giggled. "She hates shopping."

"I know, that makes it the perfect punishment for her."

Ronnie pulled up to the diner, and Rafe went quiet and looked scared. "What's wrong?" Ronnie pulled the door open and lifted him out.

"We had ice cream here before my daddy hurt Auntie Ells." Rafe buried his face in Ronnie's neck.

"This is where you ate after you went shopping?" Ronnie hadn't known that, or he would have picked somewhere else. "Want to go to a different place?"

Jace grabbed hold of his other hand and held tight, his face showing fear at what Rafe had said. Even though Rafe hadn't answered, Ronnie made the call to switch locations. He looked back at the windows and saw the lawyers, motioning them out.

Once outside, Ronnie settled Rafe back into the SUV and had Jace get buckled in. "We need to go to a different place. I didn't know that this was where Airiella and Rafe were before they got kidnapped. He's scared."

"Not a problem, Mr. Byrne," the older man said as he pointed at a car. "That's ours, we'll follow you."

Ronnie nodded and climbed back in. "Still want ice cream?" He looked back and saw Jace holding Rafe's hand. Rafe nodded, but it was slow. "I know a perfect place."

He drove to the outskirts of town where there was a small burger joint that made shakes. A tiny little hole in the wall he had stumbled on a couple of months ago. The boys were quiet as Ronnie got them out of the SUV, but Rafe no longer looked scared.

Ronne still carried him, shaken by the effect the diner had on the boy. He handed the envelope to Jace and led them inside, the lawyers trailing after him. He got the shakes ordered and sat down at the small table.

"Any problems with the in-laws?" Ronnie asked them.

"No. Not after what the investigators presented them with the information your friend Stolas had gathered."

Ronnie smiled at that. He knew Stolas would be

thorough and make sure that Chrissie wouldn't be bothered by them again. "Sad that they are so willing to give up rights to these kids. They are pretty fantastic."

"Yes, well, they come across as the type that status means more than anything else, their son's records is a blight on that. Also, your friend is quite intimidating and intense. If he talked to them, I could see why there was no hesitation."

Ronnie frowned; he was pretty sure Stolas hadn't talked to them. If he had it would have gone very differently, and there would be a couple more souls joining Travis in Hell, he was sure. He glanced at Jace, who hadn't been paying attention to the conversation.

"Jace, let them look through the papers to make sure we filled everything out correctly," Ronnie prodded.

Jace handed the envelope over and waited while they went through everything. "Looks good. Once she signs, you'll have to file them and then go before a judge. We'll get everything set up for you once it's all signed. Have you met with the advocate?"

"I did. I checked all the boxes on my end and am highly grateful for friends in strategic places, but you didn't hear me say that."

They laughed, and the lawyers left after going over all the steps again, leaving Ronnie with Rafe and Jace. "Anything you two need to do before we head home?"

"Are we going to see where Dracula lived?" Jace asked out of the blue.

Ronnie had forgotten that the show had aired an announcement about their upcoming European investigations. Someone at school must have said something to Jace. "We will. Does that bother you?"

"No. One of the kids in my class asked about it."

"Were they picking on you?" Ronnie tried to figure out an angle that a kid could have used to torment Jace.

"No, they thought it was cool."

Grinning, Ronnie relaxed. "I'm kinda excited about it. I'm excited about all of it. There's a lot of history to the places we are going. You'll get to see things a lot of these kids will never get to see."

Jace smiled. "And I don't have to go to school."

"How about we stop at the store and get you both cameras so that you can take your own pictures?" Ronnie suggested.

"Cool!" Jace got excited. "Would Uncle Jax teach me how to take cool pictures, like he takes of Auntie Ells?"

"I'm sure he will. What do you think, Rafe?" Ronnie glanced at him.

"I don't have to share?"

"Nope, I'll get you your very own camera," Ronnie promised.

"Okay," he agreed.

Ronnie went to the nearest discount store and found the electronics department, showing them the different cameras and let them each pick out what they wanted. As they got back in the SUV, Jace thrust the envelope at him. "You better hold this."

"Put it in your backpack with the ring. Hide it in your suitcase. After we get back, I'll show you both how to use the cameras. You can practice at Smitty's wedding."

"How will we see the pictures?"

"At the end of the day, we'll plug them into our computers, and it will take the pictures you took and save them, and we'll be able to see them all. If there is one you want to have printed, we can do that too and have it mailed to your class."

"That sounds cool." Jace looked like a kid for once with the grin that lit his face.

Chapter Twenty-Six

Chrissie got up and got dressed, wondering where Ronnie had gone. The sheets were cold, so he'd been gone a while. She peeked in on the boys who were still asleep and let them be. It was a weekend after all.

She went down to the kitchen to grab an orange and go over everything one last time before things started to get crazy again. Even a small wedding was a lot of work. The cooking would be done by Airiella and Jax, at least, so no caterers to worry about this time.

She would have Ronnie go pick up the cake and flowers, Jax was going to take the photographs. Taklishim and Tama wouldn't be coming since she just had the babies, but Degataga and Onida would be here, as well as the producers. Smitty's mom and Jillian's parents would be arriving before noon.

Jax had the same hairstylist coming for Jillian, and Smitty had already taken care of the music, the same way that he had for Airiella's. She thought all was taken care of; Jax and Ronnie would take the chairs down to the beach and bring them back, and Father Roarke was still here.

Chrissie sat down on the back porch and took a

moment to relax. She felt Ronnie come up behind her and hummed in pleasure as he wrapped his arms around her. "You are sweaty," she cried as he rubbed his face all over hers.

"Just the way you like me." He laughed softly.

"Were you in the gym, or did you go for a run?" Chrissie settled back into him as he sat in the chair behind her.

"Gym. Couldn't sleep, so I went to work it off," Ronnie admitted.

"Ells have another nightmare?" Chrissie wondered.

"She did. It wasn't as bad, and she came out of it faster, but my brain wouldn't shut down afterward."

"I didn't even notice," Chrissie mused.

"You were in a sex coma."

Chrissie pinched his leg lightly. "Stop bragging."

"It's not bragging if it's the truth." He picked her up, startling her.

"Hey. Put me down."

"Oh, I will," Ronnie said, kissing her. She couldn't help it; her eyes closed as she sunk into the kiss. Only to fly open and then squeeze shut as cold water enveloped her. The damn ape had jumped in the pool!

"Ronnie!" Chrissie gasped as she surfaced.

"You look good, all wet," he said and he splashed her.

"I'm not going to stop her from hurting you," Airiella called out from her balcony, Jax standing behind her. Ronnie wanted that so severely with Chrissie that the thought distracted him enough, so the giant splash of water in his face made him sputter.

"You look good, all wet, too." Chrissie snuck up

behind him. "But, you are in trouble now and cut off from all extracurricular activity."

He turned, and she wrapped her legs around him to keep her head above water. "Why is that?"

"Because now I have to shower again and try to get my hair fixed somewhat normally for the wedding."

"What if I showered with you to save on time?"

"How is showering with me saving *me* any time?" Chrissie ran a few light kisses up his jaw.

"Keep doing that, Chris, and we'll be putting on a show."

"Jillian told me you were good in the pool, and I was wondering how she would know that. She only smiled, but I am pretty sure that the answer is on the balcony."

"Watching us too." Ronnie grinned at them. "See how they are standing like that? Waking up and stepping outside to watch the waves close together like they are the only two people in the world? At least until I threw you in the pool."

"Yeah, I saw them. What about it?" Chrissie had thought it was sweet.

"I want that with you. What would you say if I asked you to stay in my room every night?"

Chrissie couldn't help the giggle that burst out of her mouth. "Are you asking me to move in with you, Ronan Byrne?"

"I guess I am, Chrissie Nielson."

"I'll think about it," she said slyly and pushed away from him, climbing out of the pool. "Now, I have to go shower, and so do you, because I am putting those glorious muscles of yours to work today."

"Showering together *would* save time then," he said

and followed her out. "I knew I was right."

Chrissie felt Ronnie behind her. She squealed when he lifted her and threw her over his shoulder, giving her a spectacular view of his backside as he carried her inside. "Are you a caveman now?" she asked, fondling his ass. His only response was a grunt.

He took her to his room, locking the door behind them and set her down, his eyes that emerald green color that stole the air from her lungs. She pushed him into the bathroom, so they stopped dripping water on the wood floors and undressed him.

"Your turn. You got the clothes wet; you can take them off me." Chrissie held her arms up above her head.

He peeled her clothes off her slowly, his mouth searing a path on her skin. "I love the way your skin tastes. The way you feel under my lips and my tongue, and those tiny sounds I don't even think you know you're making."

She reached over and turned the shower on, her legs shaking as she stepped in then pulled him in with her. "I want you hard and fast," she said and she kissed him and then turned around and bent over.

"Fuck, you undo me. Hold on, baby," he growled, sliding in slowly, and then gave her exactly what she wanted.

Chapter Twenty-Seven

R onnie went over the research one last time before heading out to set up chairs. "Jax!" he called out. "Out back," he heard Jax respond.

Ronnie grabbed the papers on top and jogged out to his friend. "The castle is still standing. I sent an e-mail to the registered owners to see if we could have access. That's where I want to do it at."

"Is it in good shape?"

"No idea. Even if it's in ruins, that's still cool. It's old as hell. I can ask Father Roarke to check it out. He's flying back tomorrow."

"He can prep it for us if it's close, make it somewhat romantic at least. I don't think Chrissie's had much of that."

"I got the same feeling. I'll talk with the priest. He might be able to recommend someone that could do it for him if the owners allow us on the property," Ronnie mused.

"Is it still within your bloodline?"

"I don't know. I didn't get that far into it. If it is, the owners are distant cousins at best. Their last name isn't Byrne." Ronnie showed Jax the papers.

"Is that what the family crest was?" Jax pointed to the design on a flag.

"Yep. I incorporated it into the ring, on the band." Ronnie grabbed a stack of the chairs, followed Jax out to the beach, and got them set up. "It's hidden in Jace's suitcase."

"Sorry that Ells weaseled it out of you."

"It's fine. I didn't give our angel any details." Ronnie shrugged.

"She's thrilled, Ronnie. She was so worried you were going to be unhappy, she almost called off the wedding twice."

"I still love her, so much it's scary. I think I love Chrissie more, which is even more terrifying. Chris loves that I'm protective, which is a nice change of pace for me." Ronnie rolled his shoulders and puffed his chest out.

Jax laughed. "Ells likes it too, it makes her feel safe, even if she doesn't let you do it."

"Married life suits you. I know it's only been a week, but there's a subtle change to you. I want it so badly I can taste it. Is it weird that I love them both so much?" Ronnie deflated a little, and they continued setting up.

"No. I think that everyone Airiella meets falls in love with her. The bond you two share is special, and you both need it. You need her as much as she needs you. You just now also need Chrissie, it's a different bond. Going to sleep and waking up every morning with her, knowing she is yours in every way that matters, it's fucking amazing, Ron."

"Well, now Smitty will be joining the ranks. Wonder if I can convince her to marry me while we are there?"

"My advice? Get the license and bring it with you. Imagine a wedding in Italy."

"You think Italy is better than Ireland?" Ronnie asked stupefied.

"No, they would be equal in my eyes. But if you are proposing in Ireland, we wouldn't have time to plan for a wedding within the time frame we'd be there. But we could plan for Italy, which could give her enough time to find a dress."

"I'll get the license Monday, then. What do I need to do?" Ronnie decided immediately.

"Google it." Jax laughed. "I'm not doing this for you. Put the work in."

"Jackass."

Ronnie turned and saw Airiella standing there behind him with an eyebrow raised. "Are you harassing my husband?"

"What if I am?" Ronnie taunted his angel.

"I'll zap you," she said and she grinned, calling lightning to her fingers.

"You love me too much to hurt me," Ronnie said warily, remembering she had zapped Taklishim.

"I do, damn it. Stop calling my bluff, takes the fun out of it." She wrapped her arms around him. "I've kind of missed you lately. Missed this."

"Am I neglecting you, angel?" Ronnie felt guilty in an instant.

"A little, but I'm okay with it. I understand why now. Just hug me every once in a while, please? There's still nothing quite like a hug from you."

"Don't let this go to your head, but there's nothing quite like an angel hug either." Ronnie kissed the top of her head. "Are you sure you are okay with all this?"

"I am. I think I was just a little unnerved from the

nightmare last night," Airiella said quietly.

Ronnie shot a look at Jax as he held her a little tighter to him. Jax's face betrayed him. "I thought it wasn't as bad?"

"The nightmare itself wasn't as bad as the others, but the way it left me feeling has me on edge." She looked up at him. "Jax knows; stop shooting him dark looks. I talked to him."

"But, you still feel this way?" Ronnie felt like he was missing something here. "Jax, I'm gonna steal her for a few minutes," Ronnie called to him.

"Okay."

"Climb on my back, angel. That way, you can still say you wrapped your legs around me and have it be true." Ronnie grinned at her to lighten the mood that was striking him. "Open the connection, please."

Airiella climbed up on his back and wrapped her arms around his neck. "What if I'm afraid to let you in right now?" she whispered in his ear.

"Then, it will make me get all protective and pushy with you, and I'll bug the shit out of you until you finally give in." Her sigh told him she knew he'd do it too. Ronnie strode back to the house and felt her open the connection.

Dark fear flooded his mind like physical pain, and he had to stop, or his knees were going to buckle under the onslaught. This sensation wasn't a common fear he was used to feeling after one of her nightmares; this was entirely different.

Smitty, Aedan, and Mags came flying out of the house, their faces concerned. "I've got it. Go do what you need to do," Ronnie called out. "Angel, you are going to talk to me whether you want to or not."

"I'm here with you, aren't I?"

Smitty jogged over to them. "Baby girl, did something happen?" Ronnie felt her shake her head in response.

"Go get ready, you've got a wedding to attend." Ronnie gave him a guarded look. Smitty narrowed his eyes at Ronnie, but Airiella must have said something to him because he nodded and walked away.

Chrissie came flying through the door next, her eyes wide. "What's wrong?"

"It's okay, Chris. I just need some time with Airiella," Ronnie cautioned as she came closer. Whatever this fear was, he didn't want Chrissie a part of it. Ronnie knew Airiella heard that thought, and her silence told him that she might already be a part of it. He kissed Chrissie's head and walked into the house.

"My room," she told him quietly.

Ronnie didn't question her, just went to her room, closed and locked the door behind them. "No interruptions," he said as she slid down his back, but didn't stop touching him. "What the hell is going on? That fear is dark, and you are clingy right now. Which, I don't mind, but combined, it's more than a little concerning."

"Sorry, I'm not trying to be clingy. The safety I get from being with you is something I crave right now."

"You don't feel safe with Jax?" Ronnie asked sharply.

"I do. It's just different from you."

"Are you trying to protect him from something?" Ronnie looked around the room. "Keep touching me; I'm just trying to decide on the bed or a chair."

"Chair," Airiella answered and tugged him towards

the chaise lounge.

Ronnie settled down, and she climbed on top of him, resting against his chest. "Talk to me, angel." He slid his arms loosely around her.

She slid her hands up his shirt, and he couldn't hold back the smile. She was still his, too. "Something's coming. For me, for us."

"What do you mean?" Ronnie did his best to keep his voice controlled and even.

"One of those premonition nightmares. Only it was dark, hot, and smelled like Bael. I couldn't see anything."

"Are you sure it's a premonition and not just something your mind conjured up because of everything else that happened?" Ronnie hated to ask that; it made him sound like he didn't believe her, which he did.

"I'm sure. That's what Jax and I talked about." Ronnie felt her tense up. "Right now, I just need you. I need to be vulnerable for a moment." Airiella said it so quietly Ronnie had to strain to hear her.

"I'm right here; you have me. What's going through that beautiful mind of yours?" Ronnie pushed for answers.

"Everything. I just got married, what if whatever's coming takes Jax away from me? What if it takes you away from Chrissie and me? What if I lose Chrissie; what if you lose Chrissie? Smitty is getting married today, what if something happens to him and Jillian? Why can't we just have some downtime and let love wrap us up in its warm hold? I'm tired, Ronnie. Tired and scared. What if I fail you all?"

Airiella's shoulders shook as she finally let the tears he knew she had been fighting come. Her last question was what he knew was at the root of it all. She might be scared by whatever was coming, that much was obvious, but she was more afraid that she would fail to keep them all safe.

"You know, as much as I hate that you don't let us help you, I have never once felt like you couldn't keep us safe. I have never felt like you failed us. You've made us all stronger. Try to think of a way we can help and still allow you to keep us safe," Ronnie suggested gently. "You don't have to shoulder every battle alone."

"What if you get hurt?"

He tightened his arms around her. "Then, I get hurt. It's not the end of the world. We still heal." He moved one of his arms and tipped her chin up, kissing her softly. "We face things together. Remember those vows?"

"Can you kiss me again?"

Ronnie chuckled and kissed her again. "Better?"

"No, but it felt good. Like I haven't lost you."

Stunned, he shifted his head to look at her. "You felt like you lost me?"

"Yeah," she admitted. "Then, I felt selfish for feeling that way."

"Because of Chrissie?" Ronnie wasn't sure why she felt that way.

"No. I'm so beyond happy that I can't even describe it. I think it's because I haven't had any of this time with you lately. It's not your fault; it's my own."

"Have you taken time with any of the others?" Ronnie pushed her, his mind clearing as an idea formed.

"A little, here and there. Not like this. I should, I feel disconnected from everyone, but it was you most of all. Jax thinks it's because we haven't fed the connection, is how he put it."

"He might be right. Maybe once a week, we need a

you and me, day." Ronnie kissed her again. "Angel, I'm still madly in love with you, that won't change. I just made room for Chrissie. I want what you and Jax have, and I want it with her and those boys."

"You'll have it." Airiella's voice was sure on that. "A me and you day, sounds perfect. I don't think it needs to be every week. Even a couple of hours in the gym with you would work, I think."

"Doesn't feeding the connection involve touching like we are now?" Ronnie felt like he needed to make sure she understood that he was okay with this.

"Maybe? I don't want to intrude on your time with Chrissie and the kids."

Ronnie shifted her until she straddled his lap and faced her. "The sudden insecurity has red flags waving in my head. You had moved past this." He tapped her head gently. "This, I think, is coming from the shit with Travis. It's thrown you off, and understandably so. Angel, every person in this house understands, accepts, and loves the connection they share with you." Ronnie tugged on it. "I wouldn't be planning to ask Chrissie to marry me if she wasn't okay with this. Neither would Smitty be marrying Jillian. He made that abundantly clear to her at the beginning."

Airiella's face crumbled. "What if Travis broke me again?"

"He didn't. He just dented you." Ronnie innately knew that she needed Jax right now. This conversation was getting into territory that Airiella responded to best with Jax. Or Smitty, but he was getting ready for a wedding. "Right now, we are going to feed your connection with the others. See if we can push that dent out a little bit. Sound good?" Ronnie swiped his thumbs across her face and sat up to kiss her cheeks.

"They are all busy. I'll be fine."

"Angel, that bullshit is why you are feeling this way. You need to be secure enough to tell us when you need us. That is missing from you right now. I can feel it in you." Ronnie pulled her down to hug her again. "I'm going to go get Smitty before he gets too wrapped up in things. Even fifteen minutes will help."

"I'll ask him to come up," Airiella conceded. "Stay with me until he gets here?"

"Wait five minutes. I want to hold you a little bit longer." Ronnie nuzzled his face into her. "Did I tell you I found my ancestral castle in Ireland? I am going to propose there." He let her in on that part of his secret.

Chapter Twenty-Eight

Chrissie saw Ronnie come down out of the house, and she beelined for him. "What was that?"

"A combination of things. Airiella said her nightmare last night was a premonition one and that something is coming, but she doesn't know what. So please, be on guard at all times and tell the boys to stay back here only while we are home, and abroad, they are to be with one of our group at all times."

"That was fear?" Chrissie prodded at him. "What aren't you telling me?"

"Nothing, I swear. Airiella doesn't know what it was, but that feeling was fear, yes. I think this is more than just fallout from Travis, but that is a part of it. She said Jax thinks we aren't feeding into the connection enough, and he may be right. There's a lack in her I can feel. She said it was mostly me, but it's true for the others. So I'll need to be better about scheduling time with her, same with the rest. I'm sending them in one at a time. You'll need to go too."

"I'm not one of her connections," Chrissie argued.

"No, but she still needs you and the feeling you two share." Ronnie kissed her. "On guard at all times. I've learned to trust those instincts of Airiella's. I'm going to finish helping Jax. When Smitty comes down, send Aedan up if she hasn't called for him."

"Okay."

Chrissie finished up what she was doing and went to check the crockpots Airiella had going and stirred them all. Then, she sat outside, unsure of what to do. She felt partially at fault for Ronnie not spending time with Airiella.

Chrissie saw Aedan heading up, and Smitty came down, sitting next to her. "Airiella said to tell you it isn't your fault; it's hers." Smitty patted her hand.

"That's going to take some getting used to," Chrissie mumbled.

"It does. The stronger the emotions, the more Airiella will pick up on the thoughts that go along with it. Practice the blocking techniques she showed you." Smitty looked at her. "I mean now."

"Oh." Chrissie focused on walls around her mind. "Okay. I have no idea if it worked or not."

"Okay, here it is. The thing with Travis has knocked Airiella back a bit. She's withdrawing and not telling us when she needs us. She doesn't want to be a burden or intrude on the new starts we are making. We don't all know everything this connection requires, so it's a learning curve we are all on. The withdrawal, though, is due to Travis. It's caused some of Airiella's old insecurities to surface. It's not you, Chrissie. It's not what you have with Ronnie," Smitty laid it out for her.

"Are you sure?"

"I am. The order of Airiella's connections in strength is, Mags is the weakest, then Aedan, followed by me, then Ronnie, and Jax is the strongest. I'm assuming you know what each of us brings to her."

"I do."

"Then how you can help is when you sense something off, figure out which one of us can help, and get us. It's not on you, that's not what I'm saying. Airiella needs to ask us, but if you see her not doing it, then step in."

"I can do that. That's helpful, thank you." Chrissie was learning as much as she could about these connections too. Airiella had a massive weight on her shoulders, and Chrissie wanted to ease it. "Go get ready. I'm fine. All the parents are here now."

"Thanks for all your help on this." Smitty kissed her cheek and took off running.

Chrissie sat there while Mags went up, and Aedan came back down, sitting in the spot that Smitty had vacated. "Airiella hates being the center of attention and asking for help," Chrissie told him gently. "It's not because she doesn't think you can't help her."

"I know that now. It took me a while to figure it out. I don't like that Airiella has this burden to carry all the time. I want for her the same things she wants, to be free just to live." Aedan sighed heavily.

Chrissie sat forward. "When you all are here, between jobs, locations and it's just all of us, she's the happiest I've ever seen her. Jax is probably on to something with the whole you all need to spend more one on one time with her. Not when something bad happens, and you all freak out and can't stay away, but one on one time on a normal basis. After all, isn't that why we are all living here in the same place?"

"Thanks, Chrissie. I think I needed to hear that. I'm going to talk to the guys about it. Sometimes, I still get tripped up over the whole needing to touch someone other than Mags, even though I'm aware we are in an odd circumstance."

"Feels good to be around her, doesn't it?" Chrissie asked softly.

"When she's not hurt, yes, it does. Do you feel it too?"

"I always have. We've never needed words between us, we just know. I know that you guys need the words sometimes, and she isn't always easy to understand, it takes time. She has to learn you guys too, and that it's okay to ask for help."

"We've been trying to drum that into Airiella since the beginning. We'd made some progress with it; now it feels like it's gone. It's because of what happened with your ex-husband, isn't it?"

"It is. Give it time." Aedan kissed her cheek and headed off to find the guys. Chrissie waited a few more minutes then went back inside until Airiella called her.

Chrissie went upstairs and found a teary Mags curled up with Airiella on the bed and sat down in front of Airiella. Mags sat up. "I'm going to go get ready," she said and she pecked Airiella on the lips. "Love you, Airy."

Her willowy frame beelined out of the house. Chrissie brushed the hair out of Airiella's face. "Let's get ready together."

Chrissie drew on the feelings she got from Airiella and smiled because she hadn't lied to Aedan, they didn't need words. Being with each other was a salve for both of them. Airiella started to feel better, and so did Chrissie.

They rejoined the others and sat to get the wedding underway. Both Smitty and Jillian wanted the traditional ceremony, with the traditional vows, which had surprised Chrissie. She had thought they would have gone the route that Jax and Airiella had. It was still beautiful and went smoothly. Jillian looked like a dream.

Chrissie noticed that all of them had been more relaxed after spending time with Airiella, and she filed it away as something to start to pay more attention to with them. Jax began to grill and got the chicken Airiella had been marinating going, while Airiella got the rest all situated and placed out on the tables.

"You did it, two weddings in two weeks. Simply amazing." Ronnie's lips grazed her ear.

"This one was easy. I'm glad I could help." Chrissie tugged his arms, so he wrapped them around her. "That's better."

"Did you spend time with her?" Ronnie nodded at Airiella.

"I did. Our time is different than yours. Something might be coming, but I think Airiella's going to be okay. The turmoil I felt in her earlier is settled after spending time with all of you."

"You are okay with this? Me needing to be with her? That she kisses me?"

Chrissie smiled and lay her head over his heart. "I truly am Ronan. Since you talked to Ells about you and me, I've seen the way you two kiss, and it's nothing like how we kiss. Even if it were, I'd be okay with it. I wasn't sure at first, but I am now. After each of you left her earlier, the load she bears became spread out a little more. I know she still carries most of it, but you were all able to take a bit off her. That matters to me."

"I love you," he murmured in her ear.

RONAN

"I love you too," she replied, listening to the steady beat of his heart. "This whole giant family thing here works."

Chapter Twenty-Nine

Ronnie couldn't believe it; they were in Ireland. It was strange and beautiful, and a part of his soul recognized it. Airiella's senses were going crazy, and she kept picking up on odd little energy signatures that she swore up and down were fairies.

The boys were tired and so far unimpressed with the beautiful scenery, but were looking forward to the castle they were vising the next day. Father Roarke had sent him pictures, and it was incredible. Part of the buildings was nothing more than ruins, and there was still a whole part of the castle that was still intact.

Ronnie couldn't wait to trudge through the ruins and explore the house his ancestors used to live in so long ago. He'd pulled Airiella in to help Chrissie pick a sundress or something to wear that was a little nicer, but she couldn't figure out how to sell going through an old castle wearing a dress. She suggested that Ronnie tell her to bring something to change into before they left citing they would be going to dinner.

He'd agreed. They spent the day in their little groups getting settled after the long flights and agreed to meet up in the morning. They'd forced food on the boys before letting them crash, the jet lag claiming them, and he and Chrissie spent the night on the balcony looking out over the city.

Ronnie waited until she fell asleep and grabbed the ring from Jace's backpack, slipping it into his pack that he'd be bringing with them and tried to make himself sleep. He got a few hours, but the excitement kept him awake, and he ended up talking most of the night with Airiella through the connection.

After a day spent doing typical touristy stuff, they finally set out to the castle he'd told them about and broke the news that it was a castle where his family had lived hundreds of years ago. The boys got excited then, at least Jace and Rafe had.

"Your family had a castle?" Chrissie was stunned.

"Yep! I found it when we were researching the locations. I knew my roots were from here and dug in a bit. It's pretty cool. I didn't trace it to the current owners, but my guess is they are distant cousins."

"That's so cool!" Jace crowed, from the back seat, fidgeting with his camera.

"Indeed." Chrissie smiled.

They pulled up, the rest of the team behind them, and the boys took off at a run, straight for the ruins that Ronnie could see from where they parked. "Hey! Slow down and watch your step," he cautioned them.

Chrissie grinned at him. "Good luck with that one."

They waited for the others and followed the boys, roaming around through the grounds, finding an old cemetery off on the rear quarter full of headstones with the Byrne name. Chrissie trailed her finger over some of the stones that had the crest on them.

"What's this design?" Chrissie asked.

"A family crest." Ronnie came up behind her, his hands on her hips. "I saw it on a flag when I did the research. Kind of cool."

"Very cool," Chrissie agreed. "Intricate. Something about these Celtic designs that are just fascinating." She trailed her fingers over another one. "So much history here. Living history. I keep thinking about what it must have been like to live here."

"Come on, let's go check out the castle part." Ronnie tugged on her. His nerves suddenly present. "I heard that some of the impressive rooms are still intact. That car that pulled up must be the owners."

"Boys, come on," Chrissie called out. "We are going to the castle now."

Grab the extra clothes; Ronnie told Airiella

On it.

They went through most of the rooms, listening to the history the older couple told them, showing them armor and other heirlooms that were remnants of his family history. Smitty and Aedan were all over it, flinging questions around as fast as they could think of them.

After a while, it was apparent there was only one room left to see, but Ronnie needed her to go change first. He became flummoxed about how to approach it.

I don't know what to do! He told Airiella.

I've got it.

"Chris, come with me. We need to change before dinner, and I don't want to wander around this place alone. It's cool but kinda creepy."

Chrissie laughed. "You are afraid of ghosts? *You?*"

"Shut up. Don't make me go pee with one of the guys."

"Big baby. Let's go then." Chrissie held out her hand for the bag Airiella held. "What's this place we are going to for dinner anyway? Something fancy?"

"I don't know. Jax said to wear girl clothes."

"You didn't argue?" Chrissie gave her a weird look.

"It's me, of course, I argued."

Ronnie watched as they walked away, then ran to the closed-up room and opened the door. The current owners smiled at him, their accents thick, but understandable as they told him the things they'd had done.

The room had hundreds of candles burning the older man had lit while they had been looking around, dozens of red roses placed throughout the ancient room. The lowering sun in the sky was streaming through the stained glass windows giving the room a surreal glow.

"Damn, Ron, fit for an angel," Jax said quietly.

"Chrissie is one, maybe not literal like our other one, but still, she's one to me." Ronnie breathed out in wonder.

Jillian and Smitty stood quietly in awe with Mags and Aedan in the corner of the room. The antique candlesticks on the pedestals giving the place the old feeling of history remembered. At the back, an antique grand piano sat, worn with age, sitting as if it were waiting for its master to rejoin it.

Ten seconds, Airiella warned.

Ronnie turned toward the door, his stomach fluttering madly as Jace, Rafe, and Bryce stood right next to him. There she was; in a simple dress, the color of cherry blossoms, her blond hair filled with waves and a soft smile on her face as she took in the room.

Airiella moved off to stand next to Jax, and Ronnie stood utterly still as Chrissie walked in the room. "This is beautiful! Like a fairy tale!"

Ronnie reached down to hold Jace's hand as Chrissie came up to them. He laced his arm through hers and walked over to the light coming from one of the stained glass windows.

"Chrissie, I love you. I've waited my whole life for this moment, right here. An Irish sunset streaming through the window on to your beautiful face in a home my ancestors built that has a room perfect for this. I'm so nervous that Jace has to hold my hand." He held up his hand, holding Jace's.

"Why are you nervous?" Chrissie didn't get it.

"I thought Airiella was going to be the only love of my life. She was just preparing me for this; for us. I don't want to wake up without you, go to sleep without you. I want forever with you, with them." Ronnie nodded to the boys.

A light flickered behind Chrissie's eyes. "Mom, Ronnie asked us if we would be okay with him marrying you. My answer was yes. So was theirs," Jace told her.

Ronnie got down on one knee and held out the ring. "Chrissie, will you marry me? I'm not good with words, and all I want is you and them. I guess that means you get the rest of these guys as well since we are all a package deal. Will you officially join our family?"

Chrissie burst into tears. "You want to marry me?"

"More than anything." Ronnie could barely hear over the sound of his thudding heart.

RONAN

Chrissie looked at her boys. "What do you think?"

"Say, yes!" Rafe cried, jumping up and down excitedly.

"Yes, Ronan Byrne, I'll marry you," Chrissie whispered.

Ronnie surged to his feet and swept her up into his arms. "Thank God! I thought you were going to say no, and I'd have to have Airiella zap you."

Ronnie set her down and slid the ring onto her finger. "Is that your crest?" Her eyes widened as she took in the band.

"It is. Do you like it?" Ronnie felt nervous again; he'd taken a play from Jax. Ronnie had the ring made with the boys' birthstones, his own, and hers, with a diamond in the center. It made a flower. The small and delicate colored stones, combined with the band's intricate work, made it unique.

"I love it."

Jace stepped forward. "When Ronnie asked me for my permission, I asked him for a favor," Jace started. His years were not showing in his exact words; he sounded far older than eight.

"You did?" Chrissie looked down at her oldest son.

"I asked him if he would adopt us." Jace looked like he was going to cry. "He loves us, and we love him. He never makes us feel bad, and he takes care of us. He makes you smile and laugh."

Ronnie felt his heart clench up. These were Jace's words, not something that he had told him to say, and they touched something deep inside him. His eyes welled up with tears as Jace retook his hand, and Rafe came up on the other side of him.

"I want him to be my Daddy," Rafe added. Bryce didn't understand what was going on, but since his brothers were clinging to Ronnie, he wanted to as well, and he hung on Ronnie's leg.

Chrissie sobbed as she knelt in front of them. "You asked him to be your Dad?"

"I did. It made Ronnie cry." Jace wiped Chrissie's face. "Like you are doing. He said they were happy tears."

"They are happy tears, baby." Chrissie looked up at Ronnie. "You want to adopt them?"

Ronnie nodded. "I told them yes as long as it's what you wanted."

"We talked to lawyers and everything," Jace told her, his voice cracking. He dropped his backpack and pulled out the envelope. "I want a real family with Ronnie and Auntie Ells and Uncle Jax. Uncle Aedan and Uncle Smitty."

Chrissie turned around and looked at Airiella, who was openly crying and clinging to Jax. "I didn't know, I swear," she blathered. "I only knew he was going to propose, that's it."

"You honestly want all this?" Chrissie asked Ronnie quietly.

"I've never been more sure of anything in my life." Ronnie gave her the unbridled truth.

"Then I accept all of it," Chrissie told Jace.

Jace threw himself at Ronnie after hugging his mom. "I told you!"

Airiella, Mags, and Jillian swooped in and circled her in a hug, all of them crying. Ronnie looked at Jax and shrugged as he picked up Bryce. "I don't have your words, and I'm sure I could have done that better, but I think Jace stole it."

"That he did." Jax picked up Rafe while Aedan scooped up Jace.

"Know what this means?" Smitty smiled at the boys. "There are more boys than girls now, boys rule!"

"Auntie Ells has wings; I think she still rules," Jace said wisely.

"Smart boy," Airiella called out, laughing.

Ronnie howled in laughter. "Uncle Smitty lost his mind if he thinks we will ever rule over these women. Come on, let's go celebrate!"

Chapter Thirty

C hrissie was so happy she felt drunk. She couldn't keep from staring at the gorgeous ring and touching Ronnie every chance she could. Jace had stunned her with his adoption request, but she wasn't about to deny him his opportunity for a family, however odd it might be, it was pure love.

"Okay, sorry. I have a few more surprises up my sleeve." Ronnie stood up at the dinner table and looked at Chrissie. "What would you say to a wedding in Italy?"

Chrissie didn't think she could be more shocked. "Isn't that two to three weeks away?"

"It is. But Airiella would have to help you plan it along with these two other lovely ladies," Jax supplied.

"Doable," Jillian said.

"I'm in," Mags agreed. Airiella only narrowed her eyes.

"What's the other surprise?" Chrissie smothered a laugh at how wary Airiella sounded. "And you both know I'm not good at planning parties. Chrissie deserves better than me."

"Can it, Ells. I know it will be just what it should be

if you are behind it." Chrissie softened her words with a smile. "Married in Italy, it is then."

"Okay, the next surprise then." Ronnie looked at Jax, who only shrugged and grinned. "Since Jax is too scared to admit he decided something without Airiella, I'll have to take the fall for this one. The owners of the castle approached me with an offer to sell the castle; since I'm blood-related, they are elderly and have no children, they want to ensure it survives. Apparently, I'm the last of my line. The price was ridiculously low, but Jax agreed to go in on it with me and get it restored, so it becomes a place we can use as a vacation home."

Chrissie felt her mouth drop open. "I'm marrying someone who will have a castle?"

"I'm married to someone who decided to buy a castle without asking me?" Airiella added, just as shocked.

"We get to have a castle?" Jace practically shouted.

Ronnie laughed nervously. "Thoughts?"

Chrissie looked around the table and saw Jillian and Smitty whispering furiously to each other, and Aedan and Mags both had their heads bowed murmuring. Airiella was giving Jax a strange look, and Ronnie wasn't sure how to react.

Jillian cleared her throat. "Smitty and I would like to go in on the castle too."

Aedan nodded. "Same with Mags and I."

Ronnie looked relieved. "That makes me happy since we'd all have to come, or deal with separation pain. Angel, you are surprisingly quiet."

"Well, I'm shocked a little bit. We now get to have a castle in a magical place where fairies live, and my husband didn't tell me. Or my number two. I mean, this feels like a plan an angel should have been in the loop on," she deadpanned.

Chrissie burst out laughing. "You guys should see all of your faces right now. You don't know her as well as you think you do if you can't tell that she's just messing with you and is about to pee herself from excitement."

Airiella giggled and rested her head on Chrissie's shoulder. "She gets me; this is true love."

"I can only hope that this doesn't mean I'm going to end up wearing a cotton candy-colored wedding dress to get married in the most romantic place in the world," Chrissie stated.

Jax snickered. "I'm not gonna lie, I had the same thought. That is something she would do."

Airiella tried to look affronted but could only laugh. "Well, that was my thought about the wedding party dresses."

Jillian snorted. "This is why we are helping her," she said to Mags.

"I'll talk to Father Roarke and see if he can officiate and suggest a venue to use near where our shoot will be," Jax told Ronnie.

"By the way, where is that?" Airiella looked at Jax.

"Venice." He grinned at her.

Chrissie gasped as Airiella squealed. "Really?!"

"I'm going to get married in Venice?" Chrissie whispered dramatically.

"Venice was one of my favorite places when we all went. The glass there is amazing," Airiella babbled. "There are hotels right along the canal, and at night, it's so damn beautiful you want to cry."

"You are so beautiful I want to cry," Chrissie heard

Jax tell her softly.

Her heart melted, and she looked at Ronnie, who was looking right back at her, a sexy smile on his face. "Are you happy, babe?"

A wide smile split her face. "Ecstatic; this is so much to take in."

"Okay, last surprise. I got informed by Jax over there, acting all sappy over his wife, that I had to plan our honeymoon, since he did this, and we would all be going. Weirdest honeymoon's ever, right?"

Smitty laughed. "It's working for me."

"How do you all feel about Hawaii?" Ronnie looked around the table. "A bit more relaxed. I was thinking Kuai. Plenty of nature for Airiella to lose herself in without dragging all of us along with, since we will be on an island, and it's not all that big so that the separation thing won't be an issue. The rest of us can laze around on a beach, snorkel, go to luau's, or even island-hop."

"I'm good with that." Airiella grinned. "I love Hawaii."

"I've never been," Chrissie admitted, overwhelmed. "Sounds great to me."

"Ditto." Mags grinned. "Man, I wish there were more of us to marry off so we could just keep vacationing in all these great places."

"No complaints here on Hawaii." Smitty sat back in his chair, his arm thrown around Jillian's shoulders.

"I'm done then." Ronnie put his arm around Chrissie. "Kids will have a blast in Hawaii; there's lots of fun stuff to do. I love Oahu, so maybe we can island-hop, the kids can see Pearl Harbor, and I can take a stab at North Shore."

"You know how to surf?" Chrissie wasn't sure why that surprised her.

"Not well. I can get up on the board, both Jax and I can, but neither of us can do what most surfers can do."

"Somehow, that translates to being good enough to take a stab at North Shore? Isn't that the famous Banzai Pipeline?" Chrissie raised her eyebrow.

"Don't worry, Chris. I'll use my water powers to either keep him off the board or ride it so far into shore that he'll wow the pros, then when he falls off trying to do it again, they'll be confused," Airiella teased. "I'll think of something to get him back for having me plan your wedding."

"Just don't drown him, at least not until the castle gets restored," Chrissie told her with a straight face.

"I'm slightly scared, right now." Ronnie looked at the two women. "Jax, help me out here."

"On your own, bro."

Chrissie laughed and nuzzled Ronnie's neck. "Are you really the last of your line?"

"Blood, yes, according to the couple. After I adopt your boys, there will be more Byrne if they want to take my name. We haven't talked about that."

"I'll let them decide. As for me, I will, of course, be taking it." Chrissie brushed her cheek against the stubble on his face. The rough texture was invoking some primal urge to stake her claim on him in front of everyone. "Maybe we should go back to the room."

"Why is that?"

"Because I want to strip you down right here in front of everyone and do all sorts of naughty things to you to make sure that all the other women in the room that keep checking all of you out know that you are not available."

Ronnie's voice deepened. "They wouldn't stand a chance against you and the angel. Throw in Mags and Jillian, and you just might end up on Irish TV as the most powerful women in the world who destroyed a restaurant. I'm all for the naughty things part. Bryce is about asleep in his ice cream, so it works out well."

"I got this, Ronnie, go take the kids back," Jax overheard.

"We start the torture tomorrow, Chris. Wear your have-patience-with-Airiella shoes." Ells grinned sadistically.

As they all stood up and headed to the front of the restaurant, Chrissie saw Airiella stop and looked back to see her staring at Stolas, approaching them with a frightening expression on his face. Chrissie moved to Airiella's side, as did Jax and Ronnie.

"Something's wrong," Airiella cautioned unnecessarily.

"Indeed there is." Stolas stopped in front of them all. "Stay together. I might not get much notice, but something has shifted below, and people in higher places of power are watching you, preparing something."

"Higher places of power?" Chrissie repeated.

"Some of the princes, possibly the boss."

"What does that mean?" Jax looked worried.

"I don't know, only that he is aware of you, love." Stolas looked at Airiella. "My instincts say it might not be a good thing; I can't be sure."

Chrissie saw Airiella's face blank out. "War is coming."

"Um, Ells..." Chrissie waved her hand in front of her face and got no response.

Stolas looked at Jax and Ronnie. "She may be right. Stay together, with her and on guard. I will do everything I can to keep you all safe."

Chrissie grasped Ronnie's hand. "Her nightmare," she whispered. Ronnie only nodded.

Smitty tugged on Ronnie. "Let's go, as a group."

Jax and Smitty hustled them all out, and as Chrissie got the boys settled in the car, she looked at Ronnie. "Maybe we should put the wedding off?"

"No. We don't have a timeline for whatever is coming; we will go on as planned. We'll just alter plans so that we are all together, as Stolas told us. Have no worries, Chris. Whatever is coming, we are on the side of an angel. You will be my wife, and we will be a family within a family."

Chapter Thirty-One

Y ou okay, angel?

I guess. Tell me how you envision this wedding going?

What do you mean? Ronnie was confused about where she was going with this.

When you picture it, what do you see?

Oh, he got it now. *Romantic. Jax said he doesn't think she's gotten much romance in her life.*

My man is astute. That's a good start; It gives me a few ideas at least.

I wasn't asking if you were okay with planning a wedding in two weeks. I wanted to know if you were okay after Stolas came to see us, and that weird little trance you went into declaring war.

I know. I didn't want to think about it. I'd rather think about happy things instead. I wasn't kidding when I told you I was tired of fighting.

That's why I asked, angel.

I'm scared, Heracles.

Tell Jax to let me in; I'm coming over.

Ronnie leaned over Chrissie. "Chris, wake up

a minute."

She looked at him, groggily. "What's wrong?"

"I'm headed to talk to Jax and Airiella. I didn't want you to wake up and find me gone. If you feel something, or get worried, yell in your head as loud as you can, and out loud." He kissed her.

"Is everything okay?"

"Yeah, it's fine. Just going to talk, that's all. Go back to sleep. I love you."

"Love you," she mumbled and drifted back to sleep.

Ronnie checked on the boys and quietly slipped out the door, making sure it was shut and locked behind him. Jax had opened the door for him, and he entered, his eyes landing on Airiella first. She patted the bed next to her, Jax wearing only a pair of shorts sitting on her other side.

"Angel, you know we all have complete faith in you, whatever is coming our way," Ronnie stated, kissing her cheek.

"That doesn't help." Her voice was soft yet teeming with an internal pain he'd caught glimpses of before. "I can't fight the devil. That's a whole different level of insanity right there. I'd likely get you all killed. I can't live with that."

"Siren, we might not have a choice," Jax reminded her. "I also think you are worrying before you even know what we will be facing."

"Remember our talk? You need to let us help you. It's not for you to fight on your own, that's why these connections are here." Ronnie stroked her hair, his fingers winding through the new shorter length.

There was a soft knock on the door, and both Ronnie and Jax rose. Jax opened it while Ronnie stood in front of Airiella. Smitty and Aedan came in, and Jax looked down the hallway before shutting and locking the door again.

Airiella took a deep breath and looked each of them in the eye. "I think whatever will happen, I need to deal with on my own. You all stand to lose way too much to be involved, and I can't even function thinking that something could happen to one of you. I can't. It needs to be just me."

"Bullshit," Jax growled at her. "Look at it from our point of view and what we stand to lose if you get hurt. You are my life; what happened to we face things together, make decisions together?"

Ronnie felt the roller coaster going on inside her and was alarmed when she started to glow. "Jax, give her a minute." Ronnie put a hand on Jax and tentatively one on Airiella. "Angel, he's right, and you know it. Take a minute and breathe."

Smitty got in her face. "Look at me, baby girl." Her only response was to close her eyes, and two tears slid down her face. "Not working for me, open those eyes, and look at me."

Aedan pushed Ronnie out of the way and sat down, Smitty and Aedan gripping her hands. Ronnie stepped back with Jax. "Let them work on her; I think our emotions are compounding hers."

"How am I supposed to act when my wife tells me she is leaving us all behind to fight a war with the devil?" Jax was borderline chaotic.

"You calm the fuck down and let the two logical ones get her head back where it belongs," Ronnie growled back at him. "You know damn well not one person in the room is about to let her do that shit. Stolas wouldn't let her do it either. Not to mention Chrissie, Jillian, or Mags."

"Jesus Ronnie." Jax dropped to a chair and put his hands on his head. "Do you know what my heart did when she said that?"

"I can imagine," Ronnie muttered. "It's not happening tonight, so how about we live for the moment and continue to believe that she is stronger than whatever is coming our way."

"Would it be true?"

"No idea. You've gotta focus. Airiella's way more scared than we are, and we aren't helping her by reacting. We are here to do the show, honeymoon, and now plan a wedding and get me married off. So that is just what we are going to do. We will take it as it comes, and we will fight tooth and nail to retain what we have. Together."

"A day at a time," Jax agreed softly.

"You two under control?" Smitty's voice was gruff.

"Yep." Ronnie shot another look at Jax.

"Now, have one of you assholes noticed that we are all glowing, not just her?" Aedan remarked acidly.

Ronnie looked back at Jax. "Shit, no. I didn't notice."

"Stolas said that means we have more strength and will be harder to kill," Smitty continued, his eyes now focused on Airiella. "If you react, it makes something happen with us since we are all tied to you. If we were in danger right now, you'd know. We all trust that."

"Maybe you shouldn't," Airiella muttered.

"Stop it, Airiella," Aedan demanded. "You have not failed one person in this room or our family."

"We are going to do what asshole number two suggested," Smitty went on. "We will do just what we came here to do, and we will roll with whatever happens as a team." He tapped on Airiella's head. "Understand? Together. You vowed it to Jax, don't break your promise."

"You are going to plan a wedding with our wives to marry off asshole number two." Aedan glared at Ronnie. "While you are doing that, they are going to learn how to control their emotions better so that it doesn't make things worse for you when we are outside somewhere, and all start to glow because they triggered you."

"Hey, we weren't trying to do that," Ronnie argued. He wasn't sure how he missed that they were all glowing.

"You also weren't reading the signals that were getting sent out," Smitty pointed out. He looked back at Airiella. "You off that edge, baby girl?"

"Not entirely. But the only thing that will bring me back is some intense sex, and since you all cut me off, that leaves me with my husband."

Aedan burst out laughing. "Mags and I didn't cut you off; you can come and sleep with us."

Ronnie saw that seemed to snap Jax out of whatever had a hold of him. "Sleep with your own wife," Jax said possessively.

"Sex, wedding planning, castle restoration, show filming, fighting the devil. It looks like my schedule is full," Airiella replied sarcastically, ticking the items off on her fingers. Her face softened. "Sorry for the freak-out. I need a break from the doom and gloom. Can you all just stay here for ten minutes and touch me?"

"I wasn't planning on leaving yet." Ronnie sat down in front of her and grabbed her feet. "I was going to be mean and make Jax wait to have that intense sex you were talking about."

"Go ahead and watch." Airiella laughed. "You might learn a few new moves."

Ronnie felt the tension in the air bleed out as they all touched her, the connection sparking between them and fighting against the darkness, trying to pull their angel out of their grasp. Something terrible may be coming, but so were good things, and Ronnie was going to focus on those instead. He had a future to look forward to now.

Michelle Lee on the Web

Michelle on Facebook at
tiny.cc/MichelleLeeWrites

or write to
MichelleLeeWrites@gmail.com

Also by Michelle Lee

The Raven's Journey
Book 1: See Me
Book 2: See Me Revealed
Book 3: See Me Go
Book 4: See Me Believe
Book 5: See Me Overcome
Book 6: Hawk
Book 7: Ronan
Book 8: Stolas

I S.P.I.
Supernatural Paranormal Investigations
Book 1: Surf & Turf
Book 2: The Doxy Proxy
Book 3: You're the T*ts
Book 4: Cop Out